The Late
Matthew Brown

The Late
Matthew Brown

Paul Ketzle

Apprentice House
Loyola University Maryland
Baltimore, Maryland

First Edition

Printed in the United States of America

Paperback ISBN: 978-1-62720-051-6
E-book ISBN: 978-1-62720-052-3

Design: Lorena Trejo-Perez

Cover art: Shadow 62x117 Oil on Canvas by René Romero Schuler, represented by Jennifer Norback Fine Art, Chicago and Paris. Section icons by creative commons - attribution (CC BY 3.0) the noun project.

Author photo: Brian Kubarycz

Published by Apprentice House

Apprentice House
Loyola University Maryland
4501 N. Charles Street
Baltimore, MD 21210
410.617.5265 • 410.617.2198 (fax)
www.apprenticehouse.com
info@apprenticehouse.com

for Lyra and Raia
for daughters in search of fathers
for fathers in search of daughters
for all those simply searching

"Turning and turning in the widening gyre
The falcon cannot hear the falconer"
—W.B. Yeats

"A thing is not necessarily true because a man dies for it."
—Oscar Wilde

In Media Res

Across the pool deck, my daughter lies stretched out on a towel far from the water's edge, head bobbing to earphones that barely contain the noise, pretending to idly thumb the pages of a magazine while she watches the swarming masses around her through the corners of her yellow sunglasses. Unmistakably, unapologetically twelve.

All around us along the patio, the lives of other families overflow. Children scurry between the worn, scattered lawn chairs and sunning elderly men whose dimpled heads shine, bright and blinding. Young and hyper and semi-medicated, the kids shriek as they play, the pitch of fright and uncontainable joy, tossing themselves hurly-burly into the shallows. The air resonates with the call and echo: Marco. Polo. Marco. Polo. Rascals dodge and duck, burn toes on the concrete, deftly slide across pale blue tile. They ignore the posted signs and bored warnings from lifeguards. They pierce the water's surface, human cannonballs and arrows, so slick and deadly. The only survivors are the balanced and the silent.

These are the fleets of summer, reliable and trying as the season. I watch them, water level, reclined and adrift upon my inner tube, seared by the heat. From this position, I can take all this in: Thin boys balanced on each other's shoulders, grasping and clawing and falling all over themselves—Damp, whirled towels snapping at exposed skin—Girls huddling by the shallow steps and across patio chairs, coconut oil making their earth-toned flesh glisten—An elderly woman tipping an equally elderly man toward the water beside the diving board, a look on her face suggesting long-overdue payback for some distant indiscretion; and as he falls, he reaches out and catches her arm, her desperate shriek cut short as she plunges under the surface.

The screams, the laughs, the bright chirp of conversation.

My daughter flips through the pages of Smithsonian, lingering on the glossy text of articles, the dark, elegant photographs. For a moment I feel she might glance over at me, but she does not look up. So I drift, waiting, harboring a hope for some kind of acknowledgment. When she lifts a hand, I instinctively raise mine in a responding wave, though she only scratches her neck, then casually turns another page.

Into my carefully managed life of solitude she has abruptly appeared, full-blown and nearly adult, full of what my folks had called moxie and a wealth of attitude to spare, not to mention those unpredictable hand gestures that just leave me hanging. And in just these few weeks, she's led me to my ruin, driven me to my death.

Less than a year ago, we each had no idea of the other. We did not know that we even existed.

Part I.

one

Commuters filed out of the terminal, many with the frantic look of those who have let time escape them. They spoke into their cell phones with a running staccato—yep, no, uh-huh, no way, sure, sure—as they wound through the impatient boarders, the well-wishers, the anxiously waiting friends and family. A red-headed woman in her pink blazer and retro cat-eye glasses stood slightly behind an elderly minister, stiff and collared and sucking on a piece of hard candy, or maybe a breath mint, while about his waist a troop of Brownies swarmed.

A young girl walked out of the gate. Ratty overstuffed duffel slung across her back, thick hair pulled into tight, though unruly, braids. She matched her mother's description over the phone to a tee—Faded denim jeans with a patch over the knee. Lips pursed and forehead wrinkled. Her expression, a mixture of interest and serious concern. She had refused to have a picture sent, insisting that our first glimpses had to be face-to-face. And in that moment, I remember thinking that she looked so completely like herself, like a celebrity whose face you'll never mistake.

Her airline chaperone asked me for some kind of identification, a license, a passport, any legal document at all, and then asked me to sign for her. As I did, I could not take my eyes off her.

"Wow," I said, once we were left alone. "Wow." Nothing else came to mind. I opened my mouth, expecting, hoping something more natural or appropriate for a first meeting of father and daughter to emerge. All I managed was, "Look at you. You're here."

"Yep," she said, matter-of-fact, shrugging her shoulders and holding me in a steady, not unfriendly stare. "I'm here."

"Well, then," I stammered. She was expecting something more, I could tell. I would have expected more in her place. Perhaps she was disappointed with me. Our first ever meeting, face-to-face. She let her expectations hang there, loose but close, like her carry-on. "So...," I said, still searching. "Shall we...."

"Close your eyes," she said, abruptly.

"What?" I laughed.

"Just close your eyes. Please."

She seemed serious. Her voice held the unmistakable weight of command.

"All right," I said.

All around me, I could sense the bustle of movement, a human energy. Somewhere close, the beep-beep of a tram carting perhaps some disabled person from one gate to the next. Someone laughed across the terminal, forceful and loud, but with little mirth. And I at once sensed that I did not know if she was still in front of me, or where she was at all. I imagined her using this moment to run off, hurrying off to a different gate with a ticket secretly stowed in her bag for the emergency return flight. Just in case.

Finally, she asked, "What color are my eyes?"

"Your eyes?"

Her voice was still directly in front of me. Behind my eyelids, I could picture her clearly, a small form staring up in curiosity, her long brown hair, her green patched shorts, her fingernails bitten to the nub. Her eyes, though, were a complete blank. "Your eyes," I said again.

"Sure," she said. "You were just looking right at me."

"Yeah, but..."

"What color are they?"

I've always hated tests, the bulging pressure of knowing something for certain—the shame of being wrong. In that moment, I saw eyes, of every sort and shade—peering, probing, various.

"Brown," I guessed.

"You're guessing."

"Green, then."

"They are not green."

"Blue?"

I heard the disappointment in her sigh.

"No. You were right the first time. They're brown."

"Didn't you say I was wrong?"

"I said you were guessing. It doesn't matter."

"Can I open my eyes, then?" I asked.

"I'm sure you can...."

I opened one eye in a squint to see her still standing in the same spot while the flow of the crowd streamed around us. "You sure you're only twelve?"

In anticipation of my daughter's first ever visit, I had purged my home, then restocked it with what seemed to me the more proper vestiges of fatherhood. At the used bookstore, I loaded up a hand cart with as many hard-bound and dusty classics as I could carry, a complete works of William Shakespeare in thirty-seven volumes, a Holy Bible the size of a phone book—items suggesting a moral fortitude and cultural grace that I thought best to pretend I possessed. From the bottom of the closet, I discarded all the automotive and semi-pornographic magazines; I placed all sharp objects high out of reach. I piled my low-grade alcohol into large crates and stored them in the basement, behind the exercise bike. Then I removed the exercise bike to a makeshift at-home gym, really just a converted shed, which I soon filled with free weights, a bench press, an 80-pound punching bag, and a used Nautilus, circa 1984.

It was only a month-long visit. I figured I could assume the mantle of perfect fatherhood for that long at least. Lacking any experience with pre-teen girls, I called upon my closest friend, Janice, to counsel me.

"You were a young girl once," I said. "A while back."

"Thirty years ago. Thanks for reminding me."

"What do I do? I want to make a good impression."

"You should aim lower. Settle for a decent working relationship."

"I'm going to decorate a room just for her."

She sighed and said, "This can only end badly," then hung up.

I wanted to create a sense of belonging, the feel of home, despite the fact that we were total strangers to each other. I pillaged Toys R Us, absconding with a cart full of stuffed creatures. Hippos. Bears. Androgynous sprites. A case of dolls, some talking, some mute. Then, I acquired a bed to place them on, as much as a place for her to sleep, a pink and white floral canopy with matching comforter, dresser, chifforobe, hope chest and vanity. And flowers, flowers everywhere. Hand-painted, glow-in-the-dark stars and smiling planets decorated her ceiling.

But with her first look at her room, my daughter just laughed.

"You're joking."

"No joke," I said

"What'd you do? Call in a cheerleading squad?"

"I thought it was nice," I said.

"It is," she said. "So very nice."

"I thought you'd like it."

She paused, fixing me with her stare, as if still trying to sum me up. She put a hand on my forearm.

"I can see this is going to take some work," she said with a heavy sigh, pushing me back out of the room and closing the door between us.

My daughter's name is Hero.

There is no part of that sentence I feel any responsibility for, but some things simply cannot be helped. The subtle events of life, those small, unnoticed moments that at the time seem so remote, come back to you in the most unexpected and frightening ways. Past overtakes present. It returns in the form of twelve-year-old girls who look upon you with pursed lips and oh-so-skeptical frowns; who avoid your eyes when you walk into a room; who stand noticeably apart from you reading grocery store tabloid banners, laughing quietly to themselves without sharing the joke, while you hunt frozen dinners and avoid the prying disapproval of other shopping parents.

I navigated the food aisles with an overladen grocery cart, the left front wheel whirling and spinning without ever seeming to touch the floor. The cart stubbornly veered to the side, and I nearly took out a display of cereal boxes, then a tattooed stock boy pricing cottage cheese, before ramming into an open freezer resting in the middle of the aisle, scattering its stacks of fish sticks out across the linoleum. Mothers shook their heads and turned away while a pair of college students, drunk or stoned, burst into giddy fits. My daughter, circling in an orbit that kept her far from me, focused her attention elsewhere, leisurely brushing her fingertips along a row of soup cans before sashaying around the corner and down another aisle.

If you live in a place long enough, it begins to occupy two spaces in time at once, or sometimes even more. A row of neat, multicolored condos now, but formerly a high vacancy office plaza. A multiplex movie house that once had been a mini-golf arcade, which had been built over an old mom and pop grocery. Once, a field of tall thin pines, where impatient teens would throw caution and clothes and themselves to the knobby ground—now, a deluxe supermarket with pharmacy, sushi bar and three-level parking. They're all here. Pasts encroaching upon the present, reasserting themselves in a swell of memories.

Once an independent, childless thirty-something. Now—

They tell me I am Hero's father, confirmed by tests that go all the way down to our shared DNA. Less than a year ago, I'd received the subpoena, lawyers requesting that I donate "material" for a paternity test in a divorce proceeding—for a woman I could only vaguely remember. Oddly, I hadn't thought much of it at the time, hadn't seen a reason to refuse or protest. I'd believed the whole thing impossible, absurd. A mere lark, a simple mistake from which the wonders of modern science would surely absolve me. Then the results had come back positive.

I was apprehensive about parenthood, my relationship with my own parents consisting mostly of a rocky and unsettled series of misunderstandings and doused hopes. I'd moved in with my grandfather when I'd turned 18, into the very house where I now lived. We had resolved most of our disagreements, though, by the time my parents died in an accident several years ago, on their first cross-country trip in the new RV after retirement, never knowing they had a granddaughter upon whom to dote.

Watching now as Hero lifted grocery bags into the truck with me, always reaching first for the heaviest, I found myself still wary, doubtful, perplexed by her stout form, muscular through her neck and shoulders, her dark freckled complexion, her flowing brown hair, her bruising wit. These traits came from somewhere, but likely not from me. Perhaps from Hero's mother, Val, though she was only an obscure, possibly invented, memory to me, an impression of a gloriously drunken evening of debauchery thirteen years before. When I asked if she had a picture of her mother, Hero had noted that if I couldn't remember the mother of my child, she certainly wasn't going to help. Still, whomever it comes from, you could see that strength everywhere in Hero herself, her arms, her calves, her face. Sweat ran in streams across her forehead. She'd wrapped her long hair atop her head in a whirl and secured it with a pencil. She'd tied her long-sleeve cover-up around her waist. A rolled-up new copy of The New Yorker was stuffed into her back pocket. I could not bring myself to ask her if she'd paid for it.

I must be in there. Somewhere.

We drove along the Augustus Parkway, the capital's main artery connecting east and west, grown rough now with age and randomly patched with black gravel squares and ovals. Cracks and potholes littered the highway. People were jerked along in their cars beside us, bouncing awkwardly in their seats. Inside the cab of my deluxe 4x4, we could barely feel a ripple.

"If you could be any person from the 19th century, who would it be?" she asked.

"Another study, is it?"

"And it can't be a political figure."

I unwrapped a piece of gum while we sat at the light, offering a piece to Hero. She turned it down. A blue Chevette came up close behind and nearly rammed our bumper.

"Which century is that?" I asked through my chewing.

"Eighteen-hundreds."

"Nonpolitical?"

"Politicians are too easy," she said.

"You're telling me."

Ever since her arrival, she'd deluged me with what she called her "studies": short exercises in empathy, guessing games, tests of logic— the works. You never knew what was coming. She flew through them rapidly, never staying with one for more than a day or so, and never revealing their results. I don't know where she found them all. Mined, I suppose, from the depths of her imagination.

"Eighteenth century, huh?"

"Eighteen-hundreds," she corrected. "Nineteenth century."

"Right."

She liked to keep the purpose behind these projects a mystery, but that didn't keep me from pressing. Somehow, I felt she wanted me to ask.

"What's this one for?" I asked.

"I can't tell you that. It would spoil the surprise."

"Just a hint. I'm very slow."

"I've noticed."

"At least tell me why it has to be the eighteenth century."

"Eighteen-hundreds. Nineteenth century."

"I'm not cut out for this," I said. "I need help."

She leaned forward in her seat, her hands clasped together in front of her, forearms twisted. "You're looking for someone who is more like an idea than a person. Someone you can't just pick out of the blue. And it can't be a politician. If you could pick a president, say, you'd just choose someone like Lincoln. This takes a little more thought."

I slowed at a stop sign, then rolled through it.

"You sure you're only twelve?"

"That's what they tell me," she said, leaning back, folding her legs underneath herself. "But how would I know, really?"

We passed a clearing filled with busted and rusting automobiles. Buicks and Hondas and Chryslers and Plymouths, each smashed haphazardly upon the next until only a smear of blue green orange. You could almost feel the vines and tall grasses stretching up through the floorboards, before they came up under and through the hoods, running out through broken windows and crooked frames. The clearing bordered a nearly completed strip mall, newly tarred and painted parking lot, crisp and glistening in the sun. Then another mall. Then a gas station. The pace of the construction was frantic, eating up the open spaces and the plots of wild growth. Stores were going up and out of business faster than people could shop.

Saddled between a fast food joint and the foundation of some new building, I spied a farmer's field, rows of shaggy crops and a wooden shack with a sign erected by the curbside. I pulled the Toyota off the road in front of it, coming to a sudden stop.

"Why're we parking?"

"I always used to do this with my family. It's a sort of tradition round here."

"So was slavery," she said.

"It's my heritage."

"That doesn't make it mine, you know."

Placards announced U-PICK corn strawberries peas tomatoes whatever's-in-season. Dollar-a-pound. The man inside the shack handed us two wooden baskets without uttering a word. His face was creased and leathered, caught in a perpetual grimace.

"You want anything in particular?" I asked, handing her a basket.

"How about cotton."

"I'm partial to corn."

"Didn't we just buy food? It'll probably go bad in the hot car, you know?"

"This is good," I said. "This'll be good for us."

"I don't have to like everything, you know," she said. "It's okay if I'm bored."

The summertimes of my own childhood had been filled with now-cherished episodes of bloody knees, runny noses, sweat-plastered hair, and the gathering of vegetables. On simmering Saturday mornings we'd load up the baby blue Impala, the three of us piling in each upon the other across the felt foam interior, the well of a trunk jam-packed with coolers, end-to-end—and we'd comb the fields, following row upon row upon row of corn stalks and tomato and strawberry plants and sprawling melon vines.

"You haven't answered yet," she said. "The study."

"Let me think. What's the rush?"

"No rush. Just no cheating."

"Seriously, who am I going to ask?"

We wandered out into the field, my daughter and I, buckets under our arms and each in our own direction. I struck a path down the rows of corn stalks, which had grown brown in the drier-than-usual summer. The ears were stunted and coarse. Nothing much looked good, to be honest, but I picked anyway, walking around for half an hour, up and down the rows, rummaging through the dead and the sun-dried vegetation.

When I finally came across Hero, she was squatting beside a patch of once-hoped-for watermelon. Most had succumbed to blossom-end rot, half-grown and rounded like softballs.

"I don't think I've ever seen melons growing," she said.

"This hardly qualifies."

"Still. Call me impressed."

She stood, unwinding herself upward and stretching. I handed her a shriveled strawberry from my basket. She ate it whole. An elderly gentleman in broad suspenders ambled by us through the rows with a nod of his head.

"Mark Twain," I said, to which Hero cocked a sly eyebrow. "Your question."

She frowned. "He's the only one you can think of, right?"

"What are you implying?"

"Try again."

"He was a writer, right?"

"I'm reluctant to offer any assistance," she said, turning away.

I balanced my basket on my hip. "This is hard, you know."

"No, you're right. It's fine. Next time I'll give you something easier."

We carried our laden containers back to the shack. Hero had filled hers with beans, and only beans, a couple pounds worth, at least. I went for variety: tomatoes, carrots, and as much corn as I could lift. We'd never eat it all, even if it hadn't been dried out. This was my experience. Most of it would end up rotting in the fridge or given away to friends. It was really just for comfort and for show.

"There's Robert E. Lee," I said, suddenly inspired, setting the bags in the truck bed.

"That's your answer?"

"He wasn't a politician. Right?"

Hero shrugged. "That could go either way."

I started up the engine and rolled back out onto the highway toward home. Hero reclined her seat and curled up away from me with a yawn.

"To tell the truth," she said, "it didn't matter who you picked. I was just testing myself. To see who I thought you would pick."

"Who did you expect, then?"

She smiled. "That I don't have to tell you."

two

Magnolia Grove, the neighborhood in which I live, is a transitional community, marching slowly but certainly toward complete self-sufficiency in my lifetime. The neighborhood was not designed this way; it was actually not designed at all, at least not as a unified community. The plots are irregular, as if haphazardly drawn and placed, as are the roads, which wind creek-like through the clusters of dense foliage. Structures sprawl, outwards, upwards, asymmetric and geometric dreams of genius and hazardous whimsy. No serious limitations guide their constructions but for gravity, and even that appears in some cases to have been an afterthought. Many of the homes here predate the War, while some date only to the suburban boom of the fifties, though even most of these owners have modeled their homes to the antebellum period. There's no room here for anything new. Frank Lloyd Wright designed a house here somewhere, I'm told, buried deep behind a thicket or glade, off some overgrown drive. The owners want its location kept secret. We understand, the other homeowners—that overarching desire for privacy and seclusion, to turn away from the bustling outside world and recapture something we've lost.

This desire was, in fact, what led us to make our collective decision. Nearly all exiting streets, those that led directly out of the neighborhood, would be blocked off. Too many automobiles, uninvited and suspicious, ventured past our homes at night while we peered out from behind our drapes and blinds. Too many commuters cut through during rush hours to avoid the expressway.

Too many west-siders, unwanted, unwelcome. We needed to close ranks, establish our independence and community solidarity.

Our best option, at least at first, was to make entrance and escape a more difficult proposition. Initially this was done by simple barricade. Drivers, though, apparently found these obstacles too constraining. Not a week would go by without someone running down the wood and metal stops. I understood the temptation, found myself on several occasions, with each wrong turn, suddenly facing the steady blip of orange, taunting me, teasing out the impulse to accelerate swiftly and grind down the obstructions.

The ever-increasing rebellion was cured for everyone eventually, once construction crews were brought in to erect concrete dividers, the perpendicular median strips that blurred any notion of continuity. This path ended; another began just beyond. Roads were renamed to further obscure past associations. Fifth Avenue became Sycamore. Third became Greenwich. Lafayette became Oak. Calhoun became St. Francis.

One homeowner, a self-employed landscape artist, oversaw the layering of grasses, flowers, trees, to give the barriers an untouchable quality, like fine china. These end-stops became, in most cases, aesthetically far superior to the yards they bordered. The landscaper left fliers wedged beneath door-knockers, between iron gate railings, under doors and into vase-lined hallways. Discounts for all community members. In response, homeowners on some dead-ends, annoyed by the seemingly ceaseless leafleting, tore out the daylilies and St. Johns wort and creeping thyme and replaced them with mammoth aloe plants and flowering cacti. Tempers flared.

Traffic out of and into the remaining opening has grown as a consequence of our roadblocks, and the single lane has slowed travel time down to a trickle. Left turns are restricted to low-volume hours. Trucks fifteen tons or over, or above ten feet in height, are prohibited. We welcome the rule of law. We've discussed widening the entrance to four lanes, plus a fifth for left turns. We considered petitioning the city for a traffic signal.

"This is all just so dumb," Hero observed immediately upon her arrival. "You can't just lock everyone out."

But as I explained to her, that was the idea.

Someday soon, our community will be guarded by a gate, a swinging mechanical arm, a sequence of four numbers, and a speaker phone by which guests can contact their respective hosts. But there's more. The plan, from what I'm told, is for this neighborhood to withdraw even farther, to finally sever our bonds with the outside world, to become, in some sense, completely self-reliant. We will have our own grocery stores, our own gas stations, our own movie theater. I imagine we'll need our own office buildings, our own airport. Auto factories to make our cars and parts. Our own ranches and fields of crops. Slaughterhouses and textile factories and newspapers and universities. A new South, wholly self-sufficient.

Homes in Magnolia Grove are upper end, in price if nothing else, when there are actually ones for sale. But this happens rarely. I have only ever seen two houses here on the market. Despite this, the homeowner's association still produces promotional materials, perhaps if only to keep public interest and property values high. The latest bulletin describes, among other things, the neighborhood's goal as:

Building a New South for the 21st Century

The pamphlet's cover is glossy, with a color photograph. A family barbecues in their rolling, green backyard, smiling, young children bouncing on a trampoline. Spanish moss drapes elegantly across the boughs and awnings. The father wears a white chef's cap and sauce-stained apron. I knew him. Not well, but enough to nod as our shopping carts passed each other down grocery aisles, by the condiments, the charcoal, the bleached white breads. Bill Dreiser. A civil service engineer from three streets over who, rumor had it, made enough in a sudden stock windfall to buy this same pictured family a second home somewhere in the Pacific Northwest, near

Portland or Seattle or somewhere in Northern California. Rumor had it he also bought a sailboat.

And then, while clear-cutting his new property one afternoon last summer, a tree fell on him—crushed him in the flash of an instant. When his family couldn't find him for dinner, they searched the grounds, only to discover a trace of his shirt under the fallen log. And when, after several hours of cutting, they were finally able to remove the colossal trunk, using two pickups and over a dozen men, there was nothing recognizable beneath, nothing distinctly human for his grieving widow and children to claim—only bone and hair and pulp.

In his still-smiling photograph, I notice Bill's graying mustache is trimmed crooked, angled upward on one side. I seem to remember this about him in person, too. One of the young girls on the trampoline, wearing a cartoon print T-shirt of a blue genie, appears caught in mid-fall, slightly blurred, frozen in time and space, as she gleefully shoots us the finger.

Hero arrived in the middle of what she mockingly termed "The Reconstruction." At 407 St. Francis Avenue, the two-story manor house I inherited a few years ago after my grandfather's death, the structure of things is in perpetual flux. It's a long-term renovation, piece-by-piece, as I have sought to restore the home's original splendor. In its 170-year history, mirroring my own family's evolution from Southern aristocracy to significantly poorer but quietly respected, the building has evolved dramatically as generations of my family have sought to move the structure farther and farther away from its roots—dragging it, awkward and uncomfortable, into their present. Officially, no new work had been done on the house in a hundred years—no zoning permits, no building plans of any sort; yet the house I now occupied bore little resemblance to the one laid out in the original blueprints I'd recovered from the county clerk's office, which to the untrained eye revealed only the faintest traces of its early eighteenth-century roots.

A variety of odd additions had been made to the back and sides of the building, including a den with three walls, an attached chapel with no walls (just a stucco oval without windows) and a glass dome for a greenhouse out back. The only thing I found that seemed still directly connected to its past was the crumbling family burial plot, with its newest addition, my grandfather Devon, as Old South as they come, joining seven generations of decomposing Browns.

Most of the additions were shoddily done. My first inspection revealed mismatched lines running throughout the structure, water damage and other sure signs of leakage, irregularly shaped doorways and windows. The upstairs bathroom was missing a section connecting the sink to the drainage pipe, and half the sand dollar tiles had been stripped from the walls with what might have been the tip of a Phillips screwdriver, leaving trails in the plaster like asterisks, drifting off into incomplete thoughts.

When I learned I'd inherited this house, I couldn't wait to move back in, despite these unsightly and potentially unsound changes, because I knew just how rare it was to find a vacancy in Magnolia Grove, and someday living in Magnolia Grove is the goal of every authentic Southern son who grows up knowing its name. But it will take years, perhaps decades, to finish restoring the place to its former glory as our family's traditional antebellum manor house. A lifetime, even. I began almost immediately after taking possession, and six years later I still felt that I was only just getting started, the past still far out ahead of me.

In the cool of the mornings, Hero and I took our breakfast on the cracked back patio, which I hoped soon to demolish in favor of the original wraparound porch. The newly retro-designed kitchen was still on the planning board. So much was still on the planning board. I'd blown through a large chunk of my inheritance just to complete the few projects I'd started, and I was already beginning to venture into debt. It was worth it, though, I reasoned, and someday, Hero would be able to stay in this house of our ancestors, maybe even live here herself once I was gone. All of this assuming, of course, that we survived this first visit.

"Why don't you have a pet name for me?" Hero scowled from across her newly discovered favorite breakfast: cheese grits.

"What do you mean?"

"I mean, other fathers call their kids dumb things like Sugar or Pumpkin. All you ever call me is Hero."

"Which is the name you came with."

"So?"

"You want me to give you a pet name?"

"I want to know why you don't call me anything."

After almost a week of meals filled with blank, silent stares, we decided something had to be done, so we developed this method of discussion: In the morning we asked each other a question, some tidbit about our respective pasts, presents and future dreams. Those little joys and tragedies that gain significance by sheer accumulation. Nothing too personal. Then after dinner, during dessert, we'd ask a follow-up and sift for some significance amid the random flotsam gathered in our nets. This was Hero's idea, so naturally her questions were better. I would ask some banal question about her school or friends, carefully avoiding any area that might seem too personal. She, on the other hand, like any good predator, knew how to go for the jugular.

"You hate my name. Don't you."

This was after dinner and partway into dessert. All day I'd been struggling with our morning session, foolishly hoping she'd let the matter drop. I swallowed uncomfortably and scratched my knee.

"Why would you say that?

"I don't know. Something in your face. Your nose scrunches up when you say it. Like you've eaten something sour."

"It doesn't matter what I think."

"I didn't say it did. I'm just asking."

"Fine. I probably would have picked something else."

She smiled. Once again, as had happened so often during her

visit over the past week, it occurred to me that I might have found just the wrong thing to say.

"And what would you have called me?"

"One thing at a time," I stalled, taking an earnest spoonful from my bowl. "I'm still working on the pet name... Puddin'."

She frowned over her grape Jell-O.

"That's the best you can do?"

"It's a start."

"That's barely even trying. Why don't you call me Hamburger? Or, wait! What'd we have for dinner last night?"

"I'm doing my best."

"Spaghetti! Or how about Meatball?"

"You're the one who suggested Pumpkin," I said.

Hero's face puckered. "That was an example."

"I'm just saying."

"My sweet Noodle," she mocked, bracing her chin on folded hands. "My darling little Marinara."

"Marinara's kinda nice," I said. "Let's go with that."

As evening set in, we walked the neighborhood. It was for exercise, so naturally her idea, and it was a rare opportunity to explore the place I lived. After six years living here again, I had not found the time or been pushed by strong inclination. Most often, I was either racing to or from work, or buried deep in one project or another, observing the necessary detachment from streets and houses and landscapes beyond the borders of my front lawn.

But here at the close of the day, we had time to meander with no expressed purpose or design. Up and down the blocks, past shaded and glowing windows, perfectly tailored lawns and next year's luxury automobiles.

My next door neighbor Alfred was clipping hedges below his front windows. Alfred was a veteran, a widower, and seemingly obsessed with how I organized my affairs. He was not only my Magnolia Grove block president, but also vice-chair of the entire Neighborhood Association. He saw to it that the rules were

followed, and when they weren't, he made sure a penalty was paid.
He also took a surprisingly dim view of my reconstruction plans. It
wasn't the retrofitting that was the problem, given the popularity of
neoclassical homes; rather, he found my insistence on an authentic
renovation perplexing. In a neighborhood perpetually reaching
toward modernity, there were specifications and regulations to
follow, security elements to maintain, beautification standards
to meet, and my idea of a historically accurate home was, as he
put it, "potentially depressive of property values"—all of which
explained why he, along with everyone else on my block and the
Neighborhood Association itself, was in the process of suing me out
of house and home.

He stopped clipping to wave and smile. I waved back.

"This place isn't what I expected," Hero said, as we climbed
the set of meandering public stairs into the upper level of the
neighborhood. "Not at all."

"Worse, then?"

"Hard to say. My expectations were pretty low."

I nodded, but said nothing.

"When I think of the South, I picture everything in black and
white. Fire hoses. Police dogs. We Shall Overcome."

"That's the Old South. Things are different now."

"It's so lush here. The trees, the vines."

"We're doing our best to change that. It's a constant battle for
supremacy."

"And it's got all this history. But what's freaky, though, is how
much of it isn't different at all. Standing around, sometimes, I think
I could be anywhere. I mean, that could be anyone's McDonalds and
Jiffy Lube."

"Is that a compliment or a criticism?"

"I'm not sure yet."

We walked side by side, her hands swinging loose. I started to
reach out to hold one of hers, then laid my arm on her shoulder
instead. She let it rest there for a moment. Then she stepped forward

with a shrug—gentle, but firm and definite.

We passed a series of lawns with poster board signs for competing political campaigns—judges and congressmen and governor.

"You should know I don't blame you for all this."

"The South?"

"No. My birth. It's not your fault," she said, walking ahead of me. "Wait. Strike that. I should say, it is your fault. But I still don't blame you."

"Look on the bright side," I said, feigning cheerfulness. "You're a girl with two fathers."

Hero shook her head. "Right now, I'm a girl with no father."

"I see."

I didn't argue with her, even to protest for my own sake. The man she had spent her whole life up to this point believing to be her father was Geoffrey Grace, a community college professor and Val's now ex-husband. What little I knew of him had come from brief and bitter rants over the phone from Val. Hero hadn't really talked to me about him at all. As we strolled about in the fading light, I began to wonder if her coming here was turning into something of a mistake. Just another in a long line for me. In a short three weeks, we'd be facing an unspoken reality: we had no plans beyond this moment and no need, either. Our lives could continue on as before, as if we didn't exist. Once she left, we could easily never see each other again.

There were times, like this one, when it felt like this choice might even be best.

"You sure don't talk like the stereotypical Southerner."

"Not folksy enough for you?"

"No," she said, "it's not that. You've got a nice but subtle twang."

"Thanks. Been practicing my whole life."

"You just don't sound like a dumb hick."

"Fair enough," I replied. "You don't sound twelve, either."

Hero paused in front of an expansive yard. The house was a good thirty yards off the sidewalk, largely hidden from view behind a cluster of palms and extensive tropical landscaping and iron fencing. On every avenue and lane, the remnants of long-deposed Southern aristocracy lay cloistered.

We moved deeper in, left on Summit Avenue, past Coral Court, up Inspiration Drive. The roads sloped upward, toward the crest of a hill that gave Magnolia Grove its towering quality. In a countryside otherwise flat, it had a feeling of regality that I'd always admired. Heavy rains barely touched us here as waters ran slowly, gradually downhill and downtown. But it was the aged and rising trees that gave it a presence, its soaring majesty.

Our path took us around and through the lavish and overwhelming. The streets wound and curved about. Everywhere deserted and still but for the occasional motorist, the slam of a door, the sputter and jerk of the automated sprinkler systems. Dim figures in windows watched as we passed, cautious and concealed and searching for signs of suspicious activities, for loitering, for an errant step onto private property. Mobile phones at the ready. Eyes following our every move.

three

My position as associate director of the State Department of Corrections was a point of contention between my daughter and me. It was my job to ensure that our convicted thieves, rapists, killers, and casual drug users were clothed, fed, warm and moderately—just not especially—content. Hero made no secret of the fact that she wasn't especially pleased with this career choice.

"I'm just not sure I can get that excited about having a jailer for a father."

"It's not like I'm passionate about it. It's not like I'm doing cell inspections. Shackling the inmates. I'm a paper pusher. A petty bureaucrat."

"Look at me," she said. "Swelling with pride. Really."

Corrections was merely another step on a ladder, I pointed out, another in a string of political appointments I'd ridden for the past decade, and one I'd been doing for only the past year, at that. I'd worked for campaigns, think tanks, and, of course, other departments in government. Prior to Corrections, I'd been director of the Bureau of Environmental Study, which, I quickly pointed out, made me a friend of the earth and all its small and defenseless creatures.

"Don't patronize me," she said.

Bureaucracy was my trade, but more than anything, I was a political animal—or, more accurately, the scion of political animals. I was following a life of government and politics that had run for generations in my family. My father had started out as an aide to a state legislator before taking up a lobbying career in the textile industry. My grandfather Devon had worked for a governor and run the Public Works Agency for decades, and off some downtown alley, there was a small office building dedicated to him. And on and on, back to before the War. I was following in a tradition as rich and antiquated as this place itself.

We lived in the era of the New South, but the Old South was still remarkably persistent, more enduring than mere memory, enshrined in its crumbling and rebuilt structures and traditions, its registry of cherished landmarks, its mansions and battlefields and overgrown natural wonders and sense of inherent majesty. The original Capitol Building was a symbol at the crossroads between old and new. Built up from the charred ashes of the War, it had frustrated and bored the politicians and lobbyists who roamed its corridors for over a hundred years. Those who wanted change dreamed of state-of-the-art, longed to be the envy of our neighboring states. For those who had to work there, change was about practicality, with nostalgia a mere afterthought. And finally, after decades of wrangling and debate, an actual proposal had been put into motion. A new capitol was to be commissioned—a high-tech symbol for these modern times, a sign of just how this New South had put its past behind it. As for the old building, it was to be razed to the ground. That was the plan, at any rate.

Radically new ideas flowed slowly through these legislative halls, and the halting process gave time for opposition to grow. Soon the preservationists were clamoring to save the old capitol, upset that the new one was to be built over the foundations of its predecessor. A local historical preservation society marched onto the Senate floor and dumped a hundred-thousand signed petitions across the dais. A chapter of the Daughters of the South mounted the steps of the old capitol building and chained themselves to the bronze statue of a Civil War cavalry soldier. It was the lead story on all three local newscasts and one national.

The ultimate compromise left no one entirely pleased. The two buildings would both remain, side by side, nearly overlapping. The past and the present. The new capitol towering over the old—the old refusing to give ground to the new. And so it was done.

The Department of Corrections stood next door to this two-headed monster of government. Each workday, as the tall, thick shadows stretched across the parking lot, I'd look upward at the newly completed building, its twenty-five stories rising straight up, and every time it appeared to be collapsing down upon me.

In the office, my associate Hal Wallace stood beside an employee's desk, his leg propped up on a trash can, leaning over the shoulder of our new assistant, a young woman whose name I had had to ask for, and then forgotten, probably a dozen times now. We made eye contact, Hal and I, and I waved. He nodded but didn't stop talking. His western-style holster flashed, its tanned leather cut, its ornamental curlicues plainly visible at his waist beneath the flap of his coat. Hal always wore that sidearm to work, an ivory-handled revolver that had been handed down to him by his G.I. father. He was an assistant director of the Department of Corrections, technically one step below me, though he'd been there much longer, nearly seven years, with a degree in criminal justice —and now he'd advanced to the top of the civil service heap, where the only ones above him were members of the political establishment, like the director and me. That he held such an important position, or for that matter that the government building he worked in forbade weapons of any sort, had no bearing on the matter for him, nor apparently for the security guards downstairs, or anyone else. Ours is an open-carry state. We don't care if you want to bring lethal weaponry to work. We just want to see what's coming.

Also, as a well-to-do black man in the South, Hal said he preferred letting everyone know that he was armed. It not only fed the frustrations of the old guard Klansmen, who could never have imagined the sight a generation ago, it was also a much safer way to walk down deserted and dark streets at night. Multi-ethnic gang violence had been on the rise for years, and for anyone with a hint of status, whatever your race, it paid to watch your back.

Through the haze of fluorescent lights, I navigated the padded cubicles to my office unmolested. The many faces of my coworkers looked up as I passed, then quickly looked down again without acknowledgment. Hal insisted that they were still getting used to me, that eventually I'd fit in. A year, though, seemed like a long time looking for a fit, and I was fairly convinced that whatever opinion they were going to have of me had long ago been formed and set.

During my year at Corrections, I had instituted my routine of delegation, a style of management that had served me well throughout my administrative career. I rarely attached my name to anything directly. I signed few documents. I wrote vague and brief letters. I avoided email and conveniently forgot my government-issued electronic address. As a result, my career had thus far been a rousing success. Only in my early thirties and already I was holding my second executive administrative position, a swift climb of the state government ladder and on pace to surpass all my relatives. And my accomplishments, while admittedly slight and largely cosmetic, were testament to the fact that the true currency of management wasn't success, but change. Or, in my case, taking credit for the changes happening around you and the labors of others.

Hal suddenly popped his head through my doorway.

"Christy wants us."

"What about?

"You know how he likes surprises."

The director of the Department of Corrections, Christy Donaldson, was, like me, a political appointee, having been in and out of government for the better part of thirty years. His faded blue sports coats, his thinning gray comb-over—he was a holdover from another era, the heyday of the Old South political machine, his only qualification for the job being his fierce partisanship. He was standing in front of his desk and smiling as we entered, and before we had even settled into our seats, announced that the governor was going to sign a warrant of execution.

"No shit?" Hal laughed, then caught himself as if embarrassed.

"There's a presser set for this afternoon. Going to be a big deal. Fits nicely with the overall campaign themes: Justice for victims. Crap like that."

I was as surprised as Hal. Due to a variety of reasons, the state hadn't managed to execute anyone in more than a decade. A moratorium following the last, admittedly disastrous, series of executions was no longer in effect, but the long appeals process had kept some of the more promising prospects from coming due. Two strong candidates for the chair had both recently had their convictions thrown back to the lower courts. Another had been the subject of a recent Dateline special, casting overwhelming doubt on his likely guilt. Executing him now would have been a public relations nightmare.

"We sure this one's not going to fall through?" I asked.

Christy just smiled, handing me a case file.

Andrew Carl Adler was just the killer everyone had been waiting for: a middle- aged white man whose brutal and premeditated rape and murder of a local college student had only been eclipsed by his grotesquely comical attempts to cover up the crime. The fire he'd hoped to use to obliterate the evidence had scorched several apartments in the historical district where she lived and severely injured two firefighters, yet hadn't harmed the girl's body, left partially insulated in the tub where he'd strangled her. Though he denied it, genetic evidence had tied him to the murder, the arson, and also the theft of the victim's car, which he tried to sell through an ad in the local paper. The trial had been a media sensation, the verdict quick, and his lack of public remorse for the death of an innocent young woman had only further inflamed public passions. If ever there was a slam dunk case for capital punishment, everyone agreed, this was it.

"Now, I'm going to be on the road for the next several weeks almost nonstop," Christy explained. "The governor has called in just about everyone to help with the campaign. So I need you to put this thing together."

"What do we have to do?"

"There're a lot of little details to arrange—hiring someone to pull the switch, settling things with the warden. Not to mention the press. Our first execution in ten years. Matthew, I want you to personally arrange all the details."

"What makes me so lucky?"

"We don't want any accidents, like what happened last time. This is going to be a three-ring circus, and you're the perfect public face for this."

"I've never done anything like this."

"Consider it a personal challenge."

"I would have thought Hal seemed like a more natural choice. His experience."

Christy shook his head. "Hal's been tasked with a top-to-bottom department review, so he's not going to be available. Besides, you shouldn't need any help. You're a former director, so you're the natural choice. Just do a job like you did with the Work for Justice program and everything will be golden."

I didn't say anything but managed a tight smile. Hal was stoic, his fingers tracing the embroidered lines on his holster.

The Work for Justice program was part of an intense effort to bring the state correctional system into the 21st century. Having evolved well past the age of stocks and racks, thumb screws and iron maidens and pickup basketball, our modern prisons were productive and cost-efficient and privately run. For years inmates had been working the phones, processing complaints, taking orders, if only for later billing. But the slew of high-tech convictions had enabled us to up the ante: we now incorporated web design, system troubleshooting and computer assembly. A complete line of office and antivirus software was scheduled to hit the market in six months. There was an entire industry here, a conversion of labor, an enabling of the idle. The response from business leaders who were looking for an inexpensive labor solution or deals of cheap software had been overwhelmingly positive, and except for a few human rights activists and the nervous competitors who accused us of slave labor, Work for Justice had turned out to be a rousing success.

But it had nothing to do with me. It had been my good fortune to be there to take credit for a decade of others' planning and work. Plans had long ago been put into motion by previous directors to better utilize the changing face of the incarcerated population. My entire contribution had been to go out on prearranged local media junkets—TV and radio and cable access. A business magazine profiled me, also the local television news. For a brief few weeks, I was a mini-celebrity. Everyone else at Corrections, except Christy, it seemed, understood that Hal was the engine of our department. He'd been at Corrections for ages, while my qualifications were limited to that three-year stint at Environmental and my knack for having the right political connections. Learning to stay out of the way was perhaps my greatest contribution to my department.

"Seems I have no choice," I said.

Christy clasped his hands together with a slap. "All right, then. That's settled!" He started shuffling through the papers on his desk, which was our sign to leave. "How's the baby?" he asked absently, without looking up. "I hear you have a new daughter?"

"She's twelve," I said.

"Amazing, isn't it, how fast they grow."

We wound our way back through the beehive of cubicles. When Hal walked, though, everyone slipped aside, his barrel girth parting the streams. Rather than heading into his own office, Hal followed me into mine, easing himself with surprising lightness onto the corner of my desk while I took my seat.

We sat like this for a moment, no one breathing a word.

"Yes?" I said.

"Nothing," Hal said. "Just looked like you had something on your mind."

"I know nothing about executing someone," I said.

Hal shrugged. "Before my time, too. That was a whole different crew, then, a whole different administration. Bunch of fuck-ups."

That wasn't an exaggeration. The last guy they tried to kill, Maxwell Carpenter Jaspers, had a barely functional IQ, and in the months leading up to his execution, this very fact had brought condemnations from human rights groups of every stripe, plus a majority of world leaders, including the Pope.

"I don't know that I could stand up to the Pope," I said.

"He ain't so tough. Give yourself some credit. I'd give you at least even odds."

All of these factors would have been bad enough, but then there was the malfunction with the chair. The first jolt hadn't succeeded in killing Jaspers, and the sight of his wheezing, smoking body had caused one witness to faint. A second electric shock then set Jaspers' mask on fire. By the time they had shoveled his blackened corpse from the chair, several of the witnesses had become physically ill. Public protests only became more pronounced when another convict later confessed to the crime.

Some believed that the state was done with killing people for good, at least those who put little stock in the emotional power of vengeance and its ability to drive voters out to the polls.

Hal wasn't leaving. He rocked on the edge of my desk, still tracing his pistol, staring at the series of old photographs on my walls. "Why do you think Christy is so intent that I do this? I'm serious. It should be you. You're the nuts and bolts guy."

"Sometimes you got to just let things go," he said, absently. "No point in making a fuss over what you can't change. Besides," he shrugged, "I've got bigger fish to fry."

"What's up with this review, anyway?" I asked.

"You haven't heard about the investigations?"

I shook my head. I rarely paid attention to work gossip when I could avoid it. I never watched the news.

"Several agencies are being investigated by the special prosecutor's office. It's all pretty hush-hush, but it's got Christy spooked. Word is, they've got teams of investigators running around, asking questions, poring through the paperwork. You know Jordan Thatcher, runs Food and Agriculture?"

"Vaguely. Small guy. Beard."

"Indicted. Last week, on charges of bribery, misuse of office and a few other things I'd never heard of. They're apparently widening the net. Heard they're going after Commerce, Health, Environmental."

"Environmental," I repeated.

My three years as director of the Bureau of Environmental Study had been a dull, uneventful, if largely pleasant experience, though my tenure there had not ended happily. Some resented my decision to up and leave so suddenly, taking me for the political opportunist I certainly am. The governor's office had "requested" that I move to Corrections, for reasons they did not specify, and I could read the situation well enough to know not to appear as anything but perfectly compliant. The assistant they'd picked as my replacement, C. Bernie Morr, was my opposite in every respect, too. Where I was hands off, he was micro-managing; where I was disinterested and unqualified, he was passionate, with twenty years of experience and a degree in Environmental Law to draw upon. He was also a fierce and loyal partisan for the political machine in contrast to my compliant ambivalence. It was difficult to imagine the department running into trouble under his watch, and though I'd made few friends there and remained close with no one, I didn't like the idea of my former staff suffering under the weight of an investigation.

"You still know anyone working at the bureau?" Hal asked.

"A few, I think. Not that they'd want to talk to me. But I don't see what that's got to do with us and your review."

"Nothing, we hope. For all our sakes. But better to know about it before they do." Hal lifted himself heavily from the desktop. "Besides, it's pretty obvious the political guys don't want me anywhere near this execution. Just imagine how the voters would react to my beautiful face. Adler may be a killer, but he's still white."

I laughed uncomfortably. "You can't be serious."

"Think about it. That wouldn't sit so well with certain important constituencies of the voting public. You don't think this was Christy's idea, do you? I've been here long enough to know that he's got very specific instructions."

"So you think it's all about race," I said, leaning back in my chair.

"You think if Adler was black they wouldn't be putting me front and center? Of course it's about race. They'd be crazy not to make it about race. I'm not saying I'm happy about it. But they need you, buddy. Should make you feel special."

"I hate this. I'm not a racist."

"As long as the next word isn't 'but,' we're cool."

I paused, then began: "I don't like playing these kinds of games."

"I spend all my day around white people, and I've never met a single one who was a racist."

"That seems hard to believe," I said.

Hal lifted his large shoulders and pointed a finger at me with a nod. "Exactly," he said.

Over half our inmates were white, but a disproportionate number were black. Hal had walked me through a memo on this after I'd been on the job only a few days. Someone would ask me about this, he said, so don't be surprised and don't pretend it isn't true. Just nod sadly, he recommended, and point out that our job is to incarcerate, not judge. And, now, of course, to kill.

"I just don't know that I'm qualified," I said.

"That's the thing about institutional memory," Hal said, leafing through the dusty volumes on my bookshelves, most left there by my predecessor and untouched in a year. "Lose it and you're starting over from scratch."

"I've got to get some help from someone. What about the new girl? What's her name? Jane. Kate. The blonde."

"Everyone's pretty overwhelmed right now, but maybe you could find someone to pick up your slack. Anyway, you should probably learn their names before you start asking for favors."

"I'm not sure they know mine. Lord knows they don't trust me."

"They're just still getting used to you."

"They should know by now. I'm not the enemy. At least you know that. Besides, I come from a long line of cowards."

"They're protective is all."

"What are they protecting?"

"They'll get used to you," he said, without conviction, and surged out the door. "Don't worry."

four

Outside Hero's room, a pile of mutilated stuffed animals was growing. To the stacks of billowy entrails and tattered appendages she'd added the comforters, the lamps, the floral picture frames— every item I'd selected especially for her. She'd been nice enough to ask for permission to change things around, which I'd granted. I was surprised, though, by the swiftness of her response. Her quick resolution to demolish everything I had done. I secretly admired her certainty of purpose.

I knocked on her door and waited through a prolonged pause before her cheerful voice told me to come in. I found her sitting on her floor, wading in a sea of fluff and balled up T-shirts and scattered magazines and books. Two comically tall pigtails were affixed to the top of her head.

"Up to no good, I see?"

"Always," she grinned. These gestures were hard to read. I'd been taken in before, thinking that she was starting to warm to me, only to be blindsided a moment later. Clearly, she was still sizing me up, just as I was trying to understand her. She seemed to be making more progress.

"What would you do if you had to keep someone in jail you thought was innocent?"

"Another study, is it?"

"Would you try to work within the system to bring them justice or would you quit in protest, hoping to effect a change from the outside?" She picked up a notebook from somewhere under the foam of cotton and drew out a pencil from her hair.

"Or I could just go to work and do my job. Why do I have to be a crusader for justice?"

She frowned. "You aren't serious."

"See. This is why I try not to get involved with the inmates. Lots of second-guessing. Who needs that kind of stress?"

"Still," she said, tapping the pencil on the notebook, "you could pretend to be a noble figure, for the sake of your daughter, at least."

"Then not measure up and risk disappointment?"

"I'm not sure I'm capable of more. Indulge me."

She tapped the page with the pencil, then pushed it aside to pick up another toy. She ran a seam ripper around the neck of a rainbow-colored rabbit and pulled off its head.

"Is that necessary?"

She shrugged, tossing the head to the floor. "You're stalling."

"My daughter is slaughtering defenseless toys. What parent wouldn't be concerned? What would your psychiatrist say?"

"Wouldn't you like to know," she said.

"As much as I'd love to sit here and debate these complex moral questions, I have to go. I'm late."

"Hot date?"

"Just a function."

"A date is a function. Business or pleasure?"

"Now, what possible motivation would I have to tell you that?"

At this, she just grinned.

"I'll only be a couple of hours," I said. "Tops."

"Don't think this gets you off the hook," she said as I closed the door behind me. "I'll expect your answer by bedtime."

Tonight, I was expected to attend the A&M's fundraising campaign kickoff cocktail party for its new Criminology Building. Launched in partnership with the Westlind Corporation, the School of Criminology was hoping to find donors to help it pay for the other half of this state-of-the-art structure, which would come complete with high-tech crime labs, as well as endowing at least two new chairs and establishing three new criminology programs. I had drawn the short straw to see who'd have to be the requisite departmental public face.

By the time I arrived, small clusters in formal attire loitered around the buffet table, a smorgasbord stretching across the width of the lawn, open bars at each end. Servers in tall white cowboy hats assisted from behind the tables. The mosquitoes were out in force, swirling thick about in the air like clouds of dust. They followed close on the heels of a storm that had left the ground still soggy, water pooling upon the tables, the chairs, everything. The runoff flowed along the yard's gradual slope, out to its edge, where it dropped off precipitously into a dense ravine, cluttered with brambles and vine.

I stood beside the edge, captivated by the falling water, nursing a mint julep. The light was slipping quickly from the landscaped yard, and the young black men in white tuxedos, mostly students from the college, were setting up torches to fend off the encroaching dark.

A short man with a shiny bald head greeted everyone with a smile as we came in. This was the president of the A&M, Walter "Wally" Alvarez, and it was his job, like mine, to be here, to schmooze with potential donors and alums. It was his primary responsibility and greatest qualification. You'd think he knew everyone, for his warmth and good cheer. He had approached me with a bubbling smile, a fierce handshake and a gentle lead toward the bar, all before I'd had the chance to introduce myself, having never met him before in my life.

Through the dusk and flickering torchlight, I saw a woman approaching. She was a washed out silhouette, but her familiar step, the confident swagger, the glass of wine carelessly tipping—I knew long before she come into the light who it was.

"Starting a second career as a philanthropist, Janice?" I said.

"Not counting it out," she said, arriving with a grin. "I have fond memories of my own college days, as you well know. No amount is too great to give."

"But you're cheap. And poor."

"True. But that's not how I choose to live. One of the great perks of being both a writer and professor is schwag, and I take full advantage when I can. Especially when food is involved. Yesterday, someone offered me a week-long hunting package."

"You don't hunt, either."

"You're never too old to start a new hobby. I have an irresistible fondness for listening to dull banalities given as speeches."

"Not as much as they like giving them."

"Secretly, though, I'm conducting research on the political fundraiser."

"You seem to be misinformed. They're just raising money for the college. You know political rallies make me physically ill."

Janice handed me her wine glass, then pawed through her purse until she found a cigarette and lighter.

"See that man over there?" she said, exhaling thick smoke and gesturing toward the milling crowd by the bar, faces losing distinction through the dark and distance. "That's Hugh Gillespie, state senator from Woodrow County. A real firecracker, as they say. Second most powerful man in the State house, which is impressive, since he never seems to be in the majority. There's not a function he attends that doesn't involve political wheeling and dealing. There are more than a few ways to get around finance laws."

"Is he one of ours?"

"Ours? You forget to whom you are speaking. I am an independent."

"I think the word you're searching for is 'professional antagonist.'"

"Political affiliation is such a fluid concept. I do believe Hugh has been, in no particular order, a Republican, a Democrat, and a Dixiecrat, as well as briefly flirting with both the Natural Law Party and the Libertarians. Not that anyone up on the hill cares. The party is apparatus. What matters is your district, how much money you have, how many connections you have. Not a soul or ideal they wouldn't sell if the price was right."

"You're ruining my faith in government."

"You're the most naive political appointee I've ever met, Matthew. It's a wonder you've survived this long."

"I just choose to believe that others have more integrity than I."

"I suspect that may be your undoing."

Scandal currently rattled the state's halls of government. The previous governor had recently been driven from office for offenses that thirty years ago would barely have merited a headline. A long career of bribes and cronyism, which had served so well to put him in office, ultimately had come back to destroy him. And it was Janice who had been the architect of his destruction, as well as of most scandals political and massive in this town, though most people didn't know it.

As a political stringer for the Capitol Times, Janice DeTreffant penned a weekly column under the pseudonym "Jefferson," which kept her a relative unknown to the powerful figures in State government whom she routinely skewered. The pseudonymous "Jefferson" was a perpetual burr on their backside, as the House Speaker once labeled her, an honor she valued highly. Though the most powerful had long since ferreted out her identity, most casual observers in the capital—and even a significant number of operatives—had no idea she was even a woman, and even those who learned the truth were often too sexist to believe it. Just as many claimed that Janice herself was a front for some other, even deeper undercover investigative reporter. All of this gave her ease of movement, and the opportunity to pick up on pieces of information from relaxed legislators who might otherwise have been more careful about what they were saying.

Janice and I weren't connected by politics, though. We had met when I was still a struggling undergrad and she was in the process of revising her dissertation into a book, Political Tribalism and Cultural Identity in the American South (1865-1965). After achieving tenure, though, her interests had turned more forcefully to politics and reporting. Her association with the college was fairly perfunctory and tangential these days. She was also the closest thing in the world I had to a real friend, though I saw her infrequently of late and never bothered reading the copy of the book she signed for me. We could do each other considerable harm with the things we knew about each other, which had only helped our friendship grow.

"How's fatherhood treating you?"

"It's not exactly what I expected."

"What, exactly, has ever been what you expected?"

"I mean it's hard."

"I don't think you fully grasp your situation."

"I grasp it."

"So where's Junior?"

"At home."

"I'm guessing without a sitter."

"I'm not concerned. She's pretty mature for a twelve-year-old."

"That's why you should be concerned," she said, pushing her hair back away from her eyes. Her most prominent feature was that thick, brown mane of hair, arching and irreverent; she draped the length of it across her shoulders, so it lay thick and billowy, in the style of a '40s movie starlet. No one would mistake her for a screen legend, however. A car saleswoman, perhaps. An evangelist. A sixth-grade teacher. She could easily be someone who makes children stand in front of a classroom and work long division on the chalkboard.

"I'm feeling generous with advice today," she continued. "Get out of politics, Matty, before it kills you."

"I'm not the one making enemies out of the most powerful people in the state. Remember, Governor Roberson sent a goon squad after you."

"Ex-Governor Roberson."

"Was it an ex-goon squad, too?"

"People always blow these things out of proportion," she said with a sigh, taking a long drag. "It wasn't a squad. Just two guys coming round the newsroom making trouble. They were kinda sweet, too."

"Sweet goons, with guns."

"Pea shooters," she said, flicking the cigarette butt into a small shrub. "Pathetic, really. Even I'm better armed than that."

"That's why I feel safer just standing next to you.

She cocked an eyebrow. "You shouldn't, you know."

Back under the lights, Wally was rambling, thanking everyone for recognizing the important role that higher education served in our community, for opening up their hearts and wallets to such an important cause. It was the usual speech, and like the best of them, you knew the next word even before it left his lips. It made you feel smart and superior. You could recite along with him.

"By the way, I hear you've got a special assignment. I'll have to buy you a black hood or something."

"News travels fast. I only found out this afternoon."

"You could see it coming. Governor Van Garen is a novice, paying for the sins of his predecessor and in the fight of his political life. Nothing like a little show to satisfy the masses."

After dealing with the execution all day, I didn't exactly have a strong desire to talk about it again. Instead, I asked Janice if she knew anything about the investigation at Environmental that Hal had mentioned

She leaned in close. "Nothing to be worried about, I hope."

"Why does everyone keep asking me that?"

"Sorry. Occupational habit."

"I'm just anxious in a general sort of way. So you haven't heard anything?"

Janice shook her head in disinterest, almost bored, then took a long sip from her refreshed drink. "Don't you think it's time for you to quit this whole politics thing?"

"This is my career. And I'm pretty good at it, if I say so myself."

She said nothing for a moment, starting at me with a curious look on her face. Finally, she said: "You see that unassuming fellow over there, Matthew, the one in the bow tie talking with the two Supreme Court justices? That, my political friend, is Bertrand Walker."

The man she pointed toward was a thin rail, his suit obviously too short for his body. He wore rounded wire frames low on his nose. He, too, could have been a school teacher.

"Name sounds familiar," I said, which only made Janice produce an exaggerated sigh.

"Bertrand Walker. He is the proverbial 'man behind the throne.' The governor's top political advisor. A more powerful person you will likely never meet in this state. They may have ousted Vern for his lawbreaking, but nothing seems to touch Walker, though his fingers are in everything. He was the power behind the last governor, this governor, probably the next one, too, whoever that ends up being. Anyone who expects to get anywhere politically in this state owes some kind of debt to him. You already do, whether you know it or not. And he's not the kind of person you want to be indebted to."

"I'm too young to owe anyone anything."

"People like Walker are untouchable. They aren't scared of the law. Like all cockroaches, they're scared of the light."

"That's not a little bit paranoid, Janice. At all."

"Trust me, Matthew. This kind of work isn't for you, and it's going to get you into trouble some day. You aren't a politician. You aren't really even a fixture of the party. If you were, you'd know everything there was to know about Bertrand Walker. Nothing will ever touch him. The best I will ever be able to do would be to foil his schemes. What you are—or are becoming—is a career bureaucrat. There a hundred people in this town who could do the job you are struggling through better than you." Before I could answer, she cut me off: "Don't bother protesting. You know I'm right. Sure, you're smart, which is fine, but the truth is, this isn't exactly your cup of tea."

"I'm doing all right."

"Don't get defensive." Janice took a long drink, draining her glass, then carelessly dropped it onto the grass. "I'm just saying you're not good enough."

"At least I'm not out there destroying careers. Brought down any more governors lately?"

"Sorry. One a year is my limit."

"Come on. Not even a little bit of scandal?"

"Always," she said. "The kind of thing that wrecks careers, marriages, country club memberships."

"Not showing a bit of conscience, are we? That doesn't sound like you."

"Believe me. I'd write about it if I thought anyone would buy it."

"Sordid, I take it."

"Graphic!" She beamed. "Amazing what a college student will do for a little money."

"Perhaps that's why our lonely legislators keep raising tuition."

Janice raised an eyebrow. "You'd be shocked by what the desperate will say for a little bit of cash in hand."

"To you, or to Johnny Senator?"

"Take your pick," she said, gesturing toward the silhouetted crowd.

"Really?"

"Matty, Matty, Matty," Janice tsked.

In the bright lights near the house, a brown haze had settled in, churning and blurred—gnats and mosquitoes and moths and other bugs drawn in by the lamps and the warm, alcoholic bodies in the evening air.

Then something suddenly dropped out of the sky into the midst of the gathered crowd. Soon another half-dozen, diving, spinning, tacking in a majestic display of aerial acrobatics. Bodies shuffled, gently laughing, the power brokers and politicians, the institutional philanthropists and their hangers on. We refilled our cocktails and reveled in a collective humor, gesturing wildly at the blur of wings streaking through the slaughter and cool night sky.

five

Once a year, nearly every year for the past one hundred and fifty, people gathered for a reenactment of the Battle of Blossom Ferry. These were the history buffs, the fifth-generation locals, the desperate and desolate still clinging to the cause. Without this, they could see what they had left. Though I'd lived in the county my entire life, I had never attended, and Hero decided that this oversight should be rectified.

"An honest to goodness redneck celebration?" She jumped on the foot of my bed in the morning, while I was trying to will myself back to sleep. "Who'd want to miss it?"

"Me," I said. "I'd like to miss it."

"But it's a tradition around here."

"That doesn't make it mine."

"I don't see your point," Hero said.

Hero had gone ahead and invited Janice, who in turn offered to drive the three of us. She was the only one of my friends whom Hero had met and liked. Though, as usual, there were caveats.

"She's killer," Hero said, as Janice pulled into our driveway. "Just don't ever trust her."

"She's the most honest person I know."

"Exactly my point."

Blossom Ferry was nothing more than a footnote reference in any history of the Civil War I'd ever seen, of the ones that even bothered to mention it; but the way the throngs turned out to watch and participate, you'd think it was the pivotal battle in the entire war. Perhaps that was because it was the only major skirmish to occur within a hundred miles of the city. Or possibly because it was a Southern victory, at a time late in the war when so little was going the Confederacy's way. In truth, though, it is only staged as a victory. Historians are quick to point out that it was more accurately a draw, and a messy one at that. It might even have been more precisely described as a strategic victory for the Union, since while the Confederate forces refused to give ground, their casualties were so great that the Northern troops simply marched through the same territory a few weeks later with hardly a scuffle.

At the site of the battle, Southland Enterprises was in the midst of construction on SouthWorld, a massive theme park and a sort of tribute to the Confederacy and the Antebellum South as a whole, as the billboards lining the drive in proclaimed. When completed, it would have "historically accurate" portrayals of "average pre-Civil War Southern life," a claim most minority communities found borderline offensive and said so. In addition, there would be restaurants and craft shops and live performances and artisans, residential housing, executive accommodations, and nearly a dozen rides, including The Rebel Yell, "the largest roller-coaster this side of the Mason-Dixon." Coming Next Summer!!

We arrived early to the battlefield. Plaques and paved paths directed visitors around the dense growth. What for the invading armies had been a treacherous and unknown wilderness was now a carefully laid out tourist attraction. Trees that might obstruct the path had been cut down and sawed into manageable sections. Janice pointed out that one of the primary difficulties during the war for the north was a lack of good maps. Were the war fought today, they could arrive at a trailhead and check out the etched and detailed map with its restrooms and major highways and obligatory red dot:

YOU ARE HERE.

The field of battle itself was mostly clear, and in the background, a row of condos. On one balcony, a party was raging, with people cheering and heavy music splitting the morning stillness. The re-enactors, the purists, were visibly perturbed, shuffling around in an uneasy silence while awaiting the start of the festivities. We waited along with two-dozen other onlookers. The rebel soldiers around were a motley bunch dressed in drab, mostly middle-aged, mostly white. Then a young man in a knock-off Colonel Sanders suit whistled for everyone's attention and announced to the small crowd that the coordinator had been delayed, but that they would be starting anyway in a few minutes.

"They should be black," I said. "That's one of the few things I remember from history class, the irony. The Southern army defending the Confederacy was black and the Northerners were all white."

"That's baloney," Janice said, taking up a position between me and Hero.

"No, it's true," I said. "They'd been promised freedom by the Confederacy. Once it became clear that the South was losing the war, the leaders had a choice: Either free the slaves or lose their own freedom. For some, that was when the South actually lost the war, even though they hung on for a while longer. It's the moment when the aristocracy decided that they weren't fighting for ideas any more. Just themselves."

"Quite a sanitized narrative, isn't it?" Janice said. "The idea that in some benevolent Southland, we weren't fighting to maintain a corrupt system of enslavement. I think it makes the whole thing much more romantic, don't you?"

"Can't you let us hold on to some of our treasured history?"

"History knows no saints," she said. "Who doesn't love a good story? Black soldiers defending the South? Trust me. All fiction."

"They say truth is stranger than fiction."

"They also say lots of things that are bullshit. I'm a historian. I should know."

"You're a journalist. Who used to be an anthropologist."

"People would know it's B.S., too, if they bothered to read and didn't just want to believe the story they liked best."

The battle was starting. The blue coats had retreated across to
the far side of the field, to the south, and the ragtag Confederates
stepped behind a line of trees to wait.

"There wasn't even a ferry," Janice added.

A whistle sounded somewhere behind us.

"How do you remake history?" Janice was saying. "You can't
recapture the essence of a battle. The fear. The unknown. All you can
get is choreography."

"Maybe they're frustrated dancers," I said.

Hero stepped hard on my toe. "Do you two mind? I'm trying to
watch a war."

The Union troops were coming into view. They were running
across the field, screaming at who knows what. The Southerners
behind the trees were having trouble keeping from laughing. Soon,
the pop of blanks exploded, and a half-dozen figures running across
the field simultaneously clutched their chests, spun around and
fell to the ground. A moment later, a few of those dead stood up,
apparently loath to be dead so soon, and continued the charge.

Meanwhile, the Southern conscripts were obviously getting
anxious waiting for their counterparts to arrive. One older soldier
let out a hoarse yell and raced out of the trees to meet the oncoming
troops. I saw three bluecoats take shots directly at him, and when he
didn't slow, they threw their arms up in disgust. When he reached
the Union troops, he shot at a couple point blank. No one fell. In
the middle of the battlefield, a brief debate began. A few errant
blanks fired here and there, but the overall battle had come to a
sputtering halt. Some just stood shaking their heads, leaning against
the support of the rifles. The organizer in the white dandy suit had
slipped through the trees and joined in the discussion.

The quiet conversation soon became more intense and evolved
into an argument, with pointing and shouting and arms thrown
up in frustration. Finally, one blue coat raised the butt of his rifle
and smacked the lone Confederate in the face, knocking him to the
ground.

The remaining line of Southerners charged out of the undergrowth in response, no longer firing shots, but hurling rocks and swinging their guns like clubs. The line of spectators took a step back as the playacting transformed into actual violence. One family rushed off toward the cars, the father with two kids saddling his shoulders. A band of Confederates separated from the melee and raced into the dense brush, immediately chased by four beefy Northern corporals. The lines were completely blurred now, as both sides became enmeshed in their individual fights. Large out-of-shape middle-agers wrestling around in the wet grass with energetic twenty-somethings.

We took cover behind a low hedge, nearer to the fighting, but clearly out of bounds.

"You know, this is a little bit more realistic than I'd expected," Hero observed.

Janice pulled out a cigarette. "It's human nature. In the pitch of battle, when things get really intense, who's there to keep people in line? Once you're up close, there's very little to do but try to beat the crap out of someone else."

By the time we'd had enough and were ready to leave, after nearly half an hour and innumerable counts of assault, the police had arrived, as well as the absent choreographer, who was still trying to salvage something of the original battle's history by coaxing the Northern troops to retreat toward the east again, and convincing most of the remaining Southern troops to lie still upon the ground long enough to be reasonably considered dead.

"Don't get the wrong idea about Southerners," I said to Hero on the ride home. "We're a laid-back people, mostly. We don't like to rock the boat."

She propped her elbows on my seat back. Our eyes met in the rearview mirror. "I thought this was the land of Rebels, stuff like that."

"That's propaganda," Janice said, gunning the engine as the light turned green. "Honestly. We're harmless."

We drove past three billboards in close succession—two of them told us we should repent our sins; the other advertised discounts for laser corrective eye surgery.

"Didn't you start a war or something?" Hero asked. "I think I read that somewhere."

"What choice did we have?" I said. "They invaded us. You can look it up."

"I also read somewhere that you might have deserved it. But really, I just want to know what it is with you people and living in the past. Can't you just let it go and get on with things?"

"That's the old South. This is the new one."

Hero leaned back in her seat. "I'm still trying to figure out the difference."

six

The ground beneath our feet was collapsing. This was the summer of sinkholes, and they were ubiquitous, popping up everywhere unexpectedly and with a seemingly intentional flair for the dramatic. Despite the brief and torrential afternoon rains, the water tables were running low after years of below-average precipitation and our thin aquifer ceiling was brittle and crumbling. With the slightest weight or pressure, it could break. There was no telling where or when it would strike.

It began one afternoon when a section of the Augustus Highway caved in during the height of rush hour, taking out a semi at full stop and sending the trailer-load of pigs squealing into a twelve-foot-wide crater. Most of the pigs survived the fall, however, miraculously pulling their chubby bodies onto the highway—and right into the oncoming traffic. Cars everywhere braking, suddenly swerving, piling and compounding.

A few days later, a much larger disaster, also miraculously without fatality (human, at least). A trailer park, three homes sucked underground. Every last bit obliterated—trailer, lawn gnomes, plastro-turf, large-bulb outdoor Christmas lights. Neighbors hovered together around the pit, thanking God that no one had been at home, placing arms around the returned families grieving and staring blankly down into the disaster, the sudden loss beyond their comprehension. The assembled memorabilia, the private stashes, custom-groomed suburban front facades, crumbled and scattered. Once, a row of homes overflowing with life. Now—

A week later, a man died while waiting at a bus stop. Witnesses said it was as if the earth just swallowed him up.

There was no way to know what might go next. Watch your children, authorities said. Drive with caution. Pay your premiums and make sure all of your affairs are in order. Downtown among the semi-high high-rises, few dawdled or loitered. We walked with lighter steps, slipping into our buildings, fully aware that it might be for the last time. I eyed the long shadow of the new capitol building with appropriate distrust.

In my office, I found two men waiting, neither of whom I knew. The younger of the two was looking at the picture frames lining my wall. They were old photographs I had collected of the capital's downtown over the decades—horse and buggy streets, unique building architecture and signage, the sparseness of a small town that had since overrun itself. The man was leaning in close, lifting up his thick-framed, heavily tinted lenses.

"These are some crazy pictures," he said, without looking over as I came in. "I don't think I've seen ones like them."

"Thanks," I said, walking over to my desk. Another man, gray fraying about his temple, sat in front of my desk in the leather chair, wordlessly tapping a pencil on the leather molding.

"Old pictures like this," said the man by the frames, "I'm always curious to see what I can recognize. It's not discovering what's missing that is so fascinating, but seeing that something has endured after all these years."

"The more things change, as they say," I mumbled, not sure what else to say. I shuffled uneasily, waiting for either of my visitors to get to the point, any point at all having to do with me. "Can I help you gentlemen with something?"

"Bill Stanton," the younger man said, stepping away from the pictures and toward the desk; but rather than hold out his hand, he reached into his jacket and pulled out a card. "Special prosecutor's office."

The older man was still quiet, still tapping his pencil on the armrest without looking up, and it seemed clear to me now that they'd made an agreement about who was to do the talking. He was obviously displeased with the arrangement. I imagined the politics between them, of the young up-and-comer pushing aside the aged veteran.

I gestured Stanton toward the other chair by my desk and set down my briefcase. "Should I be worried?" I attempted a carefree laugh.

"We just want to have a conversation," Stanton said, trying to make it sound lighthearted, but still something made him seem grim. There was a graininess to him, like a figure in one of those old photographs, just out of focus. But you could tell in an instant—here was a man who took the measure of things. A man of sums, someone for whom everything would eventually add up.

"You are currently associate director of the Department of Corrections?"

"If I'm not, I'm in the wrong office," I joked.

Stanton smiled lightly, and his partner just rolled his eyes.

"Now, you used to work at the Bureau of Environmental Study."

"Over a year ago," I said. "I was the director for about three years. Is that what this is about? The investigation at Environmental?"

The older man looked over at his colleague, shifting in his seat uncomfortably. "We're not at liberty to say."

"I just want to know if I'm being investigated, too, for some reason."

The two men sat quietly for another moment, neither taking eyes off of me.

"We aren't at liberty to say."

"What are you at liberty to say?"

"We were hoping you might be able to help us with any information from your time working at the Bureau of Environmental Study."

"What sort of information?"

"Anything at all that might be of interest."

"I don't know about anything illegal, if that's what you're talking about."

"Did you ever come across anything unusual in your time working there? Did anyone ever ask you to do anything that you considered ethically… questionable?"

"Not that I recall."

Stanton and his partner exchanged a quick look, but didn't say anything.

"I guess that sounds incriminating," I added quickly. "I'm not good at this kind of thing."

"That's fine."

"I mean, I don't think so. I just don't feel comfortable speaking in absolutes."

"That's fine," Stanton said again.

"I mean, my job was pretty benign. No one really ever asked me to do anything. It was a lot of paperwork. A lot of signatures. Boring stuff. Looking over recommendations and reports from the actual scientists. I wasn't really qualified to pass judgments or anything. Basically, I just followed the recommendations that came across my desk. Pretty simple, really. I think I'd remember if someone made a special request. But I can't be sure."

Never having been interrogated before, and feeling the absurdity of trying to defend myself for having to defend myself, fear wasn't really at the heart of my experience. I stood outside of myself, looking in on these men who seemed so clearly to want me to tell them something, yet unable to realize that I had nothing to tell them.

"What about your replacement. Mr. Morr?"

"What about him?"

The older man sat up. "When he was your assistant, did you ever ask him to bend the rules?"

"Guess that depends upon what you mean by 'bend.' " I smiled, but neither man smiled back. "I mean, no." Slowly, it was dawning on me that my innocence wasn't any kind of protection, and I sunk back into myself. "I'm suddenly feeling a little anxious here," I said.

"We're just having a conversation."

"I wasn't some guy with an agenda. I had no reason to bend the rules. I don't even know what rules we're talking about. Much less why I'd want to bend them." I didn't mention that I'd have had very little idea how to do so anyway.

Both men said nothing. The younger man, Stanton, seemed on the cusp of speaking, but then tapped his colleague's sleeve.

"Well, we've taken up enough of your time, Mr. Brown. We do appreciate your cooperation. If we have further questions, we hope you'll be available." They shook my hand, Stanton's handshake less firm, but congenial.

As they left my office, they passed by Hal, who was hovering by the door.

"I'm an idiot," I said, watching Stanton and his colleague follow the cubicle maze out.

"No argument here. What'd they want?"

"They're not at liberty to say."

"They asking about Corrections?"

"No. Environmental. I just hope they aren't also interested in me."

"Ready for lunch?" he asked, brushing past my concern with a dismissive cock of his head.

"I just got in."

"Gotta eat sometime."

"In an hour, maybe, sure," I said.

"Sure, sure."

As Hal left, I paused to consider my brief interview with Stanton and his largely silent partner. The truth was, I didn't have anything to tell them at all, and despite my clumsy attempts to incriminate myself, I consoled myself with the thought that they were most likely merely fishing for information. I had nothing to offer them, though, and so my contributions to any kind of investigation of the Bureau, especially of current personnel, were likely minimal. What I knew about Bernie Morr, especially over the past year, was even less, and if they hoped to use me to get to him, they were going to be sorely disappointed to discover my overwhelming ignorance.

My in-box was beginning to fill with requests for media credentials for the upcoming execution. With the date now set, one month away, the media was starting to jump into the fray. Ten years without the state killing anyone had made my task especially difficult. We lacked any kind of clear procedure.

Of all my tasks, the most bizarre was the matter of the last meal. I held Adler's request card, boxes marked, crossed off, blurred and smudged eraser marks, finally double-starred to indicate exactly which choice he wanted. The special request lines were filled with looping, bubbly characters that might have been drawn by Hero were she of a different sensibility, the sort who would have appreciated my bedroom design efforts, instead of the brutal killer that Adler was. He wanted a steak, medium rare, lobster (or shrimp, if that wasn't available), BBQ chicken, dark meat, fruit salad—no bananas—grape juice (wine and other alcoholic beverages were not allowed), pecan pie, a single glazed doughnut.

I phoned Hal and told him I was ready to go eat.

We often took lunch at Early's, a small kitchen crowded between rusty warehouses, two blocks from the train tracks. This proximity had always bothered me. It felt too easy, obvious: a living cliche. The line bums. Shanty houses. Pounding rhythms rising from shuffling boxcars. Poverty spreading over everything, onto us, like an odor, scents compelling and repulsive, stench of garbage and the billowing hickory smoke.

Early's stood between the Murat Gun & Pawn and the Country Feed store—an oasis for lunchtime travelers. Early himself was a lanky, lean black man of indeterminate years. His face seemed young, but both hair and voice carried hints of graying age. Today the dining room bustled like a marketplace or the floor of the Stock Exchange. Short bursts of laughter cut through the overlapping conversations, Early's sister Edna's great bellow carrying most from her position at the register. A brilliant red scarf engulfed her yards of thick hair. The place was just now opening after being closed for two weeks during an investigation concerning food poisoning. Rumor placed the blame on the ox-tail soup.

I ordered the grilled possum on toast, with a side of greens. Hal eyed my plate with distaste.

"My mother used to make that stuff. Nasty, man. Really."

The crispy cut of meat was draped with spiced apples and rested on a mountain of sweet potatoes. The thin bread, charcoal black and sopping with grease and juice, poked up from the bottom.

"I can guarantee you that my mother never even imagined you could make this stuff," I said. "I'm branching out. I want the whole Southern experience."

"Give it up, Matthew, my man. You're never going to be black, no matter how hard you try."

"Patience. I've only just started."

We found an open spot at the end of the long picnic bench, the only form of seating in the whole place. Hal had invited one of his assistants, Becky, who slid in silently across from us with a smile.

"This white guilt thing is going just a bit too far," Hal said. "On behalf of the brothers and sisters everywhere—and I believe I'm speaking for Becky, too—I'm asking you to just butt out. Leave Soul Food to those who've got soul. Look at me. You don't see me out trying to co-opt your damn French restaurants."

"I hate snails," I said

"Do you see possum on this plate? I order the chicken."

Becky sat staring blankly into space while we talked, dragging her fork along her plate of dirty rice, dipping into her bowl of peach cobbler and eating whatever she had scooped without looking. This was her third month at Corrections, and I had yet to hear the woman speak. Hal kept asking her to lunch with us because he wanted to make her feel included. I had begun to consider, despite Hal's assurances to the contrary, that she was a mute. Hal said she didn't like to chitchat, that she was waiting for something really good to say. She was, as he put it, choosing her moment.

"Can't a man eat his meal in peace?" I asked.

"You done with the execution yet?"

"I'm choosing my moment," I said. "Right now, I'm dealing with his last meal."

"Anything especially bizarre he wants us to bring him?"

"I just don't see how they choose."

"Or do they get a list?" Hal asked.

"How does someone select his last meal?"

"How did you pick this one?"

"That's what I mean. Exactly. This is totally different. For my last meal on earth, I wouldn't be eating possum."

"Famous last words, man. You'll probably step out of here and get hit by a bus."

"You're quite an optimist, Hal."

"Look at it this way, man. At least you've narrowed down your choices."

"But I'm not choosing it to be my last. The condemned—what do they base their choices on?"

"There are two kinds of people in the world." Hal set down his fork and cracked his knuckles. "There are those in the gluttony camp, who figure that they want the last taste of anything they could ever possibly have."

"That's definitely Adler."

"But then there's the ones who seem to be more palate-conscious. They want foods that go well together. They'd never mix shrimp Creole and Yoo-hoo."

"Sounds lovely."

"Cold tomato juice on your Fruit Loops."

"Oysters and milk," I volunteered.

"Hot dogs and chocolate sauce."

"There's no accounting for taste."

Becky looked up as if she was about to say something, but she just smiled and turned back to her food. Hal scraped the bottom of his plate with his fork.

"If those investigators come back, you let me know. We've got to watch our backs, my friend."

When we returned to the office, we found the streets and parking lots overflowing. Police tape wrapped up the courtyard. A half-dozen squad cars had run up onto the sidewalk in front of the new capitol building. News trucks arrived close behind us. WKCL. WRND. WWWN. Reporters began to gather, clutching their sheets of important-seeming papers and brushing back the grooming hands of Make-up. They fought for position at the dais, by the mermaid-sculptured water fountain, by the State seal, any recognizable landmark to prove, via live feed, that they were in fact "on the scene." Camera lights flooded the terrace, and everyone but the reporters was bleached into oblivion. Officers milled about in the doorway, periodically glancing back at the mob, either to spy a television celebrity, a reporter, even a weatherman, or simply to encourage questions. They carried the authority of the moment, the law. We don't have all the facts yet, but our people are investigating.

Someone, we heard them say, had barricaded himself at the top of the capitol, inside the observation gallery. He had a list of demands that needed to be filled. First: he wanted doughnuts, Krispy Kreme, in equal parts glazed and jelly-filled. Second, pizza, anyone who delivered, for the officers forced to wait out his siege. He also wanted world peace and equality for all.

Clearly, authorities announced, they were dealing with a subversive element.

Hours passed uneventfully, until the ranks of the press finally began to deplete through attrition. Then, in the haze of late afternoon, Special Forces punctured the glass and launched a canister of tear gas. The sputtering terrorist, actually just a local junior college kid with a history of mental illness, was remanded to the custody of Mental Health. He was placed under a doctor's care, though he fought for his right to not be forcibly medicated.

Landmarks and Monuments announced the floor would be closed for a week to remodel.

seven

From my upstairs study window I saw them coming, The
van rolled to a careful stop at the end of the block and parked,
and then they embarked, first fanning out, then encroaching
slowly, house by house, in teams of two, three. These are the only
solicitors still allowed in Magnolia Grove. They are evangelicals
who come a-knocking, bringing with them their good books, their
denomination-specific suits or robes, their grim certainty and the
airs of right and righteousness.

The week before it had been young men in orange skirts and
T-shirts, heads shaved close but not quite. Before that, the teenage
boys in white shirts and ties who called themselves Elders but really
just seemed so desperate to talk with anyone about anything that
we barely got to religion. Today, it was a troop of elderly gentlemen
in warm brown suits, inching their way up the walks. You could tell
from their grim huddle and gaze that they meant business.

I let Hero deal with them when they knocked on our door
and instead retreated upstairs. In the hallway outside Hero's room
hung perhaps the earliest known picture of the house. No date, but
based upon the clothing and styles, it appeared to have been taken
some time around the start of the 20th century. My grandfather
had pointed it out to me on several occasions as he gave tours of
the house. Truth be told, the building in the photo, or at least the
incomplete portion that was visible, bore little resemblance to its
current form. There was a porch, for one, which stretched along
the face of the building and a row of evenly spaced cookie-cutter

windows. The whole frontal façade was different, too. In fact, if my grandfather hadn't been so certain, I might never have believed that this was the same house. But then, I'd since seen a map of the original footprint of the house. You could easily make out the other neighborhood houses that were at least that old. Everything around us was identifiable. Ours was something else entirely. My grandfather had explained that this was due to "The Fire," which had taken out most of the upper floors and caused considerable damage throughout the structure. Paused in front, several black people in raggedy dress, most likely former slaves from the plantation or their children, stood cold and sullen, their eyes passing judgment, insisting we not forget.

About the house now, the Reconstruction was continuing, albeit intermittently. I'd recently hired a contractor to begin some of the more elaborate work. But as they'd begun restructuring the gables to match the original façade, they'd made a curious discovery. A kind of passageway had been walled off for decades, most likely also damaged in The Fire, as my grandfather reverently referred to it. His oddly fervent insistence that he had no ideas about the cause of the blaze had always left me with vague suspicions that he knew more than he had ever let on—and the uncovering of this secret enclosure held out promise for more revelations.

But the reality was far less interesting. Within the walled-off space, there were mounds of shingles and wood and nails—the residue of a decades-old re-roofing project. Under the dust and debris lay a trove of historical incoherence—an old washing basin and an electric sewing machine; a horse team harness and a car jack. Turn-of-the-century newspapers stacked atop a package of unopened floppy disks. Two unopened burlap sacks of pinto beans, one of flour. In the corner stood a three-legged desk, a mirror frame atop, though no glass, and an old corroded woven straw basket. Scattered about were fully intact olive jars, tins of cough syrup and soda, some lightly lacquered with the dried residue. In one corner, rolls of poster advertisements for items such as Queeg digestive gum and Legent pomade; an arrowhead, a necklace of shark teeth, a brass door knocker, and a nearly complete set of broken china. The treasures of someone else's age.

The exterior wall was now torn away, and in its place, a blue plastic tarp was all that separated our upstairs from the elements, secured to the new gable's wooden frame. I hadn't seen the workmen in several days, the contractor in over a week. As I sorted through the piles of old shingles and nails that were scattered about the floor, I could vaguely hear the sound of voices downstairs. Hero was talking, the strangers answering. It didn't end quickly. They were engaged. It sounded as if they had left the front door and entered the living room. Hero was rummaging in the kitchen. They laughed together, chatting away the afternoon.

I stayed hunkered in the debris for nearly an hour, sorting, waiting.

When I finally heard the front door open and shut and peered down to see the two men retreating down the walk, I came out. Hero was carrying drained glasses with half-melted ice back to the kitchen.

"You should have come down," she said.

"What did they want?"

"Saving the damned. Money for their trouble."

"Same old, same old."

"It can't hurt to be nice," she pointed out.

"Sure it can."

"My father, the heathen."

"It's just a waste of time. Theirs and ours."

"Maybe not," she shrugged, then filled the cups up and left them in the sink.

"I somehow didn't expect you to find that kind of stuff intriguing."

"I'm exploring," she said "I'm at that age. I've got questions."

"Keep in mind that you may not like the answers."

"This is the Bible belt. I would've figured you'd be more

enthusiastic. Or at least supportive."

"I just don't like people trying to tell me what I should believe."

"I think you just don't like anyone to question your faith."

Growing up, my own family had been devoutly semi-religious. My father said we were "Periodicals," as we hopped from congregation to congregation in no discernible pattern. Lost sheep in search of a fold. Methodists, Presbyterians. Catholics, Unitarians, Baptists, Lutherans. Either the regimen was too strict or too loose, too intellectual or too vapid, and ultimately we left our confused and wearied spirits to drift leisurely, without mooring. But even when we did find a place to settle, we never went very often. Easter, Christmas, and perhaps six other assorted times throughout the year.

Hero and I stepped out through the sliding door into the backyard. This had become an increasingly hazardous endeavor. Nails and screws and splinters of shaved metal and wood littered the patio slab as the wraparound porch began to rise up at the edges. If I wanted to be perfectly authentic, the cement slab, too, would need to go, but I was waffling. It was something I wanted to discuss with the contractor if he returned tomorrow. I made a mental note to call him again, even if he refused to answer. Just so he'd know I knew he wasn't there.

Barefoot, Hero defiantly walked straight across the patio and out into the yard. The back line of my property was overgrown, dropping quickly into a steep ravine, an undeveloped and presumably undevelopable swath cutting straight through Magnolia Grove—each year creeping a bit closer. The sky above was threatening with heavy clouds, and the afternoon was turning dark.

Hero flopped down onto the unmolested long grass and gazed back up at me with a gray face.

"I hear you're going to be killing someone."

"Is that what this is about?"

"I think that's kind of a big deal."

"Janice told you, I suppose."

"About the killing," she said. "Yes."

"I'm not killing anyone," I said, bending down beside her. "I'm just arranging the execution. It's entirely different."

"Not for the guy dying," she said.

"I'm pretty sure it doesn't exactly matter to him who does it."

The thick overgrowth loomed in the twilight, and through the buzz and creak of the insects, we could make out sounds of small, slow movement—a neighborhood cat, most likely, or squirrels, raccoons, armadillo, the only roaming animals left to the city in this century. And us, teetering on the fringe of the wild.

"You're leaving in a week," I pointed out.

"I know."

"We don't have much time to sort all this out."

"Sort what out?" Her eyes were closed, her lips drawn into a soft smile that might have been satisfaction.

"Us. As in, how do we proceed from here?"

"Maybe we just wait and see."

"Wait and see what? What is there to see?"

She opened her eyes and stretched her arms out over her head into the grass with a large sigh. The pose struck me with a sense of my own vulnerability, facing the danger of a looming pounce.

"Does it bother you," she asked, "what you do?"

"What do I do?" I asked, crouching beside her.

"Your job. Locking people up."

"Someone has to do it," I said. "Imagine if we didn't."

"I'm still collecting data on you."

"You make me sound like an experiment."

To this, she just shrugged, as if to say that this seemed fairly obvious. I eased the rest of the way down onto the grass beside her. A bright flash of lightning and a swift low rumble told us we didn't have long before the storm.

"Maybe I should have given those missionaries money. God seems displeased."

"Do you believe in God?" she asked.

"That was a joke."

"But I'm being serious."

"Then, yes. Of course, I believe."

"But which god?"

"Now, that's the kind of question I'd expect from a teenager."

"Don't try to change the subject."

I sighed. "You're overwhelming, you know."

"You're still changing the subject."

"I just want to know how we're going to do this, the father/daughter thing."

Her eyes darkened. "I thought we were doing it."

"You know what I mean. Visits. Holidays. That kind of stuff."

"Let's not get ahead of ourselves."

"You're leaving."

"And you're rushing." Hero sat up and stared out into the thicket, cross-legged, tearing at the grass. She didn't sound upset, but the playfulness was lost into the silence. "Maybe coming here was a mistake."

"What do you mean?"

"I mean, maybe we aren't ready for this. Me. Maybe I'm not ready."

I didn't want to ask if this was about Geoffrey, but I felt fairly certain it had to be. I couldn't imagine what it would be like to be rejected by your father, the man who'd believed he was your father for your entire life. Val had insisted that the two of them had been very close and very similar. Two peas.

"We don't have to do this all at once," I conceded. "Maybe we're just trying too hard. We have time."

"Matthew," she said suddenly, the use of my name sounding so odd coming out of the blue. I may never have heard the word from her mouth before. It carried a desperate and ominous urgency, a plea to stop before we went too far. "I think we should consider the possibility that this may be all there is. And maybe it's fine to just leave it at that."

She laid bare the artifice of our relationship. Two people, bound together by a faith in something we couldn't begin to understand, who perhaps had no business being together at all. I was trying to be a father to her, but I could never fill that role as I imagined it. Twelve years had passed, and that time belonged to another person. There was no reclaiming it. But I was her father still. Somehow, we had to make this work.

"Maybe," I said, just as we saw the dark sheet of rain fold across the dense forest. "Don't give up on me yet, though."

"I didn't say I had."

With the arrival of August, the storms had begun to roll through, swift and overwhelming and threatening. You could set your watch by them; they never varied, punching through the thick afternoon at four, rumbling deep to the core and shading out the sun. The intermittent flashes, the occasional strike of lightning. As the winds kicked up and the horizon began to darken, everyone started taking cover, setting up in their usual seats. We settled by the large front window. The evangelists sprinted about with uncharacteristic and unbecoming panic beneath nature's wrath. Down the block at the senior center, the elderly wheeled indoors onto glass-enclosed porches and lined up by the sill in rows as always to watch the show.

When the rains began to fall, they came in scattered, heavy dollops, along with clipped gusts that rattled branches. Limbs whined under the stress. By the time it was a full-on downpour, puddles and streams ran inches deep everywhere. A knot of boys raced out in shorts, over their mothers' yells and the steady rumble of thunder, carrying large squares of cardboard. As the ditches and streets filled, they were surfing across the sheen, running hard and jumping onto their sagging boards, flying headfirst into grass and gravel, young blood mixing with the mud and the water and the cheers.

eight

At a church thrift store, Hero purchased an old guidebook of the county for 25 cents, which she then used to set up a series of excursions for the two of us: an antique car museum, the longest-running continuous outdoor flea market, the Woolworth's Civil Rights Memorial Lunch Counter—though the Woolworth's itself had long since been bought out, and in its place a Waffle House had moved in. (Hero ordered the grits.) After a nonstop barrage of these trips, I thought we'd seen everything there was to see. Then one evening she said she wanted to go visit a graveyard.

"Did you know that we have a family mausoleum? Apparently, someone was a pretty big deal and had the money in the end to prove it."

"I didn't know. I thought we were all buried in the plot out back."

"Apparently there are also monuments to war heroes. A few moderately famous but impoverished writers. Maybe even the unmarked grave of a rock star." She insisted that we go at dusk. "To set the right mood."

"What mood would that be?" I asked

"Solemn. Reverent. Junk like that."

"Couldn't we just go in daylight?" I asked.

"Why? Aren't you a little old to be scared of the dark?"

"I just thought it might be more productive if we could see."

Dusk it was to be, though, since I was still fairly pliable to her whims. I grabbed flashlights, much as Hero found this, as she put

it, "infantilizing." I complimented her on her vocabulary and loaded
up the truck. Our destination stood at the northernmost border
of town, and Hero had chosen it, she said, particularly because her
guidebook had indicated that some Napoleonic general had been
buried there after having retired to the quaint isolation of America
following the final exile to St. Helena. Dead French generals, she
assured me, were a passion of hers.

The light was failing as we drove, a night-flowering vine
streaking by our windows in a ray of blue as we raced down the
highway. We were passing through the outskirts of town, the fringe
that bordered the vast tracks of swampland. New subdivisions were
just beginning to branch out here, where a new breed of ambitious
developers had begun dredging the bogs and crafting man-made
lakes and waterways, with pre-stocked fishponds and boat docks.
This wasn't the fastest route to our destination, but I preferred this
way because it was so empty, still rugged and mostly untouched by
the capital's rapidly expanding population. We'd see one or two cars
out here in total, maybe an occasional farmhouse, and not a heck of
a lot else.

When we arrived at the cemetery, it appeared deserted. A mist
was gathering, weaving in and out of the twisted oaks and the
dangling moss. The low, rusted fence served more as border than
barricade, as evidenced by the scattered collections of beer cans,
condoms and toilet tissue.

"We're not the first people here." I said lightly.

"Disrespectful."

"They're dead," I said. "I doubt they care."

Hero frowned. "The drunk hicks. They don't respect themselves."

"May I remind you, I am one of those hicks."

"No," she said, "as a matter of fact, you may not."

Our family mausoleum stood crumbling on a hill in the center
of the graveyard, towering over the low tombstones—granite and
sandstone and alabaster. I took a step closer, reached up to touch
the old weathered stone. It was cold, nearly like ice, and I felt that

creeping dread of death run up my arm.

"The name above the door says Wultz-Schmitt," I pointed out.

"We don't have any Wultz-Schmitts in the family? Hmmm. My mistake."

Hero drifted out among the low stones and stood in what appeared to be an empty section of the field, starting at something obscured by the crawling vine.

"This one, on the other hand, is pretty interesting," she said. "Take a look."

It was a cement rectangle set in the ground, like a plaque. I leaned down and pulled away the weeds that had grown over it. The name—GARRETT JAMES LONGMAN—was fading, but you could easily still make out the short inscription beneath: May God Have Mercy On His Soul.

"He was young," I said, observing the dates. "Just twenty."

"Wonder what made him a killer," Hero said.

"A killer?" I looked over the gravestone but didn't see any other mark. "Where does it say that?"

"Didn't I mention?" she said. "We're standing in Murderer's Row. This is where they bury all the bodies of the people that get executed for capital crimes, the bodies no one wants. That's what the guidebook says, anyway. Hanging. Firing squad." She paused. "Electric chair."

"I see that you're going to make this some kind of object lesson."

"Think of it as another study," she said. "The effects of consequence on a guilty conscience."

I nodded. "If only there was something for me to feel guilty about."

The mist was thickening in the twilight, but Hero demonstrated no hurry to leave. Instead she led us through the unkempt grass, pointing out a variety of other convict markers, pausing over each to make sure I read the name out loud. This was, I imagined, her way of trying to guilt or goad me into some acknowledgment of my culpability. And I confess an eerie feeling began to fall over me, but in some ways this tour only made the whole experience feel less real. Adler was going to move from a name on a page to a plaque in the earth—I felt just as detached as always, but at least there seemed in this place to be an end to my task, which couldn't come soon enough for me.

"What do you imagine this is supposed to do for me?" I asked.

"It makes them more real, doesn't it?"

"I'm not a killer," I said.

"No," she said. "You just pull the lever."

"No, I pick the guy who pulls the lever. Like I said, it's completely different."

By the time we left, night had fully descended. As I drove, Hero was mostly silent, and I didn't feel any need to interrupt this calm before our inevitable storm. I gunned the engine until the whole of the cab rattled and threatened to shatter.

As the road curved right, I flipped on my brights to better make out the space ahead. Oncoming headlights filled the windshield, impenetrable and brilliant, overtaking everything. Rushing behind them, the powerful engine, the determined driver, the road growing more tiny and unsupportable by the second. Then, the lights passed in the rush of a small car I could just make out in my peripheral vision—bass turned up high, windows down, jamming its way through the night. Right in the path ahead of us, I saw the shine of eyeballs. Instinctively, I jerked the wheel, slightly but suddenly, to the side. Maybe it's wrong to say I didn't see it coming, because I used to see it coming all the time, every close brush by a semi on the freeway, every slick moment when the tires lost their grip—I just had no reason to believe that this one was going to be the one time it really happened.

As in a dream, the road swayed and two faint red dots ran streaking across my rearview. Somehow unreal, we were swerving. The truck fishtailed, a lumbering, heavy thing. Soon, we were full-on spinning, and there was nothing I could do but watch everything swirl and fall away. Then we were off the ground, airborne, soaring, and for this moment of incline, nothing seemed unattainable. Hero and I and this heavy, speeding machine, were breaking all the rules. A high squeal sounded—a voice or engine, it could be any one of us—and then we were falling.

I have no memory of hitting the ground.

❧

"Hero?"

I couldn't see a thing. I had no idea how long we'd been sitting here. The engine was silent, and the cab was still. Beyond my door, I could hear the fierce chirp of wildlife that was no longer concerned about us. We might have been sitting here for hours.

"Hero?" I said, this time louder.

Still nothing.

"Um… Marinara?"

"Keep trying," she said, quietly. She might have been sleeping.

"You okay?"

"I think so. Just a little achy all over. You?"

"I don't know," I said honestly. "Fine, I suppose."

In the blackness of the cab, I couldn't see myself. Beside me, I could just barely make out my daughter—a mere silhouette with an occasional dull outline of a feature—a cheek, a frown, the curve of ear.

"Why am I sitting in a puddle?" she asked.

"Good question," I said. "Me, too."

The well of the cab had filled with water that gathered around our thighs. I'd been aware of it for a few minutes now, subconsciously, but her question reminded me that this was odd. I wondered if I had a concussion, then wondered if someone with a concussion could wonder that. A cloudy sheen coated the windows, but even after Hero wiped a spot in the fog clear, there was nothing but more blackness to see.

"We'd better get out of here." I said finally.

Hero choked a pale laugh. "Ya think?"

"Seriously?" I said. "This is the time to joke?"

Escape was not so easy to accomplish. My shoulder ached when I tried to move it, feeling both stiff and constrained. My legs were completely submerged in a dark muck. I kicked against the flooring, trying to gain leverage. All around was the inescapable stench of bog, and crickets chirping in powerful, sharp chorus. That last moment played again in my head— the bright lights, the swerve and jump, the crash.

We were off road, "out there," somewhere, probably twenty miles from civilization, in the untamed and night-consumed wild. When I tried to sit up, I found myself bound where I sat.

"I think I'm trapped," I said.

"Freakin' jeez."

"Can you unlatch my seatbelt?" I asked. "It hurts to reach."

Though she was leaning in close over me, it felt strange that I still couldn't really see her. I wondered if perhaps I'd hurt my eyes. Immediately after Hero unlatched the belt, I felt the pressure lift. I could move with relative ease.

"My door won't open," Hero said.

"Try the window," I suggested

I turned the key, which faintly lit the dash, illuminating us like neon-green ghosts. Hers wouldn't roll, but mine did, weakly and slowly, about two thirds of the way down before jamming to a stop. Using my legs and pulling with my one good arm, I managed to crouch on the seat. The truck pitched as I leaned out the window, and Hero shrieked.

I tumbled out into the thigh-deep bog, water and muck swallowing my head in a swoosh. I thrashed about, digging myself back to the surface, afraid that the truck itself was about to fall on me. But the rig had just shifted mildly, listing at a slight angle before settling back down. As Hero pushed out of the window, I tried to ease her down into the water, but pain shot through my neck and shoulder and I dropped her.

When she came back to the surface, she was laughing.

"Good catch. What's wrong with your shoulder?"

"Nothing," I lied.

I reached over to hold up my arm to alleviate the pain. Something was seriously wrong with it, but I put that aside for the moment. For the first time, we could look around and survey our situation in the quarter light of the moon. The truck appeared to be lying relatively flat, as if parked, but still slightly tilted and buried deep in the muck halfway up the door, its tail flush against a tree where it had crashed to a halt. The bed was a crumpled accordion.

A little ways away, Hero was looking around. I could see her slightly better now in the partial moonlight. Her vague face was covered in splotches of dark mud and grime, but she didn't seem scared, for which I was thankful. Perhaps, like me, her anxiety and adrenaline were keeping her energized and focused. Whatever was driving me was fading, though, and I knew we needed to get out of here soon.

"Where's the road?" Hero astutely asked.

In the dark night, everything had a particular sameness. We had spun around so many times, we couldn't use the truck's angle to determine direction. Finding a flat and narrow stretch of pavement, one devoid of streetlights or civilization, seemed impossible. I pulled my phone out of my pocket, but it was waterlogged, dead.

"We can't stay here," I said.

"I think I see it," Hero said, hopefully. "Over there. You see? Off to the right."

I didn't see it, but I was beginning to feel an exhaustion or concussion come over me, and if I gave in to the strong urge to sleep, I feared I might never wake up. So we struck a path for the possible highway, as quickly as we could, wading through the swamp. My clothes were heavy with water, and the pervasive dampness brought a chill from the otherwise warm night air. The path ahead of us wasn't really a path at all, as we forced our way across the cypress knees and shallow pools. Clouds rolled in and hovered thick above, faint moon pillowed behind, no stars for the night sky.

"Should I be worried about alligators or anything?" Hero asked.

"Alligators? No," I said. "But let me know if you see any snakes."

Hero moved right up alongside me, saying nothing.

I was already weary of the marsh. I wanted solid ground. The power of traction. The dry and the green, the warm touch of gravel and pavement. Then I stumbled and fell face first into the muck, managing somehow to avoid dragging Hero in with me. Pushing myself up, a stench washed over me, and I realized I'd wandered across the corpse of an animal, warm and rotting. At one time a deer, perhaps, though it seemed far too marshy for them out here. Probably mortally wounded by some hunter, but it kept running until it was irretrievable. Bits and pieces now nibbled away. The stench, the thought—both left me heaving into the marsh.

"What is it?" Hero hissed.

"You really want to know?"

"We should have gotten there by now, the road," Hero said with frustration. And she was right. How far could we have flown? We'd been walking for how long now (Twenty minutes? Half an hour?) and hadn't found a thing. "This is crazy. We should have stayed by the truck. We're going to fall into quicksand and die." Her usually confident voice was starting to crack slightly.

Then I remembered the flashlights, the ones I'd insisted on bringing and yet somehow had forgotten to grab in our moment of greatest need. Looking back through the darkness, I couldn't see the truck, nor our path back to it. We were, it seemed, abandoned by ourselves.

"No one's going to die," I said, convincing not even myself. "We don't even have quicksand." I pulled myself up onto a cypress knee, gritting down the pain I didn't want Hero to know I was feeling. I wasn't strong, but I was going to fake it for her sake, as well as my own. My hope was to keep an eye out for the unmistakable gleam of streaking headlights, though given the seclusion of this highway and the hour, I knew it was a long shot. Hero did not ask me what I was doing, even after several minutes passed in silence. She merely found a stump to sit on, curling her legs up underneath her.

Then, I saw something. A light, far off to the left. At first I thought I was hallucinating, and even after a few minutes I still couldn't say I wasn't. I waited for it to get closer, but it didn't. After a while, I decided it had to be something permanent, a fixed streetlight perhaps, certainly some sign of civilization. I slipped back down into the bog and fetched Hero, who was beginning to drift off herself.

"Follow me. I think I see a way out of this mess."

I led the way with a certainty of purpose I did not feel, a confidence that this too would end up another mirage, wondering in desperation if we would find a way to make it through the night.

Hero suddenly spoke:

"If you had to choose a way to die, what would it be?"

"Now?" I said. "Really? I don't know that I'm in the mood."

"Come on. It's the elephant in the bog. I don't want to walk around feeling sorry for myself."

"Well," I began, hoping to filibuster the moment, then gave in. "I wouldn't want to starve. I don't even like being a little hungry."

"Oh, yeah, maybe let's not talk about food," she said. "What about drowning? I hear that's nice."

"I'm scared of boats," I said. "Water rising up to your chin. No thanks."

"There's always the gas chamber. You wouldn't even see it coming."

"That could be okay," I said.

"Electric chair?"

"Now stop. You really should lay off me. It's my job."

"I'm just asking. Would you feel comfortable killing someone in a way you yourself wouldn't be prepared to die?"

"Don't kid yourself. These people are pretty evil. Electrocution is probably too good for them. The condemned get a choice, anyway. A limited one, anyway. The only thing they can't choose is not to die."

"Just like us, apparently."

It certainly was beginning to seem that way. I'd lost sight of the light through the trees. With one arm, I pulled myself up on a low-hanging bough to take another look. Much to my surprise, we'd made excellent progress. Another few minutes and we'd be there. "There" was not the road, however, I could more clearly see now, but a suburban complex of townhouses. They rose up and out of swamp on a foundation of dirt and grass. A gush of light flowed out into the emptiness around it.

When we got there, we could see a short white fencing bordered the property edge. It was laughably inadequate—something that would never have kept out alligators or anything else, merely decorative—but in our condition it proved to be moderately difficult. Hero bent down into the grass and dragged herself under the lowest beam. Unwilling to crawl anymore in the dirt, I struggled with pulling myself over. Hero reached across to help me balance, and as we wandered into the already lit backyard, a motion-detector fired up another nearly blinding halogen.

"My head is killing me," she said. We practically shined under the halogens and could finally see each other clearly for the first time since the crash.

Hero's face was drenched in red. Below her left cheek, the skin was shredded, blood mixed with muck and grass and a variety of unknowns. Across her forehead, a lock of hair had slipped beneath a large, squarish flap of skin that dangled delicately by one edge.

"God," I whispered.

"Is it bad?" she said. "It doesn't feel too bad."

"My God. I…" She seemed aware, alert. But her head was horribly mangled Instantly shredded and torn with devastating permanence. "Jesus."

"Well, shoot," she said. "You mean it's bad."

"Come on," I said, hurriedly, dragging her toward the back screen door. I started shouting and knocking, and soon an alarm sounded throughout the house and the indoor lights came on. A middle-aged woman in a nightgown quietly answered the door. "My daughter," I said, pointing to Hero, who waved and smiled despite her gruesome wound.

Events began to flow together for me in a stream. The woman led Hero to the kitchen sink, whispering comforting words and offering the robe off her back. She took a towel from the refrigerator door and dampened it, then wiped futilely at the mud and blood. Fortunately, there was no mirror there. We both seemed to intuitively understand the need to keep Hero from seeing herself. She seemed perfectly fine, otherwise, her shock sustaining her all these hours in our trek through the wild. Aside from the whole of her forehead, it was difficult to tell where to blot, her face a brown spongy mass soaked in blood. The woman gently removed the lock, pressed the flap down and held a hand towel up to Hero's face, covering it entirely.

"Hold that there," she said with a robotic sweetness, then turned to me with a too-audible hiss. "She's got. To get. To a hospital."

"Car wreck," was all I managed. "In the swamp."

She nodded. "I have small children. Take my car. Don't worry about the blood," she comforted. "Well, try to worry a little about the blood."

Her Lexus was parked in her home's two-car driveway. The wide, pristine manufactured streets were well lit and totally empty. Despite the situation, I found myself looking around enviously for a moment before my eyes fell upon Hero again and the urgency returned.

I drove with the nervous power of adrenaline. It wasn't exactly panic—more like the certainty of purpose I'd previously lacked. As we got closer to town, I wove around and past cars in my lane that seemed to be moving infinitely slowly. Everything seemed so incredibly simple. Artificial constraints applied to us not at all. There were no lanes. There were no lights. There were no limits. No obstacles at all.

"You wreck this car and we're through," Hero snorted from where she lay in the back seat."

"Try not to bleed on the cushion," I said.

At the emergency entrance, I nearly took out a man in a wheelchair and swerved to avoid the young parents strapping their newborn into a car seat. I slammed to the curb, then carried Hero in my arms to the front desk, all while she insisted she could walk for herself. The duty nurse looked up slowly, took one disinterested glance at Hero and handed me a clipboard to fill out. They wanted information, and I simply put down the first thing that came into my head. When I handed it back, she told me to please take a seat without bothering to meet my eyes.

Seconds ticked by. Then minutes. I dug at the hole in my seat cushion, picking out small pieces of foam and tossing them to the floor. Every five or ten minutes, they called another name, but the gathered mass never seemed to thin. After a while, Hero started walking around, reading newspaper clippings framed on the walls, her hand still holding the cloth to her head, talking and laughing with other patients and people waiting with them or for them.

When they finally called her name, I found I could barely stand up. My knees now weak and unsure, I teetered in place for a moment, then forced myself forward.

In the intake room, the doctor smiled and apologized. According to the clock, we'd been waiting for over an hour.

"Now, that looks pretty gruesome, young lady."

"I've had worse."

"Skateboard?" he asked. "We see lots of skateboard injuries."

"Something like that."

He pulled out sponges and dabbed her face. She grimaced as the doctor swabbed the mangled skin. He began to wipe away the mounds of caked-on blood. Everything seemed suddenly less dramatic and frightening as her face came clean, mostly intact and whole. He injected anesthetic at two points on her forehead, and then after a few moments, began to gently scrub the wound clean of mud.

"Can you see the bone?" Hero asked, looking at me.

"I'd have to say yes," I said.

"Can I see it?"

The doctor pulled a handheld mirror out of a drawer and gave it to Hero. She lifted up her head to get a good angle on her injury. The doctor peeled back the flap of skin.

"That's your skull," the doctor said.

"Wow," she said, raising a finger and nearly touching the exposed bone. "That is so unbelievably gross."

"You had to look to figure that out?" I said, shading a hand over my own eyes.

"How often do people get to look at their own bones, face-to-face? I'm just taking advantage of the moment."

"Your mother is going to kill me."

"Don't worry," Hero said. "She'll find a way to make this my fault. She's always said I'm a walking death wish."

"It is all my fault, though," I said, letting the consequence of everything wash over me.

"Good God," Hero said, handing the mirror back to the doctor. "Of course it's your fault. But look on the bright side. At least you're beginning to develop an appropriate level of parental guilt."

The doctor threaded a needle and began stitching up Hero's forehead, carefully matching up the ragged edges of the torn flesh. "Casual disregard for your own well-being is different than wanting to be dead," he said. "You may be missing the self-preservation gene, though."

He winked and passed the needle through her skin. Numbed, she bore it much better than I. She insisted upon keeping the mirror around so she could watch, even making me hold it while I turned my head away. Stitch by stitch, he put her back together, and when I peeked back I saw the pattern of her injury become plain. Not so big as it appeared, nor so horrible. The black line of thread outlined the wound. I steadied myself on the counter and the shooting pain up my arm made me whimper.

"Maybe you'd better get yourself checked out, too," she suggested.

"That might be a good idea," I agreed.

As it turned out, despite Hero's exposed bone, I was the worse for wear. Though her skin was dramatically torn, the stitches and some pain medication pretty much took care of her. I, however, was diagnosed with a grade-two concussion, as well as a bruised collarbone and a separated shoulder. It would be weeks before I was fully healed, according to my doctor, a young resident in a ponytail who herself looked only slightly older than Hero. She fashioned for me a sling and told me to stay off my feet for a few days and to make a follow-up appointment.

Janice picked us up at the emergency entrance. It was late, but when she had answered her cell phone it had sounded as if a party was going on in the background. It took some convincing to get her to come pick us up, but she did so cheerfully once I finally made it clear that I wasn't going to be allowed to drive home from the hospital.

"Cool stitches," she said, holding the door open for Hero.

"They tell me I might even have a scar!"

Janice grabbed me by my arm to help lift me out of the obligatory wheelchair. "Good job, there. Those parenting genes kicking in yet?"

"Not now, Janice. We could have died."

"You always focus on the negative. You're alive. Let's go celebrate!"

In front of the hospital, the hazard lights of the Lexus were still flashing. Its two right wheels had jumped the curb where I had abandoned it, a half-dozen feet outside of the loading zone, and several tickets fluttered on its dash in our wake.

nine

Hero slipped downstairs, wrapped only in a burgundy towel that dropped down merely to mid-thigh, another towel draped over her shoulders and her hair winding down the middle of her back. Her dark, freshly scrubbed skin glowed, and everything about her was so startlingly youthful. Against this backdrop, her wound caught my full attention. In the days since the accident, I'd never seen her without a bandanna wrapped across her forehead. But here it was, in all its glory, swollen and dripping and yellowed at the fringes.

"Jesus," I said. "Is that normal?"

"Doctor looked at it yesterday, said it was fine. Wounds do this sometimes. Maybe every time. Who knows?"

"It looks worse than before."

"You're a real help," she said, pulling the towel from her shoulder and wrapping it around her head. "You're going to make me self-conscious."

"Maybe you should be. That's pretty horrifying."

"You really have a way of easing a girl's mind."

Though it was a Saturday, I needed to head into work. There were two reasons for this: first, I was interviewing a candidate for executioner, and since this was an anonymous position, it was best to do this while no one was around; second, Hal had told me that he'd seen the investigators poking their heads around the office again, and I wanted to avoid any further conversations with Stanton and his partner, if possible. Not that I had serious reason to believe I had anything to worry about—but it seemed best to avoid further exposing my incompetence.

Hero slipped into a chair in front of the TV. "It's odd. I just realized this morning, I never thought about death while we were out there. Not once."

"That's not how I remember it," I said. "You seemed pretty sure we were going to die."

She shook her head. "I mean, I didn't think about death. Being dead, not whether I would be."

"I confess, the thought did cross my mind."

"Guess I really do think I'm invincible."

"It's a hard habit to break," I said, picking up my keys. Hero stretched out her full length on the chair, then twisted so she was looking at me upside down.

"I blame video games," she said.

"See you in a couple of hours."

With my deluxe four-wheel out of commission and no word yet from the insurance company, I was left with my grandfather's old dilapidated Ford, rusting for the past few years in the high grass of the backyard, windows sealed shut. With a little bit of coaxing, it had turned over with surprising ease. Air for the tires and oil for the engine and it was puttering along at a noisy but efficient pace, his old shotgun still firmly mounted across the back windshield.

The Corrections office was mostly dark, but for the pale glow of the emergency lights and the fluorescent glare from the break room, where the switch had long ago broken in the "on" position. Seated across my desk from me was a big man, though soft-spoken. A banker by trade, father of three, a degree in the applied sciences. His hair was longish, and it seemed he was trying out a beard. He was listed by the pseudonym "John," but I had a full and complete record of his previous experience, which though in another state, still recommended him highly.

"You understand the need for discretion here. You've done this before, so you know."

"My wife doesn't know about this. I've done, what, four people now, and she has no idea. I tell her it's a card night with the boys. Not one clue."

"Good. It's for your own protection, too."

"I'm not a saint, you know. I don't pretend to be a saint."

"We don't expect," I mumbled, wondering why a saint would apply for a job as an executioner.

"It's just. It has to be someone, and I've already got blood on my hands."

"It has to be someone," I agreed.

He shifted in his seat. He seemed very self-conscious of his presence, hunching over to make himself smaller. I hadn't even told Hal about the interviews. The fewer people who knew, I thought, the better.

"I don't enjoy it."

"I don't follow."

"There are some sick people out there. Get off on killing killers. Hard to tell the difference between them, to be honest, the killer and the killer. Both of them got their reasons. For me, it's a job. It's some money. I don't feel one way or the other. It has nothing to do with me."

"What would your wife say?"

"She'd divorce me. She hates when I kill a bug. I don't think she'd let me off the hook for this one. Though more because of the lying than the killing. She has principles. It's why I love her."

"We could find someone else," I said.

"It should be me. What's the date?"

I'd interviewed only two people for the job, after culling through about three hundred, mostly outrageously unsuitable applications. And he was right: most of them seemed far too eager and excited at the prospect. The only other acceptable applicant was fine—single, blue collar, just inexperienced. I would have preferred someone with fewer family connections, but I'd decided upon "John" because of his know-how, an executioner for whom this would not be their first. There should be at least one of us who knew what he was doing.

"Last state I worked in, they moved to lethal injections. Didn't need me at all anymore. Had to use a doctor."

"I'm sorry," I said, and wondered why.

"It's a better idea, I think. Not like gassing folks. That was weird."

"Why weird?"

"If you're gonna kill someone, should be hands-on. Electrocution is good, but injections, that's more like it. It's much more like killing someone."

"This seems close enough to do the job."

"It's about responsibility," he said "We're too good at turning killing into nothing. You have to get your hands dirty. You have to be responsible."

"What about firing squad? Or hanging?"

"I said closer. You talk about shoving a needle into someone's veins. You talk about strapping them in, placing electrodes in all the appropriate spots. Shooting someone? It's a fucking video game."

"Maybe we could try poisoning them," I suggested.

"That's not the point," he said, signing his name with a flourish.

After he'd left, I found myself leafing through my cabinets, file by file, looking over the scattered notes that had been left by my predecessors about previous executions, final meals, problems and successes, notes about the crimes that had been committed.

Javier Quintana. Premeditated murder of a co-worker. An alleged disagreement over a woman. Final meal: Scrambled eggs, toast. Gallon of ice cream (mint chocolate chip). Sweet potatoes.

Forget the problem of choosing a meal. How do you eat it? How do you hold it down? What sort of strange tradition places so much emphasis upon food? We cannot grant other last requests, other necessities of human existence. I'm told that there was a time when the condemned would get a last night with a lover, or, barring that, a prostitute. Not anymore. We want the pensiveness that comes with digestion, not the throes of passion.

And Javier Quintana was the last death by hanging in the state.

Too humane or perhaps impatient to let him suffocate to death, they had to drop him five times before his neck finally snapped.

Marcus Shepperton. Final meal: Penne pasta with sun-dried tomatoes in alfredo, two loaves garlic bread, fried oysters, tiramisu, coffee. A certain, if unimaginative connoisseur. He'd been involved in a street fight that had taken the eye of one participant and left another one dead.

Marcus was the first to experience problems in the chair. This was less a defect of the chair itself than the executioner, who had done a poor job of attaching the electrodes to the condemned. Two jolts of electricity caused his left hand to catch fire, which was quickly put out with an extinguisher but hadn't done the rest of the job. A quick conference between officials determined that the processes should continue. Through Shepperton's moans, they reattached the charges and went again. Three separate shocks of one minute each finally finished him off.

Robert Cutler, age 97, because they apparently got tired of waiting for time to take its course. Final meal: Chicken and dumplings, cabbage with malt vinegar, angel food cake; savory, bitter, sweet. Convicted of killing his second wife with rat poison.

One jolt of electricity, a mere 30 seconds long, and he was done. His body given up the ghost. Over and out.

ten

Hero's mother was missing.

This wasn't some sudden discovery on our part, but more of a slow realization and acknowledgement of this reality: Val had disappeared. She'd been fairly simple to reach for a time, and Hero had kept in periodic contact with her. After the accident, however, Hero tried unsuccessfully to call her. As the date of Hero's departure neared, we had tried periodically to reach her by cell phone and at the number of their house in Michigan, but now that it was nearly upon us, there was still no answer to our voicemails, no machine picking up at the house, no sense at all that she even existed anymore.

"Mom's a flake," Hero said, "but what can you do."

"I'll take your word on that," I said. Hero's return flight disembarked in two days, and my anxiety was accelerating with each hour Val remained absent.

"Figures," Hero said.

"What does?"

"She's always doing something batty."

"Like this, batty?"

"Sure. Why not? Just dump your problems onto someone else for a few weeks. I'm sure the freedom has made her a little greedy. Who wouldn't want to have a vacation from me?" Hero stared at me with those deep brown eyes that I still struggled to read, lightly scratching the skin around the cut on her forehead. The swelling had gone down, finally, and the doctor's promise that it would leave hardly any scar was beginning to seem much more believable.

Then, abruptly, Hero asked: "Why do you assume I am your daughter?"

This was a break in the ground rules we had set. Over a game of Scrabble, we listened to the TV playing reruns of old sitcoms while we ate apple pie, covered in chocolate syrup. She said it was her favorite, and I could only take her at her word. I have never felt more in need of trusting anyone. Hers wasn't a follow-up question, however, but something new. I wanted to protest but thought perhaps in the wake of Val's absence, Hero and I were beginning to steer a new course.

"Because you are my daughter," I said.

"According to who?"

"Your mother. For one."

"And this would be the same woman who for nine years also told Geoffrey he was my father."

"Unreliable is what you're saying."

"Can you think of any reason to trust her?" she asked, laying down her letters, double word score. The word was ekphrasis. I made her look it up to prove it was real.

"There's my lawyer," I pointed out.

"I rest my case."

"You're just being difficult. Are you suggesting that you aren't my daughter? How many fathers does one girl need in a lifetime?"

"Don't get defensive. I'm just asking. These are lawyers we're talking about, right?"

"Untrustworthy, you mean?"

She threw up her hands. "I'm just asking."

"He made them verify it. Tests. DNA. That sort of thing. It's not like my lawyer is my doctor. I gave them a strand of my hair. Val gave them something, too, a fingernail, maybe, or blood."

"Or hair."

"Maybe that."

Hero yawned. "I don't know. If I were your daughter…"

"But the test proved you are my daughter."

"Maybe I'm just not convinced."

"Well, what would convince you, then?"

She frowned, an expression of earnestness and focus, the same look the cat would make, intent upon some prey hiding under our refrigerator. I added a couple letters to make the word recreation.

"I don't know," she said at last, after it seemed she was finished speaking. "It just seems that after all of that, what do you really know? Do you even understand how DNA testing works?"

"It works like a fingerprint."

"They can't even say something is you. They can only say that a certain number of people aren't you."

"I think it's more like a fingerprint."

"I just mean it's not foolproof."

"In my experience, fools seem to do rather well for themselves."

"It would just be nice to know. I mean, for sure."

"They are sure."

"Good to see that you have faith in something."

Val's disappearance, beyond concerning in its own right, also left me with a quandary: What was I to do with Hero? Without knowing where her mother was, I knew I could not let Hero leave, not without the knowledge that there was someone waiting for her at the end of her journey. She was only twelve after all, I reminded myself, however difficult that was to believe at times.

Hero herself was unfazed.

"I don't need a stupid babysitter. Just send me back home. It'll be fine."

"But you'll be all alone."

"I'm alone all the time. I'm the Queen of Being Alone. You leave me alone while you're at work."

"That's different. I know that I'm coming home. And this is my decision. This isn't open for debate."

"Everything is open for debate. We have a disagreement. That's the reason they invented debates."

"You're not going. That's it."

I carried our plates to the kitchen, and Hero followed behind, settling into a stool at the counter and leafing through the day's mail. Since the accident, I wondered if I was seeing something different in her reactions to me. Before, all her banter seemed curious, trying to wrest information from me. Lately, she seemed much more interested in badgering me, as if trying to convince me of something. Whether that was to start taking a more active role in her life or to admit we weren't related at all seemed to vary daily.

"Ha!"

Hero sat with her mouth agape, a letter open in her hand. Her eyebrows were raised as she looked up at me, easing slowly into a mischievous smile I was coming to know all too well.

"What is it?" I asked, my familiar acute anxiety bubbling up.

She handed over a formal-looking letter. "Apparently you're dead."

It was from my life insurance company, informing my next of kin and beneficiary—in this case, Hero—that my policy was to be paid in full, due to my recent accident and subsequent departure from this earth.

Hero shrugged. "I'm thinking that's got to be a mistake."

"It's not funny," I said firmly.

"Oh, I'd say it's pretty funny."

I looked over the letter. Someone, somewhere must have checked the wrong box on my claim. There's something remarkably unsettling about seeing yourself listed as dead in a formal document—a permanent mark of a very impermanent life. I felt lured by what I read on the paper in front of me, felt myself seduced by its certainty.

I had gone out with the insurance adjuster to inspect the damage in person. As it turned out, the state troopers had found my truck resting a mere thirty feet from the road. From the dirt shoulder, you could just make out the cab through the scrub and trees. It seemed impossible that we could have traveled so far, or avoided impaling ourselves on any number of protruding trunks or logs jutting out between here and there. It seemed equally impossible that we could have missed the road from where we'd landed, even if we had been trying to.

"That's a lot of money. Thanks, Pop."

"I thought you had doubts about whether I was your father."

"Something about all these zeros is giving me a little more faith."

"Some of that's for a funeral."

"Screw that," she said, fanning herself with the letter. "I'm loaded."

"It's not funny."

"Whatever you say. The Late, Great Matthew Brown."

In a fit of responsibility and new father panic, I had made Hero my beneficiary shortly after learning of her existence and the seemingly indisputable confirmation of our relationship. It wasn't some act of generosity on my part. I wasn't trying to make sure her life was secure, though undoubtedly it would accomplish that. My entire life I had carried insurance, as a matter of course, and never once needed it. I felt a kind of relief finally to have someone to give it to. I merely expected to be gone before the money arrived.

"We'll sort this out later," I said. "Just don't cash it."

"You're no fun. You know that?"

As Hero retreated upstairs, chuckling softly to herself, I washed the dishes by hand, staring out at the TV without really focusing on anything. I was feeling the anxiety of my decision to keep Hero with me—all that it would require of me—rather than send her home without knowing where Val was and when she'd be home. I was counting on this being a simple mistake. But what if it wasn't a mistake? What if something had happened to Val? What if this wasn't a temporary fix, but something permanent? Paranoia began to settle in. What if Val was simply playing me, dumping a daughter she no longer wanted upon her newly discovered father, if—as Hero suggested—her father I even was. Our four weeks were up, and in many ways I felt that we were back to square one, with her perpetual harassment about the upcoming execution and ridiculous studies that I hoped might someday offer her some confidence in my suitability as a father.

And now I was dead. Things decidedly did not appear to be looking up.

Scrubbing plates with a ritual detachment, my mind wandered across this familiar terrain, running over and over these questions without answers, repeating them to myself like a mantra, as slowly my eyes focused on the television screen. Reporters broadcasting from a scene in the afternoon, now tape delayed, with interlaced commentaries. A pattern so recognizable, it could be any night, any place. Men in dark suits and sunglasses marching into a building, searching through files, questioning suspects. All so familiar, and yet, as I looked closer, too familiar. Not just some random generic government office, but a building I knew intimately from my years of working there. In the background, I could make out familiar faces, my old executive assistant, Shirley Sue Robinson, along with a few others whose names I'd never learned. My replacement, Bernie Morr, was talking to the television reporter, condemning this intrusion in the people's business while simultaneously vowing full cooperation with authorities. A fierce red banner ran across the bottom of the screen announcing that investigators had locked down the Bureau of Environmental Study. The video showed officers removing boxes of materials from the building and loading them into awaiting vans. All of this passed by in a few seconds. Investigators declined to comment.

Something big was going down, obviously, but perhaps it shouldn't have been too surprising given the rumors that had been flying for weeks and the specter of special investigators running all over town. The bureau, like so much of the state, hadn't yet invested the money necessary to convert to an automated system, so everything had to be sorted by hand, which meant that in order to investigate, they would have to get their hands on the files eventually. But in truth, everything about this investigation and its rippling effects throughout the government I found perplexing. There were no leaks of any kind, nothing to indicate where this process was heading. I reassured myself that I hadn't worked at the bureau for more than a year, that my tenure had been low-key and uninspiring, that I had, in fact, made a point of doing very little while I was there.

Then I saw the other familiar face on the screen. It was a blip, really, only a second. Still, there was no mistaking him, with his thick frames and heavily tinted lenses and rumpled suit. Special Agent Bill Stanton had been calculating his sums. Something, it seemed, was starting to add up.

Part II.

eleven

Kids shuffled about the school ground, huddling together, pulling apart and drifting about aimlessly. Clique upon clique upon clique. Movements and associations far too complex for me to decode. I had the sense that these patterns were something I should know, that I might once have known in a long-ago childhood, but that now were only lost knowledge. An unused skill that has dulled from lack of use. Hero could teach me a thing or two, if she's learned it herself, or not yet forgotten how.

Two weeks past Hero's scheduled date of return and still no word or sign from Val, I felt I could no longer hold off the inevitable. We had come to sign Hero up for school.

"You going to behave yourself?"

"Hell, no."

"That's my girl."

Once inside, we quickly became lost, meandering through corridors and, in the absence of elevators, carefully ascending dim-lit back stairwells, following general signs painted on the walls, pointing arrows, and the running commentary of the graffiti. Bemused students in denim and black fell in behind us. They wore concert tees, strange gothic characters I couldn't make out, with dyed and slicked hair, pierced and angry. They offered no help. One look from Hero suggested that, for her sake, I not ask for any.

When we did finally reach the main office, we found pandemonium partially contained. Phones ringing nonstop and secretaries hurrying from one task to the next, their desks piled neck-high with files, boxes of supplies, textbooks. Unable to catch anyone's eye, I took an enrollment form clipboard from a stack on the counter, and we settled into a row of waiting chairs to fill it out.

"Name."

Hero frowned "Please."

"Date of birth."

"Make something up."

"Fine. You're twenty. But you could pass for eighteen."

"That mean I get to drive home?"

Allergies, medical history, educational history, contact names, phone numbers, addresses, extracurricular interests.

"Look," I said, "I don't know anything about you, apparently. Why don't you fill this out. I'm going to see if I can talk to an actual person."

Though the room was filled with people, they carried with them a nervous, anxious energy that discouraged all human contact. They didn't ignore me as much as seemed completely unaware of me, as if my presence made no impression upon the work they were focused on. I was nearly bowled over by a woman pushing a cart overloaded with copier paper. She apologized without meeting my eyes, then pushed on without another word.

This could have been my own office for all the attention they paid me.

Along the back wall of the room, I found the administration offices, principal, vice principals, guidance counselors. One black woman was sitting in her office, a short, middle-aged VP, stern and earnest and unapproachable. I knocked on the open door.

"My daughter is new to the school," I said. "She's starting today."

The woman stared at me for a moment, as if considering what I said carefully, before pointing with her pencil toward a chair and rummaging through the stacks of folders on her desk. She had large, fleshy arms that shimmied as she moved.

"Here at Jefferson Davis Junior, we treat all our kids the same."

"I hope that means well."

She set down the papers. I noticed a flicker of crossness on her brow as an old but familiar chill ran through me and for an instant I was twelve again. "I know sarcasm, sir. Don't you think I don't. I'm up to my neck in it every day. It's all kids today understand."

"She's supposed to be with her mother. We just don't know what's happened to her."

"Drugs?"

"Flake. She's gone missing. And I'm new at this fatherhood thing. You understand."

"Afraid I don't, quite," she said, brow wrinkled.

"It's a long story. Let's just leave it at that."

"I'm sorry. I can't do that."

She leaned back in her chair, an overstuffed leather recliner that I envied for its general ease. She tapped a pencil on the edge of the desk as she looked me up and down.

"I know your type," she said after several moments.

"You don't understand."

"A disinterested parent. A working man without the time for his own daughter."

"I'm not a type."

"This isn't a daycare. Schools are not places where you go to dump your problems onto someone else. At Jefferson Davis Junior we try to teach the whole child, you see? It's a matter of commitment. It's a matter of principle. It's about the love and care of a community."

"We met some of your loving community in a stairwell a little while ago. They wanted to bond with switchblades."

"Everyone must contribute for this to work. Teachers. Parents. Everyone. I'm afraid I'm not going to be able to 'leave it at that.' What we require is a little bit more from you on the commitment end."

"What do you need from me?"

"Just a little honesty," she said, marking something in the notebook spread out in front of her.

"Fine."

"That, and at least two hours a month helping in the classroom."

I watched her watching me. It was a showdown of sorts. I decided to open up.

"Her mother is missing. I don't know where she is. I can't just send her back unless I know someone is there. She could easily turn up tomorrow and be gone in a day, but I just don't know."

She was back digging through her files. "Does she have any extracurricular interests? Music? Athletics? Drama?" It didn't seem like she had heard what I said.

"You could ask her, I suppose."

"We will. But children can be less forthcoming with strangers. If you could just help us..."

"I'd say she's melodramatic. Does that count?"

I led the vice principal back out to where Hero was finishing up her form.

"How many els in delinquent?" she asked as we came up.

The administrator smiled broadly and held out her hand. "I'm Mrs. Forrester."

"Hero," Hero said, shaking it.

"I'm sorry?"

I felt uncomfortable leaving her behind in this place. My own memories of junior high were largely unpleasant, filled as they were with scenes of beatings and perpetual embarrassment in front of the opposite sex. But if anyone could survive the difficult transition to a new school, Hero could.

"Don't leave me here," she said, as I headed for the door. "This place sucks."

"Think of it as an adventure."

"More like a prison."

"It's not a prison," I said. "Trust me. I know."

twelve

A special government courier arrived at the office carrying an envelope for me. I knew right away it had to be from someone in the administration, and it was: A request from the governor's office for a standard meeting that afternoon at 3—though by request I knew they meant a requirement and by standard I knew they meant trouble. I felt a stark unease about being called down. The last time I'd received a notice like this, I was asked by one of the governor's aides to leave Environmental and take this new position at Corrections. Whether they had been trying to open up my former position for Bernie or expected me to fill some special role at my new one, I had no idea. But I did not ask any questions, which I'm sure was one reason they found me useful.

In light of the trouble at Environmental, though, I wondered if I needed to start asking more. Bill Stanton had the whole political establishment falling over itself. Hal was mostly a blur these days as he pored through department records and personnel interviews. Each day I came into the office, I cautiously pried open my door to see if a man in thick, tinted glasses was waiting for me with handcuffs.

I had no idea what I might be guilty of.

What I did know was that the governor himself had been spending the last two months zipping from one end of the state to the other in an effort to secure his reelection, and I was fairly certain that he had little or no interest in me personally, so whomever wanted to see me, it wasn't him. Everyone else in the party, in and out of government, was working full bore on making sure that he was reelected or keeping themselves out of jail. His opponent had threatened to "clean house" if he won, which we appointees took to mean that we would be looking for new jobs. Perhaps someone wanted to know what little I knew about the investigations. If I was being called down by the administration right now, with all of these other preoccupations, I knew it could be for no small thing.

I entered the new capitol building and, as instructed, took the executive elevator up to the nineteenth floor—everything over seventeen was reserved for the Administration's top level staffers. A secretary at the ground level had to use a key to access the floor, and when the bell rang and the doors slid open, I could see why. I wasn't facing out onto a corridor, but a plush and private office. I'd seen the governor's own offices before, but this was much nicer, much more posh. A place where important things happened. Sitting behind the desk at the other end of the room was a man I had seen but never before met: Bertrand Walker.

"Glad you could come, Matt."

"Of course."

He rose from his desk to shake my hand. I recognized him from the fundraiser, where Janice had pointed him out, and he may very well have been wearing the exact same ill-fitting suit. He was disarmingly pleasant, too. I was surprised to note, based upon his accent, that the man at the center of our state's power wasn't himself even a Southerner. He adopted a folksy twang he might even have thought sounded authentic, but only he and maybe another non-Southerner would have fallen for it.

He motioned toward a large couch at the side of the room.

"How're things down at Corrections?"

"Just fine."

"Interest you in a scotch? Beer?"

"Scotch, sure."

Walker pulled two glasses down from the small bar by the couch. "Things are touch-and-go right now, I don't need to tell you," he said. "The governor is in a tight race. Things are pretty delicate right now, and we have a winning strategy, but we need every contribution we can get. That's why you're here."

"I'm not much of a campaigner," I said. "Nor a politician."

"For now, no. But right now, you see, that works to our advantage."

"I don't follow."

"Politics is the art of managing perception," he said, handing me a glass and steering us both toward the couch, where we took a seat just below a massive painting of unintelligible swirls. "And you are perceived as a nonpolitical figure. There's nothing more valuable during an election than appearing impartial."

"I still don't understand what this has to do with me, though. What am I supposed to do?"

"You're organizing the execution of Andrew Carl Adler."

"That's right."

"This execution, it's an important symbol for the campaign. We need to make sure that it is central in the minds of the electorate. We're going to make sure that everyone sees Governor Van Garen as the enemy of lawlessness."

"So, you'd like me to do what then?" I asked. "Send out more press releases?"

"The governor is going to move the execution back, and we want to reschedule it for shortly before election day for the maximum positive impact. This has to be much more than just an execution, Matt. We want an event. Something grand, impressive. We want everyone to be talking about this, and only this, for the next month and well after the governor is reelected."

We could have been talking about the weather or our families rather than death and elections.

"Is this a good idea?" I asked. "Won't people just say we're exploiting the suffering of others?"

"We have every confidence in you, Matt, and your ability to put the best possible spin on this. We saw how well you did with the Work for Justice program. Handle this the same way and we should be in great shape."

I crunched on a piece of ice, nodded slightly, but said nothing.

"You know, Matt, we're looking for capable young people to serve as the next generation of party leaders. You've managed to put together a nice career in a short amount of time. And we appreciate all that you've done for the party, both at Corrections and at Environmental. We've always been able to count on you."

"I don't know that I've done all that much. I'm just doing my job."

"Exactly. Exactly. That's what impresses us. You aren't a boat rocker. You don't make waves, but you handle the press very well. You've been on our radar. That's why we told Christy to put this execution in your hands."

"You did."

"And you should know that we're already considering our slate of candidates for the next election, and I think you would have to be at the top of the list when it comes to lieutenant governor."

I choked on my scotch. "You're joking."

"Never joke about politics. It sets a bad precedent."

"But there must be others more qualified," I said.

Walker shook his head. "The more experience you have, the more enemies, the more ammunition to be used against you. Like I said, politics is about perception control. So far you've shown a keen ability to manage those perceptions. Lieutenant governor is a good proving ground. Low profile. Not much responsibility. But you have the potential to be a top of the ticket guy someday, I think."

"The press will see right through something like this, won't they? Like Governor Roberson?"

"I don't care what they see," Walker said with a smile, "I care what they do. Governor Roberson came from an older school of politics. Explicit extortion, straight up bribes, brown paper bags of money and cracking heads. He was sloppy and stupid, two traits that served him well for a long time. Things are different now. It takes a different kind of leader. The ways of the Old South are dead."

I sipped my drink, the ice cracking in the glass, droplets of moisture appearing around the base. Walker went on:

"You're young and if you keep your nose clean, the sky's the limit."

Something about the way Walker said this suggested the larger issue under the surface—one about which I felt certain he knew far more than I.

"What about all these investigations?" I asked. "At Education. Environmental."

"What about them?" His face was unchanged, pleasant but unreadable.

"I was director at Environmental for three years. What if they come after me?"

"Now why would they do that?" Walker said in animated surprise. "You don't know anything about this, do you?"

The question seemed more genuine than anything else that had come out of his mouth all afternoon.

"Not a thing. Actually, I hoped you might be able to tell me what all of this was about."

"This is an independent investigation. We don't exert any influence over the special prosecutor's office, as I'm sure you know."

"So you don't know anything?" I asked, disappointed. If even Bertrand Walker was in the dark, what hope did the rest of us have?

"Rumors," Walker said. "Nothing much more than that. I'd be surprised if there's anything really going on. Not that that will stop them from looking. Or finding something. Generally, you're better off telling these kinds of people as little as possible."

"That's just it," I said. "I don't have anything to tell."

Walker stared at me for another moment, then finished his scotch in one swig, and stood up and started back toward his desk. I found myself staring up into the impenetrable painting beside me, its colors violently splattered and caked.

"Just give the governor his corpse, Mr. Brown. I guarantee, the rest will work itself out."

thirteen

With its fortifications and towers, razor wire and mud-filled encircling trench, Yahnakundra Penitentiary's imposing facade begged comparisons to the European castles of earlier centuries. Not the fairy tale sort—far different from the mountaintop palaces in Luxembourg, or even the cartoonish spires of Disney World. This was a gritty, pragmatic fortress guarding the British Isles. The graceless beauty of the practical. Except this was not a fortress, intently scanning the horizon for signs of invasion, but rather a keep, looking back upon itself, determined if anxious, as if confirming that the invaders of this age usually come from within.

The prison was privately built, owned and operated by the Qual-Tech Corporation—another of the state's market economy approaches to services. The jail sat in the middle of a large field, 200 yards from one of the town's major traffic arteries. Across the street stood an open-air strip mall, with outlet stores and a supermarket. A little farther on, row upon row of suburban homes, fenced yards and gardens and low-rising hedges, children on swings. I passed a cluster of kids playing freeze tag in the prison's field. One girl was frozen stiff beside the road, limbs contorted, awkward and perfect. She stuck out her tongue at me as I passed.

The prison's large visitor parking lot ran right up to the fence gate. It wasn't paved, and the grass was overgrown in spots. A dozen cars filled the spaces when I arrived, despite the fact that this was not a visiting day. It was here that the builders were starting to set up the stage. I'd arranged for a full set, with sound system, to accommodate the schedule we were developing for Adler's execution night. It was going to take weeks to put all this together. Today, I was here to finally meet with the prison's warden and work out the logistics of Adler's fate. More than two hundred press credentials had been sent out. And though only a dozen witnesses would be present during the electrocution itself, our task was to make sure that everyone else wanted to be on hand for the first execution in the state in a decade.

Precedent had always been to ensure that two witnesses were members of the press. Perhaps just to make sure we followed the rules, or maybe to make sure he was really dead. Or to generate good copy. Everyone loved a happy ending.

Though none of late, the state had killed a lot of men over the past century, more than thirty, along with two women and six children (all boys, all before 1940). Though information about the execution procedures were scant, in the county records building I located more information about the killers themselves than I ever expected to find. Case files, or copies of them, were here. Trial information and appeals. Prison reports, medical updates, daily habits, and, of course, last meals. All that remained of these transgressors and criminals and monsters, the infamous and the forgotten.

A guard greeted me at the metal detector and asked me to follow him. Yahnakundra was the autocratic domain of its warden, J.J. Creighton, who I found pacing the dining hall, watching in a what appeared to be solemn satisfaction over his charges with hands clasped firmly behind him. He was a round man, built low to the ground. Tubbish, but with thin, sharp lips. He was known for his firmness, his devoutly religious lifestyle. Up on capitol hill, his golf swing was legendary.

He shook my good hand and asked if this was my first visit.

"Here? Or jail in general," I asked.

"Either."

"Never had much reason before."

"I've come to believe that everyone should spend at least a brief time in a prison. In one capacity or another."

I nodded. There didn't seem to be a natural response to this statement.

He led me through the barricaded passageways. Everywhere we walked, I found a perfect whiteness, the antiseptic cleanliness of a medical facility.

"I have certain expectations," he said. "My way of doing things."

"Perfectly understandable."

"I have expectations, but we haven't done an execution here since before I've been warden."

"Never done this before myself. Turns out it's harder than you'd think."

I'd been calling around, reaching out to several states with a good track record for this sort of thing, but found little in the way of consensus. No two did things exactly the same way, these snowflakes of ritual. After a couple weeks of searching, I felt more lost than when I had begun. Too many choices, and you're certain to change your mind.

"Moving the date back. That's causing some problems."

"Unavoidable, unfortunately," I said. "Procedural issues. You understand."

"I do expect a certain amount of control. I like to think of this as my own personal space. I don't like a lot of outsiders poking their noses in."

"Of course."

"You've got a job to do. I understand that," he said, with obvious difficulty. "I just have my own way of doing things."

I nodded. "The way I see it, this is your castle."

"This is my castle. Exactly right. So don't fuck with me."

He took me on a complete tour of the grounds, and the whole while, I was running the coming event through my head. Logistics. Where would Adler start? In Block D. D for Death Row. It seemed pretty simple. There were only three blocks here, the others L, for low risk, and H for high. No one would confuse them, either by their consonants or their occupants. These stood on the other side of the prison, across the courtyard from Death Row. Adler wouldn't need to walk by them at all, or anyone else. There was a holding pen he'd stay in for the days leading up to his execution. He wouldn't walk down dim-lit corridors, past crowded cells of convicts, rows of the future condemned, while the priest leads the way. He wouldn't even need to see another soul.

Not quite the classic image I had imagined, but I rolled with it.

"Where is he?" I asked as we crossed the sparsely populated prison yard. "Adler."

"He's not allowed out, except for a brief exercise session, half-hour a day. There's a small yard back behind D Block."

"But his cell?"

"Second floor. Up there." The warden gestured generally toward a row of round, tiny windows that provided their occupants' only natural light. I felt suddenly self-conscious, the recognition that we were talking about a person who was nearby. I felt a pressure to speak in more hushed tones, to whisper our plans as if this were some kind of plot.

We approached a small single-story building at the end of the courtyard. The warden pulled out the large set of keys attached to his belt loop and slid the bolt back. "It didn't always used to be so complicated," he said, pulling open the heavy door. "Too many rules now. Too many people poking their noses into everybody's business. Used to be you could do whatever was necessary to maintain control. There are a hundred ways to deal with problem prisoners."

"It's a different world, I guess," I said.

"Used to be you could be creative. Prisoner gives you trouble, you give him trouble back. Someone tries to escape, they meet with an unfortunately accident. You put a knife in their hand, no one asks questions. Self-defense. Those were the good old days."

The warden kept walking, but I slowed down. "Should you be telling me this? Should I be hearing this?" It was as if I was suddenly caught in a conversation not meant for me.

"Sometimes a beating goes too far. But you just replaced the bruised body with another one. Easier than you might think to find a body, if you know where to look and who to ask."

"Jesus," I said, dryly. "You've got to be putting me on."

The warden stopped at a small, indistinct door and rifled through his keys again. He laughed to himself and shook his head.

"You are putting me on," I said.

"Just too damn easy." He punched me roughly in the arm. "Dumbfuck pencil pushers."

He led me into the chamber. We stood behind the glass, in the witness room, staring out into the bare and tiny room where one single chair sat. As familiar as I was with the electric chair from pictures and graphics, I had never seen one up close. It was all wood, constructed by inmates nearly a hundred years ago. Recent events had raised the question of the humanity of the procedure, though the only solution discussed recently had been whether to commission a new, high-tech chair made of premium alloys, designed to conduct electricity with the greatest of ease. No doubt our skills have come a long way in a hundred years.

Here, everything was obvious and simple.

Since I'd been forced to take on this task, I'd found myself wondering at times what it would take to kill someone. Physically. The actual act itself, not the emotional or psychological preparation. What if I had to manage it myself, alone. The emotions were there, of course, always. They hovered and pried. They hid their faces, changed complexion. But the physical act, like a knife to the chest, what would that take? A knife must cut something, tear away at the flesh and into the vital organs, shock the system into stopping. Even a bullet shot, it must rip, puncture. You must hit exactly the right parts, in exactly the right way. Far from fragile—I marveled at our near indestructibility.

The primary victim in Adler's case had been strangled, but not before she had been raped. There had been no fingerprints, but there were fluids and hairs, and this was what had given him away. Police were convinced Adler was guilty of more than they could prove. There are many, many other undetectable things he might have done.

Lately, I've been getting caught up altogether too intimately in my task.

The warden led me back across the large courtyard, shepherding me toward the exit. Nearby, a crew of prisoners played pickup basketball. It was the most integrated part of the prison I'd seen. Each team had one or two token whites. Just a pickup game, but competitive and fierce. As we passed, I tried to identify the really dangerous ones from the crowd hanging around in the exercise area. No one loitered near the outside wall. The guards in the tower all faced in, fully involved in the game as they gazed down. They shouted. They cheered. Their guns inadvertently pivoted back and forth with them as they followed the action.

Beyond the wall, from out in the moving world, sounds drifted in. The cries of the children playing in the field. A plane overhead. The chatter of a radio announcer. A squeal of tires across pavement, a muffled crash, the shattering of glass.

fourteen

Janice suggested that we spend a night out on the town. She accused me of being too staid of late and unwilling to engage with the people around me, including my own daughter.

"Let me take you out into the world. Just you and me and the seedy underbelly of the city."

"We have an underbelly?"

"More like a foreskin," Janice said. "Serves pretty much the same purpose, too."

Through the doorway of the club, all I could make out was part of a dance floor, overflowing with gyrating figures, vague and luminescent through flashing strobes. The man with the shaved head at the door checked my ID, his face expressionless, accented with nose ring and silver rods shot through his eyebrow and lower lip. He handed my license back to me without a word and turned to the next person in line.

This place, The Club Palmetto, had three levels, and we were entering on the main floor. A floor below was a pool hall, where people tipped beers and girls with cues leaned across green felt tables in plunging tops and high heels and low-rise blue jeans, while their boyfriends and admirers held their beers, their smoldering cigarettes that dangled an inch of ash. On this level, the dance floor, it's the college scene. Bodies squeezing together in a grind, grooving to the rhythm.

Janice and I burrowed through the roiling jam to the upper floor, the lounge, with its torn vinyl couches overflowing and crooning piano man in a light blue polyester jacket, its long padded bar that ended somewhere off in a haze of drunk businessmen and nuevo-chic alcoholics. Club Palmetto was a multi-tiered cornucopia, here to swallow up everyone in this big small town. For those in search of a good time, there's really nowhere else to go.

But I don't dance. I don't even like to flirt. Too many people in one place make me uncomfortable. Janice, on the other hand, enjoyed the sport of it all, bringing with her a pocket notebook and a tiny pencil. She kept meticulous records of the conversations, the clothing, the grasping at a lost youth.

"You're looking pretty good for a dead man," she said to me.

"You'd be surprised how complicated it is bringing yourself back to life. It's not exactly easy, I've discovered."

"Nothing worth doing is," she said as we settled into a table against the wall

"That's only half the problem. Just when I think I've taken care of it, I turn up dead again somewhere else."

"Bureaucracy."

"The left hand is fixing the problem while the right hand is mucking things up again. It's a vicious cycle, and I don't see the light at the end of the tunnel."

"To use an expression."

"You wouldn't believe how these things spread. Found out the other day that my video rental membership somehow got cancelled. I'm not sure how they'd have known to do that, even if I really was dead."

Janice scribbled something in her notebook. "What'd you do with Junior?" she asked, turning away from me to watch a tall couple saunter by—the woman's mini-dress rising slightly above eye level, the man's untucked shirt wrinkled and stained. She made another note.

"Nothing," I said. "She's at home. I have cable."

"Excellent. Glad to see you've managed to adapt to the perks of modern parenting. Haven't you ever heard of a sitter?"

I ignored her. "What do you think you have to do here to get a drink?"

"Seriously. What if she gets into trouble? There are laws against this sort of thing. I think I read that somewhere."

I stood. "I'm going to see if I can get some help at the bar."

All around, I found people of my own stripe, and there was a desperation in the room that felt both familiar and personal, one that the low lighting and heavy music could not mask. It was in the uncomfortable laughs, the surface-level banter—Do you like sushi? Have you heard his latest album? You are too beautiful for that drink. It was in the thirty-somethings pressed into dresses and pants too tight, shoes too high, and cologne by the bucketful. Everyone, every inch, shined up to a spark.

But it was also as if I'd stepped back into the space I'd occupied as a young man in college—those nights of beer- and gin-soaked indulgence, without a need or thought of the future. All we had was the night, and the years pushed out beyond us into infinity. And on one of those nights, a night probably a lot like this, I'd met Val, without a clue of what that would mean all these years later. The past overtakes the present with promises of more of the same.

A troop of women stood at the counter. I waited for my chance to slip in, but there always seemed to be someone else, another body filling in the space and, not surprisingly, I couldn't catch the bartender's eye. The attractive young woman next to me, her elevated hair reaching up like a spire toward the ceiling, asked me for a light.

"I don't smoke," I said.

"Then you can buy a lady a drink."

"Sorry. I'm here with someone," I said, turning back to the counter. I had no intention of recreating my past mistakes: a bar, a strange woman, an unexpected daughter 12 years later. The lone bartender was being accosted from all sides, and I found myself unable to catch his eye as all the women around me pushed in.

"Screw this," I said, backing away from the bar and heading downstairs. The dance club level had several bars, and each was swarmed, but unlike upstairs was serving quickly. Patrons were more focused on dancing than drinking, their faces bright with the thrill of discovery and exertion. A space at the counter opened, and I quickly signaled to the bartender for a beer and a vodka tonic.

"You don't have to be a jerk, you know. I was just trying to pick you up."

The young woman from upstairs was standing right beside me, pressed up against my back due to the crush of the crowd. She had that manufactured wounded look I'd seen Hero use a few times, when you know she just wants you to admit you've done wrong.

I didn't know what to say.

"My drink?" she said, holding up an empty glass. "Whiskey Sour. Neat."

I just stared at her, and she cocked an eyebrow with a smile, obviously amused by my confusion.

When the bartender returned, I ordered a Whiskey Sour.

She sipped from the tiny straw in her glass, and as I looked at her more closely, I wondered for a moment if I knew her, though from where I couldn't imagine. She was mid- to late twenties, with an angular beauty and sharp blue eyes that ran all over me, with an unspeakable quality whose attraction was difficult to resist.

"You're too old to be a college student."

"Good guess," I said.

"Thank God. College boys are tedious. Not to mention exhausting."

"Are you aware you are speaking out loud?"

"We haven't slept together before, have we?" she asked casually.

"I'm sorry?"

"You just look familiar is all I'm saying," she said.

"I thought the same thing about you."

She tossed her hair playfully. "Well, they pay me to be memorable," she said, in an obvious tone that suggested I should know what she meant.

"I don't follow."

She set her glass down hard on the counter, looking at me with an incredulous smile. "You don't know who I am, do you?"

"Did we go to high school together?" I asked.

She lifted her cup again and snorted into her drink.

I downed Janice's tonic in one gulp, then waved for another one. Around us, the churning masses had started to shift. In one corner the dancing had mostly stopped. A small ring had formed around one couple. They were a hefty-girthed pair, every bit of them shaking and convulsing, and it became quickly plain that they were not merely dancing. They still moved with the beat of the music, but in between flashes, we could see his leather pants were down around his ankles, and her short length of skirt was scrunched up above her waist.

Everyone was suddenly watching, intentionally or not. A few turned their heads, and a few more pushed off into the crowd, but most just stood there, transfixed. It was impossible not to be a voyeur. We were all witness, collectively, to the act, and it was hard to turn away.

No one made any motion toward them.

I don't know how long this went on. The music kept playing, the lights continued to strobe, and their bodies writhed together in a passionate desperation. We were closing in on something. You could feel it. But at last the bouncers made their way through the crowd. I recognized the one with the piercings from the door, and it was he who pulled them apart. I could barely make out their faces, which showed neither excitement nor shame. Mostly, they appeared confused, as if something had happened to them, as if we all had somehow done something to them that they couldn't quite understand. They were hustled off the floor quickly as janitorial came in with a mop and bucket.

I picked up my drinks and tried to slip away unnoticed, but my companion quickly spied me out.

"Oh, no. I'm not letting you go until I see the girl you're brushing me off for."

I headed back upstairs to find Janice with my new friend in tow. I felt that I had had enough nightlife to last me until my 40s. She was still sitting at our table, leaning back in her chair with her notebook in her lap as she sat discreetly listening to the conversation of the people behind her, brow creased but pen still. As I walked up with this stranger at my hip, Janice turned slowly, and I placed the drink down in front of her and took a seat. The woman sat down in the other empty chair and pulled out a cigarette.

Janice smiled broadly.

"Now, look who you've gone and found."

"She found me, actually."

"Still," Janice said, lighting a cigarette. "I didn't know you had a thing for local celebrities."

The woman leaned in toward Janice, reaching for a cigarette, which Janice gave her. "He has no clue who I am," the woman said, bending forward to the table candle for a light.

This made Janice smile even more widely.

"Matty, I swear. You are unbelievable."

"So you go by 'Matty?' What are you? Twelve?"

"Matthew," I corrected. "Brown. My dear old friend seems to be the only one who manages to forget that."

"Only when appropriate, darling."

"Wait," the woman said, catching her breath and turning to me. "Matthew Brown? Oh, God! Right! I interviewed you."

Janice shook her head. "This is priceless. You two. Seriously."

Then, of course, it hit me. Angelie Hart. Channel 4 Action News Reporter. She'd lobbed a few softball questions my direction several months ago about my High Tech Con program. The hot lights had left me parched and exhausted. When we had finished, she had them take a series of reaction shots of herself, practiced expressions of looking concerned, thoughtful, engaged, amused.

"That's right. That's right," she said. "You're a kind of government-somebody."

"Government nobody, actually," I said. "Though we can be

tough to tell apart in a crowd."

"I can change that," she said with a raised eyebrow.

"I saw your piece the other night on party clowns," Janice said. "I guess I never realized the depth of the personal dramas that drove them. Perhaps I would have been less frightened of them as a child."

"Who's your sarcastic friend, Matt? She's quite a sweetie."

"Janice," Janice said, flipping her hand across her forehead like a salute.

"Don't mind her," I advised. "She's like this with everyone. Just ignore her."

Angelie didn't seem inclined to ignore anything. "I'm actually pretty proud of that one. Human interest stories are the lifeblood of television news. That and car crashes. And the occasional child abuse story."

"Gotta keep the people entertained."

"You'd prefer we bore them to death? What good is it to make news if no one watches?"

"I don't like clowns, myself," I interjected. "I heard that no one really does, really. Why they keep torturing kids is beyond me."

"Television news is a business, of course," Janice said. "I just don't subscribe to the idea that good also has to be boring. I think it's merely harder."

"You take the stories as they come. I don't know why I'm trying to justify myself to you."

"I prefer game shows to news, myself," I said. "Less depressing. Sometimes people win."

"The camera loves you," Janice said. "It's a gift."

"Thank you."

"So why aren't you out there knocking down doors? Getting the big stories? I think it's a waste of talent."

Angelie laughed. "That's either an insult or a compliment."

Janice blew a steady stream of smoke through her narrowed lips, then said, "It's both."

The two women stared each other down, engaging in rituals

of animosity I couldn't even begin to grasp. Something was going on there, a clear dislike, even hatred, that seemed fully formed at the moment they were introduced. Hero had tried to convince me recently that girls were always in competition with each other, even when they were friendly. I suspected she might be right. Women, perhaps, too, it would seem. The complexity of the moment was unsettling for its unknowability.

"So tell me, what is it that you do," Angelie asked Janice at last. "Are you a writer or something? You sound like a writer."

"She's a tenured professor at the A&M," I chimed in. "In anthropology."

"Egghead," Angelie said. "Same diff."

Janice hadn't moved, still wearing that same confident smile she'd had on since Angelie had sat down. Janice never unmasked herself in public, preferring instead to lie shrouded in the anonymity of her pseudonym. For a moment, though, I thought she was going to out herself, for shock value if nothing else. I wondered what our new companion would say if she knew that the woman sitting beside her had just recently toppled the mightiest political figure in the state. She'd done it essentially alone, too, covering a story that had disinterested the rest of the media until she'd exposed the whole of the crime and the police and DA had swooped in to finish him off.

"It's true. And like all good professors, I'm a self-important, self-righteous ass," Janice said. "In fact, that's my best quality."

"Apparently," Angelie said.

There are people who have a star quality, who carry it around with them unconsciously. Or perhaps they are always conscious of it, never willing to let down their mask. And there are people like Angelie who have a mysterious quality, who in person always perfectly resemble themselves. Any picture, any hairstyle, any sheen of fashion—you would always know it was her, even when you couldn't remember from where.

Janice stood up with an unexpectedly sudden jolt. "My work here is done," she said loudly. The people in the tables beside us looked over dismissively. "I'm off." She leaned down as if to kiss my cheek. "You'll have to give me a full report later," she said. "Take good notes."

"Are all your friends like that?" Angelie said as Janice disappeared through the crowd.

"Janice is all my friends."

A waitress materialized through the crowd, and I ordered the two of us another round of drinks. Angelie and I chatted through the evening, airy nothingness, words neither of us meant or cared to remember. She laughed at everything I said, and I felt myself slipping back into an old familiar pattern. I couldn't move my eyes away from her. She touched my hand lightly. I inched up close so our knees brushed, and she didn't move. She touched my hair, moving aside some stray strands. I was acting more drunk than I felt and continued buying rounds to catch myself up. When we stood in the end, we used each other for balance. My hand wrapped around her waist. She brushed her lips across my neck.

We were into the morning hours, and she asked me for a ride without specifying a location. At that moment, I thought of Hero, who only made me feel old. Angelie, quite the opposite, was taking years off my life.

In the close and tight confines of my truck, we traced each other's surfaces, following each line and intersection, a body geometry. We had exhausted our language and still knew nothing about each other. I was grateful for a time to forget my own history, to put aside mistakes of the past for those of the present.

We quietly crept up the stairs into the house. The night streamed past, and through the fumbling and smiles, I gradually let myself go, abandoning the cautious reserve and throwing myself full-on into an unknown.

fifteen

The work crews showed before first light. You could hear them unloading the trucks, the beeps of reverse, the shuffle and laughs, the clanking and crashing as they set up for work. The early hour was a necessity. Not even nine o'clock and they were already perspiring heavily. Out-of-doors work around here always started early and finished before noon. Each year, the deaths of several workmen across the county were attributed to a combination of the physical work, lack of water, heat and the ever-dense humidity. So far, I'd been lucky. I hadn't lost a one.

After weeks of inaction, the contractor had mysteriously reappeared without a word of explanation and set his team loose on the house. These half-dozen or so men were continuing their work renovating the exterior of the home, returning it to its previous façade. Lumber was moving, nail guns firing, music from a radio cranked up uncomfortably loud. The partially constructed wraparound porch was taking shape, and the 20th-century exterior features were melting away into a polished antebellum home. It was grounding, settling back into a landscape and time from which subsequent generations had torn it.

Everything was bustling.

I found Hero eating breakfast, watching the crew work from our seats at the kitchen bar. She told me she wished to cut her hair.

"I want it short," Hero said. "Shaved almost to the skull."

She smiled, then, a partial smirk, twirling a long strand around her thumb and forefinger, gestures that might have signaled pre-teen shyness, or, just as possible, barely contained laughter. I could not tell if she was serious about this or not. I did not have enough experience with her to know for certain when she was teasing me, testing my responses, and when she was being comfortably earnest.

Her mother had claimed experience, in Hero's case, would prove itself useless.

"What would your mother say?" I asked.

"I think the question is: What do you say?"

Hero's hair ran all the way down to her waist, when she wasn't wearing it tied up in a bun. There seemed no part of her that came from me. Her strong young body, her dark complexion. I was struck this morning by the idea that she was beautiful. And this wasn't just fatherly vanity, some genetic reaffirmation of my own pride. She was utterly different and apart from me. Beautiful and distressing.

She was waiting for me to say something.

"I'd say: talk with your mother."

"Nice try. She's gone for the duration, apparently."

"Speaking of that, I'm beyond just concerned about her. I'm thinking I perhaps ought to call the police."

"I told you. She does this all the time. I'm just disappointed that you felt the need to pull out the 'other-parent' card."

"Sorry. Best I can do."

Hero's glee unleashed itself, spreading up into her creasing eyes. "Fine," she said, picking up an orange from the centerpiece bowl and digging a nail into the skin. "So, are you going to tell me who the naked mystery babe is spread out on your bed?"

None of this was what I expected fatherhood would be.

Hero seemed contented for the moment to skin her citrus, leaving me to stew. I pretended to ignore her and leafed through the paper. I could feel her eyes boring into me, sensed her pert smile, but I kept my attention on the pages, slurping from my coffee mug loudly to illustrate my lack of regard.

"Really," she said, at last. "I don't want any siblings."

"It's not like I planned on you the first time," I said.

"Exactly my point. Tell me you used protection."

I buried my head in my hands. "This isn't a conversation I want to have."

"You and me both," she said.

Angelie appeared then, as if on cue, stutter-stepped past the workman at the base of the stairs and shuffled into the kitchen, her head a yawning, tangled yellow mesh. She slipped into the chair between my daughter and me. Hero had nearly finished stripping the orange; the peel lay in tiny chunks on the table in front of her. She gave the other woman a mocking look and turned to me, shaking her head.

I ignored her, giving my grapefruit my full attention.

Angelie was, thankfully, at least partially clothed, having drawn one of my dress shirts from the closet, though she had apparently decided against pants. She did not appear to even notice Hero, much less her quick and contemptuous looks, and laid her head, cheek down, upon the table.

"Don't I know you?" Hero said thoughtfully, after several long minutes of silence, biting into a wedge, chewing with exaggeration, juice dribbling down her chin.

"You seem to get that a lot," I said.

Angelie lifted her head sleepily and turned to squint in Hero's direction. "Shit," she said. "Kids."

She tilted her gaze back to me, glaring and shaking her head slowly. Then, sitting up, she pushed her jumbled blonde hair back out of her face. "Angelie Hart," she said, holding out a hand to Hero. "And you?"

My daughter took her hand firmly.

"The price of poor contraception," she said, standing, then carried her orange slices out onto the back porch.

"Lovely," Angelie said, rising and staggering over to the steaming coffee pot. "I didn't know you had kids."

"Surprised me, too."

"Quite a charmer," she said.

"She takes after her old man."

Coffee in hand, Angelie settled back into her chair. We sat across from each other, avoiding then catching gazes. After a long sip from her coffee cup, Angelie finally said, "Thanks for a fun night."

"You, too," I said, reflexively, though I wasn't sure if it sounded like I meant it. "She's right, though. This was how I got in trouble last time."

"Don't ruin the moment. Sex is life affirming."

"I just don't get to do it that often."

"Me, neither. And boyfriends are a pain in the ass."

"That's why I don't have one myself. Among other reasons."

She stretched, her long torso twisting and arching beneath my shirt, catching every curve and dip. Her hair tangled in a frizz on her left side, the side where she'd curled up against me while we slept. Yet there was still some self-conscious hesitation in the way she turned away and tried to pry something out from between her teeth. This was all so stunningly normal, the moment rich with our domestic airs.

Someone knocked on the front door. Angelie and I exchanged a look.

"Well, don't expect me to get it. I'm not even dressed," she said, pointing toward her bare legs and the shirt riding up her thighs.

I stood. "I'm sure they don't mind at all," I said, gesturing toward the line of construction workers who were taking a break, loitering on the half-constructed porch by the glass door and facing the kitchen. Hero stood beside them, talking in muffled, laughing bursts, pointing back in our direction.

My next-door neighbor, Alfred, stood at our front door, which I suspected one of the workers must have left open. Alfred wasn't the sort to barge in unannounced. Not that I'd observed that he felt any kind of respect or reticence toward me. Six long years of residence in Magnolia Grove still made me a newcomer, still deserving of the condescension of the old-time landed aristocracy. Alfred was one of those, and his overly friendly demeanor always succeeded in putting me immediately on the defensive. That, and his propensity for bringing lawsuits against me at the drop of a hat.

"Morning, Mr. Brown."

"What can I do you for, Alfred?"

"I'm here representing the Neighborhood Association."

"I figured this wasn't a courtesy call."

"There has been an increase in nighttime burglaries, three in the last four months alone. Now, the association debated hiring a security guard to patrol the streets, but we've instead decided to authorize the institution of a neighborhood watch program, made up of locals who want to help stop this rash of crime."

"I see. And you are looking for volunteers."

"Twice a week, two-hour shifts. The more people who get involved, the less work for everyone." He handed me a flier.

"Thanks," I said, with a wave.

Alfred just stood there, making no motion to leave.

"Anything else I can help with?" I asked.

"Now that you mention it. I see you've been moving ahead with your construction."

"Nothing gets by you, Alfred."

"Now, just as a piece of neighborly advice, I thought I'd point you toward the Neighborhood Association rules about unapproved structural work, noise ordinances, and approved work hours. I can get you a copy of the handbook if you need it."

"I already got the two you left in my mailbox. Thanks, Alfred."

"That's section four, article twelve through seventeen."

"I'm sure I'll find it."

"The Association's meetings are every other Saturday at the county library. That's when we can consider new motions."

Alfred stared past me into the house, his curious gaze no doubt searching for some new violation or indiscretion. I tried to distract him.

"I like the new brochure, by the way," I said.

"Well, thank you. Shame about Bill and the logging accident.

Tragedy. A good man. Very respectful neighbor. Great picture, though, so we still went with it as a tribute."

"Darn shame," I agreed. "I didn't get to know him very well myself."

"Guess he was a little before your time."

"No," I said. "I've been here six years."

"Really?" Alfred looked surprised.

"Positive," I said. "I'm sure I have some legal fees going back about that far."

Alfred smiled, somewhat less warmly. "Let's just see if you can keep from racking up any more."

Closing the door on Alfred with an apologetic shrug, I returned to the kitchen to find Angelie with her feet propped up on my chair, her back turned to the construction workers, who had nested on the porch in large numbers for lunch despite the early hour.

"They still out there?" she asked.

"I think you could start your own congregation."

"Lovely. Not that I have time for this. I need to bolt."

"What's the rush? It's a weekend."

"Can't. I have a shoot scheduled for noon, and these things take a while to set up. Plus the editing. I'm booked solid."

She stood then and walked over toward me, leaning in so her hair fell across my face, and kissed me very slowly and certainly on the lips. I could feel all the eyes on us, these voyeurs, and I embraced the empowerment of envy.

"Thanks for a fun evening. Call me tomorrow," she said softly, "and we'll see if we can work something out."

She turned toward the door without a glance toward the workers, motions of nonchalance as she sipped from her coffee cup and made her way toward the stairs.

"I thought you said boyfriends were a pain in the ass?" I yelled after her.

"They are!" she shouted, without turning around. "Total pain in the ass."

Behind me I heard a throat clear. There, standing in the hall doorway, was Hero, my electric razor in one hand, scissors clipping empty air impatiently in the other.

"Do I have to do this myself?" she said.

sixteen

James Wilson Caldwell was a night janitor for the Engineering Department at the A&M, working slowly through an apprenticeship program at the local vocational college, one course a semester or sometimes less. He was missing the tip of one finger on his right hand, lost during an accident with a power saw. An unmarried father of one, he lived with his eight-year-old daughter down in the Hive, a poverty-stricken area on the east side of town, close to the university campus, which had started as a community of ex-slaves and slowly been swallowed up by the expanding city. A Fourth Street regular at Harriet's Lounge, good for a beer or two nightly and the occasional scotch and soda. Sometimes he got in fights with other patrons. Sometimes he drove home those too drunk to drive themselves. His circle of friends was small and rowdy, but loyal. He was a simple man, if difficult for others to know very well. No one could be said to really know him all that well.

The same day that his daughter learned that her class project had been accepted into the county fair, the police showed up at his front steps. The little girl answered the door and fetched her daddy. They read him his rights, loaded him into a squad car and rushed him downtown. It was his first arrest, which put him somewhat behind the ball. Hardly a man who lived in the Hive had avoided arrest for one crime or another, real or imagined. Incarceration had become a fact of life, a right of downward passage.

There had been a murder behind a local supermarket. The victim had been an elderly man, well-off and white. No one knew why the victim had come to the Hive, where few white people still lived, and none of the ones who did had any money to speak of. Perhaps drugs, perhaps prostitution—the Hive had plenty enough of both. Or maybe he'd just come to look around, to see how the other half lives, only to discover how they died.

The suspect was placed in a witness lineup. Then he was placed in another one. Detectives questioned him relentlessly, for hours on end. He never asked for a lawyer—he didn't have one, didn't think he needed one, didn't know what he'd do with one if he did or how he'd afford it. They gave him cup after cup of water. He wasn't allowed to use the bathroom. He admitted nothing. Before the afternoon was done, police had charged him, set bail at $100,000 and left him in the hold to stew.

The trial was short. The only witness, the only evidence that tied him to the crime at all, was a woman who had seen the last stage of the crime. A robbery, a knife, blood, mayhem, the running away. The defense pointed out that no money had ever been found. No blood found anywhere associated with the accused. As for evidence tying him to the crime, there was literally nothing at all.

The jury deliberated for a half-hour before finding him guilty. Then they sentenced him to death.

Twenty-five years behind bars, asserting his innocence along with the chorus of his fellow prisoners. Appeal after appeal, and spared time and again only by slight technicalities. Twice, he was nearly executed, before the state stopped the practice because of the botched electric chair incidents, the stays coming from some slight slipup in the process, here or there. Each time, the court made a point of stating that their ruling should not be misconstrued as a judgment of innocence.

Then, the grace of divine providence. A law school student took a passing glance at his case, a pet project for his free time. And the more he read the information present, the more he was troubled. He looked at the testimony, spoke with people involved. He began doing his own research and joined the public defender's office as an intern. Overloaded with casework, they let him help. He requested transcripts from the trial. He sent out for DNA testing of blood from the crime scene.

He presented his findings to the court: Even based upon original trial documents, it was shown that the crime had occurred long before his client had left the bar for the night, and the fact that he'd driven home one of the other patrons confirmed this fact. Tests also identified blood at the scene of the crime that matched neither the defendant nor the victim. This was, as he put it in his brief, a miscarriage of justice. His appeal was rejected, as was the next, before the case made its winding path to the State Supreme Court.

Hal and I were holed up in his office when word came down from on high: a reversal of verdict, by a vote of four to three. An aggressive dissent pointed out that, regardless of the innocence or guilt of the party in question, the issue before the court was whether prosecutors had acted improperly and whether it was a lawful conviction. It was not the purpose of the court, they said, to substitute its opinion for that of the jury. By ignoring the law, they wrote, the majority was showing contempt for precedent and the whole judicial process.

But none of that mattered. By order of the majority, Caldwell was to be freed immediately. The split majority opinion read its release from the bench, along with an apology, commenting with regret that nothing could give the man his years back.

"It don't mean he's not guilty of something," Hal pointed out in agreement with the minority.

"Who isn't?" I replied.

Someone had to get down to the prison to put a public face on the release, to show no hard feelings on our part. Seeing Hal's general attitude, I volunteered, though immediately regretted the decision. I wasn't sure how I felt about having to face the man we'd apparently wrongly imprisoned for most of his life.

The warden met me by the metal detector, his face contorted into a cross between a frown and a smile. He looked pained. He didn't speak, and I felt certain he was not a man who liked to admit that mistakes could be made.

Caldwell came down the hallway, recently changed into the same old suit he'd arrived in twenty-five years before. Though only in his 50s, he appeared elderly and bent, shuffling into the room at no great pace. He didn't smile, but collected the personal items that had been held for him for the past two and a half decades.

"We wish you the best of luck," I said.

"We'll keep your cell warm," Creighton added.

"Thank you," he said to me, his voice far stronger and deeper than his body seemed, weighted perhaps by the years of a life that only might have been. "Thank you."

Caldwell stepped out onto the front walk. Camera crews were waiting, and flashbulbs popped. I walked beside him for a ways, holding his arm. A family was waiting at the end of the walk, a mother, father and children—relatives, possibly; perhaps even his daughter. There was little visible emotion. Everyone seemed uncomfortable and unsure. I stepped out of the way as he stepped forward and embraced the woman; his fingers clutched her jacket, holding her there, refusing to let go. A perfect image. Lights flashed. Voices shouted out questions. The freed man whispered into the woman's ear, and they slowly made their way toward the parking lot.

The next day's front page capturing the instant, the color photographs, the articles, the quotes, the graphs, the banner headline blaring. The story noted that Andrew Carl Adler was soon to be the state's first executed prisoner in 10 years, the implications of its inclusion hardly subtle.

"Says here that Adler was convicted only because of DNA evidence," Hero observed, reading aloud Caldwell's narrative with punctuated outrage across the dinner table.

"That's what I understand," I said.

"And you're comfortable with that?"

"I'm not not comfortable with that. I haven't really given it much thought, really. What does it matter?"

"What if it had been this guy you were killing instead of Adler? He was on death row a lot longer."

"But the system worked," I said.

"They decided this guy should die when he was actually innocent. Someone just happened to have evidence to clear him. If that's the system working, I'd hate to see it broken."

"Nothing's perfect," I said. "We're only human."

"So, doesn't it bother you that you're letting something so monumentally important like the life of another human hinge on something you don't know anything about?"

"Why do I get the feeling your outrage isn't really about Adler?"

"Why do you feel comfortable killing someone? Since I'm just supposed to accept the word of scientists that you're my actual father, I'd like to understand what makes you tick. And I don't get you."

"It's not like I'm pulling the switch. Someone has to do it. I'm just doing what they tell me to do."

"They made the same excuses at Nuremberg, you know."

"What kind of 12-year-old knows about Nuremberg? God. Why couldn't be you interested in makeup rather than murders?"

"Who says I can't be interested in both. But don't change the subject. You are part of an entire system that's corrupt to the core. Did you know that you're more likely to be sentenced to death if you're black, more likely than someone who's committed the exact same crime but who is also white?"

"They still committed a crime," I pointed out.

"Like Mr. Caldwell committed a crime? Those eyewitnesses were certain he was guilty, but he wasn't. Eyewitness testimony is some of the most unreliable in the world. You should go look at some of these cases. It's shocking what can get you the death penalty."

"We're just trying to protect people."

"But there's no reliable study that shows that the death penalty reduces crime. It doesn't even make sense. Seriously, what criminal commits one crime and not another because the penalty is less? Seriously. You think any of them expect to get caught, for goodness sake? It's just so dumb."

"Let's just trust that smarter people than you or I have thought through this."

"They have. But those people are the ones arguing that the system is broken."

"When did you suddenly become an expert on the death penalty?"

"I've been reading up on this for my vertical file at school," she beamed. "And my opinion is that you should just cancel the whole thing."

"Cancel what? Adler's execution? I can't do that. I don't have the power to stop anything."

"Have you tried?"

"I have responsibilities. I can't just decide not to do something. If I didn't, someone else would."

"Then let someone else do it," Hero said gently, picking up both our plates and carrying them around the bar to the kitchen sink.

"It's part of my job, Hero. The guy had a trial. He was convicted, and he's been sentenced. That's how the system works."

She started dumping the residue from the plates into the disposal. "Your job is to support a corrupt system. Imagine what would happen if you resigned in protest of the system. The system doesn't work. Look at what it did to Mr. Caldwell."

"He's alive, isn't he?"

"That's one way of looking at it," she said. "Alive, but more than 20 years of his life taken from him."

"Better than the alternative," I observed. "He could be dead."

"Exactly," she said. "That's exactly my point."

"I think you're still mad at me because I didn't let you cut your hair."

Hero smiled, settling back into her seat at the table then burying herself behind the paper to continue reading. "There's that, too, yes," she said.

seventeen

Death, it turns out, comes with a few unexpected perks. For one, the dead are exempt from jury duty. Credit card offers through the mail drop precipitously. The deceased do not have to pay taxes—though I believe the government is not above trying—and in some districts they are still encouraged to vote. I enjoyed the various fruits of being departed, but in most other respects, my death was beginning to get out of hand. Much to my surprise, my recent expiration had provided innumerable financial opportunities for a wide array of people. We received notifications and phone calls from organizations I not only hadn't ever been a part of, but some I never even knew existed, all of them citing my recent departure, with a hope that the survivors would remember me with a contribution. We received endless mailings from funeral homes and charities. Mysterious and unexplained debts suddenly came due.

It was no simple matter proving that I was, in actual fact, alive. It was simple enough to prove that I was born, and there was a large volume of mounting evidence that I was deceased. But there were no affidavits or similar options to prove that I was still living. The best evidence I could provide were eyewitnesses, anyone who could testify that I was indeed the so-listed "late Matthew Brown." But even those testimonials usually required an investigation, and the results were typically nontransferable. Each new agency required me once again to prove myself. Despite all my efforts, the process was only partially completed: some records had me listed alternately as both "expired" and "active."

All of that would have been enough to drive me crazy. But the most problematic aspect was still the recurring glitch where, after I succeeding in convincing people I was still living, something else would come around to kill me off again. Agencies where I had completed the entire process were turning around and re-listing me as dead, leaving me to begin the process all over again. I wasn't paranoid, but the calamity of it all felt far from accidental. At the very least, some fundamental dysfunction, a bureaucratic ghost in the machine, was hounding me. For each step I took returning me to life, two more would appear to bury me. It had become a bizarre and endless cycle, rapidly transforming me into the living dead.

And it was beginning to invade my professional life. I first noticed this when I tried to check out Adler's files from the Hall of Records one afternoon.

"Your ID has been invalidated. I'm sorry."

"But you know me. I'm associate director at DOC. Of course I have access to these files."

"I'm sorry, sir. The computer says."

"But think. It doesn't make sense."

"I'm sorry, sir."

"Would you believe you were dead if the computer said so?"

"I'm not paid to ask questions, sir."

Shortly after this, I no longer received my weekly paycheck. At first, the federal government stopped taking its money out, which was a pleasant surprise; but then the state itself had come to the conclusion that I was no longer alive and therefore no longer in need of pay. My social security number was archived, with no survivor benefits payable, information that was then transferred to the state, which in turn was voiding the checks for my salary. Or, rather, that was the best guess of what happened. Human Resources claimed they were powerless. Christy phoned from a noisy hotel on the campaign trail to apologize for the inconvenience and promised his full help when he returned. My calls to Bertrand Walker went, not too surprisingly, unreturned.

"So, have you told your girlfriend she's dating a dead man yet?" Hero asked one afternoon as I sorted through a stack of funeral home brochures that had arrived marked "Dearly Beloved Survivors of Matthew Brown."

"She's not my girlfriend."

"From the inappropriate noises you guys make at night, I would've guessed 'Dearly Beloved' at the very least."

"We don't like labels," I said.

Angelie and I had been meeting for the periodic date for the past two weeks, slipping into the house unnoticed after Hero was asleep, then out before she awoke. Or at least, we thought so. This was the first Hero had suggested that we hadn't been as successfully duplicitous as we'd thought.

"You aren't fooling anyone, you know," she went on, "except maybe yourselves. So just stop it."

"It's complicated."

"I take that as a 'No, I haven't told her.' "

I dumped several days worth of unopened letters into the garbage. "What would I even say?"

Hero crossed her arms and stood in front of me. "I want to meet her."

"You've already met her."

"We're talking about my prospective mother here. There are many, many questions that need to be resolved. I think I'm entitled to a formal introduction. You know, one that involves pants."

"I'll see what she says."

"And it's my choice. I get to pick the setting."

My plan from there was to stall, hoping Hero's mother showed up before anything could be arranged. Val was now a month overdue, and we were fast approaching the formal appearance of fall. Hero, unfortunately, wasn't content to wait. She found Angelie's phone number in my cell phone, then issued a formal invitation in my name to a dinner for the three of us the next night.

"That was a little uncomfortable," Angelie admitted to me later.

"I didn't really see as I had much of a choice."

"She's the champion of the ambush. If we stick together, I think we'll be fine."

"I could always break up with you before tonight."

"Then you'll spend the rest of your life wondering what you missed."

"I can live with that."

Fine dining in the capital had changed dramatically over the past 20 years. When I was a child, my family had dragged me to every diner, greasy-spoon, and warm counter-top to sample the Americana fare, but what ethnic foods were to be found were primarily domestic in origin. Now there were a handful of Cantonese restaurants, at least as many pizza shacks, several dozen seafood spots, a Cajun cookhouse where it was Mardi Gras 365 days a year, and one Spanish restaurant, which never appeared to have a single customer. More than a few locals suspected the lukewarm beans and rice were nothing more than a drug-front. If one wanted a fancy meal, though, there just wasn't anywhere to go.

The exception, of course, was improbably named Chez Chateau, and this was Hero's choice for the setting of our three-way interview. She kept our destination a mystery from Angelie and me, but we probably should have guessed from her instructions to dress "to the nines," something she herself made certain to do. I don't know where she found the green dress she wore, with what Angelie told me was an empire waist, and embroidery and ruffles overflowing—perhaps a thrift store or some other graveyard for prom dresses. She would trip on the hem, which bunched at her feet, and in the end just gathered up the excess material and draped it across her arm.

"Let's boogie," she said.

After driving literally from one end of town to the other, an hour-long trek without air conditioning or working windows, she had us pull off down a dirt road that wound around to the Old World-styled scattered cottages that made up Chez Chateau. Its owners were locals, neither of whom, by their own admission, had ever been out of the States, much less to France. They'd imported a first-class chef, however, and the food they served was almost as famous across the region as the outfits their staff were required to wear. We were greeted at the front by our hostess, who wore a dress nearly as elaborate as, if better fitting than, Hero's. She led us down a long hallway decorated with highly ornamented picture frames and heavy gilt-brass chandeliers and out to a multi-leveled dining area that was largely deserted. It was early still, just barely 6 p.m., and our table was set next to a set of open French doors that led out onto a patio. Peacocks wandered the grounds, heads and tails low as they pecked at the cracks in the stone.

In the brief distance, you could see the bordering swampland, the cypresses butting up against and draping leaves over the patio. We were all hot after our extended drive in the hermetically sealed confines of my truck. It was several minutes of draining our water glasses before anyone spoke.

"This place seems nice," Angelie offered. She was probably the coolest of us three in her sleeveless dark cocktail dress. My shirt, tie and undershirt made my every movement feel stiff, and I was scorching under their constrictions. I had never been here; had never really even felt the desire to come. I didn't know anything about French food or the culture. I didn't know if Hero did, either.

"Ms. Hart," Hero began.

"Please, just call me Angelie."

Hero scooted her chair. "Okey-dokie, Angelie. I was wondering, who's your favorite non-Christian religious figure?"

"Excuse me?"

"And not the Dalai Lama. Everyone says the Dalai Lama. For a monk, the dude gets too much publicity."

"Are you joking?" she chortled. "I don't think I would even know…"

"I'm taking out Gandhi, too. He's not even a religious figure. People just get confused. I think it's because he didn't wear clothes and didn't want to kill people."

Angelie just sat there for several seconds, meeting Hero's unrelenting stare with her own expression that was part bemusement, part terror. I inched closer, aspiring to somehow anchor myself between them.

"Don't mind her," I said. "She's just looking for a way in."

"It's research," Hero insisted. "I'm a dispassionate scientist."

"You're twelve."

"She's fine," Angelie said, easing back in her chair with a laugh and picking up her menu with a wink at my daughter. "I was that age once. Besides, if it gets too rough we could always change the subject and talk about her boyfriends."

"Fine. Let's!" Hero said, slapping the table.

"Let's not!" I groaned.

"Can I start you all off with some drinks?"

Our waitress appeared suddenly over Angelie's shoulder, chipper and smiling, serving tray propped on her hip. Her long hair was braided and wrapped in gold and green festive ribbons, the neckline of her dress swooped low and her breasts pushed upwards and outwards, such that everyone's eyes were inescapably drawn to them.

"I'm speechless," Hero said.

"I doubt that," I replied.

I ordered a bottle of the house red for Angelie and myself and a Coke for Hero, along with some pommes frites and goose liver as an appetizer. These were things I recognized, even if I didn't like them, familiarity serving as the better part of valor.

"What are your intentions with my father?"

"My intentions?" Angelie laughed, then cut short as she pondered whether Hero was serious.

"Are you going to make an honest man of him?"

I rested my head in my hands.

"I don't know that I have intentions, Hero. That's kind of the point of dating. But I'm dating him because I like him. And he likes me, from what I understand." The more Angelie spoke, the more animated and pronounced her moderate Southern accent became, the subtle North Carolinian slipping into something more grand and Texan—her point of origin maybe lying somewhere within that span. But it made me realize how little I knew about her, how little our relationship had managed to expand our knowledge of each other. And the truth was, there was no need. We understood everything we needed to know being around each other—in the times that we were actually together, which were also rare. We probably spent more time together "virtually" than in the same room together. Over the phone, through email—an account I created only so I could have an excuse to communicate with her—and "messaging," which I was still trying to understand, every imaginable technological communication was employed to give the semblance of relation.

The appetizers arrived and we ordered dinner, all without excess words. Hero seemed to be biding her time, choosing her moment, waiting perhaps for another sign of weakness to strike. I assumed now that she was out to destroy Angelie, or destroy what relationship we had together, whether she understood that herself or not. I had begun to suspect that Hero's seeming calculations were nothing more than instinct and unbridled, limitless wit.

Most of the way through dinner, Angelie set her napkin down on the table, "If you all will excuse me, I need to visit the little girls' room."

"I'll join you!" Hero said, standing up. "A little girl talk will be nice away from the menfolk listening in."

"What men? There's just me," I pointed out.

"Deal with it, Matthew," Angelie said, taking Hero's arm. "You're a minority now. The girls are gonna talk shop." With that, my daughter and presumed girlfriend walked off together, laughing and chatting softly such that I couldn't make out a word. I somehow doubted they were discussing Angelie's favorite non-Christian religious figure. I wanted to shout to Angelie not to trust her, but that seemed unnecessary anymore—not merely that Angelie was prepared for the assault, but rather that after only a brief while she seemed to fathom Hero much farther than I after these many weeks.

Looking out across the patio, I watched the sun drop down behind the cypresses, burning the pooled water and long grasses red. A sharp jab at my feet made me aware of the peacock that had sidled up next to the table. Feathers were frayed about its neck, and its left eye was missing, along with several sections of tail feathers. Suddenly, a waiter in black slacks and a cuffed and buttoned white shirt lunged at him from around a corner of the patio and continued to kick at him as he scurried away. The young man, not more than twenty, then walked over to our table, picked up the two loose cloth napkins on the table, folded them quickly into crowns, then took my credit card for the check.

It was a long while before Angelie finally reappeared, but by herself, and settled back down into her chair.

"She's a good kid," she said.

"That a relief to hear," I said. "I was afraid that if only one of you came out, it would be her."

"A little screwed up, maybe. But who wouldn't be. She's been through a lot."

"I know. We've just had a difficult time understanding each other."

"My father never understood me. But I don't think he even really tried. Good for you for trying."

"And failing," I added, finishing off the last of the wine.

"Well, I get her," she said softly. It wasn't clear to me if she was even aware that she was speaking out loud. "She tells me you're going to be executing Andrew Adler."

"That's Hero," I said. "Always out to help her old man with his relationships. I suppose she also mentioned that I'm dead."

Angelie smirked as she lifted her glass. "Might've mentioned it."

"It's no big deal."

"I'm actually more interested in Adler, though. Any chance I can use my considerable influence with you to get an interview with the man?"

"Have you tried talking with J.J. about this?"

"The warden has Adler locked down and won't let anyone near him. I just thought you might be able to pull some strings, grant me some kind of special access. Come on, Matthew. You're associate director. That's gotta be good for something."

"Have you met the warden? He's not someone you want to cross."

"Think about it? For me."

"What do you say we walk the grounds while we wait for Hero?" I asked, shifting the focus onto the landscape.

"Sure."

We stepped out onto the patio, and I could quickly see that there was much more to the property than I had thought. The right side wrapped around the main building, but then stretched off into a wider courtyard overgrown by tremendous oaks and beside a mammoth glass pavilion. The inside was set up for some kind of large function, a wedding reception or some such, though looking through the smoky glass, we could see that it was currently empty, the chairs neatly ordered, tablecloths piled in the corner. Following our way around, we broke out onto a stone pathway between the buildings and leading out toward other small cottages. Paper lanterns over electric lights lined the path, and with daylight fading, we instinctively followed them.

I imagined Hero and myself crawling up out of the swamp into this little oasis, all bloody and bruised and stained, like something out of a horror movie. We'd likely have sent the patrons scrambling for their lives.

Wandering these paths, though, it was easy to feel that we truly had stepped into another world. Coming up from the swamp or from the comfort of the capitol made it no more or less surreal, either way. It was as if we'd been transported somewhere entirely alien. Angelie appeared to be thinking the same thing.

"There's no way I'm getting stuck in this podunk town the rest of my career," she said. "No way. No how. Europe. Asia. Once I get my big break, the sky's the limit. Big time reporters get sent all over the world."

"Nice knowing you, too," I said.

"Don't be stupid. We can still date. I like the idea of being with someone who knows me before I become too famous."

"You ever known a long-distance relationship that worked?"

"What the heck is long-distance anymore, anyway? We could be together every weekend even if I'm working half a world away. You could bring Hero."

"Hero?"

"Sure, why not? The three of us, rushing around Paris. Try and tell me she wouldn't like that."

"I'm not sure how I'd like it," I said.

Angelie kept walking, slowly, finally stopping to lean against a cottage wall and stare up at the sky. "You've always lived here, Matthew. Always been comfortable. I know that feeling. But the world's bigger than this. And I can help you with Hero."

"Help me?"

"Girls her age aren't easy. I know. I was one."

"That's just it," I said, pausing beside her. "Should you be helping me with Hero?"

"Sure. Everyone needs help. You yourself keep asking for it."

"I'm just having a hard time sorting through everything." Listening to Angelie go on, I had started to feel caught in a tide, pulling me along as I struggled to keep my footing. "Hero and I don't really even know each other yet. I can't help feeling that struggling like this is good for us. It sounds ridiculous, I know, but you could actually make things too easy."

"So your problem," she paused with disbelief, "is that I get your daughter?"

"We've got to sort out the father-daughter thing. I need her to myself."

Angelie closed her eyes and shook her head. "Good lord, you have issues."

"I think she and I just need a little time. So we can get to understand each other better."

"Fine," Angelie said with obvious annoyance after a moment. "It's election season anyway. You weren't going to be seeing me much as it is."

The peacock-kicking waiter was approaching us quickly, my credit card in one hand and for some reason a phone in the other. He handed both to me, and I put the receiver to my ear.

It was Hero.

"Thought I'd give you two love-birds a little time to yourselves. So I took a cab."

"What? Where are you?"

"I'm at home. Don't stay out too late. And try to be quiet when you get back. I have school tomorrow."

Angelie walked carefully back to me as I spoke to Hero, then stood in front of me with her arms crossed, hip cocked. She seemed about to say something as I hung up, but instead merely let loose a large sigh, shook her head, then turned away from me and walked back toward the restaurant, calling back over her shoulder:

"Take me home, Matthew."

eighteen

A bell rang out across the courtyard and, on cue, the children were released, streaming out of the building and racing full tilt across the patio to the buses, the waiting cars, and out into the jammed streets. We were lined bumper to bumper, and no one was going anywhere anytime soon. A large woman wearing dark sunglasses and an orange vest carried a stop sign with her out into the traffic, trying to redirect the flow up and out. But no one was listening. Some were scanning the mass of kids for their own. The woman in front of me was reapplying makeup in her rearview, puckering and dabbing, when two boys suddenly charged up, opened the back doors, and jumped in. A car beside me at the curb inched forward into my lane, and I slipped into the rare spot.

After the first mad dash came the more leisurely, the socializing groups, chatting, pausing, and gathering in circles and other, more amorphous shapes. There was nowhere they had to be but where they were. At one edge of the yard, young toughs stealing each other's baseball caps or sitting cross-legged on the walkway, huddled over their homework, nervous smoke rising. On the other edge, the boys and girls dressed as young professionals fumbled with backpacks and textbooks and flipped protractors around like switchblades. They carried an air suggesting the Ivy League schools that were still five years off, but their futures had been calculated into numbers that were, even now, whole and without remainder and oh so certain.

I spotted Hero through the crowds. She was mingling, walking slowly with a horde of girls, four or five, each dressed similarly to her, but in jeans and tops slightly more tight, hair slightly more combed through. Despite the similarities, they didn't strike me as her type, and she herself, with her paisley scarf wrapped around her head and faded, torn denim, looked a little out of place walking with them, and if I noticed this, I was sure her peers did as well. But to all appearances, they were actual friends, and I could not help but feel some sort of satisfaction and even pride that she had found a way to fit in, comfort knowing that she was not alone and isolated. They moved casually down the sidewalk toward where I was parked. I suddenly regretted my decision to surprise her. I cringed low in my seat as they approached.

Hero recognized my run-down truck immediately. She pulled open the passenger side door, but stood on the curb with hip cocked.

"Aren't you supposed to be at work?" she asked.

"Who's going to miss me?" I smiled, but she did not as she turned to look over her shoulder.

"We're going to hit the mall, okay."

"Do you need a ride?" I said.

"We can walk it."

"Y'all can ride in the bed. You don't want to walk."

"Is he offering to drive?" asked one of the girls, peeking over her shoulder. She flashed a coy smile toward me, chewing her gum cow-like, exaggerated. The other girls rolled their eyes and busted out laughing, at me or her, or both. I couldn't tell.

Hero stepped back from the door for a moment and they conversed. Then all of them, including Hero, jumped the side and climbed into the back of the truck, settling onto their backpacks.

We wended in slow motion through the congested pickup traffic, seemingly a hundred cars lining the curbs, double-parked, emergency lights flashing, everything slowed to a determined crawl. A giant flat-nosed bus was inching into the lane ahead of me, and drivers were scrambling to pull around, ahead, any way to avoid it. Things gradually began to clear out, and quite suddenly, we started to move. One second, we were paused, then full motion. There was no obstacle at the end, it turned out. Just volume.

On the open road, we could pick up speed. The girls squealed in back, the wind whipping about them. Hero banged on the driver's glass. We passed a small open-air strip mall, once overflowing with shoppers and stores, now completely vacant and empty but for the fencing that construction crews had erected throughout the lot. There was a half-demolished storefront, great piles of rubble clouded by a cement dust haze. I remembered going to the movies here, back when the theater still operated with a single screen, before it had become a third-rate comedy club, and then a community playhouse. Now, it was all a hollow shell, hardly recognizable for its dismantling.

Watching my daughter in the rearview, who was in turn mostly just watching her friends, I felt a pang of sorrow that I could never take her to this movie house, or my childhood home—that I could not share most anything from my past with her, at least not in a way that would matter to her.

The mall parking lot was largely empty. The girls spilled from the truck bed out onto the pavement with "Thank you"s and giggles and any way to draw attention to themselves. "Is that a real gun?" one said, before quickly being dragged off by her friends. Hero stepped around to my window and shrugged.

"Thanks," she said. "I'm going to need your signature later. I just remembered that our civics class is making a field trip to the capitol tomorrow at 2 p.m. to watch real government committees in action."

"Funny," I said. "It just so happens that I'm testifying before the oversight committee tomorrow at 2 p.m., too. But I suppose that's just a remarkable coincidence."

"Remarkable" she agreed, with poorly feigned innocence.

"I'll see you back at the house later?"

"Where else am I going to go?"

I decided against returning to work. I had all the materials I needed to prepare for my testimony the next day, and at work I'd just get sucked into some other unenjoyable distractions. What I needed was some time alone, so I headed home.

The house felt empty in its quiet. I took an extended pause in the doorway, listening to the familiar household sounds. The distant drip of a faucet, the faint hum of machinery through the walls.

Leafing through the day's mail, I came across a notice from the credit card company. A cancellation of my card and a lien against my account. No explanation whatsoever, but another apparent consequence of my reported death. I wondered who told them this time. These kinds of things had become so frequent, I barely registered them anymore, but still I decided to call the company for an explanation. The woman at the other end, however, had none to offer. I was simply listed in their system as deceased.

"If I'm dead, then why would you send me a note confirming that I'm supposed to be dead?"

"In case it's a mistake."

"What if no one replies?" I asked.

"Then we'd know, wouldn't we?"

Problems with my credit, however, were the least of my latest woes. Reports of my death, while obviously premature, had also become wildly exaggerated. An obituary appeared about me in the Constitution-Gazette, complete with sympathetic and heartfelt quotes from other government officials I had no memory of ever meeting. Hero too had given them a quote, a sob story about her own dejection and sadness about finding and then so suddenly losing her father. I suspected collusion between her and Janice, trying to milk it for all it was worth.

A news crew came by one morning and set itself up on our front lawn to try to interview Hero about her new life, fatherless and alone. Social services had already made two visits, and they still didn't seem quite convinced.

Much of my time in the weeks immediately following the initial announcement were spent calling up surprised relatives and friends who had sent cards and flowers expressing their sympathy to Hero, for if there had been one universal consequence of this event, it had been that everyone now knew I was a father. Not that I had been trying to hide the fact. I had simply only recently discovered it myself. But some distant relations were nevertheless miffed. There were uncomfortable silences across phone lines, a few indignant letters sent.

No one expressed particularly emphatic relief to learn that I was still alive.

Left to my own devices while Hero was out playing with her friends, I muddled through the rest of the afternoon trying to set up my new computer in the office. The cables were connected, plugs plugged. I pushed the power button, but still nothing happened. My screen stayed blank. I considered dropping the whole thing on the floor and blaming my clumsiness rather than my stupidity. Instead I shut the door and turned off the light.

That evening, Hero and I were in the kitchen together making diner. She'd come home from her mall trip with so little fanfare, I almost hadn't realized she'd returned. She was straining spaghetti noodles over the sink when she told me she had a key role in the school play.

"That's impressive," I said. "Two weeks and already you're making friends, acting in the play."

"I suspect it's just pity. They're trying to make the new girl feel loved."

"Still."

"They stick me in a drama class and insist on putting me in their play."

"What monsters."

She turned to face me. "They told me it was your idea."

"Drama's good for you," I said. "It builds character. What's the play again?"

"Shakespeare. It's a romantic comedy. Except that people die."

"At least it's realistic."

"Yes, but apparently that's not the point."

"Rarely is.

"I hate Shakespeare. That's where Geoffrey got my name. Some play."

"Which one?" I asked.

"Who cares?"

"You could always quit," I said.

She was quiet a moment, testing the spaghetti by hurling a strand against the wall. It stuck there for a second, then fell to the floor.

"That's also not the point," she said.

Still, despite her protestations, I thought she sounded pleased with herself. Perhaps this was what we could hope for, what Janice had called "a decent working relationship." It was better than nothing.

Just as Hero was setting dinner on the table, the phone rang. It was Hal, who I couldn't remember ever calling me at home before.

"Tell me you're watching this," he mumbled

"Watching what?"

The early evening news had a live feed in the front yard of a high-end home. It could have been a place in Magnolia Grove, up the block, around the corner. A man was being filmed, walking down his driveway while lights flashed all around him and the camera pushed in. Escorted by two dour-faced suits, arms pulled behind him and hands cuffed, the man was disheveled, wearing that familiar grimace of the accused that blurs all men's faces. Even so, I recognized that same doughy frown I'd seen over years of conversations across my desk.

The current director of the Bureau of Environmental Study, Bernie Morr.

Articles about the investigations had been coming more frequently, even if still frustratingly vague, since the seizure of the bureau's records, so maybe we should have expected it. Stanton's office was still maddeningly resolute about not divulging details, though, which had left everyone in government more than a little anxious. As a result, it appeared, some public figures had, in a panic, drawn attention to some illicit activities while trying to cover them up. It was enough to make we wonder whether this whole thing wasn't some elaborate charade designed by Stanton to flush out the wrongdoers. Hal, I knew, barely slept as he continued his meticulous and never-ending review of Corrections. He was determined that we would not suffer the same fate as the three other departments that had found themselves raided. I grew increasingly nervous about the whole thing. If I had any clue what I might have done, I suspect that the coyness of the investigators would have worked on me, as well.

nineteen

As I entered the committee chamber, a flash fired and instantly
blinded me. But then slowly my eyes cleared, and I could quickly
see that the large room and rows of chairs were mostly empty except
for the committee's own staffers and other legislators who where
just looking for a place where they could have a quiet conversation.
Above us stood a gallery, which was more populated, but not by
much. This was where the general public could come and see the
business of government, though in all honesty, of the dozen or so
observers, few if any were paying any attention to what was going
on below. Instead, the room was dominated by the cameras, one
perched on the balcony above, another set up behind the dais,
trained upon me. I pulled at my collar, my pinching necktie,
straining under this drab glow of attention.

A single reporter sat in the front row behind me, chin down
upon his chest, dozing softly.

With Christy still out of town, it had fallen to me to be present
for the biannual debriefing of the State Legislative Subcommittee
on Prisons, Halfway Houses, and Narcotics Treatment Facilities.
Had Christy been around, I probably still would have been sent.
The subcommittee had delivered in advance a list of questions
they wanted addressed, most of which were centered around the
forthcoming execution. So as the man in charge, I found myself
assigned by default. A lawyer from the department's office of legal
counsel had given me a briefing, but it wasn't customary for there to
be any kind of lawyers present for these types of meetings, I was told,

at least not for witnesses. If I had any questions regarding separation of powers, he said, just tell them I had to check my records and I'd get back to them later with a more complete answer. Also, he said, always call them senator. It helped to feed their egos.

The senators on the dais were dull, gray-suited, sour-mouthed. Young clerks buzzed between them, passing them notes, whispering in their ears. Water pitchers were filled near overflowing. Ice rattled. The chairman was Hugh Gillespie, whom Janice had pointed out at the fundraiser as the second most powerful man in the state. He smacked his gavel, bringing everyone to order, and voices tittered out. The bailiff came over and swore me in.

"Mr. Brown, thank you for coming. The committee has read your answers to the questions we provided and wanted to offer you the opportunity to begin with opening remarks, particularly anything you cared to discuss about the preparations for the upcoming scheduled execution of Andrew Carl Adler."

Thirty years ago, our little meeting wouldn't have been a blip on anyone's radar, and it would likely have been over almost before it started. We would have entered our remarks into the record, then all gone to lunch. That's how my grandfather had explained the whole process and its time-honored traditions of avoiding work whenever possible. Janice agreed, arguing that the ubiquity of the video camera had changed all this, as now every moment that occurred on the floor of every committee and subcommittee hearing was preserved for posterity. Politicians, never known for their forthright sincerity to begin with, were now perpetual shells. Cameras could be anywhere and, in an instant, the most benignly intended words spread far and wide, whole careers crashing down in an afternoon. None of this had made them more honest—just less authentic.

And so it was that I was made to read my statement, for the record, trying not to make eye contact with the camera, and speaking as clearly and evenly as I could while I explained all the preparations that had been made, the credentials granted, the legal procedures put into place to protect us against the very hazards that had brought the system down before. Of course, we'd already hired an anonymous executioner. A medical doctor had been hired to certify the clear expiration of the condemned. Protesters and supporters were going to be kept 100 yards from the prison in specially designated zones. Selected members of the victim's and prisoner's family would be present, as well as the warden and a representative of the department (me). A versatile chef had been hired to prepare Adler's chosen last meal—though he too would remain anonymous for security reasons.

As we moved on to questions, fairly predictable, I found myself casting casual glances around the room. That's when I saw Hero. Her class had arrived at some point after I had begun and now took up the bulk of the gallery above us. This was the first time she'd seen me in any professional capacity. I smiled, but she made no gesture in recognition of me at all. She just sat there, sometimes glancing down, other times chatting with people nearby. But from my limited position and distance, it appeared that she was holding hands with the skinny, pale boy with hair below his chin who was sitting right beside her.

I cleared my throat and took a drink of water, straining for a slightly better view without appearing to be avoiding the committee. Hero didn't have a boyfriend, at least as far as I knew. She hadn't mentioned anything about boys she liked to me, I told myself, realizing in an instant how ridiculous that explanation seemed. As a substitute father, it was hard to imagine being further removed from her.

"Mr. Brown. I was wondering if you could shed any light upon this investigation of the Bureau of Environmental Study and your involvement with Bernard Morr."

At the end of the dais, the final state senator had begun his questioning. I didn't recognize him at all, but his name plate said he was Senator Sanford Davis, and he clearly had other interests and questions than those having to do with the Department of Corrections.

"I'm sorry, senator. I wasn't really prepared to discuss details about those matters. As I'm no longer an employee of the bureau, I don't really have access to any useful information regarding this matter."

Senator Davis eased into a closed-mouth grin and tapped his pen on the paper in front of him.

"Mr. Brown, like everyone else in the state capitol, we are curious about the ongoing investigations that have seemed to stretch from one end of this administration to the other. The governor himself was forced to resign, as you recall. I believe it is in the public's interest to get to the bottom of these matters, and rather than have to call you all the way back down here for another, let's say, more insistent discussion, I would prefer it if you would be so kind as to tell this committee whether you yourself have been questioned by investigators regarding Mr. Morr?"

There were several different ways I considered answering this question, but the prospect of being called back for a full-blown hearing on the matter made the simplest answer the most appealing.

"Yes, I have, senator," I said.

I turned to catch a glimpse of Hero and her friend, but her back was turned, and she herself was partially obscured by the thickening gallery crowd.

"Do you have any reason to believe that you are a target in these investigations, Mr. Brown?"

"No, senator. I do not."

"Are you aware of any illegal activities that may have occurred during your tenure at the bureau?

"No. I'm sorry, senator, but I'm afraid I am as much in the dark as everyone else."

Senator Davis continued tapping his pen, but this time he did not smile. He merely stared at me, likely assessing how truthful I was being. I was aware that the general buzzing about the room had stopped. People were suddenly conscious that they were witnessing a moment, unscripted and poorly defended. I wondered how obvious my lack of qualifications were, whether anyone could see that I truly knew nothing of these matters, that I was merely making things up as I went along and calling my ignorance self-assurance. Hero would know how transparent I was. She could see through me, if she was even listening. This was, of course, her plan all along—to make it difficult for me to concentrate. My own personal antagonist.

"Mr. Brown, while you were at the BES, your office reviewed all of the environmental impact reports for the state, did it not?"

"We did, yes. As well as enforcement of existing state regulations and general compliance with federal law."

"It has come to our attention that certain… improprieties regarding these environmental impact reports may be related to the current investigation of the bureau. While you were director, what was your role regarding these reports?"

My role was to get the heck out of the way, I wanted to say. I had already reached the limits of my comfort zone when talking about the bureau, so I was forced to wing it.

"As I understand the process, we would contract with outside agencies to conduct most of our reports. These agencies would then submit a report to me with recommendations, which we would generally follow."

"Generally? Under what circumstances might you not? I'm trying to understand this, so forgive me if my questions strike you as simplistic."

Feeling fully exposed in my ignorance, I didn't know how to stop. When I'd first arrived at Environmental many years before, I had studied my responsibilities carefully, so I would know how best to avoid them. My primary function, in fact, was to sign off on the environmental impact reports, and I had perfected that simple task to an art. However, I could remember discussing and rejecting some recommendations with Bernie, but as for what they entailed, I had no idea. I had trusted him to know these things, a trust that, in light of current events, seemed more and more foolish.

"Not at all, senator. I'm a little hard pressed to remember a situation where we didn't follow the recommendations of those who conducted the study. I believe the bureau has some flexibility about this when there are competing considerations that need to be balanced."

All of these memories buried by the passing years.

"Are you willing to testify, under oath before this committee, that you have no knowledge of any illegal activities regarding your work at the bureau?"

"Senator, I can honestly testify before you now that I have no knowledge of anything improper regarding these reports or anything else related to my work at the bureau. My job was to follow the law and ensure the environmental safety of the public. I'm not trying to be evasive. I just don't have anything useful to pass along. If I did, you'd be the first to know."

A quiet fell over the room, broken by a cough somewhere behind me. I hadn't noticed my own voice increasing in intensity, and I realized that I appeared very defensive. I could also see why people were suddenly so attentive. In an investigation that had paralyzed much of the government for the past months but which had also been so completely silent about its movements, any public statement concerning any part of it was big news. I avoided the sharp stare of the camera eye, which was fixed on me, unmoving.

"Very well," Senator Davis said at long last. "We have your statement. I yield the bulk of my time."

With the gavel struck and people dispersing, I stood, gathered my papers and strained to make out figures milling through the upstairs gallery. A group of elderly women were still sitting, and a grade-school batch of kids were jumping on the seats. Hero and her class, however, had quietly moved on.

twenty

Everything flowed at an even pace, the movement of steady certainty, seemingly without rush or dawdle. But there was a quiet potential below the surface, a perpetual motion.

The proprietor of the hardware store sat at his chair beside the door, the figure of apparent stillness. But his eyes chased after everyone who passed him by on their way elsewhere, everyone who stepped in through his door, meandering by the washers, the nails, solid two-and-a-half-inchers on down to dainty finishing nails. He rocked on the heels of the chair, toes pushing him back, dropping him forward, balancing in between. Ready to go anywhere, anywhere at all, really, just as long as you give him time.

The woman in bright, crisp denim, waistband riding high over her round belly. She dragged behind her a toddler, who kicked at a cola cup in the gutter as they stepped out into the street. Overwhelmed by the heat, the boy sweat through his light cotton shirt, down his shining face, his bangs overgrown and dampened into thick tresses, winged like Mercury.

A smooth shopper, crisply pressed linen slacks hanging loose, his shirt a metallic, immaculate blue. He had shades, dark as his skin, and he was walking with a purpose, even if he had nowhere to go. His woman beside him, lily-pale in her floral sundress, hopped with every other step. She skipped with her hand in his, pausing only for a second to glance in the shop windows. They seemed oblivious to the random looks they received, some hostile, some just curious. Clearly, they were not from these parts.

Taking lunch at a sidewalk café, Janice and I could see just about every type of person. Everyone used these sidewalks—we were in the heart of downtown. Only a block from the DMV, squeezed between the Convention Hall and the Courthouse. Rows upon rows of shops lined the street. Apartments on the floors above us, the metal balcony above our heads looking like a fire escape, painted green, precarious.

In its shadow and the swarming heat, we sipped our Cabernet poured straight from the bottle.

The Graft House stood just across from the capitol steps, a patio barbecue joint and once-favorite haunt of legislators and lobbyists. Its original name had been the Draft House, though it had actually never served alcohol, even after the county was no longer dry, but happily charged for corkage. It had earned its more commonly used name from years of political wheelings and dealings, kickbacks, back scratching, and everyone getting their cut. The Graft House. So few people used its real name, or knew it by any other, that the owners eventually gave in and changed it officially. A large red G spray-painted on the wooden sign still dangled over the doorway. Few legislators allowed themselves to be seen coming here anymore, or on the chance that they did, would sit in the middle of the main dining room in full view. No one wanted to be caught entering or leaving the backroom booths, with their high walls and doorways and hidden compartments once useful for stashing booze.

It was Janice who had first told me the history of the place, the story lying beneath its surface, just as she tells me about everything around me I never seem to see with the naked eye.

"That was a nice display the other day in front of the committee," she said, taking a bite of her oyster po'boy.

"You saw that, then."

"My dear Matthew, everyone saw it. It was on all the local newscasts. Leave it up to you to make a dull summer more interesting. You were roundly sliced and diced."

"It's not like I said anything."

"You did better than that. You made a big deal of not saying anything. Perhaps a career as a politician is your true calling."

"I don't like smiling enough."

Bertrand Walker had made it clear, though, that this was the path I was on. As long as I followed through, my rise was nearly limitless. But generally, I tried not to think too hard about the future. Survival is a game of the moment, and there was typically enough work just trying to get by without accomplishing much of anything. This had been my model of success at both Environmental and Corrections and the beauty of bureaucracy, the wondrous mystique of three-ring binder manuals and collated memos and annual budget adjustments. Performance evaluations. Cost-benefit analyses. Outlay. Deficit. The red and the black. Conference calls and staff meetings and studies by the truckload. I was always in over my head, it was true, overwhelmed by the sheer volume of regulations over an entire state and my near total lack of knowledge.

Back then I'd learned the wonderful truth: I was utterly unnecessary.

The system continued to work even when the people in charge did not. In my case, the system even worked better when I stepped out of the way of qualified and dedicated public servants who knew what they were doing. Over my greasy basket of fish and chips, I detailed my philosophy of management to Janice, who smiled, then said:

"Did you know the man who developed the idea of bureaucracy saw it as the answer to a world of problems? It was supposed to make the world an efficient place. That may sound ridiculous to those of us who've now lived in that world, but what can you say? Alfred Nobel also believed that dynamite would bring about the end of wars. Kind of adorable, actually, if you think about it, these utopian dreamers."

"But now, of course, I'm not only superfluous in my job, but the bureaucracy has decided I no longer even exist," I said. Just the day before, one of my credit card renewals had been denied due to red flags regarding identity theft. Someone thought I was trying to steal the life of a dead man, which as it turns out, in fact, I was.

"Don't be so melodramatic, Matthew." Janice leaned back into her chair and crossed her knees, resting an elbow on the chair's arm, her chin upon her hand, a thin cigarette pinched between her fingers. "The bureaucracy is just part of our evolution. Look around you. Our South is losing its identity as a distinct culture until we're nothing more than a blur. The South, America, the world. We're being smeared together by the technology and values of the age."

"The South is still the South," I said, "new or old."

"There are a thousand ways it's slipping away. From mass production to mass media—the food, the clothes, the language. We're homogenized. The old rules don't work anymore. Just think about how everything used to be so inescapably tied to race."

"Used to be? Look around you, Janice."

"It's not that racism isn't still everywhere. It's practically its own institution. But how we deal with race is trickier than it used to be. How politicians exploit it is entirely different. We've convinced ourselves that we're no longer racist because we've put away the signs and the fire hoses. And in fairness, it's certainly less racist. Now, instead of blanket assumptions that blacks aren't as good as whites, it's 'most' blacks. And it's their fault anyway, people will tell you, unless they act as white as possible. These attitudes go by the name 'progress.' But even racism has become homogenized. The South has just learned how to be racist the same way everyone else is."

A large party of gentlemen exited the Graft House in a group, laughing and shaking heads and patting arms. I thought I recognized a senator or two from yesterday's panel and slid down lower in my seat.

Janice continued, "We've managed to convince ourselves that we've evolved. But from my perspective, it's all the same sad story. It's just the politics that's changed. The lies we tell ourselves."

"Just because we've progressed doesn't mean we're lying," I countered. "And it doesn't mean the system is coming apart. You always have some paranoid theory about something or another."

Janice lit another cigarette and took a long draft, lifting her chin into the air. "No one can be racist anymore. A Wallace gets nowhere today, at least not by standing on the front steps of a school. But because they've changed the rules, we've changed the meaning of the words. Everyone professes their love of Martin Luther King, even the very same people who made careers out of hating and vilifying him. My point is that racism has always been either a tool or a useful, if incidental, cover for the greed of those in power. But you can sense the desperation, both in politics and in the people. It doesn't work quite the same way, and we can be grateful for that. But it's in many ways just as ugly, and people are desperate to recreate that vision of Southern glory."

"What's wrong with celebrating the good parts of our heritage," I said, pouring another glass for each of us from the bottle.

"Here in the South, we constantly clothe ourselves in the past, yet we are increasingly ignorant of it. We deny what it was, but claim its rightness. And what once made us honestly ourselves is slipping into mere caricature and self-loathing."

"You gotta admit, things are better than they were."

"Drowning a man in six inches of water rather than ten feet isn't exactly doing him a favor.."

I exhaled heavily and noticed all at once my own exhaustion. There was a time, it seemed to me, that life was easier. Perhaps Janice would argue that that too was only a mirage. "How'd we end up talking about race?"

"We're talking about the South and politics. We'll always end up talking about race."

Janice knew more about the inner workings of this state's politics than almost any other person. Between her knowledge, her sources and the damning wit she displayed in her column, it was difficult not to think of Janice as the real power in town. Her opinions were read by every political player from one end of the state to the other, if only so they could keep tabs on each other. Political gossip is less a delicacy than a smorgasbord, with everyone lined up out the door.

She knew something about everyone, it seemed, and could destroy their political, professional and personal lives with a stroke of her pen. It was a perfect power relationship and I told her so.

"That's an illusion," she insisted. "It only looks like I have power. Really, I'm just as much a victim as everyone else."

"That's not true. There's not a person in those buildings who isn't scared to death of you."

"As well they should be. But every predator should be scared of his victim. We're dangerous when our lives are at stake. At the very least, we hope to give them indigestion."

"Tell that to Vern Roberson."

The state's three-term governor was just the most recent of Janice's conquests. She'd been exposing fiscal improprieties for the past decade. The list of those she'd skewered included the state comptroller, two cabinet officials and half a dozen lawmakers. She had also been accused of indirectly causing the heart attack of the state's Commerce secretary. No one, including Janice herself, had found that especially surprising.

As for the governor, he'd been handing out favors to his campaign contributors and business associates for nearly twenty years of public life. Everyone had known this. But it had been her investigations that revealed a ring of counterfeiting and graft and mistresses galore in one glorified mess. She had laid the final straw.

"Vern's a big boy. He took it well."

"Didn't he threaten to put a contract out on you?"

"That was a misunderstanding," she said blithely. "He was trying to offer me a business deal."

"You take dangerous chances."

"It always pays to hold something back. It gives you a little leverage, if handled right. Politics round here is, like sex, a game of survival. Sometimes it pays to play rough."

When Janice made her transition from anthropology to journalism, she told me that politics had seemed like a natural next step, due to her long-held interest in primitive cultures.

"I'm surprised you're not all over this big investigation of Environmental," I said. "Sounds like it would be just your sort of thing."

"Who says I'm not?" Her face betrayed no indication of her earnestness.

"Then maybe you can tell me whether I'm in trouble or not. The D.A. and his team running all over town, putting Bernie under sealed indictment. It's like Occam's Razor is hovering over my head."

"I think you mean the sword of Damocles. But actually I like yours better."

"Still."

We sat in silence for a few minutes while I read the newspaper and she fell back into her usual habit of listening in on neighboring conversations.

"Let's talk about something besides politics," I said.

"Fine. How're things going with your reporter-friend?"

"Okay," I said. "Next subject."

It had actually been over a week since I'd seen Angelie, not since our dinner, but we'd been in occasional communication through email, voicemail, texts. This distance had been helpful, allowing me to keep my relationship with Hero separate and central. Though Angelie and I hadn't slept together in weeks and our interactions were largely confined to superficial observations about our days, things were going surprisingly well. She'd become my virtual girlfriend, whom I could be certain to see each weeknight at 6 and 11. Periodically, I'd send her flowers, just to give myself some presence.

This sadly seemed to be the only successful relationship in my life.

"What about junior? You guys making any headway?"

"Absolutely. Now she doesn't think I'm her father."

"Doesn't think or doesn't want to?"

"The second one, definitely. The first one, probably. Not that

I blame her, particularly. But I feel like we're still just pecking the surface. She's been different since the accident and her mother went missing. I suspect she's feeling abandoned."

"Then you're her lifeline."

"Poor girl," I said.

I had finally hired a private investigator to see if he could help us track down Hero's mother, or anyone really, but with no success. Her father Geoffrey, I learned, had resigned from his teaching position at the junior college and hadn't left any forwarding information except for the house he no longer shared with his family. Val, too, really was missing. Their home had been shut up dark and mail put on hold indefinitely. Aside from that, there was no sign. For a few more thousand dollars, I could have paid for a more comprehensive search, but money was tight, and I had no confidence that it would be well spent.

Hero and I were still in our holding pattern. Waiting.

As Janice finished off her final cigarette and the last of the wine, she bid me adieu and sauntered off into the waning afternoon. I eased back into my chair to watch the leisurely sidewalk wanderers. Gusts of cool A/C blew out the door to make the heat tolerable. I had drunk too much, talked too much, and was just about ready to stumble back to a corner of my office for a nap when a woman who looked vaguely familiar sat down in the chair across from me, setting down a large, half drunk Draft House mug of beer on the table.

"Mr. Brown. I don't know if you'll remember me. I'm Jennifer Thorn Jackson."

She said her name with punctuation on the first syllables, as if these consonants had some kind of magical properties that might jar some memory for me.

"I'm sorry. Do we know each other?"

"That's fine. Not that I thought you would. A long shot, really. We met once, three or four years ago, at a cocktail party. It doesn't matter."

"Can I help you?"

"I was kind of hoping we could help each other. In fact, we may need each other."

"I'm flattered, but I'm spoken for."

She smiled nervously, clearly not amused by my admittedly weak attempt to decompress the serious air of the moment.

"I saw your testimony the other day, at the Senate."

I sighed and ran a hand through my hair. "Definitely not one of my finer moments."

She scooted in closer, leaned into the table and lowered her voice, though the sharpness of her words made it sound just as loud. "I work for a company that does contract work for the state's environmental impact reports. In fact, I have done dozens of these reports myself for your department."

"I don't work for the BES anymore."

"I think I may know what the Attorney General is looking for. And it's something that concerns both of us."

I felt a clutching inside, then glanced around us quickly. On a late Friday afternoon, both street and restaurant were nearly empty. I leaned in closer, too.

"What are you talking about? How did you even know where to find me? Are you following me?"

"Your office suggested I look here, which is just as well since I think we want to avoid any professional meeting. What I have to tell you isn't formally sanctioned by anyone. If my employer knew I was revealing anything, I could probably be charged with a crime."

She glanced quickly over her shoulder. I thought how odd that she should think that coming to the Graft House would somehow make her more anonymous. She'd have run into fewer powerful people in my office than here, with less chance of being discovered. But it was late, and the lunch rush had dwindled to a few college students and some shadowy figures, legislators and lobbyists, talking in isolated hush near the fringes.

"Two years ago," she began, "I was working on a local EIR for the Bureau. The title of the project was Rain Bird. The scientists were getting tremendous pressure, unbelievable political pressure, to minimize the findings of the environmental impact. Not that pressure is exactly new. It's always fairly clear how the powers that be would like for us to rule. But avoiding direct pressure is precisely why these things are supposed to be done by outside organizations. Still, word often reaches the research teams about the desired result, or it's simply obvious, which can have a minor affect on how recommendations are composed. But even I was surprised by the overt nature in this case. Phone calls were coming in on a daily basis to the science team. Someone even came down to visit, we were told, from the governor's office, to check on our progress. Everyone understood what was at stake here. Money, advancement, prestige."

"I'm sorry, but I don't see…"

"I issued a recommendation against the project. I suggested the entire thing be scrapped."

"Why?"

"The danger not just to the environment but to the public health as well was incalculable but potentially catastrophic. I told my supervisors that I could in no way sign off on a report that approved this project as written."

"I see," I said, though I didn't quite.

"People would have died, Mr. Brown. That's why I filed my conclusions against and demanded that my recommendation be adopted or I would resign. So they agreed to send the project back to the drawing board."

"That sounds interesting. I still don't see how…"

"Recently I started hearing rumors—but I can't verify for certain—about a project just recently launched called Rain Bird."

She let that sink in for a moment, taking a long drink from her mug.

"You said they scrapped it."

"I filed my finding in objection, yes, and they told me it was shelved. But I'm just a researcher. I don't see the final report, or the final recommendation."

"What is Rain Bird?"

She took a breath and looked around cautiously again. She couldn't have looked more suspicious if she had been trying. "It involved an elaborate plan for insect control. And there was an... experimental pesticide involved. That's what we were examining, its impact on the environment."

"What pesticide?"

"I don't know. My notes went with the project, which is company policy for trademarked materials. Besides, I thought I was done with this and put it out of my mind. Until now."

"And how do you know this Rain Bird is the same one?"

"I don't. It's possible that it's a recycled name for another project that has nothing to do with this one. But all this news about investigations into environmental impact reports and these men appearing at my own company wearing dark sunglasses and asking questions, it's making me nervous. If the company has falsified my results, or if someone at the bureau falsified a report, it's possible that people are gonna find themselves in serious trouble."

"So you think this Rain Bird is what's behind this investigation?"

She shrugged. "I don't know anything, Mr. Brown. That's why I've come to you."

"What do you want me to do?"

"I hoped you might be able to get access to the files, my reports or my research, to confirm one way or the other."

I thought of Hero, who might look at me in this moment and wonder what my problem was. Her sense of adventure would probably have her chomping at the bit to solve a mystery like this. For myself, I felt a bit unmoored.

"I told you. I don't work for Environmental anymore. I'm not sure there's anything I can do."

"You have to understand what's at stake, Mr. Brown. If this project really is going forward...people are going to be in danger. Some of them may even die."

The image of Stanton ushering Bernie Morr out of the bureau

office came to me then, and I could see all at once the public humiliation and the guilt of other people's blood staining me. Ignorance suddenly didn't seem like much of a shield anymore. If I was to protect myself, much less make any kind of difference, I would have to learn quickly how to be competent. That's what Hero would do, anyway, I had no doubt.

"I shouldn't even be talking with you," she said. "I just wanted to see if there was anything you could do." She paused for a moment, looking around her as if she needed to collect something, but there was nothing but her and her glass. "I should go."

I watched Jennifer Thorn Jackson walk off, cutting from the sidewalk across the empty street toward the parking garage behind the capitol buildings, and tried hard to process what she'd told me as she faded into the haze. Here was the prospect of a real scandal, and a potentially life-threatening one at that. Maybe this was the answer to what was going on at Environmental. The idea intrigued me. For the first time in ages, I felt empowered to do something useful. There was no telling what might be coming my way, but the time was right for me to try to find some answers.

twenty-one

The rush of media poured across the airwaves, occupying every channel, every digit on the dial. A young woman named Daphne King, driving home alone from college, apparently had been carjacked in the early evening the night before. A freight trucker had spotted the man jumping into her car at a rest stop, seen a brief struggle, and then they were gone. Police were alerted immediately, and soon after the freeways were being scoured in the darkness by green state troopers and circling helicopters, to no avail.

Four hours after the abduction, with no sign at all and the trail gone cold, officials unofficially began to speculate that they would not be able to track her down swiftly and that her fate would likely be a grisly one.

But then, in the wee hours of the morning, police began to receive cryptic phone calls from the kidnapper. He let his victim call her parents. He demanded money. Then he said he didn't want money, just free passage to Mexico. Then Argentina. Then Greenland. First he was going to let her go. Then he was going to kill her. Then they were going to get married. In Greenland, he said, which was supposed to be nice in the fall.

On TV, psychologists explained that it was some kind of a cry for help.

As dawn broke, a trooper spotted the girl's car just off the side of a road in the underbrush, only a few miles drive from the rest stop where she was taken hostage, its tires submerged in mud. In the car itself, they found the kidnapper and his victim wrapped up together in thin blankets, holding each other tightly and trying to keep warm. The kidnapper stepped out of the car and was immediately thrown to the ground by the swarm of cops, before being picked up and tossed all muddy into the back of a squad car. He was a married father of two from Atlanta, a medical insurance agent apparently suffering from financial and psychological difficulties. When asked why, he said he'd done it on impulse, looking pathetically into the cameras that circled the police car. Daphne was carried off in an ambulance and taken to the hospital for observation.

The whole incident had taken less than twelve hours. Half a day to change lives forever. It occurred to me then that I didn't really know where my own daughter was.

Angelie was reporting all this live, her hair sprayed billowy and arching, her cherry red Action News blazer looking crisp in high def. My whole office was anxiously watching these final events unfold in the staff break room, on the large flat screen TV, which Christy had ordered installed so he could catch baseball games without having to leave the building. Under the glare of the lights, she looked somewhat different than the woman who had, until recently, shared my bed. Not that she didn't always look like herself, but this version of her was more intense, more unpredictable. She was gunning for a local news Emmy award, but clearly trying a bit too hard, you could tell.

The sight of the insurance agent being dragged away in handcuffs also served to remind me how close I might be standing to a similar fate, a fate like Bernie's. The whole threat of the investigation, coupled with Jennifer Thorn Jackson's plea from the day before, left me anxious and ill. Something was happening, and maybe the truth was that I was at the center of it all. As much as every impulse told me to leave things alone, to let others dictate and drive, I felt the increasing urge to control my own fate for once, and maybe by doing so, end the uncertainty.

Back at my office desk, I picked up the phone and dialed.

"Bureau of Environmental Study," the woman on the other line said. "This is Shirley Sue."

"Hey, Shue."

"My God. He lives."

"Long time, I know," I said.

"I'll say. Been what, a year? Thought we'd never hear from you again."

"I need some help, if you can spare a little."

I could picture her in the old bureau office, her desk pressed up against the window, away from the supervisor's door, not that there was one there now, with Bernie out of commission. She preferred her own privacy to convenience. She was a frightfully strong woman, tall but with an non-nonsense, self-assured air and long, flowing brown hair that she nearly always kept bunched up under natural-looking wigs. It took years before I realized that it wasn't her real hair. She hated dealing with it, she said. Wigs were just easier.

"You are not a popular man round here right now, you know."

"It's important."

"Persona non grata, as they say. People think Bernie's taking a dive for you. They don't know you, or Bernie, as well as I do, though."

"I need the help," I said. "Can you spare some?"

"Depends." She always loved to keep me hanging.

"I need to get access to environmental impact reports from my tenure, perhaps two, three years ago."

"You sound thinner," she said. "Are you losing weight?"

"I'm serious. I know, it's probably not the easiest of requests."

"That's an understatement. Everything's a mess here, with the investigation and all. Couldn't have picked a worse time, honestly."

"I don't want people to know I'm looking for it. This isn't a formal request, Shue. It's a favor."

"Things are really heating up here, Matthew. Records have been seized, people are being interviewed. Everyone is scrambling to locate a lawyer. Me, I'm not worried. Worst thing you could say about me is I make a terrible pot of coffee."

"And they'd be right," I said. "Then there's nothing you can do? I'm desperate."

There was a pause at the other end of the line. I could picture her rummaging around in her wig for a pencil. She always had three or four stashed up there at any one time. It's where writing utensils went to die. Finally, she said:

"There is, of course, the old duplicates warehouse."

"You mean out on Clockwise Highway? I thought all copies were supposed to be destroyed every year or so."

"Supposed to be." She paused again, then her voice became especially soft. "All the originals here are under lock and key. I've been archiving every three months regularly, though. But if you're going to be looking for something, perhaps you should start there. They don't seem to be in any particular hurry to head out there. Maybe they haven't thought to ask, yet."

"You're the best. I owe you."

"Some day I'm going to call in one of these favors, Matthew. And you better watch out when I do."

"Thanks, Shue."

"You haven't seen the warehouse yet," she said. "It's a little bit messy."

"Messy how?"

Bordering a mile-long stretch of the Clockwise Highway, King's Storage was forty-five separate warehouses cut into the underbrush. Sandwiched between the Persian man selling antiques and the teenage rock band was a length of adjoining rooms that made up the duplicate records office of the Bureau of Environmental Study.

It took me a long while to sort through the ring of old office keys, going through them twice because the first time through had proved fruitless. The padlock was a bit rusty, but once unlocked, the door lifted with only moderate difficulty, leaving me standing in a cloud of swirling dust, my eyes adjusting to the darkness. It was a pathetic security system. The general disorder would do more to confound and frustrate the busybodies and any other potentially nosy person.

The large room, like a small hangar, was piled high to the ceiling with boxes, stored on freestanding metal shelves. Navigating the maze of shelving was complicated by the near total lack of lighting, my flashlight and the thin rays slipping around the edges of the other sheet metal doors. The dense scent of mildew, a grainy dust lay over everything.

This was where regulations dictated copies of all documents were sent for a year, then destroyed. Though the former was followed regular as clockwork, the latter hadn't happened for perhaps fifteen years or more. The system that existed to keep track of these stacks had long ago fallen into disuse.

Shue was surely right. It was a colossal mess, and finding anything was going to be a monumental challenge. But though the seizure of the original records had brought the main office to near standstill, this outpost was likely low on the government's priority list. It might even be months before they thought to secure this location. Investigators in search of information only wanted to prevent someone from hiding something, not to stop a person from conducting an investigation on his own.

At one time, there had been some kind of order, a rationale of organization. Shue had been responsible for depositing these files here, and she had obviously been busy. I understood her reluctance to come help me now, though. If she were caught here with me, a complicated situation would have become intolerable. In truth, I too felt apprehensive about drawing any attention to myself. But Jennifer Thorn Jackson had painted a dire enough picture, and I could imagine Stanton right now rifling through my old records, second-guessing, nitpicking, building his case against me one file at a time. I couldn't just sit passively waiting for indictments to come down. I knew my only chance was to beat him to the punch.

The first batch of records I came to was for personnel, and I was struck with a sudden curiosity to take a peek at my own file, which I had never seen. The problem was, I couldn't find it. Nor anything else I started looking for. The dilemma facing me slowly became plain—I had no idea what system was being used. Whether by plan or simply random laziness, Shue had certainly found a masterful way to keep the snoops at bay.

The temperate morning slipped away, and well before noon I began to feel warmth seeping in. Here in the dark, you did not answer to time. Somewhere out there, wheels were in motion. In here, you were unaware. I felt currents of sweat running down my back and my shirt beginning to stick to my skin. There was nothing to stir the air inside the large room, its cabinets and mouse-chewed boxes huddling in close. It became less and less bearable. I dropped my flashlight, but even the blackness that suddenly fell upon me did nothing to help ease the heat. It was an oppressive dark, fibrous and musty.

Somewhere in here was something I needed. And it wasn't in the stack I was poring through, a list of 1690 forms, fifth copy, a light coral, faintly scribbled and nearly illegible. Random marks crossed the pages, the errant pen stroke, the coffee ring, the enthusiastic fingernail-sharpened crease.

Off in the darkness behind me, I heard a shuffle. I froze, suddenly anxious and intent. Peering back toward the door, I noticed it stood slightly open. Hadn't I closed it? I thought I had but honestly couldn't remember. I held my pose, arms buried in a stack of files, waiting, until I realized I wasn't even breathing.

Another shuffle. The scamper of small claws across cardboard, then cement. Rats and mice. That seemed likely. But still I waited, listening for some confirmation, anything to ease my fear of discovery. Finally, I just gave up and stopped caring. If someone wanted to spy on me, they were more than welcome.

I pulled down a box from the shelf, let it fall upon the floor. It landed with a hard smoosh, caving in on one side. The lid flew off and slid into the shadows, some papers scattering across the floor. I stepped on them, felt them crinkle under the tread of my shoe and tear slightly.

The answer was here, I trusted, somewhere in this dark.

twenty-two

The school building radiated with the dim glow of after-hours importance, muted yellow lights illuminating areas around the doors, the windows, casting sporadic shadows in the courtyard scattered with the discomforted middle aged. This was Parents' Night, so there were no children anywhere, but for the occasional infant straddling a hip, a toddler dawdling behind its mother, its eyes puffed and red, mucus dribbling down the lip. There was only the periodic man, a couple couples—most were flying solo tonight, and nearly everyone carried with them the impatience of imposition. They had something better to be doing, some other place they needed to go. Overall, though, our numbers were small. Most didn't show at all.

We were greeted at the registration desk by the day receptionists, poorly masking their displeasure and lack of enthusiasm at having to work double hours and play chaperone to the parents of the trouble they dealt with during the daytime. I was given a name tag and Hero's class schedule. The evening was broken into brief periods, most no more than 15 minutes. There was no loitering, no hall passes, no bathroom break.

My first class was with the math teacher, Gladys Moore, Hero's first-thing-in-the-morning, which constituted a method of slow torture. The reek of cigarette smoke hung in the classroom, and it took a moment to realize that this came from the teacher herself, an elderly woman wearing a solid blue, formless dress. She was short, but what she lacked in height, she made up for in stern malevolence.

This evening her serious acrimony was turned on us, the parents of her ungrateful pupils.

"They do not respect authority, and that makes it very difficult to teach. How am I supposed to make them learn if they don't want to learn? I'm not a circus clown. I'm not performing tricks. Do I look like a circus clown to you?"

We looked at each other, at the floor, around the room, no one willing to look her straight in the eye.

"I'm a math teacher. I've been doing this for forty-five years. I don't need the aggravation of some spoiled little brats who don't care that they are throwing their lives away. So when they come home and complain about this and that, you should know that unless they do their work, I don't want to hear about it. I don't want to have a conference to talk about me. I'm not the issue here. I can't make them do anything. If they fail because they aren't doing their homework, don't complain to me."

This continued for nearly the full period. Hero had warned me what to expect with Ms. Moore, but nothing could have prepared me for the intensity of her monologue. No one made any attempt to interrupt her. One mother arrived late and received a harsh reprimand and a change in the course of the speech to the issue of tardiness among our children. Squeezed into the same small chairs that our children occupied during the day, it was easy to feel reduced. Memories ran by of the classrooms and teachers of my own childhood. I recognized a familiar mistrust and a perpetual longing to be anywhere else.

I tried to imagine Hero in this room. Where would she sit? What would she do while the teacher ranted about this or that? Along the walls were large cardboard numbers and mathematical symbols spelling out equations. They were bright and colorful and seductive. There was no turning away. They promised a wondrous mathematical utopia, where there remained no remainder, and everything reduced down to the lowest common denominator.

The next few classes were similar in content, if not quite style, to the first. English, P.E., German. Each speech a primal scream. Our children weren't listening, their teachers were saying, and if anyone needed to know that, we did.

There was a "lunch period" inserted as well, with refreshments served in the cafeteria. A moment carved out of our schedules for socializing with each other, in order to increase the bonds between parents. I wished I had asked Hero for some of her friends' names, that I might talk with some of my peers. But I didn't know if she even had any real friends. The girls I'd driven to the mall. The boy whose hand she'd been holding. Around one table in the middle of the room a large group was gathered. I recognized one of my neighbors, Gretta Fathon, whose son was several years older than Hero. A few faces raised as I sat next to them, but no one gave me more than a casual glance, a short smile, no word of greeting. They were intent on their discussion. They were approaching an understanding.

"Do we have any other options?" Gretta was saying as I sat. "I'm just glad this isn't East Middle. I hear that they've installed metal detectors."

"Why not?" asked a man wearing a nametag that said Randy. "I don't trust my own child, much less anyone else. These are dangerous times. Do you know where your child is?"

"You can't be too careful," an eager woman chimed in.

Several people nodded in agreement, sipping their cherry Kool-Aid, taking bites of cookie. We were confederates—our childrens' friends, rivals.

"You can't do anything at all. Kids today are emotionally dead. They watch things that would have sent chills down your spine at their age, and they don't even flinch. They are desensitized to the violence of it all."

"You don't trust your own children?" one woman said, surprised. "How can you not trust them?"

"Look at this place. Look at what they're doing. You call this an education? I could teach them better at home."

"It's the world we live in. The violence. You can't escape it."

"What would make them do that? Why these shootings? I just don't understand."

"And what would you say if one of our kids did it? Look around this table. Who could show their face? Who wants to believe that their own child is becoming a monster? You can't control it."

One couple stood without a word and wandered slowly back to the refreshment table.

"I don't buy that," another woman countered. "I was teased every day in school. "Most people I know were. And I never saw a single person pull a gun, much less plant a bomb in a school. The world's gone crazy."

"It's acceptable. We can accept it now because it was unthinkable before. Just get used to a new idea, and anything is possible. I'm an optimist at heart."

"I blame you," Randy said. "All of you. Me. Everyone. We've really fucked them all up."

"You can't blame people. You can't blame a parent for what a child does. Parents don't know. We can only guess."

"I don't know about you all, but I feel pretty successful. My child does more than I could ever hope to myself."

"Look at serial killers. The first thing that everyone says about them is that they never suspected that they were bad. Just everyday, ordinary folk. Do you think most of these parents think their children are killers? How many parents go to court and say, 'Yes, my child is guilty as sin and we all saw it coming.' Sometimes you know, sometimes you don't."

"I'm not scared of my child. I'm scared for her. I'm scared for all them, frankly."

"It takes a village."

I sat silent through all of this. How could I explain, I was none of these things. I was an interloper, a chaperone. My part was no part in the shaping of Hero.

"Maybe we should arm them in the first place," a man offered, blithely. "That might make some of those punks second-guess stuff."

"Thirteen-year-olds having shootouts in the hallways. That'll end well."

"They aren't thinking ahead," said a balding man in a polyester blue blazer and jeans. "That's their problem. They're only thinking about right now. If they thought about it, they'd realize that all of these people they hate are going to go on and have relatively crappy lives. They have reached their pinnacle, their apex, and they are only 14 years old."

"When did you hit yours?" I asked

"Sixteen. But I was a late bloomer." There was a general laugh as the tension began to break.

"You can know and still not understand," the woman beside me said.

"Just watch them," said another. "You just never know."

Around us, a few parents spoke more quietly to each other about their children. Some obviously knew each other, old and dear friends built upon play dates and school fundraisers, churches and scouting, a certain continuity in the education of their children. They vicariously shared the same third- fourth- fifth-grade teachers, gym instructors, principals and their associates. A solo woman beside me started to ask me questions about my child, trying to discover if our children knew each other. It was small talk, simple pleasantries. I confessed that I didn't know any of Hero's friends. I was pathetically underinformed, but worse, I felt that I simply didn't belong here. These were people focused on the general welfare of their children, who'd seen them take their first steps, coaxed their laughter, soothed their pain. For me, it was all still theoretical and I was the ultimate imposter.

I didn't know what to say to this woman, what to ask about her child. After a moment of silence between us, she moved on to someone else.

The bell rang and everyone drifted off toward the next class, some in small groups, the rest of us alone. But then I hit Hero's political science class. The instructor was an enthusiastic middle-aged woman who took pride in showing us the vertical files our respective children were maintaining of articles and media references to events that were going on around the world. Hero's was for the death penalty, and so far it took up an entire drawer by itself. There were a dozen articles just on Adler and my involvement, plus pieces about people being freed after decades in jail due to prosecutorial malfeasance and other miscarriages of justice, and the disproportionate application of the death penalty to minorities in capital murder cases.

"She's quite a busy bee," her teacher said, smiling at my shoulder while I searched.

In science, too, the attitude was different. Dr. Banerjee, as he made very clear he desired to be called, had put out small experiments for us to try. They were simple things, something we ourselves might have tried once long ago. But it made me remember something of childhood wonder about the world around me, a time before I realized I had no hope myself of coming to an understanding.

"We don't have much time. I want everyone to take a station." He gestured toward the tall lab tables, which were already set up with flasks and burners. The table's enamel was heavily scarred.

"These are your experiments," he said. "And you should all know that I will be grading this assignment and sending a report card home to your children, which I expect to be signed."

He said all this with a warm humor, but also an authority that no one questioned. We wore our latex gloves, our plastic aprons. One parent seemed to be taking his experiment seriously, but the rest of us did not. As I combined my ingredients, I was suddenly aware that Dr. Banerjee was standing right in front of me.

"You are Hero's father?"

"Does it show?"

"But you forget. Your nametag."

I had forgotten. It was always a strange feeling, wearing

something about your life on your chest. We were all identified
as progenitors of our own children, whose names were printed far
larger than our own. It was as if people knew all your secrets, all the
things you struggled to keep hidden.

"A unique young girl," he said, looking over my experiment,
making a mark on his clipboard.

"They broke the mold," I said. "Believe me."

"I've observed she's somewhat hostile to ideas she doesn't agree
with."

"Which would include just about everything."

"But she could also be a very good scientist. If she applied
herself."

"Isn't that true of anyone?"

He frowned, serious and displeased. "No," he said. "It is not."

Back at home after a long night of school, I found Hero with
a pitcher. She was wearing a flowery apron that I did not recognize
and seemed to be watering the artificial plants.

"How was school?" she asked. "Did you learn anything today?"

"You've certainly made an impression."

"I hate the idea that you all talk about me behind my back. It
feels creepy. If you want to say something about me, you can do it to
my face."

"They like you."

"Like they'd say anything different to you. Your kid sucks, by the
way."

I showed her my report card from science class, where I'd
received a C for my flubbed PH testing with boiled cabbage. Hero
frowned.

"Naturally, I'm not pleased at all. You should be doing better, a
grown man like you. The cabbage test is particularly easy. I expect
you to apply yourself. Now go to your room. No TV."

"I was distracted," I said. "People were passing notes."

"I may need to conference with your teacher."

"He is pretty impressed with you."

She smirked and signed the form. "I think you mean he's pretty impressed with himself. Did you know he makes us call him 'Doctor' ?"

"Us, too."

"Dr. Banerjee. He even corrects people when they don't. Imagine having all your ego caught up in something like that."

"He's not that bad," I said. "Besides, it takes a lot of time and money to get a Ph.D. Maybe he thinks he's earned a little respect."

She shrugged and returned to her watering. The base of the plant began to overflow, water spilling across the tabletop and onto the ground. "Maybe he's just trying to get some return on his investment."

I left her to her strange preoccupations, retreating to the basement. I considered, if only for a second, asking her point blank about the boy whose hand I thought she'd been holding at the hearing. Thus far, I'd avoided even the slightest hint that I'd seen anything, but found myself becoming increasingly anxious about the prospect that she was seeing someone. I could ask, of course, but nothing in my experience with Hero suggested I would get anything resembling a straight answer. In fact, ever since some time around Val's disappearance and the accident, she'd struck me as even less forthcoming, if that were possible, even as she seemed somewhat more invested in and probing into my activities. What to make of this was anyone's guess.

It was a soothing cool in the dark beneath the house. Here in my basement I stored the residue of technological advancement. A stack of televisions, newer models upon the old, black and white, surround-sound; a cable-ready, internal VCR, several years old and therefore well out-of-date; a living, functioning obsolescence. Remotes, deluxe remotes, super omni-remotes. Atari, Odyssey 2, Playstation, Xbox, video game cartridges by the bucketful. Gadgets that can change your world, most that have never seen the light of day.

On a desk in the corner sat several stacked file boxes, promising candidates I'd removed from the duplicates warehouse to search in a more comfortable but still isolated environment. Hero confessed she didn't like coming down into the basement, and I'd made up some story the other day about trying to repair some old video game console so she could see what I'd played with as a kid. For different reasons, neither of us expected that promise to bear fruit.

As I waded through the streams of paperwork, I was surprised by how unfamiliar it all was to me, these years of projects I supposedly was responsible for. My passivity had been more successful than even I could have dreamed. The volume of things that never even made it to my desk was astounding, my associates dutifully crafting policy responses for the department. Only occasionally would my signature appear, signing off on this or that, projects I had given merely a cursory read.

Staring off blankly into one dark corner of the basement, my eyes began to focus on a place where a significant chunk of the basement's inner wall was starting to crumble. Vines had infiltrated and now crept along these inner walls, burrowing deeper through weathered cracks, wrapping around fixtures. The strong concrete blocks were becoming dusty, crumbling away in places. I would need to reinforce the retaining wall, replaster the entire basement, to make this an impervious environment and remove all traces of the natural world.

Entropy touched every part of my life, breaking away and climbing back up, in search of its static equilibrium. The whole system was eroding and being rebuilt, corrupt and purifying, living and dead. I envisioned my entire house collapsing down on top of me. A sudden end to all my worry, if not my troubles. Or perhaps, it would just trap me down here, without food or water, a joist maybe impaling a limb or some nonvital organ as I withered away my days in a decaying heap.

twenty-three

In the cool of the mornings, I sorted through boxes in the duplicates warehouse, long after the weight of the previous day's oppressive heat had lifted and before another wave could crest.

Rummaging through the stacks of folders brought back memories of my time at Environmental, the three years I'd spent in my first real job, a position far above my experience level. On any given day, so many pieces to consider. Without my associates, accomplished graduates and career men in the field, like Bernie, I would have been utterly lost. I knew my role, the expectations placed upon me—the few and the low.

All I was told when I was offered the position I hadn't applied for was that they needed someone with my credentials. What this meant, as near as I could tell, was someone who had nearly no discernible interest whatsoever in environmental policies. I had never joined an organization, signed a petition, attended a rally, or really expressed an opinion about these matters, largely because I rarely considered them one way or the other. With my appointment, some advocacy groups steamed, but there was nothing in my past to demonize, no record to hang me. It was as Bertrand Walker had said: there are advantages to being a blank slate in politics. With no clear objection outside of my utter lack of qualifications, I sailed through the process. The unspoken mandate from above was perfectly clear: no new initiatives, no revisions and as few waves as possible.

I had expected to find a leftist crew at Environmental, a hodgepodge of current and former hippies, tree-hugging their way through regulations and enforcement. Instead, I found a collection of serious and lifelong bureaucrats, though admittedly with a flash more enthusiasm for their cause than your everyday office workers. But I've found that true at Corrections as well. Both agencies had the benefit of seeing the direct impact of their work. It's hard to say the same thing for the actuaries and personnel administrators, who recognize that things are working best when no one knows they've done their jobs. Of my associates at Environmental, I could say at least that they were passionate about their work.

But none of this was me. After a few years, after the governor and his administration had gone down in flames, more changes came. Another unrequested job offer, and next thing I knew I was packing up my things and moving down in title, but modestly up in prestige over to Corrections, where I'd continue the meteoric path of my expected mediocrity. No point, I assumed, in bothering to mess that up by knowing what I was doing. A better manager at Environmental might have done more, been able to shape the department around his own clear vision of what a Bureau of Environmental Study might be. And a better understanding of all these ins and outs might have made my current dilemma more manageable. I had learned more about my department in this week of sorting through papers than I'd known after three years on the job. But I was beginning to sour on the prospect of ever actually finding this study Jennifer had mentioned. There must have been millions of sheets of paper composing thousands of files in hundreds of boxes going back years, with no clear order except perhaps for the stacks of boxes themselves, accumulated layers with each passing year.

What would happen, I wondered, if I actually found something? Worse, what would happen if I didn't, and Hero got to see me carried off in handcuffs by Stanton. Who would look out for her, with her mother missing, father soul-searching, and me sitting in jail. This search took on a greater importance for me the less I found.

After days upon days of digging, I began to see some hopeful signs. Several large stacks of environmental impact reports grouped together at least suggested I was on the right track. The dates were still fairly random and weren't especially helpful. Rather, they appeared to be grouped by subject, dealing with wetlands, air quality, and any number of factors, and each listed according to the risk item: construction, industrial production, public health. None of these seemed to help me with the limited information at my disposal, but into this fertile ground I plunged, grabbing a stack of boxes, loading up the bed of the truck and carting them home.

Back in my basement, I tried to make sense out of what I had found. Project titles weren't used at all on the files. Instead, each study was designated by an alphanumeric code, of which I again knew nothing. So, I found myself reading anything involving pesticides or insecticides or something akin, hoping to somewhere come across a phrase, word, anything that would tell me whether I'd found what I was seeking. Leafing through the documents, reading about their various classifications, their active or inert qualities, the uses to which they were being put on their respective projects—they all ran together, characters and sounds that seemed like a familiar yet foreign tongue, from abamectin to buprofezin, cadusafos to famphur. Fenitrothion, methyl parathion, mevinphos, propargite, propetamphos and zeta-cypermethrin. I waded through biopesticides and bioinsecticides, herbicides and growth regulators, fungicides and nematicides. The antimicrobials. The attractants. The bactericides. The disinfectants. Every use and possible abuse and still they kept coming. Cytokinin, butylate, dalapon, monuron and vernolate. Bacillus thuringiensis to acrylic acid terpolymer to metaldehyde methyl chloride to zinc pyrithione and on and on and on and on and on.

And then one evening, I found it.

On its surface, it appeared like any of the hundreds of files I had already read. File 04-VH74739-d. There was a summary of the proposal, a list of the potential areas of environmental concern, along with detailed reports summarizing extensive research that had been conducted and attached to the file—several hundred pages worth. It was the conclusion section that explained it, though, and

I would have missed it entirely had the words "Rain Bird" not been underlined in type. Included in the file, too, was the original Rain Bird proposal that served as the basis of the study. Among the many reports attached was the one by Jennifer Thorn Jackson, warning of serious health risks and recommending the rejection of the entire project. I couldn't make any sense of the scientific arguments she made, but her numerous point returned to one particular item proposed for use in the project: Methyl zeta-adrophos (Lychroson).

I started reading the summaries of Project Rain Bird, a public heath/insect control proposal to deal with a South American fruit fly infestation expected to hit the state some time in the next few years. Included in the file were also graphs and distributions, images of the fly, diagrams of tanks and gauges and nozzles. The proposal itself was brief, a mere outline of plan, with details to be determined later. It mentioned an extensive spraying program, to be conducted at night in residential neighborhoods all across the state using tanker trucks. It was recommended that the public not be openly informed about the project lest "irrational public outcry" delay the implementation of the process. The summary itself acknowledged the concerns of researchers like Dr. Thorn Jackson, and recommended, too, that the project be postponed until further study could be conducted testing out the potential for hazardous consequences to the public.

But there was absolutely no question about it: the Bureau of Environmental Study had approved the project anyway, without stipulation or qualification. This was on the very first page, where the box denoting departmental approval had clearly been checked and stamped—signed, sealed and delivered over the objections of every qualified person who'd studied it.

My own signature clearly marked the bottom of the page.

The Dublin Laboratory Complex radiated like a beacon in the center of the wide, flat landscape. Nothing could approach or escape it undetected. It most reminded me of the prison, and I believe it may actually have been designed by the same firm—in both cases, the idea was to discourage infiltration or escape. Arriving just as a stream of employees were heading out, I parked in a space beside the main building, then walked back toward the main entrance through the shadows, close against Dublin's outer wall. Through the cement I could hear the hum of machinery from somewhere deep inside, its steady, bellicose groan. Men and women continued to funnel out through the door, some in lab coats, but more wearing gray suits and skirts of various shades. Serviceable. Nothing fancy. Most wore glasses, thin-framed and respectable. They were climbing into their fine automobiles, Saturn, Lexus, the occasional Mercedes, heading home down the dark two-lane roadway, away from the haunting glow of the laboratory.

It seemed that there should have been officials around somewhere, some sort of security personnel to keep people in line. Instead, just cameras, on every lamppost and building corner, shot from every angle. When most of the cars were gone, I pressed my way across the wall and quickly out onto the fern-lined path leading to the double glass doors. They weren't locked and opened into a standard hallway entirely bereft of character. I could have been anywhere in the world, at any time over the last seventy years, thirty years ago or yesterday. Smooth walls. No art. A few black and white photographs. Two small palm trees bordered the elevator. Overwhelming in its simplicity.

I passed by the periodic staffer, a few departing suits, but no one gave me a second glance. After wandering around for a while, poking my head in through doors and peering into dark windows, I finally found a wall directory listing Research and Development and Dr. Franklin Adams.

He was the only one in his lab, sitting with a clipboard in his hand. An older man, balding, with thin strands of wispy white hair. He smiled when he saw me and motioned for me to come in and sit on a stool beside him. The drone of machinery was louder in here and laid a steady, even soothing, background track to our conversation.

"Mr. Brown, I presume."

"Dr. Adams."

We shook hands like old friends, though we'd never before met. His comfort level suggested a supreme, unwavering confidence, the sort I had never experienced in any capacity at any point in my life, least of all at this moment.

"My apologies for asking you to come so late," he said. "I don't like to work regular hours—things get too hectic and noisy with all the other people around. And I don't really have time for business lunches."

"That's fine. I just have a few questions."

"I confess, I've not really had a visit from the Bureau of Environmental Study before. Makes me a little anxious, to be honest."

"We're just having a conversation," I said. "I'm here regarding an environmental impact study that was done for a project over a year ago. In that study, there were concerns raised over the use of a particular chemical agent that the documents in my possession suggest was created by you and your company. Lychroson."

"Methyl zeta-adrophos. Right. Lychroson is what the marketing people came up with. I think they could have done better."

"Can you tell me a little bit about it?"

Dr. Adams paused, then. "I'm afraid that confidentiality agreements prevent me from discussing these matters in any kind of detail, outside of the formal patent information, which you should already possess."

"I was hoping for a more frank conversation, not so much company secrets. I was hoping we could avoid any… formal processes, subpoenas and whatnot, and cut through the BS and red tape that might interrupt your research."

Dr. Adams sat silently for another moment, considering me and my not-so-thinly veiled bluff of a threat. But this charade was the only way I could think to get some of the answers I needed, to know if I had found the cause of my problems. Finally, with a resigned nod of his head, Dr. Adams stood and walked over to the lab door and locked it. "The bosses are a little paranoid when it comes to people asking questions," he said, retaking his seat on the stool, "but if I can set your mind at ease, I'm more than willing to do so."

"Thank you. Are you familiar with a project called Rain Bird?"

He shrugged and shook his head, so I reluctantly handed him the file I'd brought with me, my only link to this whole puzzle. But if I needed answers, this was the only way it was going to happen.

Dr. Adams pulled eyeglasses from his shirt pocket and began to flip through the documents. While he did that, I looked around the room. It reminded me of a fancier version of Hero's science classroom—the thick tables, the charts on the walls. I felt under the desk. There was even gum.

"I'm not sure there's much I can help you with," Dr. Adams said at last, setting the file down in his lap.

"What makes Lychroson dangerous?"

"That's just it. It isn't."

"But, the reports…"

"Mr. Brown, our research teams spend thousands of dollars and hours designing and testing these products for both safety and effectiveness. The end result is often years in the making. That's how labs like this work. We're scientists. We're not in it for a quick buck. We believe very passionately in what we do, and it requires patience. The product I'm working on now won't even be available to begin testing for another year at the earliest. Lychroson was the same way. It took years of research to perfect, to discover not just how to make it safer, but its properties and uses. I myself have tested it extensively. I can tell you with absolute certainty that it is not harmful to humans at all."

"And yet, the EIR says that's not true."

"Certainly you are aware of how this whole process works, Mr. Brown. Environmental testing is designed to put an extreme stress upon conditions to determine the subject's failure point. It's like animal testing. We put animals through an unrealistic scenario that doesn't exist in the real world and then see how quickly they become sick or die. And that's useful data, of course. Don't get me wrong. But it doesn't accurately reflect the real public danger. If it did, we wouldn't need to do extreme tests like this in the first place."

"I want to believe you. I do."

"Do you even know what methyl zeta-adrophos is?"

"That's what I'm hoping you can tell me."

He stood and walked over to a cabinet. Inside were hundreds and hundreds of small vials. After running a finger along one row, he pulled one container out and brought it over.

"That's it?" I asked.

He took the tube and put it to his lips. In two quick swallows, it was gone.

"Are you crazy?" I said after a moment in shock.

"Now do you believe me that it isn't dangerous," he said, handing the empty container to me. "We did far, far worse to the mice before we could even kill half of the test group. Not that I'd start a diet of the stuff, but it's pretty harmless on this scale and concentration."

"But what makes it any different than any other pesticide?"

"Not a pesticide, Mr. Brown. It's a chemical, and like any other chemical, in different quantities it can have any number of useful properties. Certainly, as in this context, it can function as a pesticide. Some of our other research suggests it may also slow the development of Alzheimer's. It can also help oils coalesce, which makes it an excellent additive for paints. It is especially useful, I'm told, in hair products. I believe we've found a dozen practical applications for it in hundreds of products so far."

"A wonder chemical."

"No, but versatile. It just depends on how you want to use it."

I pointed to the file. "What about this usage? Is this problematic at all?"

Dr. Adams looked over the pages again, frowning and nodding. "I don't see a problem. Putting it in the air would dilute it even further. It's not classified as an active ingredient in this, mind you. We're very careful about consumer safety. Regulations demand that we be. It has to pass our very rigorous codes of use."

"So the objections…"

"…are simply unrealistic, Mr. Brown. I'm sure the researchers did the best they could, and frankly it's their job to err on the side of caution. If I were in their shoes, I'd probably do the exact same thing. It's not like most of these people would know a molecule from a motorcycle. They're bureaucrats. You can see our justifications here in the file, all very meticulously laid out, as are our own studies and conclusions. The bureau has nothing to be concerned about, I assure you, at least as far as Lychroson is concerned."

After all that searching, it was all a dead end, I realized. I was frustrated, angry even, mostly at Jennifer Thorn Jackson. Her professed ignorance suddenly struck me as unpersuasive and manipulative. She had sent me on this wild goose chase, for reasons I couldn't begin to imagine. Now, I felt even more lost than before. Though my worst fears weren't realized— that I had, through my own incompetence, somehow endangered the lives of innocent people—whatever Stanton was looking for, whatever he might have hanging over me, was still out there, somewhere.

Dr. Adams handed the file back to me.

"Thank you," I said.

"Not at all. Anytime."

As I made my way back to my car, both relieved and deflated, the night wind was kicking up, gusts swirling trash into whirlwinds down the highway, illuminated by the glow of the full moon. I startled four deer that were walking through the parking lot. They bolted, then stopped mid-road to look back, perfect and still, glassy eyes taking it all in. Then they charged full tilt into the surrounding growth.

twenty-four

The air turned cooler, though it could not yet be considered cool and the temperature continued to hang high. But there was an unmistakable shift, the days less dense, the nights less stiff and still. You could move about more easily. And with the calm evening breezes and with each passing day you could feel anticipation building. Older men moved with a livelier step, young men more carefree and cocksure. Store fronts began posting specials on MREs, maps, coolers, hand-warmers, sub-zero sleeping bags and tents, gas grills, heavy coats and thick wool socks, water-resistant boots and assorted items of camouflage. Rock bottom sales on ammunition of every stripe and caliber.

Everywhere, preparations for the season. Hunters stocking up, retooling, walking out of R&R's Sports Universe with their 30-30 calibers, Brownings and Remingtons, lever-actions, their spot and scope mounts and slugs. They had their orange-lens shooting glasses and survival kits, matches and whistles. Their five-mile range, two-way VHF radios and GPS and four-star mosquito repellant. The hardcore, with their bows and steel tips, frost-free compasses, antler sets for rattling and scents of running buck and of urine. The new online, automated deer license system crashed the first day of registration, and the line of frustrated and impatient hunters wound all around City Hall and out onto the Parkway from early in the morning until well into the late afternoon.

The governor's new campaign ads hit the local stations, extolling his steely will and tough determination and featuring a grainy photo of Adler and a smiling graduation photo of his victim, Hannah. Justice is coming, an announcer intoned. This November!

As each passing day brought us more noticeably into the fall season, I had started to notice subtle changes in Hero. Since she had begun school and found peers to interact with, she'd been home less, mostly because of daily practice for her play, which went on late into the afternoon and sometimes early evening. She would come home sometimes after me, and then often head right back out again, or she might arrive midafternoon, then be gone before I came home. There were days she wouldn't be there for dinner at all, and our conversations trickled off into a sporadic flash of banter, a grunt and snort here and there. At first, she was good about keeping me apprised of her schedule. Either she'd call or leave notes, indicating some general plan she'd made with people whose names I couldn't tell apart, one from the next, saying when she'd left and when she expected to return. But soon even these slight indicators became merely occasional, an afterthought. She was drifting off into another sort of life, and I had no sense whatsoever what that life was, who it was with or where she was going.

I didn't want to restrict her, didn't want to chance the role of the punitive father. But I was being driven to it with each day. She was pushing the borders of the acceptable because she could, relegating me to the status of impotent and distant observer. We would catch at times rare glimpses of each other, shadows passing through halls in the night.

Then one day it came to a head. She'd mentioned that she would be going to the movies, then some sort of gathering. I expected her home by her curfew at 8:30. And when that deadline came and went without a call, I became restless. I tried texting her, calling and leaving a voicemail—but was greeted only with silence. Later into the evening, each sound of an automobile down the street made me jump. I settled down in a never-used couch by the front door. What does one do in these situations? Does one call hospitals? What would I say? What could I even do were she there? Should I call the parents of her friends? But I didn't know any of her friends, much less their parents. I felt utterly useless, as well as clearly idiotic for acquiescing to her desire for this much freedom. I scripted a conversation in my mind, a lecture of a sort, something fair and direct that would express my displeasure, my unbearable anxiety. The longer I waited, the harder it was to keep those thoughts straight. By midnight, I'd forgotten it entirely and drifted off instead into imagining all the worst-case scenarios and wondering how I'd explain any of them to her mother. Wading through old magazines my grandfather had stashed throughout the house over the decades, Newsweek, Life, Time, waiting on the living room sofa for my daughter to come home, I watched uneasily as the nighttime quietly slipped into morning

Hero finally wandered in from somewhere at precisely 1:44 a.m., and I was there to meet her, exhausted but conscious. She smiled sheepishly as she closed the door behind her, but there was no offer of explanation. No apology. She did not appear the least bit tired.

"I didn't expect you to wait up," she said.

"I didn't expect you to spend the whole night out like that. Where were you?"

She shrugged and walked past me toward the kitchen. I followed behind her, tall and responsible, but now that she was here in the flesh, and the relief of knowing washed over me, I was once again at a loss for words. I stammered:

"Should we be talking rules? Ground rules. That sort of thing?"

"It won't happen again."

"I didn't think it would happen the first time. You're twelve, for Christ's sake." I watched as she found some O.J. from the fridge and pulled out a chair at the table. "It's just, there are some things that have to make sense," I said. "I need to know. You understand? It's my responsibility to know what you've been doing."

"But what if I don't want you to know?"

I hesitated. I took this moment to pull a glass down and pour myself some juice, too. I tried to make it seem like I wasn't stalling, though I wasn't fooling anyone. Not even myself, and I was easily fooled. Finally, I said:

"Who talks like this? I'm being honest with you now. Who?"

"I'm being honest, too."

"Fine. You're right. I don't want to know the truth." I was sorting out my own frustrations as I spoke, uncertain if I even believed the words I was saying. "I just want the convincing lie. Can you do that for me? I already know what you do. I was young once."

"What am I supposed to be doing then?" she asked.

"I don't know. How about learning to lie better? To at least act more contrite?"

She drank her juice in one long gulp, then set the glass upon the counter. There was no humor in her face.

"No problem," she said, then brushed past me, heading upstairs.

As she left me standing there, I reconsidered. No. I was wrong about this, too. The not-knowing was worse than knowing for real. The guessing and supposition was slowly wearing me down. I really did want to know everything about her. Every action. Every thought. I feared what that would mean, but the suspicions and doubts that I had now were cloying, and her increasingly less-childlike behavior left me in constant worry.

So when I returned home that afternoon to find her gone again, I immediately slipped upstairs to her room. The comforter I had bought was balled up in the corner, along with some clothes, a skirt, some shorts, unmentionables. The decapitated stuffed animals were nowhere visible, long since disposed of or hidden. The dresser was well-used, covered with bits of jewelry I'd never even seen her wear, hair clips, and small cosmetics, lip gloss. And so on.

The center top drawer was open. A pair of dark socks overflowed. I pushed them back in and closed the drawer. I opened the one next to it, without even a conscious thought. This one had underwear, and I started to close it, then stopped. I took a deep breath and put a hand inside, feeling all the way down to the bottom, until my palm was touching the wood. There was nothing else there. I turned back to the sock drawer and did the same. Nothing at all but socks.

I repeated this with each drawer in succession, left to right, top to bottom, twelve drawers in all. Each held something of hers, a piece of her young life. Perfumed sachets, scunchies, hair clips, belts—it all seemed so absurdly normal. Perfectly typical. Without the slightest threat of lie or betrayal.

This is what real parents do, I'm fairly certain.

In the last drawer, my hand touched something solid. Something hidden. It was a diary. I felt certain it had to be. But when I opened it, I could immediately tell that it was much more than that. It was all-purpose. Random thoughts scattered among phone numbers and homework assignments, pencil sketch drawings. I sat on the corner of her bed and scanned the open page in front of me. The few focused thoughts appeared to have nothing to do with me at all, but rather a brief reflection upon the play, some advice her teacher had given her about acting, and a paragraph focusing on study habits and self-improvement. There were references to friends and acquaintances I'd never heard of: John, Madison, Taylor, Chase. Some raunchy lines of verse labeled as by Rimbaud.

A creak of the stairs made me slam the diary shut, barely breathing, heart racing. I hadn't heard the front door, or any other of the usual sounds. Holding the book behind me, I peered out the doorway and down the hall. The house was still.

I started to return the diary to the drawer but found myself thumbing through the pages while standing over her dresser. I'd only had a glimpse of a few random passages. Surely there was something more. Some detailed discussion of her true feelings, some articulation of the workings of her mind and of her heart. I felt on the cusp of something, a rare window into my daughter's unguarded mind. To peel away the layers of cynicism, the games that she played—this was the promise of the book in front of me. It was all there to be discovered.

Still, I hesitated, conscious of crossing another invisible line. But this time I couldn't push myself to continue. It was beyond even a father wanting to be a part of his daughter's life—I was trying to get inside her mind, to know her as she knew herself. And I couldn't bring myself to do it. Not like this. It was cheating, I felt, taking what is not freely given.

I needed to know. As her father, it seemed I deserved to know. But not like this. I still wanted to find another way.

From the back of her school's auditorium, crouching behind an obstruction amidst a dozen or so other casual observers, I watched her performing on stage.

I took all precautions I could to make sure she did not know I was there. I admit, I was actually surprised at this point to discover that there really was a play after all and, by all appearances, Hero was in fact playing the lead. She was a marvel on stage. All eyes on her when she spoke, when she listened, when she hung sheepishly toward the back. Even here, she was an undeniable presence.

I couldn't stay long because I knew that it was only a matter of time before she spotted me. If that happened, I planned to brush it off as my coming by to see if she needed a ride home. But she was up at the front or on stage the whole time I sat there, and people were coming and going throughout, other parents, students, administrators. I saw the vice principal, Ms. Forrester, and realizing that I hadn't yet served any of my classroom duties, I did my best to block my face. She'd left me a dozen messages on my answering machine already, her tone becoming increasingly hostile with each call.

I sneaked out with a small group of adults and then sat waiting in my car, positioned in a lot and behind a tree. This would be harder to explain, I knew, were she to see me here, so I was determined that she would not. A couple passed by walking their dog and gave me a hard look. Reflected in their expressions, I could see myself and what I was doing, but I had come this far. I couldn't turn away now.

She emerged eventually from the building, alone. It was still early, not yet four. She swung her backpack and began to carelessly skip along, her long lacy skirt twirling with each step—the frivolous movements of the unobserved. Already I felt the excitement of seeing my daughter as perhaps she truly was, without a mask for her father or her friends. When she'd turned the corner at the end of the block, I started the engine of my car and followed.

Hero walked slowly through the neighborhoods, seemingly aimless, taking leisurely glances at the homes she passed, the occasional barking dog, but she neither stopped nor even slowed. I tried to stay more than a block behind her, hugging the curb. I kept a map on my steering wheel to hide behind, to generate a more believable facade. Once, she glanced over her shoulder, a quick move, but I was equally fast. The wheels did not squeak. She knelt by a bed of flowers near the sidewalk. Then after a moment, she stood and continued walking again.

Soon it became clear that this was definitely not a way back home. She was moving in a general direction that was essentially parallel to Magnolia Grove. Where was she going? I wondered. Perhaps nowhere. Perhaps she was merely exploring the South she now lived in, venturing out into the unknown.

When she came to the train tracks, she turned down them, following the rail line south. I thought I might lose her then, knowing that she could go almost anywhere from there, and I could spend all day trying to figure out where she had gone. I had to make a choice. I stopped at the curb and started to follow her on foot.

This was not as easy as the drive. She knew what I looked like, first of all. Soon she turned back onto surface streets, and I was left out in the open. Worse, there was no one else on these neighborhood sidewalks. I also couldn't hide effectively, knowing that anyone watching out their windows would likely be suspicious of a man cowering behind a tree or a car in front of their house. So I let her move even farther ahead. I adopted a strolling gait, that of a casual wanderer out for the exercise or the air. I wasn't dressed for this, either, and my dress shoes quickly started to irritate my feet. We had entered one of the college student rental neighborhoods, a cluster of relatively low-income housing units that were still several steps above hovels. They were run-down and lower-middle-class. I smiled at the few young people I did pass, as they moved between their houses and their cars, all the while keeping a distant eye on Hero.

She started moving faster, it seemed. The space between us continued to grow. I was forced to speed myself up, jogging for short stretches, then slowing to a fast walk. The farther I went, the more I considered turning back, pretending the whole thing had never happened, but I couldn't let myself lose her or pull away. To stop now, after all that I had already done, almost would have made me feel worse than I did about what I was doing. If I was going to spy on my daughter, I rationalized, I should at least learn something for my troubles. I wasn't sure, though, if I'd be able to find my truck again.

Hero's path was slowly becoming clear: she was heading toward the university campus, whether to cut through or stop there was no way yet to tell. We'd already walked several miles from her school, and she obviously was familiar enough with the trek. We were hiking down the compromised streets, slabs of sidewalk unearthed by mammoth twisted roots. But soon we crossed from the lapsed outskirts into the groomed interior, the campus itself, with its finely manicured landscapes, its pansies and ferns and well-groomed oaks draped in Spanish moss. Generations of buildings intertwined, an incoherent mesh of styles—past, present and future tenses.

This hour of the late afternoon meant a sparse array of students, shuffling between dorms and classrooms, the intramural fields and also the Student Union, which we were rapidly approaching. Here things were considerably more crowded; a flea market had been erected, with dozens of booths and hundreds of students milling about, perusing the wares. Handmade jewelry and soaps, homemade pottery and batik shirts, dresses, jackets. Tapestries hung from rods draped across the top of one booth, next to a woman doing Tarot readings and another offering massages. All this mass made it easier to stay hidden from Hero, but also harder to follow her. She didn't appear to be shopping, pausing only briefly once as she passed a woman binding books by hand.

At one edge of the main Union patio stood a long table with steaming covered tins and platters. The orange-robed and shaved nearly bald proprietors were dishing up plates for the awaiting college students, and a sign proclaimed "Free Meal!" in a paisley twirl.

Hero walked up to one of servers, an extremely tall reed of a young man, who leaned far over as she gave him an exaggerated hug.

"Would you like a massage?"

A young woman, maybe 20, with a dozen blonde dreadlocks, smiled sweetly as I paused in front of her table. Watching Hero drop her backpack into a pile by the large assembly hall steps, I decided this might be an easy way to remain inconspicuous.

"Sure," I said. "How much?"

For a half-hour, I paid her $15 to dig her fingers of wire into my back, an increasingly painful experience that I twice prolonged by paying for another 15 minutes, occasionally peering up from the massage chair to see if Hero was still with her friends. She'd tied and pushed her hair back under a kerchief and was serving plates to passersby. Who, I wondered, were these people she seemed to know so well? John, Madison, Taylor, Chase? With a sharp dig into the small of my back, my well-meaning torturer explained that she was hoping to start massage school in the spring, but still needed to raise more cash. I paid her for another 15 minutes as she pressed her palm into my spine.

It occurred to me that Hero might have joined a cult. That, I thought, would explain quite a bit.

But the longer I stayed, the more I watched her, the less likely anything like that seemed and the less uneasy I felt about all of this. Other friends of hers appeared, less cult-like, these closer in age, a menagerie of misfits seemingly drawn together by how little they belonged anywhere else. She greeted each of them with the same generous hug, laughed with them, goofed around like you might expect a twelve-year-old to do. She seemed more natural among this group than she had with her more polished and respectable-seeming friends at the mall, less reserved, and happier than I'd seen her in weeks. Maybe even since she'd arrived to visit me.

Or perhaps, I thought, I was wrong. In my desire to be a part of this, to know her better, I'd pushed my boundary. I needed to retreat, hunker down, and let things go. I was trying to be her father, yet we were still nothing more than acquaintances, like distant relatives whom you are told you are connected to you, yet which connections never quite feel real. Those years she and I missed while she grew up, we could never get them back, and biology could not manufacture more than false affection. True feeling takes time and experience. Someday we'd have an answer for our little experiment in constructing a family out of nothing, one that offered a better answer to its own question.

I stood to pay the dreadlocked girl for my hour of torment. Looking up, I saw that Hero was staring directly at me from across the patio.

My impulse at the moment was to run, just as it had been when I'd received that call a year ago confirming a DNA match for the paternity test. And maybe if I had, perhaps all of us would have been better off. There would be no father caught between Hero and Geoffrey, her familial relationships more mysterious, perhaps, but less complicated by one. Or, consider how simple had I just let her go back home, not insisted that she was too young to be by herself and asserted my parenting responsibilities. Or, upon catching her breaking curfew, merely let her blow everything off.

But, instead, here I was, standing my ground as I watched her part the crowd and glide toward me. I'd chosen another path, and there was no backing down now.

"Why aren't you at rehearsal?" I asked when she was close, my assertiveness as much a surprise to myself as to her.

"We broke early," she offered in defense, then pivoted. "What are you doing here?"

"I'm your father."

"You followed me."

"We need ground rules," I said. "You can't just keep prancing about wherever at all hours of the day."

"You can't make me stop seeing my friends. They're the only thing keeping me sane here."

"It isn't normal for girls your age to do this."

"The executioner tearing his house apart and making it into some kind of Disneyland pioneer village is going to tell me about being normal?" She was becoming more animated. "What the heck's the point of that anyway, Matthew? You have some bizarre desire to relive a plantation lifestyle. Whaddya think? Maybe we should start rounding up the black folk."

A few of the merchants around us had become noticeably more attentive of our conversation.

"Don't be ridiculous. It's just our past, our family and history wrapped up in that house."

"You're not my father." She laughed suddenly, a sharp sound that seemed to surprise even her. "I don't have a father. The one I had doesn't even want me. And you, Matthew. I mean, heck, you were dead long before everyone else figured it out."

"Come home with me. We'll find your mother."

"Who cares about my mother? She doesn't care about us, just dancing across the world, gone one day, turning up the next. She's the one who got us into this mess."

"I want to help."

"I don't want your help. Can't you understand that?"

"So you turn to your friends," I said, gesturing through the crowd to the gathering of kids, who were beginning to pick up their bags. "I just want you to feel like you can talk to me and not have to turn to Taylor or Chase or whatever friends or boyfriends you are seeing."

I kept pushing, hoping she'd start to understand me or trust me. But she had become quiet, all of a sudden, and she looked up at me now with a perplexed expression.

"How do you know about Taylor? Or Chase?" she asked.

"They're your friends, aren't they?" I said.

"I never told you about them. Never."

"You must have mentioned them, when talking about school or something," I said uncomfortably.

Slowly, a glimmer of realization flickered across her face and her eyes widened.

"You read my diary," she said in quiet shock.

Something in her face now changed. I felt this one across my chest, a hot anxiety and realization that I'd made a pointless blunder in trying to sound like a knowing parent.

"I…"

"Don't!" she yelled, holding back a cry and holding up her hand. "Just don't," she said again, this time more softly. She turned her eyes from me, grinding her teeth through a clenched jaw. She then took a deep sonorous breath, and without looking at me, said: "I'm done. We're done. Okay?"

"Hero…" I said, tentatively reaching out toward her.

"I'm not your possession." She stepped away from me, walking backwards amid the collapsing market. More of the merchants and shoppers paused to stare, their quick assessments and judgments sweeping us both up and away. My masseuse took a few steps back from me. Hero kept facing me, though, as if unwilling to risk turning her back. Trying to defuse the moment, I took a step toward her.

"Wait…"

"No!" she hissed, her voice choking back tears, yet still fierce. "Don't even think. Don't try." She paused and took a deep breath. "Stop," she said, again calm. I had to strain to hear the words now. "We're through. I'm done. No more games. It's over, okay. It's just… over."

And then she turned from me, stomping defiantly, her white skirt kicking up into a blur as she snagged her backpack and in the same motion moved to follow a pack of her friends who were retreating in the growing dim of twilight. For a brief moment, I thought I'd still follow her, see where she was heading, hope to resolve this mistake—then I recognized how foolish I was, how foolish I'd been all along. Distrustful glances abounded. Two women were huddling across the courtyard with a security guard, gesturing my way. I turned the opposite direction, passing through the collapsing tables and boxed merchandise, retreating through the petering crowd, back to the empty streets to find my way home.

twenty-five

The mammoth RVs began to arrive midweek, decked from hood to spare in school flags and ribbons and magnetic banners. They cruised everywhere through town. By Friday, traffic hit a near total standstill as our town's small population literally doubled, between the fans and the media corps, the magnetic pull of social conquest.

The parties commenced Friday night, small affairs, the exchange of beer, the sharing of expectations, hopes and dreams for the coming contest. Saturday dawn rose misty but warm, and the gears slowly began to turn, increasing in speed with the brightening day. They crowded the parking lots surrounding the stadium, double-decker grills flaring, oil drums charred black, converted into smokers for barbecued chicken, sausage, ribs. Under the stretched canopies, card tables were layered with coleslaw, Jell-O, green-bean-and-fried-onion casserole. Two men sat in lawn chairs beside a five-gallon pot on a propane camping grill, roiling water boiling peanuts, Cajun-style. Everywhere, radios tuned to the same pre-game radio show. You could walk clear from one side of the stadium to the other without missing a moment of banter.

As kickoff approached, the crowd drifted toward the gates. Nothing especially quick or noticeable. Nothing here approximated hurry.

No particular fan of football, I had come at the invitation of Janice, to whom I'd recently revealed that I had never attended an A&M game. It was she who had suggested I arrive early to avoid the serious crunch, but I still found myself caught up in a moderate crowd. When I showed my pass to the ticket-taker, he called over a woman wearing a blue blazer and chatting nonstop into a walkie-talkie, who led me away from the growing crowd milling in the corridor. As we passed through the throngs, I caught glimpses through the portals, out onto the field, where the closeness broke out into the open air and clean green.

But she led me to the back stairs, accessible only with a key. She did not follow me, but rather ushered me into the dim-lit well, then closed the door behind me. In here, the muted crowds echoed like ghosts. I followed the several flights of stairs up to a long empty corridor, then quickly found the President's Box, which was more like a conference room with tiered seating. At the front of the seats, a large window stretched from floor to ceiling. Today was the grand opening of the new stadium complex, a $43 million project that had taken four years to complete, no expense spared. It might have been a professional stadium, as near as I could tell, paid for entirely by boosters and the occasional generous tax break. A service to the community.

The president was throwing a grand bash, which extended out onto a large patio deck overlooking the South end zone. Hundreds of people were expected—administrators, faculty, spouses, Honors students, artists in residence. But when I walked in, there were only a couple people present, and fortunately, Janice was one.

"Noon kickoffs are a bitch," she said. "Only a man who detests football as much as you would be here this early."

"You're here."

"Darling, I'm here for you. You and, of course, the bar."

More men in blue coats were laying out a spread against the back wall. It was a four-star version of what I had just seen in the parking lots, which mainly translated into smaller portions. Tiny sausages on toothpicks, shredded chicken, plus whole boiled crawfish and shrimp on ice, and jambalaya. Sushi, too, and crab puffs for good measure. The open bar served beer on tap, cocktails of your choice. A door was opened out onto the patio, where a canopy had been set up, along with a longer buffet and bar.

We chose to say in the A/C and took seats close to the top tier. Looking down upon the field, you could also see above the rows of fans in the bleachers. The sun was bright upon their heads, the heat of the day already beating down on their completely exposed bodies. Even before kickoff, I saw two different people carried away by medical personnel.

Here above them, encased in glass and steel, our churning A/C made me shiver.

"I hear you are in the doghouse with Junior."

"At least she's talking to one of us."

"I told you, Matthew. Mildly competent was a good goal. I could have told you that reading diaries was completely off the list."

"Tell me parents don't do this. My mistake was accidentally letting her know I did."

"Oh, Matty. Like that was in your top 10 mistakes. Speaking of, how's the vapid media whore?"

"You mean Angelie?"

"Are there others in your life I should be aware of?"

"What is it with everyone's preoccupation with my love life?"

I'd actually invited Angelie, who I knew was off today, to join me at the game, but she'd declined. She'd declined pretty much every offer I'd made this week, though, so it wasn't a particularly big shock. We hadn't spoken directly for longer than I could remember. Bringing Hero, of course, wasn't even an option since she refused to be in the same room, much less speak to me.

The box began to fill, but more than half the seats were empty at any one time. People were loitering by the bar, the buffet tables. Almost no one seemed aware of the game that had just started below. Janice introduced me to an older balding man who took a seat beside her.

"This is Mike. He's a lawyer."

"The good kind," he volunteered, bracing his 64-ounce beer between his knees and holding out his hand.

"Good how? Honest?"

"Poor," he said.

"It's a time-honored profession," Janice said. "It's the poor lawyers who know all the best bars. Matthew here works for the Department of Corrections."

Another man, somewhere in his forties, was working his way down the aisle, waving to Janice. She introduced him as a political science professor, whose name I missed behind a surging cheer from the crowds both inside and outside the observation room. Below, an interception flipped the field of motion and sent players rushing the opposite way. Hidden speakers around us piped in a radio announcer's play-by-play. He. Could. Go. All. The. Way.

More people came, a small crowd swelled and gathered around us, friends and acquaintances of Janice, most faculty and employees of the school. She was quick to get me involved with the conversations and make me feel comfortable.

"Matthew can't stand football," she said.

"It's true," I admitted reluctantly. "I don't know what's wrong with me."

"I was of the impression that one could not both be a Southerner and dislike football," Mike said. "Aren't those positions mutually exclusive?"

"Obviously not," Janice said, retreating toward the bar. "Matty here is zillionth-generation and jails people for a living. How can you get more Southern than that?"

"It's in the blood, though," Mike said. "He doesn't have to like all of it. Hell, I don't even like everything about it."

A young professor, younger even than I, nodded. "The old school stuff I don't understand. How could anyone have watched a game before the invention of the forward pass? Run left, run right, run straight ahead. A game of inches. Put you to sleep. Worse than baseball."

"You're treading on dangerous ground there," Mike said. "Don't malign the national pastime."

"I thought that was football. Didn't I hear that somewhere?"

Someone two rows up said, "More people watch the Super Bowl than an entire seven-game World Series combined."

"Are we really going to debate the relative merits of sporting events?" Mike interrupted. "I just want to watch someone get laid out on a stretcher."

"Helmets flying."

"Severe bodily injury."

"For me, I like to watch them miss." Janice had come back with a fresh cocktail. "That's the beauty of the game. The juke. Some young stud making a dozen guys miss, every one of whom only wants to break every bone in his body. That's as beautiful as any double play I've ever seen."

"The perfect spiral. It don't get better than that."

"Football is an identity," Mike said, suddenly standing and gesturing as if he were dissertating before a jury. "It's something that makes us Southern. And we all need to identify with our heritage. Some choose civil war reenactments. I pick pigskin."

I found myself simply trying to follow the back and forth. Play on the field had stopped. A fan had jumped down from the stands and was streaking across the field, naked and pink on a sea of green. As he approached the huddle, one of the young players squared up and tackled him.

Lawyer Mike turned to me. "As our symbolic jailer, you must have some pearls of wisdom you can share with us about human nature."

"None. I work in an office. I'm not even sure that qualifies me as human."

Janice smiled. "Matthew's the lucky soul who gets to execute Andrew Carl Adler."

"Beware anyone who uses all three of their names," another man chimed in. "They're nothing but trouble."

"It's a media thing, I think. Ask Janice why they do it. Maybe so we don't confuse them with your neighbor down the street."

"Or perhaps it's like your parents, calling you out. That's the only time anyone ever used all my names."

Mike finished the last third of his beer in one gulp. "So you get to pull the trigger, do ya?" he asked me.

"It's a switch, actually. But no. I hire the guy who's throwing the switch. Among other things."

Janice blew a cloud of smoke into the air directly above her. "He doesn't like to talk about it, as you might have guessed."

"Nothing to be ashamed of," the professor said. "The guy's an animal."

"Very true," I agreed.

"Everyone's entitled to their day in court," Mike said.

"Spoken like a true defense attorney," Janice said.

"Doesn't make it any less true."

"Besides," someone from the row below began, "he's had his day in court. Now he gets his day with the chair."

Janice swirled the ice in her glass. "You gotta wonder what drives a person to do stuff like that."

"He's crazy," Mike said sadly.

The young professor frowned. "If he's crazy, why isn't he in an insane asylum, rather than about to become a French fry? No, these people aren't crazy. They're perfectly sane. That's what makes them so scary. That's why we have to deep-fry them."

"You have a lovely way of putting things," Janice said.

"No rational person would kill another person except for money or love," Mike rebutted.

"I'm as fair-minded as the next guy, but you can't let people get away with this. It sends the wrong message. People really do start to think they can get away with murder."

"But who ever thinks they're going to be caught?" Mike argued. "Do you really think, if they want to kill someone, that they'll stop because some day down the line they might get caught and executed? Do you think they decide to go ahead with it because if they do get caught, at least they'll only be in jail for the rest of their natural born lives?"

The game was slipping away and I felt pressed into my chair, cast as the symbol of something beyond me. Yet I felt no connection to it at all—not the execution, not to Adler, not to any of these passions swirling around me.

The professor threw up his hands. "That's the problem. They know they won't be in jail for the rest of their lives."

"Then don't let them out," Mike said, punctuating his syllables by slapping the chair back in front of him. "Isn't that obvious? The problem isn't that we're not killing them. The problem is that we're letting them go."

Janice laughed. "Our good defense lawyer arguing to keep people locked up. Now I've seen everything. Except a football game, which looks like a good one, BTW."

"We're all just exercising our natural human evolutionary need for conquest," the professor said. "Most channel it constructively, like with sports. Those who break the social contract need to pay the ultimately price."

"I know these people," Mike said. "Most of my clients are guilty as sin. Many need to spend time behind bars. But the cold-blooded killers, there's something wrong with them. They are crazy, I don't care what you say."

Janice propped her feet on the back of the chair in front of her. "But you realize, Michael, that saying he's crazy only protects us from having to look at the ways he's like you and me. That makes him easy to deal with. We simply say he's nothing like us. But the truly frightening part is just how close he is to the rest of us. Rather than even consider that, we treat him like he's the devil. That way, we sleep easier at night."

The lines spoken were all well rehearsed. None of us even needed to be here.

"I never sleep easy," I said. "I don't know why Adler did it, and I don't care. I don't see this as some complicated problem. Courts determine whether he's guilty. My job is just to do my job once the judgment has been made."

Janice cackled loudly. "Amazing that a man who deals every day with the consequences of human behavior would care so little about its causes."

"What I care about is our budget."

"You say that like that makes it better," she said.

A cheer went up from the crowd below us. A swarm of players converged upon a single figure, scampering wildly on the field of play with the ball tucked firmly under his arm, and then the next instant he was frozen and quickly crushed and buried under, just as the halftime gun sounded. The teams jogged off the field. Streams of fans lined up along the ramps, in search of refreshments, bathrooms, a temporary respite from the maddening heat.

I stood and ventured out onto the patio. A waft of smoke from the grill rolled over me as I stepped out, the charred scent of burgers. I grabbed a plate and weaved through the now fairly substantial crowd, many of whom appeared to have arrived from the other side of the patio, a different stairwell, a different gate. A small troop from the band were playing over on the other side, a couple of cheerleaders prancing in front of them. The festival feeling was spilling over.

I looked over toward the bar, and there, dressed in a tight cocktail dress, entirely inappropriate for any kind of sporting event, stood Jennifer Thorn Jackson.

At first, I wasn't certain what to do. She hadn't apparently noticed me yet, and it would have been easy enough to slip away back into the viewing room with Janice, or even to leave the stadium entirely. But I stayed there, focused on her, waiting for some flash of recognition. But she was distracted, taking periodic swigs from her beer bottle, gazing out above the field and crowd into the humid horizon beyond. My weeks of searching, of plowing through thousands of documents, moving moldy, heavy stacks of boxes, all for nothing in the end, came back to me. My questions unanswered, I wanted some explanation, some justification for the crusade she'd sent me on.

I drifted casually through the crowd toward her. So distracted was she that I was beside her before she turned and saw my face.

A quick intake of breath was all the immediate visible shock she showed, but then she instinctively took a step back from me. She glanced around her, perhaps a quick check to see who else was around. I started to speak, but before I could get a word out, she brushed by me, hurrying through a circle of conversation to a door marked exit. Then she paused and looked at me with a hard stare as if to entreat me to follow her. She quickly slipped out the door.

She was most of the way down the corridor as I entered, and I nearly had to run to catch up with her. She paused by another exit sign, waiting for me to arrive, and still without a word we stepped through that door into another stairwell deep within the bowels of the building.

"You are the last person I expected to see."

"Same here," I said.

"Why are you here?"

"I was invited by a friend who teaches here."

"My husband is on faculty. I'm sorry. I'm just a little paranoid. I thought you were following me, that you had news for me."

She shifted her weight uncomfortably.

"I don't think you're being honest with me," I said. "I don't believe that you don't remember what Rain Bird is about."

Her fingernail tapped the bottle in her hand, and she cocked her hip, contemplating my face. Finally, she sighed and leaned into the wall.

"You're right. I'm not being honest with you. I just didn't know if I could trust you."

"And do you now?"

"No. I just need you to trust me."

"Why should I? What is the point of all this?"

She hunched her shoulders for a moment, chin down and looking up from under her lowered eyebrows. Then she unclenched, her whole manner noticeably more open.

"Are you familiar with Cloraserin?" she asked.

"That's some kind of poison gas or something, isn't it?"

"It's a nerve agent, developed during the Vietnam war, which was later discovered to have useful properties for use as a pesticide and became widely used."

"It was banned, though, if I remember. In the '70s?"

"Concerns about its potential impact on nontarget biota, as well as natural- and agroecosystems, habitat and food sources led to its restriction, yes. Many, many studies were done, medical records scrutinized. In some South American countries, where its use is unrestricted, birth defects and high cancer rates have been shown to correlate strongly with its use. Our government decided that strict regulations would be placed on its use and explicitly banned its use in public settings, which includes use as a pesticides."

"Okay. But what does this have to do with Lycroson?"

She took a deep breath. "Lychroson is Cloraserin."

The steady beat of drums, a brass medley, ricocheted through the cement walls.

"How is that even possible?"

"Chemically, they are practically indistinguishable. But slight modifications allowed its creators to file for a new patent. And a new patent meant it needed to go through the whole approval process again. Except this time, they were smart. They didn't seek approval for it as a pesticide. They didn't seek approval for it at all. Their own proposal lists it as an inactive ingredient, working in conjunction with the registered pesticide. They backdoored it."

"I don't know what that means."

"Whoever came up with this project perfectly understands how to exploit the gaps in the system. If I hadn't caught it, I doubt anyone would have until the dead bodies started piling up. That I even noticed was dumb luck."

"But that can't be right. How can Lychroson be that deadly? I saw someone drink it. They were perfectly fine."

"This not a poison like arsenic. If the proportions were small enough, if it were in an inert form, I doubt it would have any kind of immediate impact that anyone would see, though it certainly wouldn't be good for you. If, on the other hand, it became laced in your water every morning, then I'd start to worry. Or in the food you ate. Or in the air you breathe. Whoever told you Lychroson was simply harmless either was clueless about what's in those files or they were lying to you."

"How do you know all this?"

"I read the patent and I compared them. Cloraserin and Lychroson are functionally identical. A ninth-grade chemistry student could see that, if they were looking for it. Whoever put this together thought they could slip this by someone who wasn't paying close attention and didn't know this stuff. A bit disrespectful, if you ask me."

"Why didn't you just say this in your report?"

She took a step back, growing suddenly quiet and looking up the cavernous stairwell at a point far distant.

"It's in the findings, at least technically spelled out, if not explicitly. But I was convinced to leave it out of my summary. My superiors were adamant that we stay within our mandate. In a sense, my silence was the price for declaring the project hazardous and formally issuing a recommendation against it. They agreed to kill Rain Bird, and I would not expose their fraud. And I naively believed that my recommendation would be enough."

"And that's why you were so urgent that I find the report. Because they had brought back Cloraserin."

"Putting Cloraserin back into circulation would be bad. But this is worse."

"What worse? Worse how?"

"You need to understand how this process works. Mostly, my job is to review the scientific data that has been presented with the project and from there determine the potential environmental impact. But the data only assesses these on an individual basis, which means that our determinations will mostly be isolated."

"Sorry. I don't speak environmental impact report."

"It means we don't know how these chemicals will interact with each other or how increased exposure to multiple chemicals will affect the human body. Cloraserin was deemed especially hazardous just by itself. But most recent studies have shown that chemical pesticides can become significantly more dangerous to the public when used in combination with each other. Which, if I remember correctly, is precisely how this proposal is indicating it will be used."

There was a rumbling in the empty stairwell. We were clearly under the bleachers, and hundreds of thousands of feet began stamping in unison, flooding the cavern with sounds like war.

"Why didn't you tell me when you asked me to investigate? Why are you telling me now?"

"I'm breaking a hundred different confidentiality agreements right now. But I've heard more rumors. More than rumors, actually. I've seen other documents that make me believe Rain Bird is really happening. Right now. I know that. What I just don't understand is how this could have happened. Did you find anything?"

"The records from the office have been seized," I said. "I've been down in a warehouse every day trying to sort through duplicates." This was as much of the truth as I was willing to share at the moment.

She looked me over carefully, then finally nodded slightly. "I guess it doesn't matter why, really. It's still happening. And someone has to stop it."

"Perhaps they changed the project," I suggested. "Maybe that's how it got approved."

"I suppose," she said uncertainly, "they could have simply changed the project, substituting Lychroson with another chemical agent."

"Sounds reasonable." .

She stood silently for a while, her eyes intense upon mine, as if testing my sincerity, I thought, waiting for me to break and tell her what I really knew. And I nearly did, knowing, as I had only just now learned, the full disaster my casual disregard had unleashed.

But then she thanked me, less than sincerely, it seemed, and then exited the stairwell, back toward the patio with a few more exaggerated glances. I watched her slow stride, elegant and dangerous in her sleek gown, until she slipped out again into the bright afternoon. Surely she would keep looking, still searching for some other way to the truth. She was driven, desperate. For myself, I had had enough of games and conversations and reports and studies and executions and Janice and Hero, and the whole damned weight of the world. I turned the opposite direction, toward the stairs, and began my long, slow descent in search of a way out.

twenty-six

Lying in my bed under a blanket of down and cool dark, before the sounds of new morning chirped in, I could swear I heard the trucks roaming our neighborhood. Their engines rolled, constant and even, a gravel hum starting in the pit of my stomach then moving outward toward my extremities. By first light, the tremor reached my fingertips, which shook as with nerves or over-caffeination. My body stuttered with the possibilities—involuntary and uncontrollable motion.

These trucks were out there, I knew for certain, navigating narrow corners and cross-streets, an occasional cul-de-sac, barely slipping by tilted sign posts as they chart courses down Mayhill, past Duey, round Peacock and up Vesper Vines and St. Francis. They were stout machines with shaded windows, drivers in un-ironed denim, their workshirts sweat- and coffee-stained, with cursive name tags: Billy and D.J. and Hank. They wore sunglasses because the pale yellow streetlights hurt their eyes, and they pulled their baseball caps low across their brows. When they passed each other, one truck crossing another's slow path, they would wave, a quick salute, possibly roll down the window to discuss where they'd meet for breakfast, still over an hour away. The Waffle Shack, Cutler's Griddle House, any of a number of greasy spoons. Order some honey ham and cheese grits if you get there first, one would say, I'd like to have that waiting when I arrive.

All the while the tanks they tow behind hissed, slight and soft.

The morning mists draped thick as cobwebs across the sidewalks, the lawns, the driveways. A periodic commuter motored through, unsettling the fog into swirls of eddies that quickly resolved themselves again into stillness. The air would taste fresh, pure and light and damp like clouds. But what was left upon the tongue was a metallic hint, a residue that soon would faintly coat mouth and throat, lungs and stomach. It could have been exhaust. It could have been factory fumes. It wasn't, as I now knew. Soon you could forget it, become accustomed to the flavor, drown it out in morning tea and omelets or syrup-soaked pancakes and juice. Once day finally broke into full bloom, the mists had dried up and the bright world resumed in an uneasy sort of silence.

Late summer in the South usually brings droves of flies and fellow forms of pestilence, choirs of crickets and cicadas and congregating insect hordes. In every yard, puddles of damp, small pools renewed by cycles of thunderstorms would swell under the shade of bottle brush and schefflera branches. This was where the mosquito larvae grew and where they were born and where they'd return to lay eggs again after they'd made their way in the world. They'd become bloated full of blood before they were either splattered across limbs or escaped.

These are silent hunters, except when they ventured too close to the human ear. You'd know them from their high-pitched buzz, but by then it's already too late. They had you, while the crickets chirped on. The soft, sweet music of the season.

Yet after the trucks had passed, the mornings stood still and silent beneath the hum of freeway traffic, a sprinkler snap, and laughter rising out of someone's kitchen down the block. But for this, all across town, only the quiet of the dead.

Part III.

twenty-seven

Silhouettes moved through the darkness, nighttime figures trespassing through our streets and courts, our yards and alleyways. Another one of the reasons the neighborhood has felt compelled to lock itself off: workers from the Stewart Paper Mill took a shortcut walking home, tired strangers going home in the early evening by the shortest route. At this time, Magnolia Grove was experiencing a crime spree, as well. Four home invasions in the past two months. No one had been hurt, yet, but one night, four men had raided a family home and placed a gun to the head of the grandmother while the others cleaned the place out.

Even so, random crime wasn't my greatest concern. Ever since my conversation with Jennifer Thorn Jackson, I sensed the coming apocalypse, checked obituaries for signs and trends, and awaited the inevitable arrival of Stanton, who would cart me off for my crimes, whether they were unintentional or not, confirming or even surpassing Hero's estimation for how low I could go. All of which seemed to confirm that I had been wrong. Better to have never tasted the fruit of knowledge than to be cast out of the blissful ignorance of Eden.

Hero rapped quickly on the open frame of my study one evening as I pondered my sad fate.

"I think there's someone outside my window," she said.

"I thought you weren't talking to me.

"I'm conveying information. It was dark. There was movement. I thought it was a tree at first. But now, I don't know. I'm pretty sure someone's out there, and I don't want to die. Do with it what you will."

Under normal circumstances, I might have told Hero there was nothing to worry about, but I was in too deep now to defer to trust. I descended to the garage and retrieved my grandfather's shotgun from the rear window rack, then pressed the automatic door opener and stepped out into the driveway.

A storm was coming, I could feel it. The gusts of wind blew damp and crisp, kicking up trash and leaves into tiny whirlwinds. Outside in the dark, at the base of our walkway, I saw to my surprise the dark shadow of a man. He wasn't hiding or sneaking in any sense that I understood. He stood partway up the walk, facing my house. There was a car parked in front, too, sidled up to the curb.

I kept the shotgun down at my side, not wanting to accidentally shoot someone who was lost and looking for directions—a mistake Dr. Morgan Roberts from two blocks over learned the hard way two years ago with some German tourists.

"Can I help you?" I said.

The man seemed to take some sort of encouragement from my comment and inched forward, though not enough to fully emerge from shadow.

"I don't know. I think I'm lost. It's very dark out here. Have you considered installing street lights?"

"People don't like them. Keeps everyone up at night."

"It's very hard to see," he observed.

"I think there's an ordinance against it," I said, "but you'd have to check the manual. I have several." If he was from the state investigators, he was the oddest sort imaginable. He also clearly wasn't Southern, or even pretending to be. "Anything else I can help you with?" I asked.

"Perhaps," he said, stepping further into the light where he was revealed. He was middle-aged, balding, and his clothes were fine, but wrinkled and stained. "I'm looking for Mr. Matthew Brown. Do you know where I can find him?"

I raised the gun slightly.

"And you are…?"

Hero was suddenly at my arm. I didn't like the idea of her being out here, exposed to unknown hazards. But she took a step past me toward the man.

"What are you doing here?" she asked the stranger.

"I want to talk to you," he said.

"Haven't you heard of phones?"

"I didn't have the number. The operator claimed the Matthew Brown at this address is deceased. Don't even get me started with getting the address."

The weapon in my hands seemed to radiate its own light, a burning energy of its own potential.

Hero crossed her arms. "So you show up in the middle of the night? Are you trying to be melodramatic?"

"I wanted to surprise you."

"Surprise!" She turned to me. "Go ahead and shoot him."

"I'm sorry," I said. "We haven't met."

He held out his hand. "Geoffrey. Hero's…"

We both let the space of the unspoken word stand between us for a few moments. Hero was looking at us, her gaze passing from one to the other, as if waiting for someone to step into the breach.

"Exactly," she said firmly, as if she'd just proved some point, and turned back toward the house.

twenty-eight

Past overtakes present. Once an old rundown rail yard and warehouse district—now a series of studios, galleries, shops and, for some, low-cost housing, and in the middle of a once empty field now stood a bright red caboose, since converted into a restaurant—The Cornucopia Café—its insides gutted and remodeled, with a row of stools squeezed up close to a counter on one end, a grill and sink and chimney crammed into the other. Saturday brunch was a popular attraction at the Cornucopia, whose entrepreneur owner was an aspiring chef in her mid-twenties, crafting gourmet meals for the curious and aspiring few who managed to find her. Picnic tables littered the surrounding field, and this morning a large crowd of people had gathered. An impromptu fashion show was going on in the quadrangle of lawn outside the caboose, people modeling colorful batik clothing while an acoustic trio strummed over in a corner.

"That's quite a scar," Geoffrey noted, as we waited for our food. "How in the heck did you do that?"

"Matthew beats me," Hero said.

"That so." Geoffrey smiled.

"Oh, yes. I need the discipline. He keeps me in line."

"Mmmm."

"I think he's taking his own personal inadequacies out on me."

"Only when she gives me lip," I joined in. "I can't take anyone giving me lip."

"I'm not getting the real answer, am I?" Geoffrey sighed.

Hero smiled. "Nope."

"Mmmmm."

"How about we start with what you are doing here," Hero said suddenly, short circuiting the small talk.

Geoffrey's arrival the previous evening had startled Hero and me out of our routine of ignoring each other, but we quickly returned to form. Out on the front steps, I had offered Geoffrey our extra bedroom, which he accepted, and each of us then retreated behind closed doors to mull this new and unexpected dynamic. When we awoke, Hero announced that this café was where we were going to go in order to, as she put, "sort through this ridiculous mess."

Geoffrey touched her arm gently. "Like I said. I'm here to see you."

Hero shied away from his hand, but only after pausing a moment. "You trying to size up the competition? Is that it? See who else is out there competing for my filial love?"

"This isn't a competition," Geoffrey said calmly.

"You're telling me."

The band struck up a louder tune, the singer crooning through his amp, an almost squeezebox bluegrass melody.

"Hero's in a play," I said, trying to lighten the mood.

"Oh?" he said, raising an eyebrow and turning to look at Hero. "What's the play?"

"The Winter's Tale," she chirped.

Geoffrey rolled his tongue around in his mouth. "Mmmm. And you are playing…"

"Perdita."

"Perdita, naturally," he said nearly atop her, anticipating the answer. "Let me hazard a guess: You suggested the play."

Hero shrugged and smiled with no attempt to deny it.

"I've never heard of it," I said.

"You'd like it," Hero said. "It's one of Shakespeare's comedies. It's about a King who decides suddenly that his wife is having an affair and that his kids aren't his own."

"Sounds vaguely familiar," I said.

"Oh, it gets better. When he questions his wife's faithfulness, the Gods strike down his little son. Even though the kid really was his kid. How's that for misapplied justice."

"A bit harsh."

"It gets even better than that. Then he sends his infant daughter away to be killed. All because he felt betrayed by his wife."

"This is a comedy, you say?" I said.

"She comes back later, as an adult. Marries a prince. Shames her father. Mother comes back to life from a statue. Typical Elizabethan stuff."

"Alls well that ends well," Geoffrey added, taking a long sip from his coffee cup.

"Except for Mamillius," Hero said. "Everyone's all happy. But the son is still dead. And everyone's spent 20 years in misery. Honestly, I think the moral of the story is to try to put the best face on a bad situation."

"Sounds like it will be a fun evening," I said.

"Still," Geoffrey said, "it's not like it's a perfect parallel. Hermione was innocent, after all, and Perdita was, in fact, his daughter."

Hero frowned. "So, what you're saying is that it would have been okay for him to kill Perdita if she hadn't been his daughter? Good to know."

"Don't be ridiculous."

A gangly teenager in a torn T-shirt who apparently was our server brought out our plates, two at a time. The portions were mammoth, overflowing the large ceramic. For Hero, two thick pancakes the width of her entire dinner plate and spilling over the side, with whole blueberries peeking through here and there. My omelet was bursting with chunks of mushroom and tomato and oozed cheese. Geoffrey's huevos rancheros were piled high with black beans and sour cream and rice.

"Do I look like I need this much food?" he said, picking at his plate with his fork.

"Give it a rest," Hero said, digging in. "You know you like it."

"That doesn't mean they have to overwhelm us with proportions fit for a football player."

"Eat," she said.

"Digest," he replied.

They both smiled, amused by the lameness of some inside joke, I supposed, and turned to their food. I admired his skill with her, something fine-tuned from a dozen years of living with her, interacting, day after day. It was an odd feeling, his preeminence. When they spoke it was of the experience of a shared life. He stopped eating to ask her about friends I didn't know existed, lingering questions from their lives, references to trips and conversations years in the past. It was distressing to know that he knew far more about her than I did or was likely to ever know. He was her childhood. He belonged to her from her earliest cognition. His face, his hands, his voice. The strands of memory and connection.

"What is it you do, Matthew?" Geoffrey asked, turning to me. "You're in government, I think I heard.

Hero sneered. "He's a cold-blooded killer."

"I work for the Department of Corrections."

"Don't leave out the killing part."

I glared at Hero. "The state is in the process of executing a murderer, and they've left the details up to me. Yes."

"Nice dodge," Hero laughed.

"No one asks for this," I said, inexplicably trying to justify myself. "It's the job."

"Don't worry. Everyone's got something," Geoffrey said, glancing around distractedly, without elaborating.

Hero sighed.

"Two of my least favorite people in the same place together. How did I ever get so lucky?"

Geoffrey laughed. "All we need is your mother and everything would be complete."

"Ah, yes. The architect of all our troubles. Unless, of course, you count Mr. Brown over here."

"Me?" I said, wiping my mouth. "What did I do?"

"If you need me to explain it to you, you've got a lot worse problems than me. Or maybe there are a few more me's running around. What do you think? You sowed your oats all over the countryside?"

"Just one oat. As far as I know."

"And what about you," she said, turning toward Geoffrey. "Any pseudo-siblings I should be aware of?"

"No," he said. "But I am seeing someone."

"The ink isn't even dry on the divorce. Who is she?"

"You don't know her."

"Bull-oney."

"Fine. Her name is Alice."

"That better not be my sixth-grade teacher, Mrs. Duncan. Everyone knew you had the hots for each other."

"We'll talk about this later."

The morning heat began to overcome the thin shade as we finished eating, so we retired back to the house after first taking a brief tour of downtown and the capitol buildings. Two peas, Val had said, but watching them I had my doubts. Competitors, perhaps, well used to the other's modes and methods. They seemed perfectly suited, though, for their kind of contention—combative, condescending, abrasive. So as the morning slipped into afternoon, I plied myself from them, by default encouraging a return to their standard mode of interaction and affording myself a rare opportunity to see my life as it might have been—a normal relationship with my daughter who would never really be mine. Two months ago, I would have been perfectly fine, ecstatic even, with this arrangement. Now, I was no longer sure.

But as the day went on, it became increasingly clear that I was mostly in the way, which is how I ultimately ended up in the basement, far away enough for them to begin to sort through their issues, but close enough to not seem to be abandoning either one. On the basement table lay scattered still the remnants of the Rain Bird project file, which I shoved over to make room for the several days of mail I piled there instead.

By the light of the desk lamp, I read through a letter that had arrived a few days ago from the Magnolia Grove Historical Society. As my project continued to grow in scope and my financial resources decreased, I'd decided to pursue possible grants. The historical society had as its stated goal the preservation and restoration of the original character of the Magnolia Grove community, and a number of my neighbors had made use of these grants for projects significantly less ambitious in scope than my own. According to the letter, the society was interested in my property, especially in terms of seeing a return to the building's antebellum character. My request was being processed and I would be contacted in a few weeks about an inspection to view the property and discuss the options available.

With assistance from the historical society, I hoped that the whole process might be accelerated and the lawsuits against me perhaps even abandoned, once I had official sanction. In the dim of the underground room, I sorted through more residue of my family's heritage. Nearly a hundred years of photographs were stored in a variety of photo albums and shoe boxes, most unmarked and unlabeled, and more than a few decayed by mildew and water damage. Beyond the photographs, there were heirlooms, documents, even clothing—over two centuries of history built up within this house, which my family had occupied through every age. Its bizarre evolution into an unrecognizable monstrosity had been the slow denigration of its very identity, and something I was slowly, but surely, beginning to reverse.

It was late in the evening when I awoke from the chair where I dozed and noticed Geoffrey standing at the top of the stairs holding a six-pack of beer.

"I'm not bothering you?" he said.

"Not at all," I said. "Come on down."

He stepped cautiously down the remaining stairs, then settled onto the long sofa against the wall, stretching out and offering me a beer.

"Hero tells me her mother is missing."

I nodded, taking a bottle. "She was supposed to go home over a month ago, but we haven't been able to reach Val, and I just don't like the idea of sending her off without anyone being there to receive her."

"Interesting."

"Hero insists it's nothing to worry about, that she'll turn up eventually. That she does this all the time."

"She doesn't disappear, no," Geoffrey said, frowning. "Val can be eccentric, without a doubt. But it's not like her to just disappear without telling anyone."

"Hero doesn't seem worried, but I'm getting pretty anxious."

Geoffrey was quiet a minute, twisting off the cap of a new bottle, then taking long, drawn-out sips before he finally spoke again.

"Hero asked to come with me when I go," he said, with a hint of apology.

"I'm not surprised," I said, poorly hiding my surprise.

"She says she's ready to leave."

He shrugged, a gesture I immediately recognized as Hero's. Even as we sat there, I sensed that I was being tested and suppressed the nervous energy of being assessed.

"If that's what she wants," I said.

He rocked his half-empty beer bottle on the hardwood floor. "I told her she couldn't come."

"I'm sure Val would be fine if she did."

"You don't understand," he said. "I don't want her to come."

"I see," I said.

Geoffrey, as he explained, had known Val since before high school. Though he was a few years her elder, they had been dating by the time she had gone off on a full ride in the Art History program at the A&M, while he had finished up his master's degree at Michigan State. When she became pregnant, they decided to tie the knot and bring up their child in a happy domestic union. But their personalities were different, and as a curator, she was traveling often to acquire rare works from all across the world.

The cracks in their relationship had started to show several years before, and their small arguments had become increasing hostile and combative, until they finally decided that it would no longer be possible to continue. The divorce proceedings had only made things more contentious as they sought to sort out the division of their decade of marriage. The paternity test, he explained, was merely a delaying tactic, one he felt certain would piss Val off to no end. He had never expected the results, however.

"Maybe Val didn't know," I suggested. "She might have been mistaken."

"She knew. How could she not know? Or at least not have suspected?" he said.

"Everyone makes mistakes. Hardly an exact science."

I asked Geoffrey if he had a current picture of Val, and he nodded, ruffling through his wallet to pull out a family photo of the three of them. Studying the faces, I tried to dig beneath the expressions, what lies and secrets they concealed. Val's face was drawn into a sarcastic grimace, a look Hero herself would manage on occasion. My hope was that recognizing Val would give me something else to cling to besides my mere faith in a scientific test I couldn't even begin to understand. But mostly the image left me lost and confused. Sure, it was a more recent picture, perhaps a decade after our tryst, but I couldn't escape the feeling that I had never met the woman pictured in my life.

Geoffrey took back the photo. "It felt like a betrayal of everything, our entire marriage. It was the basis of our marriage, in fact, which only made it all that much worse. I was furious at her, furious about the whole situation. Can you imagine what it is like to be lied to about your own child?"

I just stared at him quietly.

"Oh, yes. Right," Geoffrey shook his head and laughed. "I keep forgetting. Sins of omission are still lies. Sometimes it's easy to think this is just about me and Val."

"And Hero."

"Hero. Of course. I could have handled that much better, I suppose."

"She thinks you hate her."

"No, she doesn't," he replied calmly.

"She feels abandoned."

"Yet she's the one who came running to you."

Despite the anger and disappointment between them, you could still recognize their bond, more certain than science and thicker than blood.

"I still need time to sort all this out. I hope Hero and I will still be in each others' lives. But this is a bit overwhelming, and I want to make sure I make the right decision and am not influenced too much by emotion."

What else was there to this, I wanted to ask, besides emotion?

"I really just came down here to let you know that I'm leaving tomorrow. Probably would've been better if I hadn't come at all, actually. I seem to have made things worse."

"That's how things have worked for me recently. I don't think you have to worry about competition from me. She hates me."

"If she hated you, she'd just ignore you. She doesn't have patience for lost causes. It's those she cares about that she annoys mercilessly."

"She says she's done with me."

Geoffrey stood and made his way to the stairs, then paused and surprised me again by smiling.

"We'll see," he said.

When I awoke the next morning, I found him eating a bowl of cereal alone in the kitchen, his packed bag at his ankles. We nodded silently, and I fixed my coffee. He dallied for a while, waiting to see when Hero would emerge, but the sun was rising toward midday without any appearance from her. Finally, he climbed the stairs and I heard him knock on her closed door, once, twice. His voice buzzed faintly, wisps of words spoken close through the barricade, followed by a pause. I could sense no answer.

Even after he'd gone, she stayed hidden away and did not come down at all that day.

twenty-nine

Despite the fact that I hadn't been paid in nearly a month, that the computer system no longer validated my identity card, and that our office was apparently receiving nearly a dozen resumes a week from people hoping to get a jump on the recently deceased man's job, I decided to still come to work to do what everyone expected me to do. Not every day, mind you. I didn't want to raise expectations too drastically. But there was more than enough work for me to do, what with the execution only one week away and the election following just on its heels. I rarely, if ever, saw Hal, whose departmental review left him hunkered down behind a stack of folders so thick, even his large frame was obscured.

I poked my head in to say "Hi" but received only a noncommittal grunt in reply.

My continued appearance at Corrections wasn't due to some deep-seated sense of responsibility. I went because, in the end, I simply had nothing better to do other than wait at home for the authorities to arrive.

I was sitting at my desk when Janice appeared unexpectedly in my office doorway, holding a potted plant. It was a large, sprawling thing without a leaf on it.

"For color," she said.

"It's solid brown," I pointed out.

"For character, then. This place could use some personality. Besides, what's one more piece of dead weight?"

"Funny."

She set the pot behind the door. I'd not seen her in a few weeks, but I was well used to her routine, as I'd observed over the years— to ignore people for great stretches, then suddenly appear in their lives again bearing gifts and asking questions. As much as I would have liked to believe otherwise, I accepted that I was a professional convenience for her. She never made courtesy visits to my work. More likely than not, she wanted something from me.

"What do you want from me?" I asked.

"I'm offended by the implication. Can't a friend just drop by with a gift?"

"Any other friend and I'd say yes."

"You don't have any other friends," she said with a smile. "But I accept your apology."

"I didn't apologize."

"Don't change subjects. I need some information." She lit a cigarette.

"This smoking thing is getting ridiculous. You're worse than some '40s movie star. It's going to kill you."

"Whatever kills me will be from the past 30 years, not today."

"That doesn't make any sense. Besides, you can't smoke in state buildings. It's against the law."

"What is it with everyone and these rules? You'd think I'd just strangled a baby."

"I don't make the rules."

"You just enforce them. I know."

She had recently returned from a short stint covering the candidates on the long stretch of the fall campaign trail, jetting from one end of the state to the other. Her scathing commentaries on each candidate were as depressing as they were withering. She was, as she always claimed, an equal opportunity muckraker. But lately her columns had turned from the everyday politics of the campaign toward the growing investigations of the administration and various government agencies. Our whole system of government appeared to be coming apart at the seams. Political powerhouses who had stood for decades against threats of all sorts were fighting for the salvage of their careers. Everywhere you looked, you found scandal. Two dozen agencies were under the microscope, including Environmental. The dominoes were beginning to fall. Three different agency directors had been forced to resign in the past two weeks alone. One had subsequently left the state and possibly even the country.

She leaned over and started to close my office door, but I stopped her.

"That will just make everyone more suspicious. If it's open, they'll think I'm just doing nothing. As usual."

Janice eased into the chair across from me.

"I've been doing some poking around."

"That's always an ominous sign," I said. "I've been reading your work."

"Peanuts," she said. "This state investigation is such a convoluted mess, figuring out what's driving it all has been nearly impossible. Half of these resignations have nothing to do with Stanton's inquiries. You just keep turning over rocks, you'll eventually find slithery things beneath. His people just don't want to talk, though, and those people who do want to talk don't seem to know anything. I've still managed to piece a few things together, however."

"Do tell."

"Do you know what a regulatory backdoor is?"

I shifted slightly in my seat.

"Is this a trick question?"

"A backdoor," she said, almost cross. "When a company wants to get approval for a new product, say, a new type of mayonnaise, it has to go through a whole series of steps—analyses, studies, etc—all to determine the safety and acceptability of this thing. These processes are different for various government agencies, which is fine, mostly, because there is little in the way of overlap. Mayonnaise isn't going to be used to power your car. But in cases where multiple approvals are necessary, the whole process can become very expensive, in terms of both money and time, not to mention the possibility that their products might be rejected and sent back to the drawing board. So, naturally, these companies want to streamline this process as much as possible."

"Naturally," I said.

Janice's legs were crossed, and her top leg kicked back and forth in a swift meter. "And the government, being as it is, torn between the populist desire for public policy and the corporate desire for relaxed procedures, has reached a compromise. When a new product is approved for use by one agency, the same product is essentially approved for other agencies, through the means of a backdoor."

"So, you're saying that because it is approved for public use in one agency, it's automatically given a pass elsewhere? That sounds crazy," I said, feeling increasingly uncomfortable as Janice lectured. But this wasn't the professor I was familiar with, nor the careful prose of a writer, nor even the sarcastic musing of a friend I'd known for years. She held the air of a predator. She was stalking.

"Some agencies have stricter standards than others," she went on. "And sometimes the mechanisms are practically identical. A public health benefit analysis might contain much of the same research of an environmental impact report. Rather than make this happen twice, people concluded that defaulting to the stricter agency standard is the same as doing the same study twice. You'd probably even say it makes a lot of sense."

"That certainly sounds more reasonable."

"But even the best laid plans go astray, Matthew. This probably works fine, as long as everyone is doing what they are supposed to be doing. But it also makes it far easier to slip something through. Bribing five different agencies is difficult. Bribing one director, well, that's like trawlin' crawdads on a chicken bone."

"So that's what you think this is all about? Someone bribed Bernie?"

Scatterings of ash flickered from the smoldering cigarette to the floor.

"This is far bigger than Bernie, my friend. The tentacles of this investigation stretch from one end of government to the other. With so many opportunities to create mayhem in the system, it's not a surprise that it's touching every part of not only this administration, but the last. You start to wonder if it's going to tear down the whole apparatus, which is ironic, since the people who are behind this whole scheme would probably love nothing more than to see these regulations disappear. Yet the consequence of this kind of investigation is mostly to make people skeptical of the regulators themselves."

"I had no idea about any of this."

"Tell me something I don't know, Matthew. But here's the thing: there's a reason why Bernie was targeted in this investigation and why the bureau has become a kind of focal point. Its standards are some of the most strict, which means that approval by the Bureau of Environmental Study is sufficient for practically any other agency in state government. But, as you know, the bureau doesn't really investigate products but rather the impact of various projects. The end result is the same, though. Whatever product is included in an approved proposal achieves a de facto backdoor approval for any number of other agencies."

Lychroson is a wonder chemical, Dr. Adams had said. They'd found a dozen practical applications for it in hundreds of products. So far.

"My God."

Janice raised an eyebrow. Beneath my desk, I twisted a sheet of paper into a knot.

"So I have just a simple question for you, Matthew Brown," Janice said, leaning in. "Has anyone ever asked you to change the conclusions—or ignore the recommendations of—an environmental impact report?"

This kind of inquisition from Janice was new to me—direct and unwavering and without any of her typical wry joviality. I could see how ex-governor Roberson had crumbled under the force of her inquiry. Janice, when focused, was withering.

"No," I said, relieved to be able to tell the truth. "No one ever asked me to do anything." And in an instant I finally understood my place in the grand scheme of things. No one asked me to do anything illegal. They apparently just knew I was so incompetent that I wouldn't bother reading the file in the first place.

She clicked her pen, on, off, on again.

"You wouldn't hold back on me, would you?"

"Hero says I shouldn't trust you."

Janice shoved her notebook back into her bag. "I've always said that girl's too good for you."

"She thinks you'll betray me."

"She's smart, too. Maybe she's right. Maybe you two aren't related."

"Are you trying to destroy me?"

"Don't be paranoid, Matty," she said, rising abruptly and heading toward the door. "I'm out to destroy everyone. I can't be playing favorites."

thirty

A fire truck was racing down our block, all lights and sirens, when its tires streaked to a sudden halt. A child biking with training wheels had coasted in a flurry down a driveway, speeding past the sidewalk and parking strip and right out into the street. They missed each other by a matter of feet. There was a pause for reflection and maximum effect, tall men staring down with concerned disapproval. The child pushed his bike toward the curb. Then the truck was moving again, and watching it move away from my seat by the front window, I waited for the sound of sirens to disappear into the distance.

But the sirens didn't disappear, nor even really fade. They continued to bleat into the calm afternoon.

Stepping out onto my lawn and looking down the street, I spotted the back of the truck sticking out from around the corner where it had stopped, apparently to render its assistance. Before I made it halfway down the block, the neighbors had clustered in a loose group at the corner. We nodded to each other in vague recognition, names buried and jumbled together, community meetings, Christmas parties, early morning commute drive-bys. Most of them were suing me, if only collectively through the association. I recognized some of them, though no one I knew well enough to strike up casual conversation with on any normal day, but today was different. Now we had a reason to engage. Catastrophes always serve as unique socializing opportunities.

"What happened?" I asked one of the curious, a man still in his bathrobe who I was sure I must have known. Richards? Richardson? Something Richardson. His name was right there. I had it on the tip of memory. It's something common, clipped and manly. Bill Bob Rob Ted.

He didn't say anything, just pointed toward the house with the firemen congregating on the lawn, three doors down.

Never having lived in a war zone, I was surprised by how artificial what once had been a colonial-style home now appeared. It had a sudden fictional quality. I'd passed this place a thousand times on my way out of the neighborhood, never giving it more than a casual glance. The structure still stood, but its windows were completely missing, now lined with charred black starbursts. The inside, now fully exposed by one absent wall, consisted only of dark and burnt. No mahogany dining table. No tea service. No dangling crystal chandelier. Just the blackness of carbon char. Layered across the lawn, toasted pieces of insulation, black and pink imitation snow.

More people were coming, everyone curious, and some asking questions of the police officer standing nearby, walkie-talkie chirping static at his waist. A few had heard the explosion, much more faint than you would have believed. People were paying close attention to the details, and everyone wanted the scoop. This was an event, a happening, something sure to warrant a mention in the Christmas letter this year.

I didn't really know anyone here very well. The woman beside me—Mrs. Watson? Ms. Foulk? Debbie Terri Patti?—started relaying what she knew to anyone who would listen.

"The owners are on vacation in Europe for a few months. The wife is an administrator for the county schools. Husband's an investment banker. They've been saving up for a big second honeymoon to Europe.

"So who's been there?" another woman asked. "I've seen people coming and going."

"Said they leased out their home to some college students who've been staying there this month."

"They run with a sketchy crowd," someone says. "They throw parties late. All hours."

"Meth lab," says the cop standing by the curb, chiming in. "Seen this a hundred times. It's a tricky thing, and more often than not, things get out of control and something combusts."

And where are the renters now? the neighbors asked. Probably on the run, trying to dodge the long arm of the law, and soon the wrath of the owners. What a surprise they will be in for when they return. In just the flash of a moment, your world can turn upside down and burn to the ground. Everything you thought secure comes apart.

She started periodically leaving small notes lying around, tiny comments and observations obviously intended for me to discover. Most of them simply said, Fuck off.

My days became intertwined, one with the next, until I no longer possessed any sense of time passing, just the insecure feeling that events had come and gone beyond my notice. I awoke at some point in my lounge chair, the television playing an old movie. I had no idea how long I'd been here, nor even when I sat down. Daylight shining in through the windows, but I could not tell if it was fading or growing, the distinctiveness of sunset and sunrise finely obscured. Outside of the chattering TV show, the house rested quietly with me, a weighted silence that suggested I shouldn't be sitting here. I was supposed to be somewhere else. I should have been doing something. I didn't know what. Anything.

If Hero was anywhere around, I could not sense her, and in this waking moment she seemed absolutely remote to me, as if she no longer even existed on the earth. My heart's pace quickened. Was this fear? Joy? What was this general bubbling excitement, and did it really have some sort of hotline to my unguarded psyche? And could she perhaps really have vanished from my life during a brief interim of sleep?

This feeling lasted only a moment, and the next, my senses

returned. The world does not operate in this way, I thought. Your problems do not simply disappear through wishful thinking or an especially deep slumber. They either must be confronted and overcome, or ignored and left to fester. More often than not, I preferred the festering. It gave me a confidence of my own victimization, my self-suffering. It had provided all the best excuses of my life.

There was a noise from across the house, the familiar sound of a shower turning off. I realized that the running water had been going this whole time—I simply hadn't heard it. The muting of everyday background sounds. I strained to listen, to break free and hear all the noises you have to shut out because otherwise you cannot function. Like the dogs next door, whimpering because their families have left them alone again, if only for a few hours. Like the refrigerator churning alone, making ice, keeping things cool. Like the two children calling to each other outside. They argued. One raced down the sidewalk, the other close on his heels, footfalls of sneakers clumping heavily upon cement.

This abstract world of sound.

Perhaps this is what it means to be a ghost. I had become, after all, the walking dead, unseen and unknown. I'd given up—for the time being, anyway—my attempts to resuscitate myself. The bureaucracy believed me deceased, and there seemed little more I could do than I'd already done to permanently change that fact. A little time might help, I suspected, letting everything settle down before I quietly began again. In the meantime, I was learning to adjust to my new afterlife, always on the lookout for new haunts. But mostly I hovered here, in this vaguely familiar setting, as construction migrated inward and began to reshape the interior.

In the half darkness of my living room, eyes slowly adjusting, I began to see for the first time broad strokes of the restoration going on around me. Looking close at these corners, these window frames, archways and banisters, I had a sense of what it must have been like for my long-dead family to live here—to rule their world of privilege and to feel what I still longed to feel: that they were of this place and it was naturally and unquestioningly theirs. But the corruption of this ideal wasn't new. It was carried in on the backs of abuse and torture. As much as I wanted to separate the two, I'd always failed, struck by the sterilized past that formed and glorified our Southern mythology. We were bound together, black and white, master and slave, future and past.

So I needed this house, this past, to understand wherever it was I was going.

Hero came down the stairs, step step step step step step step, then into the kitchen, where she opened the fridge and poured herself a drink—juice water milk?—then down the hall into this room. She was not dressed yet, just wrapped in a burgundy towel that came down to barely mid-thigh. Another towel draped over her shoulders and her hair fell down the middle of her back. Her scar still plainly visible, but with stitches now removed, less ghoulish and beginning to fade.

For a brief second, our eyes met. Then she turned and retreated back upstairs. Her door slammed shut.

I climbed the stairs to her room with the intention to confront her. Perhaps we could negotiate a temporary peace, at least until Val turned up. Most days, Hero would come home from school, gather food from the fridge, then hide away from me upstairs. But I'd finally had enough. I wasn't going to let another day pass without at least making an attempt.

I knocked on her door. She didn't make a sound, so I knocked again. The responding silence left me uneasy. I was fairly certain she was in there, but I couldn't be sure. She might have slipped downstairs at some point, or maybe gone out the window and down the scaffolding on the back of the house. Maybe this was how she spent her evenings, away from home and out on the town.

I tried the handle, but it was latched shut. In fact, a bolt had been installed on the door. When did this happen? I wondered. She must have come home in the afternoon and done it herself. I felt a momentary sense of pride. My daughter was a doer, a hands-on girl.

But still, my problem—I was locked out. Privacy is a complicated matter in any family, but I was certain I didn't approve of this move. I was equally sure, too, that I would never lock her out, unless I worried that she might be embarrassed to walk in on me. I didn't want to imagine what might embarrass her.

"We need to talk," I said through the door.

"We aren't doing anything. Go away."

"We can't just leave things like this."

"Give it up, Matthew. Stop trying."

"I need to talk with you," I said—shouted, really—through the door. I suppose I expected her to shout me down, to become fed up and maybe angry. Or that she would just continue in her isolating silence. What I didn't expect was what actually happened: She calmly opened the door and then stepped partially out, leaning against the frame and blocking access or even a view inside. She didn't say anything. She just stared at me, her face innocent and cold.

"What are we going to talk about?" She was eating a yogurt. She stirred around in the cup with her spoon and took a mouthful. I took a deep breath and jumped in.

"You shouldn't have gone out like that."

Hero frowned. "Stop trying to be my father."

"Forget about fatherhood. You wouldn't treat your friends this way."

"Don't try to blame me," she said. "You're the one who didn't respect my privacy."

"You locked me out. Then you stayed out all night. I didn't know what you were doing, what was happening to you."

"Whatever happened to trust?" she said, sounding almost hurt.

"That's just it. I don't trust you. You don't trust me."

"And here we are," Hero shrugged, taking a step back into her room, "with nothing much to discuss."

"I screwed up," I said, before she could close the door. "Badly."

"Yes, you did," she said, calmly pausing.

"I want to salvage what we have."

"What would that be? There is no "we," Matthew. I'm not aware we have anything at all."

"I made a mistake. I just want to move on."

"It doesn't work that way," she said. "You can't make betrayal go away."

"We should try. Both of us. We can't give up before we've really even started."

She scraped the bottom of the cup, turning her attention away from me for a torturous moment. Then she sighed.

"I was right. This was all a big mistake, coming like this. What would it matter in the world if we actually were related? Do you think being my father makes any kind of difference? What would it change? I'm not ready for all of this, and it's pretty friggin' obvious you aren't, either."

Watching her face scroll through the myriad and conflicting emotions, I wanted to offer some kind of comfort. But I had nothing to give that she would take. That mantle of perfect fatherhood I'd hoped to carry hadn't even lasted the full first day she arrived. Since then, I'd torn myself down to nothing in her eyes. But none of that mattered to me anymore, I now realized. She needed someone, and I wished I could somehow be that person—but knew I simply was not and wondered if I ever could be.

If she only knew of the thousands of people I had put at risk, of the lives that could be lost because of me, she would cast me aside. Few things made me more certain than this.

"Maybe you're right," I said at last. "But for now we're stuck with each other, and we can try to make the best of a bad decision, at least until your mom turns up."

She gave me a long and thoughtful stare, the spoon dangling from her lips.

"Have you thought at all about what it would mean if she doesn't come back? We could be stuck with each other forever."

"She'll be back," I said. "Don't worry."

"Right back at ya."

thirty-one

We lost a member of the construction crew at the house. They were completing rear roofing, after a month where we'd been left with nothing but a plastic tarp between us and the elements, when he collapsed. Dropped to the ground from the first rung of the ladder. Members of the crew worked to revive him and dragged him into the shade. It was several minutes before we learned that he wasn't, in fact, dead, just dehydrated and soon dry heaving into the hedges. But after the ambulance had come and he was rushed to the hospital for intravenous fluids, construction at the house came to an abrupt halt. The rest of the crew revolted and walked off the lot due to abusive work conditions. Word got around. Soon, my contractor was blacklisted for improper treatment and was forced to search all across the county for a piecemeal crew of any sort—legal, illegal, underage—to continue the work.

As I stood staring out into my transitional backyard, quiet and empty, I flipped through my mail. There was a letter from the Magnolia Grove Historical Society, notifying me that my grant application was in its final stages and an on-site inspection was imminent. This was fortuitous timing. It was just as well that the contractor couldn't find workers since my savings were just about depleted. I hadn't been paid in months now. If, however, the historical society deemed my residence of significant historical value, my financial problems would likely be solved. Not only would they pay for future work but all previous work completed in the restoration.

Also in the mail I found another lawsuit from the Neighborhood Association. That made three in the last six months. I made a mental note to slip over to Alfred's in the middle of the night and plow down his rose bushes.

Back in the house, the telephone rang. I dumped the mail onto the kitchen bar and picked up quickly, and an operator's voice started speaking almost immediately:

"Mr. Brown? This is a collect call. Will you accept the charges from Yahnakundra State Prison, prisoner number 466302, Andrew Carl Adler?"

I crouched down suddenly, huddling behind the kitchen table, holding the phone away from my ear, as if I could somehow push him farther away from me. After I heard the operator asking me again from the distance, I put my mouth to the receiver.

"No."

"Come on, man…" came a rough but faint voice in the background, just before the line disconnected.

I had never met Adler, and I had felt sure until that moment that I never would. Until now, I had managed to keep him at a distance. But suddenly I felt that I had somehow dodged a bullet. He had called me on my home phone. Collect. What could he possibly want to talk about? He must have known that I had no power whatsoever to change his fate. As for his immediate needs or comfort, he had the warden; or if there was some other problem, his lawyer.

I poured myself a cup of water and drank it in one gulp. My heart rate began to slow, and my fists unclenched. I felt his invasion, his attention focusing upon me from his prison cell, and it made me nervous, as if I were somehow under his control. What did he want with me? Why hadn't he simply waited until I was back at work, when he almost certainly could have reached me through some kind of normal channels at the prison, rather than wasting his only phone call for the week. If I had accepted the charges I could have asked, but there was no way that would ever happen.

Slowly, another question began to gnaw at me with greater

intensity. How had he managed to track me down? My number remained unlisted, and it ran entirely contrary to office policy to give prisoners, or anyone else for that matter, the personal phone number or address of employees. This struck me more and more as the most important question. He could have a partner on the outside tracking me down. It did not seem a stretch to think that Hero and I might be in some kind of real danger.

Adler's scheduled execution was in four days.

These thoughts, digging at me over the course of the next hour, mining for doubts and fears and frustrated anger, finally drove me to call J.J. Creighton and ask him to meet me at the prison to try to find some answers. I left Hero a note instructing her to not accept collect calls, then scratched that out and wrote another telling her not to answer the phone at all. A killer was on the prowl.

Around the parking lot and into the fields surrounding Yahnakundra, people had already begun camping out. Just a few, a half-dozen passionate people hoping to bring some attention to a cause. They had staked signs that said FRY 'EM UP and BURN, BABY, BURN, but also TURN THE OTHER CHEEK and DON'T KILL IN MY NAME. They pitched small tents or slept in the back of their cars. They toasted marshmallows over propane flames and made friendly waves at me as I pulled in.

The warden laughed and shook his head when I mentioned them. "The bugs are nasty out there this time of year. They'll get eaten alive."

"I'm just thinking of the publicity," I said. "The governor said he wanted a show."

"I know a half-dozen guys who would just love to come out here and beat the crap out of those murderer-loving bastards. They should know, if God wants to stop this execution, he's got my number."

We were in the warden's office, where we could clearly see several of the protesters out in the field tossing around a Frisbee. The execution was coming together. We had the staff, the chef, a time-coordinated schedule that laid out all of Adler's final routine, the last

48 hours. He'd just recently passed his psych exam with flying colors.

"How does a death row inmate get access to a telephone?"

"New procedures. Apparently it's cruel and unusual punishment to not allow them to phone out periodically."

"But how'd he get my number. I'm not listed," I said.

"Don't blame me," the warden said suddenly, handing me my drink.

"I'm not blaming you."

"Good. I'd hate to ruin our working relationship." The warden lit up a pipe, the rich, earthy tobacco chugging out and quickly filling the space around us. "We don't monitor calls anymore, except in national security cases. Courts made sure of that, too. Used to be he couldn't sit on the pot that we didn't know the color of his shit. Now, he could work on Wall Street for all we know."

"He could be working with someone outside. He could try to take me out. I've got a daughter."

"Don't get paranoid."

"Everyone keeps telling me that. Why can't I get paranoid?"

"We could beat it out of him."

"It seems to me a good time to get paranoid."

"Beatings aren't reliable, though. Might serve to piss him off. Could go either way."

I hesitated a moment, then said: "I want to meet him."

"No."

"I'm associate director of goddamned Corrections. That's got to be good for something."

"It's not going to solve anything."

"It will solve things for me. I have to meet him. I won't be able to rest until I know."

"What're you gonna do, ask him nicely?"

"Worth a try," I said.

The cell was tiny, one small window, no bars, a door instead of a gate, and porous cement bricks coated with a beige lacquer. Adler stood up to meet me as I came in. He was in manacles, which they'd attached just before I entered. The guard stood behind me, silent and grim. His eyes never left Adler.

The stench of the cell, of Adler himself, nearly caused me to double over. Being in his presence altered him for me. He seemed smaller in person and less crazed. And in an odd way, this made him seem much more dangerous, facing him in the pale flesh removed the sheen of celebrity. It made him merely human, which in light of his crime was all the more frightening.

"Didn't think you'd come," he said softly.

The officers set up a chair for me, but I just stood behind it and leaned into the backrest. "Seems you wanted to talk."

Adler nodded, but remained silent. He was biting his overgrown mustache, which hung down over his bottom lip. He seemed both familiar and strange to me. I knew so much about him, about his history and his childhood, much of which came from the transcripts from the sentencing phase of his trial. They'd tried to paint a human image of the convicted man for the jury, someone who was as much a victim as the people he had victimized. A child without parents. A wandering soul in search of a place to belong, ridiculed and accosted wherever he went. But perhaps the jury had had the same reaction I did—humanizing him only made his crimes that much worse.

"Why did you call me?" I asked after a minute of silence. It wasn't my first question, but I was taking Creighton's advice to not betray what I most wanted to know. Adler was just staring at me intently. "If you want to beg for mercy, I'm the wrong guy. It's not my decision."

He shook his head. "My lawyer's doing that. Thinks we got a pretty good shot at a stay, too."

"I can't help you." I wanted to believe I wouldn't, even if I could have. As I sat there, I tried to keep in mind the terrible things he'd been convicted of doing.

"I just needed to see you," he said. "Face to face."

"Face to face."

"A man wants to look his killer in the eye."

"I'm not a killer."

"I meant it as a compliment," he said.

"What the hell do you want?"

He kept on looking at me silently with his unnaturally sunken and wet eyes. Truth was, he didn't feel like a killer. He wasn't slight, but every aspect of his movement, each rattle of his chain, came with a lightness that suggested the careful and tentative. It would have been easier to see in his face the lunacy of a killer, rather than this resigned calm of the condemned.

He sighed. "I'm not looking for pity from no one."

"I wasn't offering," I said.

"I don't need your self-righteous bullshit neither. I'm a dead man, only I ain't dead yet."

"I know the feeling."

"I just needed to meet you. That's all. Now I have. Now go the hell away."

I paused a moment, not able to look him in the eye. I replayed the scene again in my mind, again placing Adler into it. The images, the fire, the wire cord snapping her soft neck. But for the face, all I could picture was Hero.

"Why don't you just admit what you've done?"

"What does that matter?" he shrugged. "All anyone cares about is that someone is dying for this."

"How did you get my number?" I asked suddenly, more urgently than I intended.

At this, Adler smiled. "It's a small world."

I tapped the back of the chair with my palm. "I could send someone in there to make you tell me," I said. I didn't sound convincing even to myself.

Adler stood up, pressing against the strains of his chains. "Heck, if you had any balls at all, you'd put a bullet between my eyes yourself right now."

Facing down the cold-blooded, brutal truth of Adler, I felt surprising calm. His death would be a final act of justice in a world where nothing much else seemed fair. But everyone should ultimately face his demons, and Adler had certainly become mine. He had silently stalked me through back alleyways and office corridors and midnight thoughts as I drifted to sleep. He was quietly overwhelming.

Through it all, Adler kept his chilling, calm demeanor.

"Who are you working with?" I asked. My death, this investigation, my daughter, now this: every circumstance conspired against me.

Adler smiled again, but remained silent, then laid back down in his cot, apparently deciding that our brief interview was at an end. I considered again, as I still stood there, taking the warden up on his offer to beat the information out of him. I wondered what methods he might use, what kind of torture would be effective. I wondered if it would make any difference.

As the guard let me out into the corridor, Adler didn't look at me. He made no motion at all. He just laid there staring at the ceiling, mouth moving, as if silently counting down the seconds.

The next morning, I was down at the hall of records, at the base of the city-county building. I showed the clerk my department picture ID and my signed letter from Hal stating that I was, in fact, who I claimed to be, whatever her computer might say to the contrary, and she went to fetch the files I requested. I sat on a couch in the waiting area, leafing through a copy of Modern Mechanics. She brought back a stack of files, those belonging to Adler, as well as the other seven men who still stood on death row. Each contained information from their respective trials—photos, depositions, police reports, interviews, newspaper articles, information about the trials, information about jurors themselves, the kind of things that should never get into the wrong hands. Reading through it all, it was clear just how little agreement there was between them about evidence, even among people who reached the same conclusions: still, they had all found them guilty. Then, for equally various reasons, they all wanted their convicts dead.

A juror said after the trial that you could see the wheels turning in his mind, that the accused was just going to bide his time. He would be patient. Killing him was the only way to make sure that people were safe.

One woman said she didn't think an innocent man would act the way he did. She said she knew he was guilty right away.

Another juror admitted that though he didn't agree with the death penalty himself, he felt it was his responsibility to vote for it. People expected it. It was something that had to be done.

This was a tough decision, another juror had said, because everyone has a mother.

The jurors would often get to know each other intimately. They'd spent a week, sometimes more, in a hotel room together, a week or more huddled in a jury room discussing the weight of the evidence, the character of the defendant, what drove people to do terrible things. They became close.

Two members of a jury met during the trial and were later married. Murder and crisis had a way of bringing people together, just as it tore others apart. Another one eventually wrote a book cataloguing her experience. It spent two weeks atop the best seller list and a major studio optioned the rights.

These seven black faces, plus Adler. Hero had said we condemned minorities for crimes we didn't for whites. What faces were missing here? I wondered. What if you didn't realize you were killing people? What if the people you killed were in the hundreds? What if it was all just a horrible, embarrassing mistake?

In Adler's file, there was a great deal beyond the material from the crime itself, which was certainly graphic enough. There were pictures of the woman's corpse, along with still photographs from her life. A sort of narration for the viewer, an animation of the lifeless, bruised flesh. Hannah Marie Salazin, twenty, single, college student. She was set to graduate in two more years. A major in

Communication. Her apartment stood directly off campus, behind and between a dormitory and a frat house. She worked at a coffee shop down the block, an income supplemental to the money sent by her family. She paid her bills on time.

She'd been strangled by a thin wire, likely a clothes hanger. Evidence of sexual assault. Some money had been taken. The body was not mutilated, and consensus was that she had been killed after the assault. All body parts still intact. The fire that had been started after the attack may have succeeded in burning out the entire front room, the second-floor walkway, and portions of the neighbors' apartments as well, but Hannah's body, resting in the bathtub in the back (pictured), had at most only grown warm.

The prime suspect: her boyfriend, Gerald Cozy, a junior, college football player, defensive end, third string. Always they suspect those closest to the victim, those with reason to feel passions strong enough to kill, because almost always those are the killers. Random violence is rare. The statistics, our leaders remind us, have been going down, down, down.

Those statistics were here, too, though likely not used at trial by the prosecution, and certainly used by the defense. There was the transcript of the trial. It was brief, lasting four days in all, before handing it off to the jury. Without a single witness placing Adler near the scene of the crime, the key to the whole case had been the sexual assault, bodily fluids being probably the only piece of evidence that wasn't destroyed in the fire. DNA tests had indicated Adler, a refrigerator serviceman with some old juvenile sexual assault charges who had done work in the apartment complex a month prior.

I took notes from the transcript, a few from the police investigation, and made a copy of one of the photographs of Hannah. Some holiday at home, a personal moment, family gathered around in festive cheer. She was grinning, foolish and delighted, draped across the lap of her embarrassed father.

thirty-two

Banners draped from the ceiling of the main hall, torn posters and flyers papering the walls. In the corridors, tables set up selling punch and potato chips, plus a candy sale by the Key Club. A chipper young girl handed me a playbill made of green construction paper, creased with care and pasted with bright red lettering. I held it between my fingertips, which left prints and a smear across the surface. Here was the result of hours of labor and dedication—a memento someone wanted to be just perfect. There's something to be said about firsts. They are the most important, and we want to get them exactly right.

There was hazard in the air, the possibility of disaster along with hopeful prayers of families and friends whispered all around.

Opening night and I sat alone in the droning auditorium, right on the aisle to assure myself a clear view. A squad of cheerleaders was on stage, tumbling and jumping before the lowered curtain, leading a half-dozen front row parents in cheers. Everything upbeat and excited. They set the tone. A man with a camcorder was staking out his ground at the front of the auditorium. He wanted front row, unobstructed, full-on. His son or daughter might be the star, or just some figure in the background, occupying space. The set designer. The spotlight operator. Pride runs deep. I recognized some of the parents from the cafeteria. Some were chatting with each other, some eyeing the parents and other children suspiciously. Security was tight, night watchmen all over the place, keeping everyone in line.

The lights dimmed and up rose a chorus of teenage whoops

and hollers. Behind the lifting curtain, rickety cardboard set pieces shaped the scene for two young boys with pitched voices to begin. I found the story difficult to follow, the language bumbling awkwardly from their lips. Mostly I didn't even try to keep up with the banter, the attempted kings and queens and dukes and ladies. I was keeping an eye out for Hero, but she didn't seem to be in this opening act. Instead, an animated teenager played a young queen in a flowing white dress that covered her feet. A large stuffed mound around her belly suggested that she was also supposedly pregnant. My eyes were drawn to her magnetic glow. This wasn't just me, I didn't think. She actually radiated a kind of light. As she argued with this boy who was supposed to be king, her face became a fiery red and her words cut through sharply, arching like darts. As the other actors fluttered in and out with lines—some remembered, some forgotten, all stammering—you could see that she stood far above them all.

A baby began to fidget and gurgle somewhere nearby in the dark. The hushed lisp of whispering voices, the occasional laugh, the silhouetted bodies standing and shuffling across rows, going in and going out. More arguing on the stage. One boy became animated. He hadn't spoken before and he was rising up at this moment, giving a performance that made most everything else seem oddly out of place, and hardly what would qualify as good. This was his one shot and he was giving it his every and his all. The next actor forgot his line, and after a minute of pause, the woman at the piano finally shouted it out. A baby began to scream horribly. The king distrusted his wife, substituting what he could not know for what he suspected. Camcorder man stood up at the front row; he was rushing the stage now, moving up and zooming in for the tight close-up, shot perfectly framed.

Everyone was adorable, children dressed up, assuming the cares and joys of not only adults, but grave figures out of the fantastical past. It was a past that didn't exist and had never happened, Hero had told me when she first got the part, and it certainly wasn't happening now.

Events turned dark, then tragic, as best we could make out between whispered and flubbed lines. The queen apparently had her baby, then later left the stage in a swoon, effectively real and heartbreaking. Soon, another girl returned to proclaim that she was dead. We hadn't reached the end of the first act, and already her part appeared to be over. Though I hadn't yet seen Hero, I felt the strong urge to leave as the other actors muddled about incomprehensibly on stage. My mind drifted as the play continued, a story long and, but for the death at the beginning, remarkably without drama. You could sense the growing impatience, a collective restlessness of the audience. Coughs and raising voices, the shuffle of bodies and bags. One family, taking up more than half of one row near the back, rose and left out the back door. Perhaps they were there only to support the dead queen.

I nearly failed to notice when my daughter appeared on the stage. Young Perdita, the little baby from the womb, left for dead, appearing now quite suddenly fully grown, complete with boyfriend. Watching her up there, I felt closer to her than I had in weeks, much like I had when following her. I was a voyeur again, but she was acting for the world and, unlike at home, I could admire her without fear of recrimination. The truth was, she was almost certainly little better than the other kids wandering on and off set. But what struck me was her enthusiasm, her dedication to her part—a role she knew inside and out.

We were approaching the end, and the dead queen was suddenly up on stage again, still and silent, frozen in place, a blue spotlight illuminating her. Both audience and actors gasped in wonder at her, so statuesque, so life-like. Didn't she move? Didn't she blink? A silence settled across the room as she came down off the pedestal; the piano struck up a chord. Some sobs across the room, in the darkness. A coming together, a queen and her king, with the uncomfortable and brief kiss of budding teens. Hero stood beside them, a long-lost daughter reunited with the father who had abandoned her and the mother everyone thought dead and gone.

Everything all aglow. The curtain closed and the house lights brightened. A curtain call with staggered bows, furious cheers. Hero bowed deep, and I thought the audience of her classmates roared especially loudly for her. The cast slipped backstage, and after the clapping did not cease, they came back, bowed once more, and were gone.

"Entertaining, at least." Janice was suddenly standing beside me as I still clapped while the crowd began to disperse. Despite the numerous posted signs, she had lit a cigarette and was puffing unconcerned.

"I didn't know you were coming."

"Like I'd miss Junior's literal moment in the spotlight."

"She did pretty well, I thought," I said.

"It's important for her father to say that. You might even tell her." She dropped the cigarette onto the cement floor and mashed it with her heel, then seemingly unconsciously pulling out and lighting another. "So. Tomorrow's your big day."

"Adler's big day, anyway. He should be just about finished with his last meal by now." Technically, this wouldn't be his "last" because the warden would make sure he ate something first thing in the morning to tide him over for the rest of the day. But it was tradition for the official last meal to be dinner, even if modern advances in killing necessitated it happen a day early. Creighton planned to sit with him and feed him some Bible verses, too. I'd asked if that wouldn't violate some church-state separation, but he said he wasn't worried whether a dead man would sue.

"Any famous last words from the condemned?"

"He called me. Adler did."

"I heard. How did he find you?"

"Maybe his lawyer did some poking around, though he denies it." With Creighton I'd perused the prison logs, but Adler's only visitors had been his legal representation and a minister. I suspect them both. It was better than the eerie possibility that there was someone out there working with him, someone who could possibly try to hurt Hero or myself in revenge. There were no copies or records of his correspondences. Creighton said they only read the mail of those inmates deemed dangerous, and the condemned, friendless man didn't fit the bill.

"Junior doesn't know you're here, does she?" Janice asked.

"She didn't ask me not to come."

"But you came without an invitation—and knowing you weren't expected to. Interesting."

"Someone has to look out for her," I said.

Janice cast me a quick sidelong look. "Oh, my! You're here to protect her! How adorable are you?"

"Please."

"I miss you, Matty. We never talk."

"I open the paper every day afraid of what I'm going to see. It's not enough that I've got the special prosecutor's office breathing down my neck."

"That's good, though," she said. "You should be more scared of me than them."

"So, I'm right that you've found something?"

She smiled wryly, taking a long drag from her cigarette and shaking her head.

"Tell Junior I thought she was great."

After Janice left, I loitered in the auditorium, long after the show had ended, and longer still after the crowds of parents had gone walking off with children in tow. I stood amid the throngs near the stage, parents and teachers and children talking loudly with heavy breaths and uncontainable smiles. I caught periodic flashes of Hero through the busy onstage rush, running there and back across the stage, adrenaline pumped, laughing and chasing other members of the company, her long dress hiked and gathered in her arms to avoid tripping. But as the crowd thinned, she appeared less and less. I pushed my way to the front, hoping to catch her eye, to show her that despite everything I had still come. But when she didn't appear, I thought that perhaps she had gone. I knew there was a cast party she was going to, a nearly all-night affair with the entire cast and crew at the director's house. But I'd thought, hoped, that she might come out looking for me, to see if maybe I had come after all. In that moment, I would have tried to tell her what it was I felt right then: that she was wonderful, that her future was bright, and that I'd never experienced the sense of swelling pride that I'd felt that evening.

When they started to shut down the lights, and the last of the crew was walking the aisles picking up trash, I finally headed back up the aisle alone.

thirty-three

Turning off the highway and down the prison lane, we found ourselves driven into the midst of a carnival—the warden and myself and a print reporter who had been chosen as the official witness. Cars filled every spot, bordered the narrow road and overflowed out into the street. We had to dodge pedestrians who were walking to join the event. There were tents set up, booths and tables and blankets. It reminded me immediately of the flea market, except for the tone, which was heavy and passionate. In one corner, a quiet group prayed intensely, vocally, candles lit and wax dripping. All around them rolled the lunatic fringe, left and right. Many were holding cardboard signs. They hollered at each other. They hollered at passing cars and walkers. They raised their voices to heaven. The cacophony was such that I half expected the skies to open up and the hand of God to reach down and smite someone. Everyone. A vanguard gathered around our car as we made our way to the gate. Perhaps they believed they would find the executioner himself in here, behind these dark windows. We were trying to arrive incognito, but that wasn't going so well.

A jumbled phalanx of bodies blocked our way.

Television reporters had gathered, including Angelie. I could see her piercing eyes through the glass and was thankful at that moment to not be the official spokesman who would have to face her questions. They were interviewing a sobbing woman, a victim's relative or perhaps just a sympathetic sinner who felt everyone else's pain, who cried for our state, our culture. A man at a booth was selling T-shirts with lightning bolt decals across the front, along with jumbo letters that said, "JUSTICE!" Another woman being interviewed had gone red in the face as she became more and more animated. She was calling for life, calling for death, I just couldn't tell.

I felt weak, impotent in the face of this swelling mass. They were the ones with power. If only they had been of one mind.

My phone rang, and I put it to my ear.

"I'm hoping you're making some arrangements for a last-second interview with Adler for me."

Angelie was standing right outside the car window, somehow staring right at me despite the opaque tinting, phone at her ear.

"You know I can't do that."

"Then how about letting me observe the execution? I'm your girlfriend, for Chrissakes."

"I thought you didn't use labels."

"I'm begging," she said, leaning into the glass.

"You're putting me in a difficult position," I said, shifting in my seat. I wanted to turn away from her, to get away from that stare, but even though the glass was totally opaque, it seemed like she saw right through me. "We already have a print journalist. The law is specific. I've told you that."

"I used to write for my school paper. That's got to count for something."

"I'm sorry. I can't." The car jolted, inching forward as the guards cleared space around the vehicle.

"Come on, Matthew. This is my ticket out of here."

"It's out of my hands now."

The car jerked forward again. She took a step forward to keep pace and punched the car door with her palm. "We are so through."

"You're breaking up with me?"

"You have no idea how much."

The security guards finally cleared enough space to let us through the main gate and into the courtyard, closing out the mass swarming behind us. We stopped in a bright corner near the entrance. There was only one door, the only other way in or out being over the wall. The thick crowd called after us as we stepped into the night air, and somewhere in all that mass was Angelie, probably cursing up a storm. How fitting, it struck me, that our virtual relationship should come to a virtual end.

Up in Creighton's office, everyone was gathered, though the crowd was small, just a few more than a dozen people: one guard, but the rest civilians. Conversation hummed in the low breathy tone of whispers. Across the desk, a plastic tablecloth was set, a pitcher of red Kool-Aid, small sugar cookies, some M&Ms.

A man about my age, with slicked-back hair, came up to me as I entered the room. He identified himself as a college friend of Hannah's, shaking my hand and thanking me, though I had no idea for what. I was a cog in this machine, a piece of a large apparatus that we perceive as justice. Adler was getting what was coming to him, finally, but it could just as easily have been Caldwell's funeral we were ordering here. If the state hadn't screwed up the other executions, it almost certainly would have been, long before anyone thought to figure out he wasn't guilty.

Perhaps I knew too much. I knew where Adler was at this moment. I knew every content of his "last meal" from the night before—and the fact that after ordering a virtual smorgasbord, he'd simply looked at it silently and not touched a bite. I knew he had finished his true last meal around 9 this morning (oatmeal, eggs, bacon, juice), early enough to ensure that his stomach would be empty by midnight. Trial and error in other states had illustrated the danger of eating too close to electrocution. He was waiting in the holding cell right then, shaven and half-naked. Just waiting. They removed every bit of excess hair from his body, in order to give the electrodes unimpeded access to his skin. I knew that, too.
I didn't want to talk with anyone. The friend shifted over to the prosecutor, who was standing nearby. I slipped into the corner by the window. Out in front of the prison, the carnival was buzzing.

The school bus was gone but the crowd continued to swell, mostly concentrated in front of the camera lights.

The warden came over to me, leaning in to whisper.

"We good to go?"

"It's your show," I said.

"Damn straight."

He called for everyone's attention and asked for a moment of silence. He closed his eyes and bowed his head and I saw most of the others do the same. People reached out to hold hands, and the woman next to me grabbed mine. The guard by the door and I stared at each other. The warden then pulled out his Bible.

"The courts say we're not supposed to do this, but screw 'em."

He read several passages, pausing between them only to turn to the next. It was earnest and powerful. There was a lot of wrath there, vengeance, too. The warden became animated. He slammed the book shut with a snap and took a deep breath with his eyes closed.

"Let's go," he said.

We migrated from the warden's office to the special wing where the execution was to take place. It was a lengthy walk across the compound. The dark night was cut a thousand ways with bleeding floodlights. One of these followed our whole path, this cluster of twelve people, huddled together in an uncomfortable clump. As we walked, I was introduced to the parents of the victim.. I recognized the father from the picture I had copied, and here he looked out of place and empty without her. The mother bore enough of a resemblance to Hannah to make it obvious. State law granted them the right to be present at the execution. I spoke to each of them separately. They did not walk together, and in fact they refused to be in close proximity to each other. Someone whispered to me that it had been nine years since they had said a word to each other. The wounds upon the remnants of their lives still raw and untouchable.

The viewing room was dimly lit but comfortable. People acted uncertain about taking seats. No one seemed to want the front row. Only half ended up sitting, everyone immediately restless. Adler's warrant opened at midnight, and we were determined that he wouldn't go much longer than that.

Twenty minutes before midnight, Adler came in, almost unrecognizable with his hair and moustache entirely shaved away. For a moment, I wondered if they'd brought the wrong inmate. He walked in on his own, looking up at all of us. The glass through which we viewed him had, until that moment, seemed almost opaque, a one-way mirror or a screen separating us from the room. We would be voyeurs, present as witnesses but absent to the scene. Now, suddenly, he was staring right at all of us, and we were forced to confront the face of impending death.

Still, it didn't feel real. We were watching someone die tonight, but it still didn't feel like anything more than a process. Not that the feeling mattered. It was happening. It would be done.

I cradled the cell phone that was my direct line from the governor, should some last-minute miracle need to come down. I made sure it was on and fully charged, but moved it from ringer to buzzer.

The guards led him toward the chair but let him seat himself. They had a bucket of saltwater, and they began to rub his arms and head with sopping sponges. Some of the water fell into his eyes. He squinted.

In that photograph Hannah had been young and happy and unsuspecting, sitting on her father's lap. I saw, too, the images from the crime scene, the burnt-out apartment, the limp and contorted body in the bathtub, naked, cold, staring.

In this moment, I knew Adler was right. I was a killer. Or at least some part of me wanted to be.

When they strapped the cap to his head, Hannah's mother released a strange sound, a nervous excitement or anxiety. Here, I thought, is where past and present would overlap. But the one person who really should be here, the person for whom this was most clearly meant, was absent: Hannah herself, washed away from the earth in one violent act. There was no passion in the act. Not even vengeance. That seemed wrong. Here, now, there was only Andrew Carl Adler and the cold force of the act. And he was not long for the world.

Strapped in, facing his executioners, his victims, his peers, the warden asked him if he had any last words.

Adler didn't respond. He sat there, jaw clenched and strained, eyes moving from one person to the next. The warden shook his head and looked to me. I double-checked the cell phone, the battery. The wall clock said less than thirty seconds to midnight. Formality dictated we let the minute stretch out to its full length.

Nineteen, eighteen, seventeen, sixteen…

We were holding on. I looked from the warden to the executioner to the mother, then the father, then to Adler.

Twelve, eleven, ten, nine…

…eight…seven…

A piercing screech of siren sounded out suddenly through the corridors. Everyone startled. Adler exhaled in a quick shout. A young guard rushed hurriedly into the room and started to whisper to the warden. Then two more, nervously looking around, rifles held high, confusion all around. The guards standing in with Adler looked uncertain. Even my executioner seemed perplexed, head jerking behind his black veil. The warden grabbed the arm of the officer beside him and began to issue terse orders quietly into his ear. Then he made a signal to the guards in the other room, and they began to unplug Adler, his body locked and eyes squeezed so tightly that he screamed when touched. As he cast confused looks around the room, they stood him up and carried him down the hall. In my pocket, the cell phone was silent.

"Sorry, folks. There's an urgent situation that has to be resolved, and we have to take Mr. Adler back to his cell for the time being."

Creighton leaned up to my ear. "We've got a problem," he said softly. Then without clarifying, he left the room and another guard arrived in a moment, this one armed with a shotgun, and escorted us back across the courtyard. Sirens were pealing into the night, searchlights circling like a circus act, chasing every shadow.

Back in the warden's office, we could finally see the trouble. There was pandemonium in the carnival. Shouts and screams elevated above the crowd. Bodies bounded across the parking lot, through the field, jumping, almost as if performing a chaotic dance in orange suits pale under the moonlight. They pushed through the clash of protestors and supporters, who found themselves quickly overrun. The mass descended upon the residential neighborhood, through suburban streets. The outlet strip mall parking lots. Bead and craft stores. Shoe warehouses. The refurbished Piggly Wiggly.

Information was coming in slowly to us, overheard conversations between the guards, who kept us locked down. Fifty-eight men from block L, mostly white collar criminals, were on the run. Junk bonders sent up for thirty years after stealing retirement funds from depression-era penny-pinchers. Accountants who'd committed corporate fraud, with children in Harvard. Wasted politicians with devastated careers and nothing left to lose. A computer hacker—a lead programmer of our office design software in Work for Justice— had somehow used his privileges through Work for Justice to find a way to open the cell doors.

Warden Creighton issued orders. He wanted every last mother's son of them taken—dead or alive.

thirty-four

In the first blush of dawn, I was being driven alone back downtown and back toward the capitols, old and new. As they rose above the tree line, they appeared to be bleeding light—reds and yellows and blues strung around and around from base to tip. Twenty-five continuous stories of flashing color. I pulled up and parked at the curb for a better look. On the grounds beneath and between the buildings, a crowd of extras was similarly wrapped up in combinations of flashing bulbs and cellophane banners. They moved hulkingly, each one dragging their weighted form around, spinning, jerking and toppling over. A few shorted out. One figure caught an arm on fire and then raced out into the gathered crowd before being thrown to the ground by technical personnel and extinguished.

Beneath the barely contained anarchy, there appeared to be a choreographed routine.

A sporadic crowd congregated at the base, onlookers, apparently unconnected with the display. Or perhaps they were part of it, knowingly or not. What is a performance without an audience, after all? There was an empty parking spot out front and I couldn't resist the urge to stop. Walking among them, I recognized many people from my office and the other halls of government. Many were as wide-eyed as I felt, like we had all stumbled across something magical and ludicrous.

Ahead of the crowd, I saw a team of photographers. They were snapping sequences of pictures, rapid-fire, too fast for anyone to keep up. Among them, one unmistakable figure stood out, with his tubbish girth, curly mop, and long colorful smock hanging down to his knees. The paper had featured a story on the artist, Richard McCormick, who was famous worldwide for his installations, which made use of well-known natural and man-made structures. Apparently, he'd seen our strange setup of capitol buildings and was "moved to create," as he put it, and now was shouting directions to the dancers, his team of photographers and a lone videographer as they made their artistic statement.

We could only get as close as the sidewalks, where people from all walks of life had gathered—the indigent, the elderly, the young, the poor, the wealthy. Most everyone appeared to be here like I was, in transition, stopping off on their way somewhere else. A young couple stood next to me, disheveled but finely dressed, he with his tux and tails, open at the collar, and for her a prom-like evening dress, oddly bunched and gathered.

I paced for a moment, looking for a way to get through the obstacles to the main entrance. I was running late and didn't really feel at ease to dawdle. But still I stood there for a few more minutes with the scattered crowds, watching McCormick prance around with an intensity and determination I had rarely seen in another human being, herding a flock of electric-light sheep across the green.

Then, I jumped the slight barricade and sifted through the extras, ignoring the yells from McCormick about disrupting the flow. I didn't have time to care. Despite myself, I actually liked the strange cellophane installation and its dancing light bulbs. In the face of the reality of the capitol buildings, and the insanity it produced in our state, I thought McCormick had perfectly captured the silliness of it all. But I was late, and so I pushed my way through, up the steps, and in through the main doors and to the awaiting, open private elevator.

Bertrand Walker's office was unchanged, except for the streaming purple and pink banners now draped outside his window, through which the morning sun cast a pastel light across the floor. Walker himself was sitting at his desk, already on the phone with the warden, and put it on speaker as I entered. He struck me as slightly unkempt—his tie pulled less tight, his shirt more wrinkled—but still fastidious to the extreme. The election was in a week, and dealing with a massive prison break, we were faced with a crisis that bound all of our fates together.

"What I need to know, J.J., is what we're going to tell people about the ones you haven't yet caught."

"These dipshits aren't dangerous. They're more likely to give someone a million bucks to keep them quiet than hurt anyone."

"Good God, we can't tell the public that. We'd never catch any of them."

Walker gestured for me to sit in the large chair in front of the desk. After a long night holed up at the prison, we'd finally been allowed to leave, but only once they'd secured all the surrounding grounds and checked every person and car in the area. I was the one who had to call Walker and inform him about both the aborted execution and the prison break. With the warden out on a manhunt, he'd wanted to meet with me first thing, and the three of us needed to coordinate the message going forward.

"How much do we need to say?" I asked.

"I think we need to downplay the number," Walker said. "Make it something far less intimidating. We are going to look like idiots if they get the real number, and we'll lose in a landslide."

"There are about two dozen still on the run," Creighton said.

"That's good. We'll focus on the number we've already caught and rounded up. As for the number on the loose, cut it in half and then again. So, we'll say about six still at large. If they ask how many escaped in the first place, just talk about the larger number that attempted to get out but were caught immediately in the prison yard. We'll let Matthew here deal with the press after that."

"When did you catch so many?" I asked. "I heard you'd only recovered about a couple when I left the prison half an hour ago."

"Just got word we caught up with about thirty of them, huddled behind a shopping mall, searching a Dumpster for clothes. Stupid sucks."

"The biggest concern is that we've lost the execution," Walker noted.

"It was a split-second call," Creighton said. "It's against prison policy to run an execution during lockdown. I don't make those rules. Talk to my bosses at Qual-Tech. They run the show."

"I thought it was your castle," I said.

"It is my castle," he growled. "I'll take out Adler tomorrow, if you want."

"The governor needed this execution,," Walker said. "That's all we're saying." Then he pressed his fingers together and leaned back in his chair. "Okay, J.J. We'll leave you to sort out the capture. Keep me posted when you find the rest."

He tapped the phone with his index finger and the line went dead. He didn't look over at me at first, continuing to lean back and stare up at the ceiling, processing the situation, before finally easing forward with a sigh.

"The timing here is the problem," he said heavily. "What's the situation with Adler? Any chance we can still squeeze this in before election day?"

"No. No chance," I said. "I've been told his lawyer has already filed another appeal in light of the abrupt stoppage of his execution. His warrant expires in 30 days and from what I understand, this latest issue will probably take at least that long to resolve. Cruel and unusual punishment to nearly put someone to death, I understand. The court may even revisit the whole question of the death penalty in this light. Not saying it'll be overturned again, but you probably couldn't even get a warrant signed and executed on another inmate. The courts would stop that right in its tracks."

Walker nodded slightly.

"We were very close. Now things are all screwed up, pretty badly. The law and order governor who botches an execution and allows the largest prison break in state history. Not the kind of press we need."

"It was beyond my control."

Walker shook his head. "I'm not blaming you. These things happen, and it's how we deal with them that matters more. We should treat this as an opportunity. We'll double down on the law and order line, introduce a new initiative calling for ten times the punishments for escaping inmates. In times of crisis, people want the guy who gives the best answers. We'll worry about who will take the fall later. There's always someone."

I felt myself starting to nod off, and he laughed softly.

"Go issue that press release and go home, Matthew. I think we'll avoid any press conference until we see what the backlash is. I think the governor can take the lead on this one."

Standing again in this office, I thought about Walker's previous suggestion of a political future. It all seemed so distant, nearly lost now behind a hedge of scandal and catastrophe and decay.

By the time I left Walker's office, it was fully light and McCormick and his colleagues had dispersed, leaving the buildings once again to their usual décor, as if none of this had happened. I walked across the courtyard, then the street, over to Corrections, filed the press release, and picked up my car from the lot where I'd left it the night before. A Sunday morning calm stretched across the city, with easy flows down major roadways, a hush upon us like the calm after an exhale. Spent, I needed to retreat, an escape back into the quiet of a past that promised me absolution.

Back at my partially reconstructed house, though, I found Hero half asleep in the chair by the front window.

"Should we be talking ground rules?" she yawned. "You should have called."

"It was crazy. It won't happen again."

"I didn't think it would happen the first time. You're over thirty, for goodness sake. Go to your room."

thirty-five

Alone, I settled into the living room couch, collapsing from the overwhelming weight of exhaustion due to the past twelve hours. I leaned back on the arm, a pillow beneath my neck, bourbon in a plastic cup on the floor. An old movie played on the television, a story I didn't recognize and couldn't quite follow with the sound down low. It starred Gary Cooper and Clark Gable. After a time, I began to wonder if someone was playing a trick on me, or if perhaps this was some comical mistake. Two different films cut together like one. It was a western and a romantic comedy, cowboys and flappers. Maybe it was some gag reel, or a documentary special about old films, but it just kept going on between the two. It could have been some arty experimental film they showed at half-empty theaters downtown. I had no context at all. Worse, it did nothing to distract me from my own progressively anxious thoughts.

I could have stood to raise the sound, but I stayed where I was.

Lying here, all I could think about was death—those near death, the walking dead and the reprieved, those still awaiting and those since gone. Adler and that look in his eyes as he faced his certain end and Hannah's infectious smile, blissfully ignorant of the brutal fate on her horizon.

This was hardly the end, even if Adler ended up winning a permanent stay. He was only the first in what promised to be a long line, now that prosecutors could seek the death penalty again. There were seven other inmates on death row, a number that was certain to grow. Did these men sit in their tiny cells and contemplate their crimes? Did they lament their actions or the result? Did they curse the people or God who put them there? Did they believe in a just world? Were they the innocent wrongly condemned or the guilty facing justice? Everyone's done something, Hal had said. So what were these men guilty of, each with their own personal crimes and misdemeanors? Seven men all waiting for their day. And Adler, wondering again when—if ever—the axe would fall.

I was more than just a part of this system, Hero said, but the enactor of the vast injustice that condemns not just the convicted, but us all. I wondered, would my own crimes of omission, in the end, make the blood on their hands pale in comparison?

The evening settled, its dark and heavy shade, people dozing on couches and in their bedrooms. People wander because they cannot sleep, cannot think, and simply moving, you hope, will do you good. The young hipsters, long past curfew, owning the streets, drag racers speeding down dim avenues, midnight bowlers, laser light trippers, convenience store malt liquor binges and long drags on menthols and cloves.

The trucks navigating the neighborhoods, the tanks towed behind whispering along with the nightly breezes.

Late at night, once the revelers dispel, it takes no time to get anywhere. The town almost spins beneath you, homes running past in a shimmering blur. There's nothing to stop you, nothing to even slow you down. Soon you're passing the hospital, the graveyards, the governor's mansion. Everything speeds past you like you're standing still, a uniform blur. This is how it goes, in dreams and flights of fancy.

The lights of Yahnakundra radiate a yellow hue, illuminating the entire lot. Not a shrub nor tree anywhere, not a single shadow. It's another daytime. There's a haze about as cool night mists are caught in the glare of the halogens and fluorescents.

Through the main gate, up to the entrance. They are watching, always watching. A buzzer opens the door and the guards are there as if they could do nothing else, perpetually sharp and alert. Walking through the metal detector, the flash and the ring. It's a part of the job, it's an understood thing. What else could they do? They call for assistance, a large guard named Eddie, twenty years on the force and he'll tell you, man, has he seen some things. He leads the way through the dim-lit halls. He could do it blind, he knows every step in the dark.

Even killers sleep the sleep of angels.

Adler in his cell, wrapped tight in the thin sheet, huddled down but facing the door. You don't turn your back here, not for an instant. Yet he sleeps, still and peaceful, a man undisturbed. The bolts to the door pull back, surprisingly soft and light, and there in the room he lies unmoving. His eyes are open, but he's not looking at anything in particular. What allows people to sleep without closing their eyes? What dreams have overtaken him, swept him up in their stories, their colors and shining lights? Where has he been and where is it he is going?

Then, the pistol fires, almost of its own accord.

All sound and smoke, echo upon echo around the room, up and down the corridors, spilling out into the streets and into the secured homes and the innocent quiet of bedrooms. Adler swallows his bullet whole, rocking back in his bed, not a word or sound. His pale open eyes then blink, as if startled out of something, in time to see the face of death, and he rolls off the edge of the cot onto the floor in a sinking heap that splatters across the dull cement.

There are guards everywhere. They seemed to crawl out of the walls, first eyes, then uniformed bodies, heads and legs and arms lifting Adler up and carrying him away. Shouts ring out down the halls. But the shot, Adler's shot, still echoes, and they yell to be heard above its call. He wheezes as they turn him over, his chest now a bloody mush. Eddie lifts him onto his back, that massive strength rising up. As he's carted by, one eye continues to stare, still and focused on nothing at all.

The quiet of those black early hours, the slow and steady retreat through unaware streets. What fears still plague people in the darkness? What fire still burns in them? What will ever make them happy? Out here, driving in the dark, up and down neighborhood avenues, creeping slowly, carefully, meandering through these streets and back alleys, searching for what you know you'll find.

The trucks are out there, with their sweet, versatile poison, slipping through ventilation, clogging air purifiers. It invades the home, hiding deep in cupboards, under cabinets, and dripping off the walls. It's silent but waiting in your household cleansers, your pesticides, your additives and preservatives, unlisted, unspecified, entirely under the radar.

Not that it matters to you, really, because you are already dead and have just about given up on ever fully coming back to life. It's far easier at this point than trying to reanimate yourself. There's no way around it. In the fog of nighttime, into the wild surrounding, you will be allowed to pass away.

But this is not the end. What else to call you now but a ghost, dead but not gone, alive but without substance. Nothing for it but to haunt. Clinging to a past that no longer exists in the present. Or perhaps a rebirth, finding a place for fatherhood and friendship and compassion, letting the avenging angel lie in his shallow grave.

A telephone rang, its metallic rattle calling to me from another life. It rang again. Then again. Then again. Then stopped. The television ran soundless—happiness now comes in a little yellow pill, SouthWorld Theme Park opens next week, the governor loves children, hates criminals, protects, defends, serves. Then Hero is standing over me, holding my cell phone, and I'm rising up from the arbor of dreams to hear the sonorous lilt of Hal, the bearer of tidings, his voice smooth, but brimming with satisfaction.

Andrew Carl Adler was dead.

thirty-six

The airwaves were thick with nonstop political ads and endorsements. Politicians knocked door-to-door, sweating in the fierce heat as the cooling drift of autumn gave way to an Indian summer. The once-regular rains had slowed to a trickle. Over the course of the month, the whole county had become crisp and dusty. Lawns had faded to a light brown. My neighbors were out early with hoses, wearing their khaki shorts and black socks, obsessively watering brown patches, spraying passing electioneers and school children speeding by on bicycles.

Adler was dead. Really dead, officially due to natural causes. Hal had explained that the reported cause had been a spontaneous cerebral hemorrhage, leading to an irreversible injury to the brain stem. This had happened a week ago now, in the middle of Sunday evening, following the botched execution. Tests were immediately run. Prison doctors hypothesized that it could have been stress-related; there was, apparently, a history in the family. Several guards who witnessed the onset had been interviewed. A freak accident, they determined. An act of God, the fickle roll of chance. With no next-of-kin to claim the body, the warden had quickly and quietly ordered it cremated, a violation of numerous state laws. But Qual-Tech policy was specific about the rules and procedure, if not the speed, even as it stood in contradiction to other laws and obligations, and with questions over the state's contract and jurisdiction, politicians would need to resolve the conflicts in next year's session. None of that mattered for Adler, whose ashes would eventually be scattered, per his request, over the nearby pond visible from his lone cell window.

They had ways, Creighton had said. It was all too easy.

No doubt, letters of protest would be sent by the requisite organizations. Reporters would stand outside the prison walls, making sad expressions, their voices filled with pity and concern. There would be a brief inquiry, with questions raised about how two dozen prisoners had died under suspicious circumstances like this under Creighton's watch over the past two decades. I could see all of this unfold, but I let Hal handle the details. His review was done, he said, and we both knew he was made for this sort of thing. As for me, I was finished. There was no returning to my old life now—dead done through.

As I sat at the breakfast table, letting my coffee infuse me, Hero walked in with the morning paper. She had it stretched out to read the front page, her face drained and long.

"What is it?" I asked.

"You tell me," she said, placing the paper on the table.

My face was plastered across the front page, side by side with Bernie Morr and four other men I knew only by their captions. Agency heads, corporate power brokers and state legislators. Stanton was pictured, too, off to one side, unlike the rest of us who were featured against the melodramatic graphic of gray prison bars.

Janice had finally betrayed me.

The exposé was titled A SYSTEM OF FAILURE, and early on it became clear that by "failure" Janice meant me. Relying primarily on "inside sources" and "those familiar with the investigation," the article was damning, but it also represented for me a kind of release, the break of thunder after a sharp flash, finally answering questions that had been plaguing me these several months. What it showed me was that things were better—and far worse—than I had ever imagined.

She explained here, as she had for me, the function of backdoors, and how various corporations—pharmaceutical companies, textile industries— aided by politicians and other government figures, had spent a great deal of effort to exploit this system, which was specifically designed to prevent these very abuses. What shocked me here was the sheer scope of the whole thing. We were talking about not just Whelks-Deprado, the makers of Lychroson and sundry other chemicals and compounds, but nearly 30 companies, representing a dozen different industries. All of these companies, Janice explained, fully recognized the value of the Bureau of Environmental Study's approval, and all of them had exploited the "inept management" to one degree or another, according to government and industry sources.

Of hundreds of reports the bureau had reviewed where allegedly dangerous chemicals were involved, not a single one had been rejected. This was true, according to Janice's sources, even in many cases where the bureau's own commissioned reports had recommended rejection.

As stunning as it probably seemed to readers, this all made sense to me. The only times I specifically remembered rejecting any project was where there were particular high profile considerations—a lawsuit, a public complaint—and Bernie and I had gone over it together. For the rest, the simple truth was that I signed whatever I was asked to sign, the hard work having been done long before it appeared on my desk. Anyone counting on me to make a decision didn't understand me well. Shirley Sue and Bernie knew my inadequacy, even if they exploited it in entirely different ways. I read little or nothing and understood less—something everyone else seemed to know about me all too well. Not that this was any kind of excuse or defense—I, along with everyone else, had trusted that these bureaucratic hoops would work to protect us, as redundancy built upon redundancy. Certainly, the idea of that security was what my entire career had been based upon—the assurance that someone else, somewhere, was on top of things. But in the end, it was a paradox—both my blind faith in the complex maze of the system and the reforms created to streamline that system—that had converged to destroy me.

All systems break down, eventually, succumbing to the entropy of time. The center cannot hold.

Janice, however, acknowledged that the specifics of the chemicals involved were impossible to verify. Though numerous people she spoke with made many allegations, most of which were corroborated independently by each other, the paper trail itself was essentially off limits, barred by copyright laws and the state special investigators, who had locked down both the Bureau of Environmental Study and the Consumer Protection Agency, raising complaints from both activists and local prosecutors that they are unable to get access to any information. Reporters' requests to investigators for copies were also denied due to privacy concerns.

"Our cases are dying," DeSilva County Prosecutor Ken Whithead said. "This special investigation is sucking all the oxygen from the room, and whether they intend so or not, the result is that they're hindering these other investigations and limiting the prosecution of potential crimes." Leader investigator William Stanton would only comment that the investigation was in process. Any further details, he was not at liberty to divulge.

I had been outed on the front page of the state's largest paper as a dupe with little natural talent of my own, a clueless lackey hopping from political appointment to political appointment, assigned jobs like Environmental and Corrections more for my lack of technical know-how than to serve any sort of dubious purpose. All true. Despite this, there was one overriding point of relief that Janice made perfectly clear.

As dangerous and stupid as I had been, my actions were, contrary to the prison-toned picture of me on the cover, perfectly legal.

The director of the bureau had full legal discretion to ignore any recommendation made by the research teams. As a result, whatever harm my actions may have caused, there was essentially no recourse to be taken against me—or anyone else for that matter, of a legal nature, anyway. Bribery, like what Bernie was charged with, was another matter. Those were simple prosecutable acts. Potentially releasing hundreds of Lychrosons upon the people in our state, at who knew what cost to the public health and the lives of innocents—none of this technically broke any law whatsoever.

I began to feel nauseous and weak. And what of the people who knew, I wondered? What of those who planned and perpetrated these acts? What of the people who had hired me in the first place, the unknowing dupe, the fool to do their bidding—someone to turn a blind eye, to stand down, to kill. What of Bertrand Walker, who certainly had to know of all this but was still nowhere to be found in this article? Small fries, like me, like Bernie, like the two-bit legislator, we were the ones being set up to pay the price. As Walker had said, there's always someone to take the fall.

Without any paper trail, she wrote, it was impossible for anyone to know the extent of the danger to the public of any of these actions.

I picked up my keys off the counter and left Hero sitting there, shouting questions at me I just ignored as I raced out the door to the truck. The wind and speed shook the old frame as I drove, rattling as if it might fall apart, engine whining and sputtering the whole way. I needed to know, needed to see what all I had done. I could tear the warehouse apart, box by box, until I knew the full extent of the damage. It was years too late, and I still knew next to nothing about my job at the bureau, but I could find people who did, like Jennifer Thorn Jackson. Like Shirley Sue. We could begin to undo some of this, perhaps even save some lives, I could maybe find for myself some measure of absolution.

However, as I slowed the truck to a stop at the storage facility, I found the hangar door already thrust open. It was utterly empty. Not one box, not one cabinet, not one file or even a scrap of paper. Nothing remained. My footfalls pounded with an echo in the now seemingly mammoth building. The floor had been swept clean, all traces removed. Not even the lock on the door remained. Everything had been carried off, either by investigators searching for answers or someone else with enough sense to realize the dangerous truths contained within.

❧

Hero was sitting in the living room, the morning's paper opened up all across the floor, laying out the multiple spreads for the article. She should have been off at school, but I was in no position to question her. I dropped myself down into the chair by the front door, tossed my keys to the coffee table, and leaned into the armrest. She was scribbling in her notebook, copying elements from Janice's story or arguing with herself—or composing another study, perhaps. She hadn't tested me at all since before our confrontation. But at least the insulting notes had tapered off recently to occasional updates concerning her whereabouts. We were tired, seeped in our mutual exhaustion. Everything had seemingly run its course.

I watched the ceiling fan spin, blades coated in a thick layer of dust.

"I told you she was dangerous," she said at last, still writing in her journal.

"As the scorpion said to the frog, it's her nature. It's what she does."

"So, does this mean your career is over?"

"Never say never," I said. "But yes. It does."

"At least you're not going to jail. There's that."

"Just a dead man. And a killer. Wonder if anyone's hiring for my special skill set.."

In these scattered remnants across the floor, Hero could see every embarrassing and condescending detail. Janice had laid me utterly bare to my own daughter and the rest of the world, or so it probably seemed. But there was still more—what Janice did not know, about Lychroson and Clorisorin, about Rain Bird and the specific deadly potential of these perfectly legal crimes.

So I told Hero everything, tired of the lies, the hiding. There was no point to them, nothing more to be gained, no honor left to preserve. And when I finished, she sat silently, knees pulled into her chest, staring blankly at the piles of slightly crumpled newsprint upon the carpet.

"This isn't your fault," she said at last.

"I kinda think it is."

"Oh, no," she said, laughing slightly. "The endangering the public thing? Yeah. Totally your fault. No," she said, gesturing from her chest to mine. "I meant us."

"I thought there was no 'us.' "

"What I mean is that I came here for all the wrong reasons. That's why I keep saying it was a bad idea. I wasn't coming out here to meet you. That wasn't the reason, not the most important reason, anyway, for me. I didn't know you, and I didn't really care about getting to know you. I didn't care about you at all, actually. What does it matter in the end, someone's biology? That's not the reason I loved my parents. But for some reason, it seems to matter to him, to you, to everyone. You aren't anyone to me."

"All right, then. Good to know."

"Wait. Listen. When my Dad, when Geoffrey…" she paused a moment. "When he left, it was as if he didn't even think about or care how much that might hurt. What that might mean to me. I thought coming here would show him that he couldn't hurt me, that I didn't need him. So, that's why I came, I think. It wasn't fair to you. It was all me, my fault."

I took a deep breath. "Maybe I'm not meant to be a father," I said. "At first I didn't think I even wanted to be. But now I'm not so sure."

"Geoffrey is the one who asked for the paternity test, did he tell you? He and Mom were breaking apart, and he said I might not even be his daughter. Why would someone do that to their kid, someone they supposedly love?"

"People do irrational things when they're angry."

Hero nodded. "It was meant to hurt her, I guess. I don't think he even considered for a second what I'd think about it, or that it might turn out we're not actually related. I can forgive that. But now he acts like something is different. Like somehow you're my 'real' father and he isn't. Like any of this crap matters. It's total BS."

"But he came to see you. That counts for something, right?"

"He didn't come here to see me. You could see that right away. He wanted to meet you, to see who you were, to size you up. Because he thinks it matters that I'm not his daughter, whatever that means. In Shakespeare, people go ask the Oracle for the truth—now we've got tests that break your DNA down to the individual rungs. And you and I just have to believe that someone else understands this because, Lord knows, we don't. I mean, we could, but no one's smart enough to know everything anymore. So we have to take some part of the world on faith. If we lived a hundred years ago, none of this would have ever happened, and Geoffrey would still believe he was my biological father. But I can't bring myself to have that kind of faith in anything."

"I don't know much of anything," I said. "Faith is pretty much all I have."

Hero leaned back, stretching her athletic arms over her head. She released a groan of exasperation. "I'm just so stupid. I guess Geoffrey told you I asked him to take me with him."

"He told me."

"When he said no, I didn't know how to deal with it. I'm still not sure. But that's also not your fault. And it had nothing to do with you. I shouldn't have taken it out on you. Obviously," she gestured to the newspapers, "you have enough problems without me making things worse. It wasn't you. It was about Geoffrey. I mean," she started, then halted again. "I mean, he's my dad. You know?"

All around us, a settling quiet, punctured from outside by the metronome chorus of sprinklers.

"I'm not the answer to your problems, Matthew. I'm sorry." She didn't sound especially sorry. She revealed little in the way of any emotion at all. She spoke the words as if long rehearsed and merely awaiting a point of release. "Whatever you're looking for, you aren't going to find it with me. I can't save you. And you aren't going to find it on a microscope slide or behind the walls of this crappy old house, even if you do ever manage to restore it to its infamous glory."

"The past tells us about ourselves," I said. "We can't deny it."

"You can't really live in it, either. Look, in the end, it's just a house. And I'm just a girl, someone who probably shares a bit of genetic code with you. But none of it really makes any difference. It has nothing to do with us."

She became silent then and wrote something else in her book while I gazed out the window. And we sat there long into the morning just like this, but with no more words left to exchange and neither of us with any will to retreat.

thirty-seven

My lawn grew without pause. It elevated and expanded. Somewhere in the dense green, my sprinkler lay rusting, unused in recent memory, long ago detached from the cracked hose and abandoned. I waded through the green blades, kicking as I went from one edge to the other until I finally gave up and headed up toward the garage.

Despite an unusually dry summer drifting into a parched fall, the encroaching vegetation had been undeterred. The time for pruning had come around again, and it felt as if it was always coming round. Less than a week after mowing, it looked as if it hadn't been touched in months. I got glares from passing neighbors. Alfred left notices in my mailbox. Random strangers in sneakers and shorts, skin tanned near black, arrived at my door and cheerfully offered to cut it for an outrageous fee.

I stopped watering. I stopped fertilizing. I left suppressing piles of clippings atop the expanse—if anything, the long grasses were thriving.

My mower was a classic. The Lawn Master 250. It once belonged to my father and was a product of a prior generation that crafted with grease and gears. The motor started on the first turn. You could feel its strength inside your chest. It jostled windows. It set off car alarms up and down the block.

As I plowed through the thickened mat, I felt a keen satisfaction watching a path emerge, feeling myself taking control again of the grassland that had grown up around my house. Despite my job at Environmental, I'd never really been much into nature. Not to say I carried animosity toward it; more just a general ambivalence. Everything was fine as long we left each other alone.

I wasted away under the morning heat, stumbling around in clothes that had over the years turned to rags. Then, while pulling the mower behind me, a section of jean below my left knee, long dangling by a thin finger of fabric, finally separated from the rest of the pant. The Lawn Master chewed up the denim and spewed the shredded blue and white threads out across the yard, then clattered to an abrupt stop.

Hero was spread out in a lawn chair, resting in some slight shade by the front walk. She sat up as I lumbered by, pulling the mower back to the garage.

"This has got to stop," Hero said, standing up. "I'm going to get you a new wardrobe."

"Oh, really. And what are you going to pay with?"

"You pay. I'll choose."

After I'd cleaned up a bit, she directed us to the Martin Luther King, Jr. Mall, with its half-dozen department stores and fully stocked food court. It was located just outside of town, on the gnawed fringe of untamed swampland and brush. They'd dammed the marginal flow, drained everything bone dry, then carved out a space in the dell, a home for The Gap and Macy's and Pottery Barn and Cinnabon.

Stepping inside, we were hit by a strong blast of cool air funneling out the door. From floor to ceiling, everything was state-of-the-art. It was perhaps the most sophisticated structure in town, and certainly much better than my own rickety office building. Rumor claimed it had better lighting than the hospital. It was three stories tall, with internal balconies ringing the entire structure, and two tiered fountains, one at each end. The food court stood at its center, jammed with shopping bags and the shoppers who toted them, the former more numerous than the latter. Here were the leisurely, the frantic, the focused and the aimless. Everyone was in each other's way.

Hero pointed toward the food court.

"I want a pretzel."

"I thought we were here for clothes."

"We're here for lots of reasons," she said.

I stood in line while Hero wandered in and out of the crowd. I had never cruised a mall before, and it quickly became clear that this was exactly what Hero had in mind.

"See those girls over there?" She gestured over her shoulder toward a group of three teens, several years older than Hero herself, walking so close together that they could have been connected. They were right on the heels of a chubby young man in his early-twenties. "Those are the merry pranksters. Every mall has them. They walk behind complete strangers and just laugh. Usually solo guys, someone dorky and insecure."

"Why would they do that?"

"I'm not sure. It's a coming-of-age ritual of some kind. I haven't figured out all the nuances yet, but I'm working on it."

"You spend a lot of time in malls, I take it."

"Mom figured out long ago it's cheaper than a babysitter."

"That's terrible," I said. "Even by my standards."

"And you wonder why I don't complain about you."

"This is you not complaining?"

With her pretzel in hand, we strolled the promenade, lingering for moments in front of display windows that Hero wanted to observe. She had comments about everything, each item of clothing, every mannequin pose and accessory. This was how we spent the day.

"What's the deal with your bimbo?"

"Angelie. She has a name."

"True. But notice I also didn't mention that her hair is taller than some local buildings. Haven't seen her in ages. Weren't you in love or something? If not, you sure had sex a lot for people who weren't."

"She dumped me."

"Hope it wasn't anything I said."

"I wouldn't let her watch someone die. Apparently, there are lines in relationships one simply does not cross."

Hero led me into a small clothing store with heavy music that pounded in my lungs. She might have been one of the youngest people in the store, but I was by far the oldest. She sifted through the racks, every once in awhile pulling out something she might wear. As she perused fashionable panties and bras, I wandered over to the opposite side of the store and leafed through a stack of classic noir film posters. After a while, she tracked me down, holding up a pair of brown leather pants, with lace ties in the crotch.

"What do you think?"

"You sure your mother would let you wear that?"

"Me? This is for you."

"You're kidding. I wouldn't wear clothes like that."

"Come on," she said. "Don't you want to be one of those cool dads?"

"Haven't we decided I'm definitely not one of those cool dads? I'm too old, for one thing. For another, if that's cool, I definitely don't want any part of it."

"Indulge me," she said.

After my protests failed to convince her, she shuffled me into one of the changing rooms. The lights were dim and flashed randomly, so it was nearly impossible to get a good sense of what you were trying on, despite the dozen mirrors that covered every inch of wall.

"I'm not coming out," I said. And I meant it. The pants were too tight. Despite the low lighting, in the mirror I saw myself as my own actual age, a thirty-something wearing the clothes of a teen. I would never be able to take myself seriously. I pulled off the pants and rummaged through the strobing lights for my own clothes.

Stepping back into the showroom, Hero was nowhere in sight.

"Excuse me." I tapped the shoulder of the attendant. She wore low-cut pants several inches below her navel and an asphyxiating top. She smiled as she turned around, all charm and sex appeal.

"I'm looking for… the young woman I came here with."

"Dark hair? Tweener?"

I nodded.

"She headed out a few minutes ago. Said you'd pay for the small stack she left for you at the register."

I found myself watching the girl as she retreated toward the counter, her slender and shapely body, her accents and her curves. A body that insisted that you watch, gnawing and impatient. She was the kind of girl I might have been interested in a few years ago. The more I thought about it, though, the more "a few years" was more like fifteen, which was longer than my daughter had even been alive. The girl herself, it slowly dawned on me, was probably only a few years older than Hero. Maybe seventeen. Eighteen. A young woman still coming into her body and life. She could even be Hero, Hero as she would someday soon be, the woman in the crystal ball.

I looked down awkwardly at my shoes, the countertop, the spinning earring display.

The small stack cost me $400, which I placed on the last credit card that still believed I was alive, but at least I now had clothes I could wear—jeans, dress shirts, nothing fancy, no leather. Still, I'd likely just return it all later, spending $300 less and ending up with more. But for the moment, I signed the receipt and gathered the bags of clothes, all without looking at the shop girl, and then went out in search of my daughter.

I walked down past the same stores we'd passed coming up, along the balconies, through the food court. Somewhere behind me, I thought I heard the quick chattering voices, the soft snickers.

Hero was sitting in a circle of benches near the main entrance, pretending to read the business section of the paper. But it was plain that all the while she was listening in on the surrounding conversations, smiling to herself. She waved when she saw me.

"That was a bit pricey," I said, slumping down beside her.

"Was that a problem?"

"I'm poor."

"You are not poor."

"I'm not rich," I said. "I have low cash flow. It crimps my style."

"You don't have a style," she pointed out.

"I would if I were rich."

"You are rich. Look around you. You just spend more than you make."

"That's true of all poor people."

"How much do you make a year?"

"Before or after I died?" I asked.

"You did receive a pretty big inheritance."

"I'm not talking third-world-type poor," I said, feeling defensive. "I mean more of a middle-class poor. Between being dead and not bringing in a salary and the expenses on the house, I definitely can't buy everything I want."

"I believe that would be called gluttony."

"Gluttony is only a type of rich," I argued. "It's when you actually do buy everything you want. I only want the option."

"I don't see the difference."

Commerce was our means of bonding, and I wanted to keep a good thing going. "Let me get you something," I said.

"Something expensive? Or are you just going for cheap sentimentality."

"The cheap one. It produces better results."

"You could try sentimental and expensive, but you couldn't find both at the mall."

After some negotiation, we settled upon a small vendor who was set up in the middle of the walkway selling various knick-knacks and odd jewelry. Hero chose a large silver-banded mood ring.

"I should probably tell you now because you'll find out eventually: today is my birthday."

That couldn't be right, I thought. "But your birthday is…" and I realized I had no idea, had never even thought to ask.

"Watch out world. I'm officially a teenager."

"Just when I thought there was no way you could be any more

trouble."

"This doesn't count as buying my love, by the way" she said, obviously quite pleased with her gift. "You can't buy it, anyway."

"I probably couldn't afford it."

"It's priceless," she said, twisting the ring around her finger. "I thought you knew."

thirty-eight

The ever-present haze of humidity at long last broke one evening after the rolling storms departed, signaling the true arrival of fall. I stood in the kitchen, trying to boil spaghetti noodles. Hero was out back with her journal, writing, lost in her own world. Despite everything, we were settling into the routine of normalcy. Beyond the pain we'd caused and experienced with each other—perhaps even because of it—we'd created a life of give and take, the rhythms and tone that bore a striking similarity to the reality of family.

Then the phone rang.

"It's Val," a voice said, somewhat sheepishly. "Sorry I'm a little late."

"Just a little," I said, my dry tone probably hiding the intended sarcasm and complete surprise. "Where have you been?"

"Well, there were more problems than we expected with the Peruvian government. Some of the art had been classified as national artifacts, which only complicated the expedition process. Not a lot of fun, I promise you."

"You've been in Peru all this time."

"I would have called, but you know how reception is up in the mountains. I know I told Hero I probably wouldn't have any access, but still. It was worth it, though. These village artists are absolutely incredible, and we're going to make a killing. Still. I'm only a week later than I said I would be."

"Don't you mean two months?"

"You're funny, Matthew. I told Hero I thought I'd be back by the first."

"You told Hero?"

"Right. Before I left." She paused. "Wait. She did talk to you, didn't she? She told me you were fine with watching her during my trip."

I stared through the newly installed French doors onto the deck. Hero was out in the yard, notebook open before her, but leaning back with her face open to the sun.

I forced a laugh. "Yeah, right. Could you imagine if she hadn't told me anything for two months? We'd be freaking out. I'd probably hire a private investigator or something to track you down and start making permanent arrangements for her to stay."

Val laughed, too.

"Right. Sorry. I'm a bit jet lagged. So how was it? Was she good?"

"At many things," I said. "She was in a play. She's quite an actress."

"The girl never ceases to amaze me. I'm glad to hear you two are getting along."

"I don't know that I'd go that far. She seems to revel in harassing me. I can't quite figure out where I stand."

"With Hero, you know she's happy when she's pestering you and keeping you guessing. Her father, Geoffrey I mean, is the same way. He never did anything without a purpose, usually one that was different than whatever he said it was he was doing. Hero doesn't like to show her cards, either."

"I've learned a lot these past few months, that's for sure."

"Look, Matthew." She became hesitant, again, tripping lightly over her words. "I guess I never really said how sorry I am about all of this, for dumping her on you. You didn't ask for this."

"I'm her father," I said, grabbing a beer from the fridge and twisting the cap. "It's not what I thought I wanted." I took a quick sip from the bottle. "And, the truth is, I'm probably never going to be more than some stranger to her. But it's fine. I try to imagine how our lives would have been different if I'd known all along."

"I'm sorry. I really did think Geoffrey was her father. Or maybe I just convinced myself of that. Don't be mad."

"That's a past that doesn't really exist, though."

"You're probably better off."

"I think I'd have been a terrible father. I never can figure out the right thing to do."

Out in the yard, Hero sat up with a jerk and slapped away at something on her arm, then resettled under the blanket of fading sun.

"Parenting is pretty much never knowing what's right," Val offered in an all-knowing kind of voice, the wisdom of years in the trenches. "As long as they come back with all their limbs, I consider that a success."

"All her limbs are accounted for. And just the one scar."

"Scar?"

Catching Hero's eye, I signaled to her. She came trotting in as I was giving Val a brief rundown of our accident. With a quizzical look on her face, my daughter took the phone from my hand as I pushed it in her direction.

"Your Mom's back from Peru," I said, matter-of-fact.

She nodded and dropped her eyes away from mine, dodging out of my way as she dragged a stool from the kitchen out into the hall, huddled up close around herself, her back to me. If she was saying anything back to Val, it was entirely under her breath—she appeared to make no sound.

I stepped out onto the back porch, closed the door behind me, and eased into the mildewed cushions on the wicker couch. The fall evening was almost chilly and I wished I had a jacket, but I wasn't about to interrupt them by trudging back inside and rummaged through the hall closet. The backyard was quiet. As I watched the encroaching kudzu that had come in and overwhelmed everything, creeping over the years as it had slowly risen up and over the trees and underbrush and spread atop like a lush green comforter, I considered the possibility of clear cutting that stretch of woods on my property, reclaiming the family graveyard, the tool shed, the borders and heights from the natural growth. Not that I'd ever really stop it, of course, but I could tame it, perhaps, if just for a brief time. In the end, it was going to win. Uprooting the old trees and ripping everything out of the earth would buy some time. I could smell another lawsuit in the offing.

The rest of the house was still. Any day now, I expected to hear from the Magnolia Grove Historical Society about my interview, which would hopefully allow me to continue, maybe even someday finish, the restoration on my family estate. As I'd watched the house progress, my imagination of the possible had grown. I could revamp the grounds, perhaps, recreate the sense of the place as it had existed in the age before the war. I could re-plot the fields, grow crops. We'd have a mill, of course, maybe hire cobblers and smiths and haberdashers and potters. Fence in a pen, then raise a barn and a chicken coop. Every need provided for, every thought and desire. Wholly self-sufficient.

Hero opened the French door, phone shut off and by her side.

"Mom's putting together a flight for me. Probably by the end of the week."

"Call me crazy," I offered, "but maybe I should confirm this with her?"

She managed a slight smile at this.

"Why didn't you rat me out?"

I shrugged. "Didn't seem much point, I guess. How pissed off would she have been?"

"Very. Probably would have grounded me until I was twenty."

"Seems a little on the light side to me," I said. "Maybe I should call her back."

Hero sat beside me on the couch, gazing out with me into the wilderness.

"After a while I thought about telling you that Mom wasn't really missing," she said. "But since I was stuck here, you'd only be pissed at me rather than the woman who wasn't coming back."

"I seriously thought she might be dead."

"I told you not to worry."

"I didn't know that was because you knew she was okay. I thought you were just being optimistic. But that still doesn't explain why you pretended she was gone in the first place."

"I thought you'd let me go home. I underestimated your resolve. But I didn't know you then like I do now."

"Was staying such a terrible thing?"

She smiled and shook her head. "I told you. I was here for the wrong reasons. Once I figured that out, once I knew that this was just about trying to hurt Geoffrey, it didn't seem fair to stay. It was just torturing you."

"It was torture. I figured your Mom had met some grisly end, that you were here for the duration."

"And what did you think about that idea? Me staying, not the torture" she asked, casting a sidelong look at me.

"I was getting used to it. I was maybe starting to care a little bit too much, if you know what I mean."

Hero took a long, slow breath. "I was beginning to get scared and wanted to leave," she said, "for pretty much the same reason."

At my front door stood a young woman from the historical society who introduced herself as Alice Nicely, a towering neighbor whose face and improbably taut hair bun I recognized from her constant television appearances, our resident expert talking about preservation issues. In the capitol flap, she'd been a constant presence, mediating the different positions. She said she lived a few blocks over, but I'd never seen her in Magnolia Grove.

Now, she stood on my front walk, rapidly snapping digital photos.

"It's a different façade, of course," she said, after introducing herself. "This kind of architecture is a 20th-century invention. No one would have built the house this way in the late 18th or early

19th century." She said this with a somewhat condescending yet still pleasant tone that made you almost want to be corrected.

At her request, I took her on a tour through the house, a maddeningly slow crawl room to room as she assessed each wall, each doorway, every buttress and sconce. Hero joined us partway through as we passed her room. Alice was fascinating to watch in her element, and as she asked question after question for which I had no good answers, I found even her annoyance charming. But with each altered square foot, her obvious disappointment appeared to diminish our chances of securing some kind of grant. I invited her into the attic to view perhaps the only space that hadn't been purposefully rearranged by human intent.

"I'll be upfront with you, Mr. Brown. The specific historical character of this house is of interest to the society. After the war, there was a period where the plantation partitioned land into rental plots, which were then, by the turn of the century, sold to developers, who founded the community of Magnolia Grove, which has all along fought for a separate status from the city proper. Obviously a great deal here has been changed over the years, Most of the work done has been cosmetic, but if you don't mind restoring some of the contemporary features...."

"As you can see, I've done a good deal already. And I'm told I might be able to get money for that work as well?"

She nodded.

"Here's the proposal, Mr. Brown. Typically, we will provide grant funds up to 25 percent of costs directly related to the restoration. What we're prepared to offer you is 50 percent of costs, plus a monthly maintenance stipend and a share of fees if you allow the home to be included on the registry tour."

She pulled some papers out of a briefcase and laid them on the table.

"That seems pretty incredible," I said, stifling a laugh. "What exactly would it mean to be on the registry tour? What would I have to do?"

"Nothing, really. We run a fairly popular semi-weekly tour of local historical homes. This particular offer is special, though, because we'd like to convert at least a portion of the interior to its original state. It's a new part of the program. Typically we are dealing exclusively with exteriors. But if we can reach some kind of agreement, I think everyone will benefit."

"As long as I don't need to use an outhouse, I'm fine."

"We don't ask people to live in the antebellum South, Mr. Brown. We are just trying to preserve the rich character of our history, both the good and the bad. We too often give in to foolish and shortsighted notions in order to be current."

"If we never did something new, though, we'd miss out on a lot of history, wouldn't we?" Hero said.

"No one is trying to stop progress, my dear. As if we could. We just want people to value what they have more. And respect their own histories more. These tours help raise awareness, help people appreciate the proximity of our past, make it a little less distant."

"I'm new here," Hero said, "but if there's one thing people around here don't seem to have trouble with it's holding on to the past."

"Everyone wants to relive the glories of the past, sure. We're trying to preserve the whole of the Southern experience, the good, the bad and the indifferent, which includes the life of the slaves. That's why we are excited about this chance for you to let us include the slave quarters for the plantation house."

Hero began to cough beside me.

"I'm sorry?" I said. "What slave quarters?"

"Your house. This building served as the primary slave quarters for the Holifield Plantation."

"That's not right," I said. "This was the original manor house. It's been in our family for generations, since before the war"

Alice tapped the plans. "Well, we've been over the original records at city hall. There's not really any question about the origins. I have the original plotting right in here."

From her bag, she pulled out a larger document with topographical markings and several buildings marked up. Despite the fact that it bore little resemblance to the place as it now existed, this was clearly Magnolia Grove. The proximity of the lakes, the three hills, the Johnston plantation near the creek that bisected the area.

"You're here," she said pointing. "And here's the site of the Holifield manor house, and several other structures. A mill over here. My own home would be in this empty stretch here. Several other slave quarters over here, though they were all demolished before anyone was really agitating to preserve them. You could even say that the random parceling off and demolition of these historical treasures were the reason the historical society was brought into existence in the first place—to preserve the character and integrity of our real past, instead of a whitewash.

The photograph of the house in the hallway looked nothing like the place we lived now; the family of former slaves perched out front, smiling.

"I'm sorry," I said. "This just can't be right."

"Don't spoil a good thing, Matthew," Hero advised. "The woman is offering you money. Dead men can't be picky."

"This just can't be right."

Alice cheerfully left us the papers, including the neighborhood map, which she said she could pick up any time seeing as she lived just a few blocks down. I told her we'd need to consider the offer. For a moment, I wondered if she was a party to these lawsuits against me, as well. Perhaps this whole thing was some elaborate plan by my neighbors to exact their revenge, their idea of a joke. But the more I stared at the map, so much that had seemed odd suddenly made sense. As a plantation manor house, it was decidedly small in comparison with others in the region. There were numerous, better spots in this area that would have been more prime choices for the original landowners. And looking upon its structure anew, I could more easily envision the contours in all of its unglamorous functionality. My grandfather had been wrong, then. We weren't the original residents at all. Our family would have arrived later, after the end of the war. It was the only conclusion that made sense.

In the backyard, the low headstones were overgrown and crumbling. Generations of Browns buried here, a family tradition honored whenever possible. Each of us building upon, becoming part of, this history. My grandfather's plot was newest and closest to the house, but there were dozens of others here. As a child, I remembered playing among them, tripping on the buried stones that stretched long out into the forest. Now I plied away the kudzu, then kneeling in the grass started to expose the older stones, brushing back a century and a half of earth to make out names, dates, secrets long buried.

Hero came up beside me.

"You'll save a fortune on renovations," she said.

"This isn't funny," I said.

"It's a little bit funny."

The older headstones had mostly crumbled away, dust to dust. But there was still enough for me to see, markers that clearly enough told a story of a family and a house, two centuries in the making and desperate to forget.

Settled down in the mangled vines, I wiped sweat from my brow. The heat of summer may have given way to fall, but today was still oppressively hot. My home, long my sanctuary during these uncertain months, was suddenly unfamiliar to me. A new past being written upon the old one now fading. I felt the suddenly urgent need to be some place else—an escape into the world, for once, rather than away from it.

"How'd you like one last swim?" I asked.

Out at the public pool again, we found the same people, the same games and competitions and fierce battles as we'd encountered during the heat of summer, just fewer of them. The season had fully made its turn. Under a cloudy sky, Hero floated, straddling a partially inflated yellow duck, its head bobbing limp in the water. I watched her, pool-side, laid out in a patio chair and sinking through the worn and broken straps. A cool breeze whipped across the water.

Just beyond the curled back chain-link fencing, a middle-aged man, potbellied and Speedo-clad, hopped across the hot black gravel, barefoot through shards of broken bottles and the tangled balls of what might have been kite string. Moms straggled in from the parking lot, concerned women shy of middle age, swimsuit fashions one decade out of date, with coolers, digital speakers, wicker handbags, transparent rainbow-colored visors. Out on the deck, a child squirmed out of one cursing woman's reach before she could apply a final coat of sunscreen. He hit the water with a sudden, painful smack. We all saw stars.

Everywhere overflowing with ragged youths in cut-off jeans and sopping sneakers, blue and white polka dot one-pieces and neon inflatable floaties.

Women in skintight suits drew towels around themselves; young boys sopping and wet and gathering in a chunk near the diving board wrapped thin arms around shoulders, teeth chattering. A swimming class for toddlers in the shallow end had spastic and crying children standing right at the edge, while their parents stood waist deep calling to them, pleading for them to jump and to trust. One dove in and thrashed about in the shallows, unable to touch the bottom. Her mother held her arms outward, but at the same time taking slow steps backward as her child began to pick up steam, until they'd both crossed the width.

Distant thunder rumbled into our bellies.

I caught Hero watching me. She wore a difficult expression on that young and beautiful face. Wheels churning behind those eyes, you could always tell.

The drive to the airport was silent. No questions or chatter of any sort. Once I thought I heard her humming, though I couldn't make out the tune. The roads were just gearing up, lines of traffic heading into town, but the airport was out on the fringe, by the farm fields and cattle ranches. We passed two men, one old and another young, sitting in a lawn chair by the roadside, a sign beside them written in exaggerated letters: "Hawt Bowled Paynuts." Both raised arms in a wave as we passed.

We checked her in at the flight counter, where a chaperone was waiting to take her all the way to her plane. At the security entrance, we stood a moment facing each other. She with her carry-on slung across her shoulder, my hands shoved deep in my pockets. After a few awkward moments, I lifted my arms, leaned down and we hugged. I patted her back, and she squeezed me awkwardly for a second or two, saying goodbye, before she released me.

This was an end. A beginning. Something in-between.

"You'd probably figure this out eventually," she said after a pause, "but I'm the one who sent Adler our phone number. I thought you two really should talk, and I told him you weren't such a bad guy. You just hadn't really thought about the killing part that much. And you aren't a bad guy, Matthew. You just have some work to do."

I leaned in close, turning us both away from the chaperone.

"So, let me get this straight," I said, carefully. "Since we've met, you've lied to me…"

"Yep.

"…and spied on me."

"Yep."

"…and given away my home phone number to a convicted murderer."

"Prrrrretty much, yep." She reached up and patted my cheek. "Basically, just a chip off the old block."

Hero slung her bag over her shoulders and turned away up the ramp. I watched from behind the large machines screening luggage as she was led down the terminal toward her departing gate.

Just like that. Gone, baby, gone.

thirty-nine

On the day before its grand opening, SouthWorld went up in a fiery blaze. The cause remained something of a mystery. It could have been that while putting the final touches on the Rebel Yell roller coaster, workers had inadvertently released a spark, which in turn ignited a small blaze that quickly became a much bigger blaze, and before the afternoon was half gone, every inch of the soon-to-open amusement park had burned to the ground. But just as easily it might have been the splinter group from the Ku Klux Klan, which had claimed responsibility in objection to the "sullying of the noble spirit of the true South." Or perhaps an irate member of the growing protest movement, which objected to the glorification of slavery. Whatever the cause, the result was catastrophic. Helicopters circled in broad sweeps, some attacking the fire, some capturing it on film. Ground crews tried containment, but gusting winds spread the wildfire across the surrounding growth and into the bordering woods and across the county. Wildlife was driven into the city and expensive homes were caught up in the charging fire and laid waste. The last two of the at-large white collar prisoners returned then, coming in from the wilderness, sunburned and starving and lonely.

A few days after Hero left, I called up Janice and asked her if we could meet. I hadn't spoken to her at all since her article was published, not since long before everything fell apart, but I decided now was the time to settle all accounts.

The west side dive she suggested was called Lou's. I couldn't imagine this being a place that Janice would return to on a regular basis, with its decaying exterior, its limited tap of stale beer and lack of hard liquor, its perpetually sticky tabletops. But though they said little and offered not much more than skeptical looks, it was apparent that the regulars recognized her as one of their own.

"I'm a fraud," I said, by way of introduction, as I slid into the booth she already occupied. "But you knew that. I mean, I come by it honestly, from a long line of frauds, apparently. My family's entire history is complete fiction."

Janice scoffed. "Please. How many millions of lies combine to make up our heritage, Matthew? We live in the land of the Lost Cause, where we tell ourselves that we fought a war that had nothing to do with slavery. We live in a South apparently entirely devoid of racists, much to everyone's surprise. We're good at nothing if not manufacturing the artifice of our history into a pleasing and glorious shape."

"But at least now I can start living the honest truth."

"Living in the past is hardly honest, my friend. This whole obsession with recreating your family's glory days was a farce from the beginning. It was never going to make you anything other than what you already are, you know."

"Whatever I am, I'm also apparently a fool, and now disgraced, all thanks to you."

"Matty," Janice sighed. "As I've already told you a hundred times, you are most definitely a fool. Just don't take it personally."

"Maybe I should return the favor. I'm sure there are a number of people who'd love to see Jefferson's cover blown."

"Go ahead. Anyone who doesn't already know couldn't hurt me anyway. I'm tenured."

"How could you do that to me? Weren't you supposed to call me for a quote or something? Isn't that the ethical thing to do?"

"I did call," she said lifting up her plastic menu in front of her face. "Your daughter couldn't wake you up, and I was on deadline. You'll see I noted that you couldn't be reached for comment."

"You've made me a laughing stock."

"Don't let that bother you. Public humiliation is a fact of life. You'll get over it."

"It's politics," I shook my head. "Public perception is everything."

"No," she quickly retorted. "Loyalty is everything. People have short memories and less patience. Most of the people I exposed a few years ago found themselves on billionaire welfare, working as consultants for the same government they defrauded. But it's all the same. Nothing really changes, my friend."

"I thought there were no second acts in American politics."

"That's true," she said. "It's all first acts, relocated to a different theater, played over and over again with the same bad actors."

"What about the investigations?" I asked. "Do you really think they were launched to cover everything up?"

"It doesn't matter. Regardless of why, that's what's happening."

"And Stanton?"

"Stanton is as pure and uncomplicated as the sweet nectar from my granddaddy's still."

From the end of the bar, two elderly men and one woman burst out with a riotous laugh that shook everyone in the establishment.

"If Stanton is not on the take, how could this be happening, then?" I said.

"You still live under the illusion that there is all good and all bad. We live with both, the good and bad, the old and the new. It's a push-pull, and mostly they even each other out, find a state of balance. Stanton's integrity is the biggest obstacle in this whole mess. He won't leak anything. He won't bring charges against anyone unless he's certain he has the goods on someone. Evidence that he's found in the process will just sit there under lock and key. Not for any nefarious purpose on his part. He's a firm believer in the system and that everyone is entitled to the presumption of innocence unless they can be convicted. I, as you know, am not nearly so charitable."

"But because there's nothing illegal about any of this…"

"Precisely," Janice said. "If you're trying to cover up a non-crime, choosing Stanton was a stroke of brilliance. First, navigating all the loopholes and vagaries of the law to get exactly what they wanted. Then, using that same law to keep anything concrete from getting out about it."

Behind this grand orchestration, I imagined some conductor stood. Walker, I supposed, who'd pressed me long ago to make sure I knew nothing. Or maybe it was bigger than that, even, some elaborate conspiracy involving corporations and billionaires and who knew what else. The imagination was the only limit. The only shocking thing about the whole affair now was that they could endanger people's lives and no one would—or even could—be held accountable.

"Janice, people will die. And it's my fault."

"Welcome to the big leagues, Matty."

"If there's pressure, the governor might be forced to do something."

"Oh, they'll do something. They'll do a lot of somethings. And some of those things might actually be related to fixing the problems I wrote about. I'm hearing rumors that the backdoor will soon be gone. But as is often the case, they're using the crisis to add in 'fixes' that will let them do a heck of a lot more damage and in more complicated ways. This time through the front door."

"But you'll just expose them."

"Don't look at me. You still don't understand, Matthew. The press has no real power unless there's really something to fear beyond public embarrassment. The only reason we got the last crook out was because he was going down anyway. The cockroaches aren't scared of shadows, I told you, only the light. They like to keep the rest of us all paralyzed in the dark. People might be outraged if they knew the details, if there was something specific to be afraid of. But the prosecutors have all the evidence, and since all of this was perfectly legal, it can't be used to prosecute them and their records will remain sealed for protect those who are innocent in the eyes of the law. The press will never see it. They played this one—and you—perfectly."

I chipped at the cracked laminate tabletop. "You said that if I'm a good soldier, if I just sit back and keep my mouth shut, despite all of this, I'm set for life."

"They take care of their own, Matthew. It's the unspoken rule." Janice took a hard drag, then shook her head with a frown. "Not that your word will do much good, especially now. The accusations of a disenchanted and discredited public figure won't hold much weight. We don't have any proof that there's any real harm. That's it. The well's run dry. It's over."

We were quiet for a minute. Janice's eyes were grayer, I thought, more deeply sunk. She struck me in that moment as much older than she was, worn down by her driving passions. She'd been pushing hard for a long while now, and I imagined it must have been distressing to know all she knew, to expose these things to the world, yet still know that we were just acting out the same drama, the actors merely changing parts and never leaving the stage.

Nothing ever changed. Except this time. This time, it would be different.

From my briefcase beside me, I removed the file on Rain Bird and set it on the table between us. It was perhaps the first and only time I'd ever seen Janice genuinely taken aback. She pulled the folder toward her and swiftly sifted through the reports contained within. I explained to her everything I knew. Every sin, by fault or omission.

She smoked as she listened, a wry smirk slipping across her lips as I went along.

As I finished, I peeled my arm from the tabletop and pushed myself back against the wall, stretching out across the bench. The bartender dropped off two more mugs, and I held mine close to my chest.

We watched the rest of the afternoon loll away, slowly working through tin-edged beer and grease-soaked burgers, chatting easily, almost carefree. And the truth was I was glad to lay down my burdens after so long. Whatever hope I'd held of keeping the life I'd made for myself was slipping away, so here I was, letting it go.

Pushing it away, in fact. My final act was one of disloyalty, for the most noble of purposes and no hope of reward. No more blood on my hands. No more me. As far as the world was concerned, Matthew Brown had finally ceased to exist, the specter of my death serving as my only substance. Finally, I knew, my peace had found me.

Post Mortem

All around lay the tattered remains of the battle, nature against mankind. Building foundations broken and sidewalk slabs raised and cracked. Street signs bent over, smothered in vines. Weathered traffic lights delicately dangling under their own weight. Yet amid all this there were signs, too, of people fighting back. Lumbering construction projects, the capitol's redevelopment. A New South continuously rebuilding upon the old one wasting away. Still, for every clear-cut lot and new strip mall, yet another overrun home, a rusted, crumbling automobile, a small stretch of the untamed wild creeping up and in and flowing over the fenced and settled lines.

In this kind of war, there was no end, no victor, just perpetual casualties and hope for better days to come.

Behind my house, the workers were clearing the wilderness. They were extracting the husks of decaying oaks, grinding the stumps into oblivion. The house itself was teeming with swarms of construction workers, remolding and reshaping the structure to its original form. The pace was frenetic, a mad dash to the past. Board members for the Magnolia Grove Historical Society would come by at times to observe the progress.

In the three weeks since Hero's departure, I'd heard not one word.

Janice gave her assessment when I told her: "She's young, Matty. I know it doesn't seem like it most of the time. She hides the fact that she's so young behind the fact that she's also brilliant. Someday she might be ready for you. Don't hold it against her. You're a pretty good guy to know and you've come a long way. Just don't spend your time waiting for her to recognize that."

My previous life was gone, but there was nothing to replace it. I was starting from scratch, reconstructing a history, along with a building, generations lost and found. I created a past without a future. In the weeks since she left, the empty space of Hero's room swallowed everything surrounding it. I closed the door and left it shut, contenting myself with the time we had already spent together. We could never recollect the past we'd never had. But what we had was enough and would need to be.

Then, out of the blue, Hero called. It was late morning on a Thursday, when she knew I would regularly be awake and still contemplating whether to go in to work, even though Christy had told me no longer to bother. She told me that she was working on another one of her studies.

"It's a big one," she said, and she needed my input. She thought it was something that would really challenge me. "It might even test the moral fiber of your very being."

I asked, but she wouldn't tell me what it was for.

Acknowledgments

I am indebted to a number of people who have, over the years, helped bring this book to fruition. Thanks to David Hawkins for his willingness to read and offer suggestions, and to Todd James Pierce, for his many years of encouragement and advice; to Katharine Coles, who was right about the book from the beginning; Rob Van Wagoner, Guy Lebeda, and the Utah Arts Council; Harvey Klinger and the Columbus Creative Cooperative; Mary Jane Ryals, for throwing a lifeline; and John Sibley Williams, for believing this book would find a home and then making that happen.

For contributions and suggestions, thanks to Heidi Czerwiec, Robin Hemley, Jenn Gibbs, David McGlynn, Mary Anne Mohanraj, Traci O Connor, Susie Petheram, Aaron Sanders, Mark St. Andre, Melanie Rae Thon, and a special thanks to Eric Brosch (whose casual observation unexpectedly helped inspired the tale).

Thanks also to Kevin Atticks, Lorena Trejo-Perez and the entire staff of Apprentice House. Special thanks to René Romero Schuler for her incredible generosity and the use of her stunning artwork.

This book would not be what it is without many lessons learned from Pam Balluck, Matt Bondurant, Jeff Chapman, C.V. Davis, Elie Edmonson, Michael Wm. Gearhart, Adam Johnson, Kelly Jones, Lynn Kilpatrick, Brian Kubarycz, Kathryn Carson, Rae Meadows, Felicia Olivera, Samantha Ruckman, Ron Smith, Erin Sweeney, Stephen Tuttle, Ryan Van Cleave, and Mike White.

I am grateful for the wisdom and support I received from Virgil Suarez, R.M. Berry, Janet Burroway, Karen Brennen, Francois

Camoin, Sheila Ortiz Taylor, Jerry Stern, Maureen O'Hara Ure, Kathryn Stockton, and Stuart Culver and the many teachers and fellow writers I've worked with over the years.

A special thanks to my parents and my brother, who have always encouraged me. Finally, I must thank my wife, Marcia C. Dibble, who has edited what must have seemed to be endless story revisions and whose brilliant influences on the writer and the text are far too numerous to list.

Apprentice House is the country's only campus-based, student-staffed book publishing company. Directed by professors and industry professionals, it is a nonprofit activity of the Communication Department at Loyola University Maryland.

Using state-of-the-art technology and an experiential learning model of education, Apprentice House publishes books in untraditional ways. This dual responsibility as publishers and educators creates an unprecedented collaborative environment among faculty and students, while teaching tomorrow's editors, designers, and marketers.

Outside of class, progress on book projects is carried forth by the AH Book Publishing Club, a co-curricular campus organization supported by Loyola University Maryland's Office of Student Activities.

Eclectic and provocative, Apprentice House titles intend to entertain as well as spark dialogue on a variety of topics. Financial contributions to sustain the press's work are welcomed. Contributions are tax deductible to the fullest extent allowed by the IRS.

To learn more about Apprentice House books or to obtain submission guidelines, please visit www.apprenticehouse.com.

Apprentice House
Communication Department
Loyola University Maryland
4501 N. Charles Street
Baltimore, MD 21210
Ph: 410-617-5265 • Fax: 410-617-2198
info@apprenticehouse.com • www.apprenticehouse.com

www.ingramcontent.com/pod-product-compliance
Lightning Source LLC
Chambersburg PA
CBHW030635020726
47493CB00006B/1720